LORDS AND MASTERS

The following titles are all in the *Fonthill Complete A. G. Macdonell* Series.
The year indicates when the first edition was published.
See **www.fonthillmedia.com** for details.

Fiction

England, their England (1933)
How Like an Angel (1934)
Lords and Masters (1936)
The Autobiography of a Cad (1939)
Flight From a Lady (1939)
Crew of the Anaconda (1940)

Short Stories

The Spanish Pistol (1939)

Non-Fiction

Napoleon and his Marshals (1934)
A Visit to America (1935)
My Scotland (1937)

Crime and Thrillers written under the pseudonym of John Cameron

The Seven Stabs (1929)
Body Found Stabbed (1932)

Crime and Thrillers written under the pseudonym of Neil Gordon

The New Gun Runners (1928)
The Factory on the Cliff (1928)
The Professor's Poison (1928)
The Silent Murders (1929)
The Big Ben Alibi (1930)
Murder in Earl's Court (1931)
The Shakespeare Murders (1933)

LORDS AND MASTERS

A. G. MACDONELL

FONTHILL

Fonthill Media Limited
Fonthill Media LLC
www.fonthillmedia.com
office@fonthillmedia.com

First published 1936
This edition published in the United Kingdom 2012

British Library Cataloguing in Publication Data:
A catalogue record for this book is available from the British Library

ISBN 978-1-78155-018-2 (print)
ISBN 978-1-78155-150-9 (e-book)

Typeset in 11pt on 14pt Sabon.
Printed and bound in England

Contents

Introduction to the 2012 Edition

'And so Armageddon began once again ...' The terrible implications of the rise of Nazism were rarely so accurately perceived as in A. G. Macdonell's prescient novel, *Lords and Masters*, published in 1936. After the success of *England, Their England* in 1933, it is this work that cemented his reputation as a trenchant satirist with extraordinary powers of perception.

Archibald Gordon Macdonell — Archie — was born on 3 November 1895 in Poona, India, the younger son of William Robert Macdonell of Mortlach, a prominent merchant in Bombay, and Alice Elizabeth, daughter of John Forbes White, classical scholar and patron of the arts. It seems likely that Archie was named after Brevet-Colonel A. G. Macdonell, CB, presumably an uncle, who commanded a force that defeated Sultan Muhammed Khan at the fort of Shabkader in the Afghan campaign of 1897.

The family left India in 1896 and Archie was brought up at 'Colcot' in Enfield, Middlesex, and the Macdonell family home of 'Bridgefield', Bridge of Don, Aberdeen. He was educated at Horris Hill preparatory school near Newbury, and Winchester College, where he won a scholarship. Archie left school in 1914, and two years later, he joined the Royal Field Artillery of the 51st Highland Division as a second lieutenant. His experiences fighting on the Western Front were to have a great influence on the rest of his life.

The 51st, known by the Germans as the 'Ladies from Hell' on account of their kilts, were a renowned force, boasting engagements at Beaumont-Hamel, Arras, and Cambrai. But by the time of the 1918 Spring Offensives, the division was war-worn and under strength; it suffered heavily and Archie Macdonell was invalided back to England, diagnosed with shell shock.

After the war, Macdonell worked with the Friends' Emergency and War Victims Relief Committee, a Quaker mission, on reconstruction in eastern

Poland and famine in Russia. Between 1922 and 1927 he was on the headquarters staff of the League of Nations Union, which has prominent mention in *Flight from a Lady* and *Lords and Masters*. In the meantime he stood unsuccessfully as Liberal candidate for Lincoln in the general elections of 1923 and '24. On 31 August 1926, Macdonell married Mona Sabine Mann, daughter of the artist Harrington Mann and his wife, Florence Sabine Pasley. They had one daughter, Jennifer. It wasn't a happy marriage and they divorced in 1937, Mona citing her husband's adultery.

A. G. Macdonell began his career as an author in 1927 writing detective stories, sometimes under the pseudonyms Neil Gordon or John Cameron. He was also highly regarded at this time as a pugnacious and perceptive drama critic; he frequently contributed to the *London Mercury*, a literary journal founded in 1919 by John Collings Squire, the poet, writer, and journalist, and Archie's close friend.

By 1933 Macdonell had produced nine books, but it was only with the publication in that year of *England, Their England* that he truly established his reputation as an author. A gentle, affectionate satire of eccentric English customs and society, *England, Their England* was highly praised and won the prestigious James Tait Black Award in 1933. Macdonell capitalized on this success with another satire, *How Like an Angel* (1934), which parodied the 'bright young things' and the British legal system. The military history *Napoleon and his Marshals* (1934) signalled a new direction; although Macdonell thought it poorly rewarded financially, the book was admired by military experts, and it illustrated the range of his abilities. Between 1933 and 1941, Archie Macdonell produced eleven more books, including the superlative *The Autobiography of a Cad* (1939), a hilarious expose of the vanity and deplorable cynicism of the wealthy.

Lords and Masters, written four years before the start of the Second World War, is disquieting in its prescience. Macdonell recognized that with the unimpeded rise of Nazism, war was inevitable. He predicts Europe's rapid descent into chaos and bloodshed, and Japan's attack on Singapore, the USA and Australia.

> So the [German] air fleets started off. And the air fleets of France, Czecho-Slovakia, Belgium, Romania, and Poland were instantly mobilized for defence against this unheard-of aggression ... And the Italian air force bombed Belgrade, and the Russians bombed Tokyo, and the Japanese, furious at their inability to bomb Moscow, took it out on Singapore and San Francisco and Melbourne, and the two halves of the English-speaking world sprang to arms and lent each other large sums of money without the slightest intention of repaying any of it....

Macdonell's characteristically adroit satire exposes the destructive madness of it all, a madness that must have been especially poignant for a veteran of the First World War.

> ... and Portugal, uncertain of the rights and wrongs of the whole affair, but knowing exactly which nation drank the most port-wine, joined in the fray on the British side, and sent an aeroplane to bomb Andorra — the only target within range which was unlikely to indulge in reprisals upon Lisbon.

But what is perhaps more disturbing than Macdonell's prediction of how the war was to unfold is his understanding of the extent to which the Nazi rot had penetrated British upper class society. He recognized that the fear of Bolshevism had given rise to fascism and an admiration for Hitler's brutal regime.

> A generation accustomed, like a hundred generations before it, to take its fences or its medicine with a debonair gallantry, can look a Lett in the face. But what it cannot look in the face is the prospect that Parker, the lifelong butler, may suddenly say "You go to hell, Eleanor Hanson; you goddam little swine," and walk out of the house; the prospect that the head keeper at Achnaclorach Lodge might put his feet on the mantelpiece in the smoking-room and drink himself into a defiant coma; the prospect that policemen, bus-conductors, attendants in parking-places, girls in shops, servants in bridge clubs, hairdressers, manicurists, telephone operators, head waiters, hall porters, mannequins, all the tiny pebbles which made up the mosaic pavement upon which Eleanor and her friends walked every day of their lives, might turn and spit upon them, and, worse, refuse to work for them any longer; that was Bolshevism.
>
> That was the Nightmare which haunted the Squares and Gardens, the Crescents and the Gates, which hung cloud-like over bridge-tables and brooded over fashion parades, which stalked invisible in Bond Street and dampened the air in theatre stalls.

Macdonell's masterful character depictions of war-profiteer Sir Montagu Anderton-Mawle and Nazi fanatic Veronica Hanson (modelled on Unity Mitford) tear into the arrogance and hypocrisy of the 1930s Mayfair monied set and their attempts to portray fascism as a reasonable antidote to Bolshevism.

> "My poor, sweet, guileless, adorable Papa," she cried, flitting round the back of the sofa and patting the top of his iron-grey head. "Do you

believe everything you see in print? All that stuff about atrocities is just lies. Communist propaganda, my pet. You know what Communists are, darling, don't you? I mean, you've been out of the world for such a long time that it's a bit hard to find out what you do know and what you don't."

"Veronica, dear," said Mrs. Hanson admiringly, "aren't you being a little impertinent?"

"No, seriously, Daddy, that atrocity stuff is all rot. Hitler wouldn't allow it for a moment. He isn't that sort of man. A few Jews have been beaten up perhaps, but that's nothing. What are Jews for, anyway?"

Potent and prescient, *Lords and Masters* remains one of A. G. Macdonell's most important and enduring novels.

In 1940 Macdonell married his second wife, Rose Paul-Schiff, a Viennese whose family was connected with the banking firm of Warburg Schiff. His health had been weak since the First World War, and he died suddenly of heart failure in his Oxford home on 16 January 1941, at the age of 45.

A tall, athletic man with a close-cropped moustache, he was remembered as a complex individual, 'delightful ... but quarrelsome and choleric' by the writer Alec Waugh, who called him the Purple Scot, and by J. B. Morton, as 'a man of conviction, with a quick wit and enthusiasm and ... a sense of compassion for every kind of unhappiness.' Such enviable attributes are displayed in none of A. G. Macdonell's works more so than *Lords and Masters*.

CHAPTER I

Mr James Hanson

One of the strangest districts of the strange town of London is the southern portion of the part that is called Kensington. It is strange for many reasons. For one thing the streets are called almost anything in the world except streets or roads. Some, because they surround a dingy shrubbery heavily fortified with iron railings and sharp spikes, are called Gardens. There are a few flowers within these railings, and sometimes there is a soot-covered lawn-tennis court with a dilapidated net, and sometimes there is the dignified cry of a dignified child playing with a ball, and always there is a crowd of little lap-dogs, and often an array of tin and enamel notices, menacing the proletariat with the most fearful process of the Law if it so much as insinuates a grubby proletarian countenance between the bars of the railings. The streets which surround these scenes of rural enchantment are the Gardens of South Kensington. No wandering pedlar may peddle his wares in these gardens, nor may a passing troubadour lift up his voice in song to praise the Lord. Both are forbidden in tin and enamel. Other streets are called Gates, although there are no gates in them and they themselves may, and often do, lead to nowhere but a blank wall. Others again are called Squares, although the measurement, and frequently the number, of their sides would have given Master Euclid, that precise man, a fit of the shivers, and others, that hardly at all resemble the sunny tranquillity of a Southern Plaza, are called Places, and yet others in an ostentatiously Christian portion of a comparatively Christian town, have been christened, so to speak, Crescents.

The houses are all exactly the same, tall, massive, fronted with pillared porches, stuccoed, gloomy, and all have been at one time or another painted yellow, except that here and there a dazzlingly new coat of white paint proclaims the occupation of a short-term tenant instead of the usual owner of 999-year leases. For the Gardens, Squares, Gates, Places, and Crescents are almost entirely inhabited by families which fully expect to outlive their leases and see out their proprietary millennium, and these naturally enough do not propose to repaint their exteriors until, say, the 927th year of their lease. When, therefore, you see a new coat of paint, shining like a good deed in a far from naughty part of the world, you may be quite sure that it is being reluctantly applied by a temporary lessee whose lawyers cannot, for all their craft, see a way to dodge the painting-clause in the short lease.

The poor sinner, wayfaring through this mysterious acreage of dingy solidity, may be forbidden to enter the magic gardens (though his disqualification is determined rather by his poverty than by his sins), may not find a Gate through which to pass, may not pace round a true Square, may see a true Crescent but nowhere a true Cross, but nevertheless he would do well to pause and, doff his hat, provided that his poverty is not so abject as to have necessitated the pawning of it. For he is standing on Holy Ground.

He is in the very heart of the Greatest Empire in the World. Nineveh, Babylon, Persepolis, Ecbatana, Athens, Rome, and South Kensington, there is no difference between them.

The whole of an Empire, from North Borneo to the South Shetlands, from Nangi Parbat to the Isle of Man, from the Upper Reaches of the Klondike River past Honduras, and Sierra Leone and Mauritius and Tasmania to the islands of the Antipodeans, white, yellow, black, or brown, baptized or infidel, pays unending tribute to London, and London pays unending tribute, through the simple device of the Preference Share, to South Kensington. The whole imperial fabric climbs dizzily to this summit. Here are the ultimate fruits of the toil of Continents. Here is the apex of culture and grace for which so many great Dominions, and so many Crown Colonies, and so many Protectorates, and, since 1920, such useful Mandated Territories, have laboured, and to them the knowledge that they have created, and are maintaining, South Kensington is its own reward. At least it ought to be.

On the strong foundation of the Preference Share, a great social structure has been erected, that is like nothing else on earth. Its chief characteristics are its passionate — I use the word in its genteelest and quietest sense — belief in the infallibility of the Conservative Central Office; its desire to shoot, with noiseless powder of course, and of course somewhere decently out of sight, President de Valera; its devotion in theory to fox-dogs and in practice to lap-dogs, and its deeply rooted, but never uttered, conviction that Galsworthy spoke a true word when he described the life of a typical Southern Kensington man, and his uncles and aunts, his daughters and granddaughters and cousins, and their respective solicitors, as a Saga. The

Religion of this great social structure is, as is seemly in the heart of an Empire which contains so many creeds, not unduly dogmatic. Indeed, it lays almost all its emphasis upon its negative rather than upon its positive beliefs. Thus it is not good form to discuss Christ in the drawing-room, but it is considered distinctly correct to discuss the Anti-Christ of the moment. This typical institution of South Kensington varies from time to time, just as on the day which is reserved to celebrate the escape from destruction of the House of Commons, the Guy of the street-urchins is seldom Guy Fawkes himself but may vary from Herr Hitler to Signor Mussolini, or from Signor Mussolini to Herr Hitler, according as those potentates pop in and out of the contemporary limelight. Twenty-five years ago the lowest hell of South Kensington's Inferno (although, of course, the local citizens would never dream of using such words to describe it; they would probably, if they had ever felt the necessity of putting words to it, have called it Dante Gardens) was occupied by Mr Lloyd George. He would have been succeeded, only that South Kensington did not at the time, and hardly does yet, admit the existence of the female sex in public affairs, by Mrs Pankhurst. As it was, he was compelled to sizzle upon the drawing-room gridirons until in 1914 the outbreak of Armageddon, by a change of fortune that would have startled the most enterprising of the old Greek dramatists, deposited a grandson of Queen Victoria (and first cousin of our own King, nowhere more beloved than in South Kensington) in his place and simultaneously raised the ex-fiend to the very pinnacle of Kensingtonian Heaven. Later on the Kaiser was overlapped as Anti-Christ by Vladimir Ilyitch Ulianov, and then when Lenin died, and the Kaiser had bolted to Holland to grow a beard, the job fell automatically into the lap of Mr Gandhi.

Since then, however, the position has not been so simple. Mr Stalin settled down as a serious rival candidate, and South Kensington has tended more and more towards an extension of its negative creed. By this extension, Mr Stalin and President de Valera remain as joint temporary Anti-Christ, just as some fox-hunting packs have joint Masters, while a permanent Anti-Trinity has been set up, consisting of Mr Gandhi, Lord Chelmsford, and Mr Montagu, with Lord Halifax as a kind of reserve. This compromise has given the greatest satisfaction.

Morally, South Kensington is as near perfection as any community in the world. It is the district not only of Museums but also of Morals. If Kensington proper has the advantage of Albert's Hall and Memorial, the Southern part, equally proper, of course, is proud in the possession of an even more significant, even more symbolical, emblem of marital fidelity, the Victoria and Albert Museum. Nor is that all. Round the corner is the School of Needlework.

.....

Number Forty-four Partington Crescent, S.W.7, was exactly like its neighbours on each side, and exactly like all the other houses in S.W.7, and it was the home of Mr James Hanson. But Mr Hanson only resembled his neighbours in that he was rich, very rich indeed. He never went to Church on Sunday mornings, in silk hat, and tight, striped trousers, and button boots, and velvet-collared overcoat of antique build, and dark grey gloves, and neck-tie secured by a large and handsome ring, carrying in one hand a fatly furled umbrella and in the other a prayer-book, as so many of his neighbours were in the habit of doing by way of spiritual prelude to the roast beef, the port decanter, and the afternoon nap that form the essentials of many a Kensingtonian Sabbath. He never displayed Conservative posters in his dining-room windows during General or Municipal Elections. And he never took a dog for a walk "round the square," a technical term in South Kensington meaning simply a walk.

But there was a very good reason for this almost freakish nonconformity to type. Mr Hanson would probably have enjoyed a fully choral Church service if it had ever occurred to him to attend such a festivity. He could well have afforded button boots, and he possessed several silk hats which he wore on the rare occasions when he visited the City. And he could easily have hauled the largest of dogs not only round the square, for he was a man of great strength and a powerfully built physique, but, being a householder and so the possessor of a key into the magic precincts, he could have hauled it into the gardens as well. But the essential difference was that Mr Hanson, alone of the dwellers in Partington Crescent, alone of the possessors of the right to herd horrid little lap-dogs into the Crescent gardens, had never practised the grand old Kensingtonian trade of Inheritor. He had made his own fortune himself, and had never been able to rely upon the lucrative amenities of the mid-Victorian factory system which has been the foundation of so much cultured ease and quiet felicity in Great Britain. Mr Hanson's grandfather had bequeathed no house property in the poorer parts of Sheffield or Bradford, nor had Mr Hanson's father drawn a single pennyworth of royalties in his life from the fifteen-hour day of Durham miners, in those halcyon days when coal was coal and Mr J. D. Rockefeller's philanthropic scheme to make the Chinese peasant oil, conscious was yet in its infancy. Neither Hanson *grandpère* nor Hanson *père* had done any of these things, nor yet had either of them harnessed women to trucks in the mine-galleries of the Midlands and driven the blithe, singing lasses up and down in the dark all day, thereby providing them with an honest means of livelihood. For the grandfather had been a clerk for forty years in a very respectable firm of solicitors, and although for at least thirty of those years there had been no clerk in the whole of Lincoln's Inn adepter in the tricky business of preparing 999-year leases, nevertheless his salary had never risen beyond the sum of two pounds eighteen shillings a week. The grandfather's son, James' father, had fared better, for at the end of thirty-seven years of clerkship in the London office of a Yorkshire firm of engineers, he had at least attained a weekly salary of three pounds and a half. But even this sum left little margin for the bequeathment of substantial legacies, and James Hanson had fended for himself ever since, at the age of fourteen he entered, through the influence of his father, the Penistone steel-works of the same engineering firm, at a salary of seven shillings a week.

But, by some queer freak of muddled heredity, James Hanson very soon proved himself to be a very different sort of person from his father and his grandfather, and fending for himself, even in the harsh surroundings of a Yorkshire steel-works in the early eighteen-eighties, presented no great difficulties to him from the very beginning. His father and grandfather were content with their station in life, and thanked God every day on their knees for His infinite mercy in supplying them with a regular income, the intellectual employment of a pen, and the refined surroundings of an office. James was a rebel at fourteen and remained a rebel. He was content with nothing and thanked God for nothing. The two old clerks had no desire to better themselves. James had. They were small, humble men with shoulders rounded from much desk work, and their mousecoloured eyes were puckered from a lifetime of tracking ciphers by the light of ancient gas jets. James was big and broad and strong, with keen, long-sighted, blue eyes. They wore high stiff collars, and shiny black suits that time had worn almost to the thinness of tissue-paper, and big black satin cravats. James wore boilersuits and dungarees. And if a fellow-clerk spoke sharply to them, they cringed, whereas if a fellow-artisan in the workshops cuffed young James' head, young James flew at him like a wild-cat.

James Hanson went steadily up in the engineering works. His pugnacity made him popular with the pugnacious and good-humoured Yorkshiremen, and his industry and talents marked him out to his employers. When he was twenty-one or twenty-two he had invented several small improvements in the processes, and had been rewarded, not with money — for that would have been a dangerous precedent — but with promotion in the shops.

But the turning-point in James Hanson's life came when he was taken out of the shops and sent as assistant to the firm's Representative in the East-European country of Cimbria. The firm's Representative for the last thirty years had been a Scotsman, Mr Thomas Macadam, and for thirty years Mr Macadam had led a blissful life. He had married a beautiful, deep-breasted, placid Cimbrian; he loved the country; he loved its peach-brandy, and its easy-going peasantry and its slow, indolent life; and he was immensely popular. Everyone loved and trusted old Mr Macadam, and they came to him for advice and for small loans, and, occasionally, for the purchase of a good Penistone plough or seed-drill or harrow. Mr Macadam was always ready with advice or a small loan, and, if they insisted, would sell them agricultural implements. But he was happier sitting under a cherry-tree with a few friends and a bottle of peach-brandy than wrestling in his office with the conversion of the price of a water-pump from pounds sterling into Cimbrian crowns. James Hanson, bursting with youth and enthusiasm and energy, soon changed all that. He hurled himself upon Cimbria and its potential buyers of steel articles like a tornado.

At first old Tom Macadam was amused, and then pleased that even the little work he had been in the way of doing was taken off his shoulders and that there was more leisure than ever for talk and peach-brandy under the cherry-trees. And so long as his vigorous assistant confined his vigour to the sale of rural implements to a rural people, Mr Macadam remained amused and pleased. But he began to shake his grey head and stroke his patriarchal beard thoughtfully when it became increasingly clear that James Hanson was not really interested in spades and harrows simply as spades and harrows. For thirty years Mr Macadam had taken a personal interest in every implement he had sold. For three months in the spring of each year, when the orchards of cherry and peach and almond and apple were a rippling sea of bloom in the valleys, and the brown bees were on the wing, and the roses were in bud, and the farmers were singing in the pale-green wheat-fields, Mr Macadam used to ride round the farms to drink with his friends and enquire after the health of tools which he had sold them, fifteen, twenty years ago. But to pushing, vehement, energetic James Hanson, a plough, a harrow, a spade, were not agricultural implements for the use of primaeval dwellers on the soil, but things made of Steel. It was Steel that James Hanson was selling, and the particular shape of each piece that he sold, and was paid for, vanished out of his mind. The transaction was complete, and only the name and address of the customer remained, as a man who, having bought a piece of steel once, might buy a piece of steel again.

Nor was James Hanson content to sell small rural tools. He began to launch out into side-lines, and old Mr Macadam grew more and more unhappy as he saw old simple friends being cajoled into buying steel fence-rails to keep mountain sheep, which never strayed from the mountains, from straying from the mountains, and being bamboozled into buying

Swiss musical-boxes, for which Hanson had obtained the agency, for their wives.

But peach-brandy and sunshine and orchards and friends go far in compensation for commercial unhappiness, and it was not until James Hanson struck up a boon companionship with the Cimbrian Minister of the Interior and landed a large contract, by a palpable use of bribery, for railway equipment for a non-existent railway, that old Tom Macadam knew that the world had gone past him and he folded his tents and resigned his post with the Penistone firm and crept away to his beloved Cimbrian hills with his beloved Cimbrian wife and settled down among his friends. And James Hanson, *persona gratissima* at Penistone and at the London office in Victoria Street where his father had drawn three pounds and a half per week in the thirty-seventh and last year of his employment, reigned in the stead of lazy old Tom Macadam.

From that day, in the lovely, blossomy spring of 1895, for nearly thirty years, the history of Cimbria and the history of James Hanson were interlocked so closely that they were practically identical. The building of the railway — and the subsequent retirement to Monte Carlo of the Minister of the Interior with a large fortune, carefully deposited through Hanson's kind offices in various Swiss banks — was the next incident in the joint history. Then came the discovery of iron-ore in north-east Cimbria and the eighty-years' concession of the mineral field to the Penistone Company, followed at a discreet interval by the withdrawal to Deauville of the newly created Minister of Mines, and a corresponding but temporary unsettlement of the Cimbro-Swiss exchange. Then in 1904 came the discovery of a great coal-field in the south-west corner of the neighbouring East-European kingdom of Suevonia. The iron of Cimbria lay within a mile or two of the coal of Suevonia. James Hanson pounced upon the coal. To his astonishment, his pounce was a complete frost. An American Syndicate was ahead of him. He tried to buy them out. They laughed at him. He pounced on the Suevonian railways. The Americans had already bought them. He bribed the Suevonian Government. The Americans out-bribed him. He contemplated a smashing financial attack upon the Syndicate, but discovered, just in time, that Standard Oil might possibly be lurking in the background. So James Hanson retired to his iron-ore and began to think.

The first result of these thoughts was the increase of Cimbrian armaments from the 1,600 old Italian rifles which had been bought from Abyssinia after the Adowa affair, and the two field-guns which fired the ceremonial salutes in the Cimbrian capital of Santissima Catharina, up to ten thousand brand-new French rifles and twenty complete batteries of French field-guns.

In 1905 and 1906 and the early part of 1907, the Cimbrian army grew rapidly in size. Conscription was introduced, and the equipment kept pace, in quantity and modernity, with the growth. James Hanson, on the urgent advice of his friend, the Minister for War, who afterwards got away to South America with upwards of quarter of a million, was appointed the sole agent for the provision of this modern equipment, and the Penistone Company paid record dividends during these years. For Hanson loyally gave his employers the contracts for the shells and the cartridges, but the contracts for guns and rifles he gave to the French firm of Schneider. Being an independent agent of Schneider, he was under no obligation to pass his handsome commission from Schneider's on to Penistone.

Suevonia at first affected to treat the arming of her rustic neighbours as rather a joke, in spite of the uneasiness of the American Syndicate. But in the autumn of 1906 or thereabouts the Suevonian Government was at last persuaded by Messrs. Krupps of Essen, that the Cimbrian army now constituted a real menace to the Pax Balkanica — as it was rather ironically called — and that it was Suevonia's duty to civilization, culture, and humanity, to say nothing of the American Syndicate, to place a very large contract indeed with Messrs. Krupp's for defensive weapons. The contract was placed, the usual loan was floated, partly in Frankfort and partly in New York. The usual exodus to the French Riviera and the Italian Riviera took place of the Suevonian Ministers concerned. But it was too late. Cimbria was ready. Suevonia was not. James Hanson murmured a word in the ear of the Cimbrian Government, and the rest is history. Every schoolboy knows how Suevonia committed an unparalleled act of aggression upon the peace-loving Cimbrians; how a horde of Suevonians massacred a poor harmless body of Cimbrian soldiers in cold blood, in time of peace, simply because they were enjoying a little rustic sport at a Suevonian village, burning a house here and there out of sheer animal high-spirits, and raping a few giggling Suevonian girls, and looting, just for fun, a shop or two; how the Cimbrians protested in a dignified way; how the treacherous and dastardly Suevonians not only proposed that the dispute should be settled by arbitration, but even went to such lengths of chicane that they withdrew their troops fifteen miles from the frontier.

This last act of aggression was more than unfortunate little Cimbria could stand. Springing to arms like one man in defence of gods and hearths and women, the peace-loving Cimbrians swept through the phalanx of the aggressor. Inexpert in the art of war, practically unarmed save for the French artillery and machine-guns, with no reserves of ammunition other than the few million Penistone cartridges and few hundred thousand Penistone shells, the bucolic Cimbrians blazed through Suevonia and dictated a just and lasting Peace, based upon justice and the reign of Law, in Santa Leonora, their enemies' capital.

By this peace, Suevonia was formally annexed to Cimbria, and the new country was christened Cimbro-Suevonia; and, under Article 426, paragraph 16, all foreign concessions that had been granted by the Suevonian Government were recognized by the High Contracting Powers to be null and void. All that, and more, is known to every schoolboy.

But what no schoolboy knows is that one of the Penistone shells, fired by a Schneider gun, and lamentably misdirected by a Cimbrian shepherd who had been conscripted from the watch of his flocks by night, killed old Tom Macadam up in the hills as he sat under a cherry-tree with a bottle of peach-brandy in his hand and his beloved wife at his side.

But perhaps Tom Macadam was happy in his death. For during the peace negotiations in Santa Leonora, James Hanson, who was holding a watching-brief partly for the Penistone Company but mainly for himself, formed a close friendship with the chief accountant of the now expelled and highly indignant American Syndicate, a young London Jew named Amschel Wendelmann. The two men had known each other, off and on, for ten years and had always liked each other. Wendelmann had been the Penistone representative in Suevonia before going over to the Americans, and naturally had often been associated with Hanson in business. They got on well from the very beginning. They understood one another. Each was the complement of the other. Hanson was swift, vital, almost recklessly audacious, incurably optimistic, and he knew the inside affairs of Penistone, of the iron-ore, and of Cimbria. Wendelmann was slow and cautious and far-sighted, and he knew the inside affairs of the American Syndicate, and of the coal-fields, and of Suevonia. So when the victorious Government of Cimbro-Suevonia granted an eighty-year concession of the coal-fields, it was not to the Penistone Steel Company, but to the newly formed firm of Messrs. Hanson, Wendelmann and Company. And when Hanson had persuaded the Penistone Company, by a mixture of bluff, intrigue, and violent threats, to part with their iron-ore concession for a comparative song (he could have secured it for nothing by getting his Cimbrian friends, overwhelmingly grateful for the French guns, to cancel the concession. But he felt he owed a loyalty to his late employers), the amalgamation of the iron and coal made Messrs. Hanson, Wendelmann & Co. into a very large concern. And it grew and grew and grew.

Yes, old Tom Macadam was happy in his death. He did not live to see the March of Civilization. Cimbro-Suevonia rapidly became a great industrial state, and the shepherds went further and further into the hills before the great strides of Progress, and the smoke from the Hanson mills mingled with the fumes from the Hanson smelters, and the dust from the Hanson slagheaps, and the grit from the Hanson cokeries, and the gas from the Hanson gasometers, to blight the orchards and wither the cherry blossom and canker the peach-trees.

So James Hanson became a great man, and when the World War broke out he became a Member of the Inter-Allied Munitions Committee.

And Cimbro-Suevonia became a great Power, and when the World War broke out, she was admitted to alliance on equal terms with France, Haiti, Britain, Ecuador, Belgium, Russia, Serbia, Montenegro, Italy, Panama, Roumania, the United States, Costa Rica, Brazil, and the rest of them, and was allowed to expend the lives of a quarter of a million peasants in the fight for Democracy and to the eternal Glory of God.

CHAPTER II

Forty-four Partington Crescent, SW7

On a sunny summer morning of 1936, Mrs James Hanson sat at the end of the breakfast-table in No. 44 Partington Crescent and purred. It was her sixtieth birthday and four of her five children were assembled together under the ancestral roof in honour of the occasion and the fifth would undoubtedly have been there too if she had not been too feverishly busy to spare the time. It was comparatively rare even for four of them to be in the house at the same time, for although the third and fourth, Robert and Eleanor, lived there, the two eldest, Nicholas and Oliver, were soldiers and their leaves seldom coincided, and sweet little Veronica was such a madcap, thought Mrs Hanson fondly, that no one knew where she was or what she was likely to do.

It was only natural, therefore, that Mrs Hanson should purr as she looked across the massive silver urns, the silver covers, the silver toast-racks, jam dishes, rose-bowls, knives, spoons, forks, fruit dishes, cigarette-boxes, and cigar-cutters, all massive, to the other end of the table where James Hanson sat, and to the four empty places which the four young people would occupy at their leisure within the next three-quarters of an hour or so.

There was something most comfortingly solid about it all, something that was symbolical of the solidity of Mrs Hanson's whole life. The daughter of a rich and worldly Archdeacon, she had never known a time when money was not plentiful, and for the last thirty-seven years, since she had met and married James, she had not known a time when money was not very plentiful indeed. And it was not only the silver fittings of the breakfast-table that were solid. The handsome gilt and pink-marble clock on the black marble mantelpiece, the full-length portraits, in oils, of the two soldier sons in the dress-uniforms of their respective cavalry regiments, painted by a famous Hungarian amateur, the picture of Eleanor as a small girl dressed as a shepherdess and playing with a real rabbit painted by a very old and well-known R.A., the high-backed heavy chairs, the thick carpet, and the great cigar cabinet which had been designed and hand-carved by a Belgian refugee, a coffin-maker by profession, during the War, all these contributed to a restful feeling of permanence.

And James himself was solid and restful. His shock of hair was grey now but it was still almost as thick as it had ever been, and his big square beard was still streaked with black among the grey, and his blue eyes were as alert as ever. His great broad shoulders were unbowed by the burden either of seventy years or of several million pounds. If ever a household was founded upon a rock, and a peaceful rock at that, it was 44 Partington Crescent, S.W.7.

Eleanor was the first of the children to appear. It was one of the basic theories of the house that "Father doesn't like you children to be late for breakfast," but of course that did not apply to the boys. That was another basic theory of the house, that of course nothing applied to the boys. So Eleanor was only ten minutes late for breakfast and she kissed her father and then her mother, and then wished her mother many happy returns of the day and handed over her birthday present, a box of half a dozen very expensive, very modern, night-gowns.

Mrs Hanson protested with a sort of fluttering gentleness at the unsuitability of the present at her age and purred more loudly than ever, especially when James smiled his ironic smile and said, "Keep 'em till you're eighty, Biddy. They'll suit you then." Robert was next, in his neat striped trousers and black coat, and he kissed the top of his mother's head and gave her the six volumes, specially bound in dark-blue leather with gold lettering, of the Monypenny-Buckle *Life of Disraeli*.

"Sorry I'm not a Jew, Bobby," said James. "Otherwise you might follow in his footsteps."

"Might yet, Dad," replied Robert, sitting down to a plate of those queer American cereals which are to old Scottish porridge exactly what the American character is to the old Scottish character. "Foot on the second rung, anyway," he added.

James looked sharply at him under his great bushy eyebrows.

"Second?"

Robert nodded, his mouth full of Chicagoan novelties.

"Step up?" asked his father.

Robert nodded again and swallowed his scientifically adjusted percentage of carbohydrates.

"Financial Secretary to the War Office," he said. "The P.M. offered it to me last night just as I was leaving the House. Fishface was with him."

Mrs Hanson gave a squeal of maternal joy and pride.

"Darling, how splendid," she cried. "I knew they'd soon begin to realize what a catch they'd got. Is it a Cabinet post?"

"Not exactly," said James while Robert was negotiating some more chemicals. Mrs Hanson's soft, sweet face fell a little.

"Well, it ought to be," she said. "And it would be, if somebody or other wasn't jealous of you. Depend upon it, there's jealousy somewhere."

"Don't be absurd, Mother," protested Robert. "I'm jolly lucky to get it considering I've only been eight years in the House altogether."

"Never mind. It ought to have been a Cabinet post," Mrs Hanson maintained. "But if you're pleased, dear boy, then I am. But tell me, I know I'm dreadfully ignorant, but who is Fishface?"

"Minister of War," said Eleanor, getting up to refill her Father's coffee-cup. On her way behind Robert's chair she smacked him gently upon his glossy, neatly parted hair, and said, "Well done, Bobby, I'm glad." She picked up his coffee-cup also and waited beside her mother while the plump, white, beringed fingers fluttered about among the massive silver. Then she took the filled cups back to her brother and father.

Nicholas and Oliver came in together, both of them yawning a little, and both of them a little apologetic that they had been so busy with their various duties, military and social, on the previous day that they had not had time to buy their mother a birthday present, and both of them sincere in their determination to repair to Asprey's in Bond Street at the earliest possible moment after breakfast.

Mrs Hanson was not in the least put out at this filial impiety. Who could expect great strong soldiers, cavalry captains, to finick around with birthday presents for an old woman?

Eleanor was faintly distressed at her brothers' carelessness, for she knew that it was only carelessness — they had spent the whole of the previous afternoon playing snooker at the Cavalry Club — but she was not distressed for her mother's sake. Her mother was perfectly happy. But her elder brothers were her heroes and always had been her heroes, and she had not missed the ironic twist of her father's eyebrows as he listened to the apologies of the cavalry captains. The cavalry captains themselves missed the ironic twist altogether, and they applied themselves to breakfast with vigour, firmly missing, however, the patent cereals and devoting themselves to less scientific eggs, bacon, and sausages.

After a few minutes of silence, during which the only sounds were the occasional rustling of *The Times*, the champing of strong, equestrian jaws, and the hissing of the tea-urn, Nicholas looked up from his plate and said, "Must say, Mother, you still feed us well."

"Keep a pretty table," concurred Oliver, and they both returned to their trenchers. Mrs Hanson's heart glowed with pride, and the glow mounted from her heart to her plump cheeks. She stole a glance towards Eleanor as much as to say, "there's a tribute, if you like." She knew that the other feminine mind in the room would understand the glory of the moment when these godlike fighting-men unbent for a brief space, and tossed her a word of praise. Mrs Hanson's domestic life was founded upon a maxim the truth of which she admired almost as profoundly as she deplored its phraseology and its authorship. She would have infinitely preferred that the phrase "Feed the Brute" should have been invented by say Bishop Mandell Creighton or Miss Maria Edgeworth or the first Lord Tennyson or even, in his later, saner days, by Mr Joseph Chamberlain, rather than by Mr Oscar Wilde. She knew very little about Mr Wilde's writings and career but she did know that he had introduced into England some strange crime — she knew not what — whether from Egypt or from some place even worse — and had been so promptly and so decisively dealt with by the Conservative Government then in office that it, and he, had been finally and forever extirpated from British shores, like rabies. It was all a great tribute, thought Mrs Hanson on the very rare occasions when she did think of anything except her husband, her three sons, and sometimes her two daughters, to Lord Salisbury.

But there was no denying the truth of the remark, whoever it was who had invented it. Mrs Hanson naturally deplored the suggestion, even when uttered by a man, about men, that anything Male could be a brute. For she had never encountered, in all her sixty years of life, anything that even faintly resembled brutishness in the male sex. A courtly deference of the minor clergy, and even sometimes of Mr Dean himself, in her archidiaconal youth, an almost cringing subservience of the Cimbrian, and later the Cimbro-Suevonian Cabinet to the wife of James Hanson, the aristocratic kindliness of South Kensington butlers, these had combined, over her sixty years, to make Mrs Hanson regard men in general as well-mannered folk.

And it was especially nice of them to be well-mannered folk, for after all were they not the lords of creation? Were they not formed in the Image of God? Who ever imagined a Female Jehovah? But although the regrettable Mr Wilde had used the wrong word in his description of the lords of creation, nevertheless it had to be admitted that in essence his epigram savoured of eternal truth. For Mrs Hanson knew very well, as her mother the Archdeaconess had found before her, that their lordships are more easily guided in the ways of reasonableness after a good meal than after a bad one, and more easily after a bad meal than after no meal at all.

So Mrs Hanson maintained an admirable cook in Partington Crescent, and the cook maintained an admirable table, both above and below stairs.

"How's Mammy's darling?" asked Nicholas suddenly, munching beautifully cooked eggs and bacon, and looking across at Robert's suavely immaculate clothes. Nicholas himself was wearing a rough tweed coat, grey flannels, brown suede shoes, and the tie of the regimental polo club.

"Pet of the girl voter," put in Oliver with a grin.

"Little Benjy," said Nicholas.

"Sweet lambkin," added Oliver.

Robert laid down the Hansard of the previous day's proceedings in the House, which contained his rather important question about the Government's policy with regard to the foreign trawling menace with especial reference to the conditions in the Moray Firth, and smiled benignly.

"Run away and sharpen your spurs," he observed.

"And little Benjamin shall be your ruler," said James Hanson, addressing the ceiling, which had been painted to represent a view of Belgrade from the Danube, as near as the painter could remember it, by a Serbian refugee during the War.

The cavalry captains went on munching. Robert looked vaguely at his father. Eleanor laughed. James' twinkling eye caught hers, and he laughed too.

Nicholas and Oliver, knowing by long experience that their Father seldom spoke, and never laughed, without reason, stopped chewing for a moment and looked enquiringly at him.

"He's your boss now," said James Hanson. "You ought to stand up and salute him."

"What the devil—" began Nicholas, but Mrs Hanson interrupted him placidly and proudly.

"Bobby's been made First Lord of the Admiralty," she said.

Nicholas and Oliver broke into loud and ribald shouts of laughter, but were brought up short by Robert's look of self-conscious assurance.

"By thunder, he's been made something," exclaimed Nicholas.

"Out with it, Benjy," exclaimed Oliver. "What is it whipper-in to the Buckhounds?"

"Or chucker-out to the Gaiety?" said Nicholas.

"Or second Lady of the Bed Chamber?" said Oliver.

"None of them," replied Robert, with all the benignity of a man of the world who knows that he has a heavy howitzer up his sleeve and is about to fire it. "Only Financial Secretary to the War Office," he said, and glanced slyly across the table to see if the howitzer-shell had exploded.

It had.

The cavalry captains needed a moment or two to absorb the news — their profession had not trained them to especially swift thinking — and while they were absorbing it, they looked a little like bewildered flounders. But when their minds had grasped the essentials of the position, they sprang to action in the most vehement manner. The sedate dining-room rang with military protests. The epergne, of massive silver, quivered under the impact of cavalier oaths.

The main theme of the outcry was contained in the words, "Well, I'll be damned."

Robert Hanson lay back in his chair and self-consciously twiddled his toast.

Eleanor leant forward and concentrated upon the pattern of the table-cloth. She was determined not to catch her father's eye, for she knew that her father was trying to catch her eye, she knew that he was trying to make her laugh, and she was resolutely determined not to laugh. For, after all, she was her mother's daughter, and her elder brothers were her heroes.

James Hanson, having failed to catch his daughter's eye, and knowing perfectly well why he had failed to catch his daughter's eye, for he knew his daughter rather well, laughed all by himself, a short, delighted laugh, and picked up *The Times* and left the dining-room.

CHAPTER III

The Box-Wallah at Aldershot Tattoo

It had been decided by Nicholas and Oliver that the great treat of Mrs Hanson's sixtieth birthday should be a visit to the Aldershot Tattoo, and as they were the eldest sons, naturally the decision lay with them. Robert might be officially superior to them in his new post, but at home he was still the general school-room fag, whose opinions and tastes did not matter, and Eleanor's assent was taken for granted. The cavalry captains had quickly got over their mortification at Robert's promotion, and all day were full of jokes about politicians and the political control of fighting-men, and how the damned little Welsh attorney had nearly lost the last War by disagreeing with Sir William Robertson, and how Robert, as Prime Minister, would probably nearly lose the next one by disagreeing with Field-Marshal Nicholas and Field-Marshal Oliver, and thank God for the British Navy, and so on. Robert accepted the chaffing placidly. After all, he could afford to. His foot was on the second rung of a ladder which stretched a good deal higher, and which could be climbed a good deal faster, than the ladder of peacetime promotion in a cavalry regiment. Nicholas had been a cadet when the Armistice brought war-time promotion to an end, and now at thirty-six, after fifteen years' service, he was only a captain of recent vintage, and Oliver, who had not even been a cadet, at thirty-five was a captain of the very latest season of grape-harvesting. It might be years and years before they attained their next rung.

But in politics things were very different. With plenty of money, a presentable appearance, a really good tailor, a gift of silence, and a profound admiration for Disraeli, there is no predicting the heights to which a young Conservative can attain.

Robert had all these qualities. He was pleasantly good-looking — not too short to be overlooked and not too tall to be unpleasantly dominating, not too handsome to cause misgivings among his male constituents and sufficiently agreeable to flutter platonically the hearts of his female ones — he patronized a most refined and gentlemanly firm in Savile Row, he sincerely admired Lord Beaconsfield, he carefully concealed, on the sage advice of James Hanson, his excellent capacity to make a public speech, and, again thanks to his father, he had plenty of money. Ten years before, when he had expressed, on his twenty-first birthday, a desire to enter a political career, he had been a little hurt at his father's reception of the announcement. For James Hanson had lifted a bushy eyebrow from one of his sparkling blue eyes and had asked:

"Which side?"

Robert, a Southern Kensingtonian to the core, as well as Trinity and Eton, had exclaimed in genuine horror:

"Conservative, of course. Good heavens, Father!"

"I just wanted to know which sort of seat to buy you," replied James Hanson smoothly.

"But, Father, I'm serious," protested the young man. "You can't buy seats in Parliament as if they were your old bits of scrap-iron."

"Can't you?" replied James Hanson, with a devilish look on his face that that Minister of the Cimbro-Suevonian Interior, long ago, would have recognized, and he ordered the Daimler and drove to Westminster. In the evening he came back shivering, as if he had got malaria or an ague, and Robert looked at him in some alarm, and Eleanor, who had never seen him shiver before, was terrified, and rushed upstairs for her mother.

Mrs Hanson came down to the study and surveyed her large quivering husband. "He's only laughing," she said placidly and returned to her knitting.

James at once mastered his emotions and surveyed his youngest son benevolently. "I've bought you Westbourne," he said.

Robert looked at him blankly.

"Westbourne," explained his father, trying hard not to be ostentatiously patient. "A safe Tory seat on the South Coast. Majority last time, thirty thousand odd. Present member retiring. Old Sir Thingummy What's-his-name. Twenty-eight years in the House and never made a single speech except once when he complained of the under-toasting of the muffins in the tea-room. It'll cost you two thousand a year to the local Tory Association. I'll pay it. Pity you didn't plump for Labour. I could have got you Stopley-le-Spring in Durham for a thousand."

"But, Father, I didn't plump for anything, as you call it," protested Robert in some bewilderment. "I'm a Conservative out of principle—"

"Oh yes, I know all about that," interrupted his father soothingly. "So am I. So are we all. Now run away and play."

"Play?" cried the now completely bemused politician. "What at?"

"Politics, of course," replied his father, ringing for a whisky-and-soda.

It was in these humdrum circumstances that Robert Hanson placed his first foot upon a very, very secure rung of the political ladder. Westbourne was a seaside resort which depended for its very existence upon the moneyed classes. It was a vast Pyramid, of which the apex was the Carlton Towers Hotel, and the base was an immovable mass made up of old folk in bath-chairs and middle-class families in boarding-houses. It lumped together under the comprehensive heading of "not cricket," Communism, Socialism, Radicalism, and milk-and-water Liberalism, and it voted solidly for Robert and would continue to vote solidly for Robert, so long as he proved his incontrovertible capacity to legislate for the country by paying his two thousand a year, in four quarterly cheques, to the Westbourne Conservative Association.

No wonder, then, that Robert could afford to smile placidly at the nimble chaff of his elder brothers, and he felt a glow of sleek satisfaction as he wrapped himself into his befurred overcoat, although it was a warm summer night, for the drive down to Aldershot.

Eleanor was enchanted at the prospect of going, for the sixth consecutive year, to the Tattoo. There was something indefinably thrilling about the masses of young men in gay uniforms, marching hither and thither, and galloping to and fro, in perfect unison, with perfect precision, and, most thrilling of all, in blind obedience to orders from some other man, also in gay uniform, controlling, directing, all-seeing.

James Hanson joined the party with the words, "I'm always on for a Vaudeville Show," and Mrs Hanson, who would really have preferred to stay at home with her knitting, professed great enthusiasm for the excursion. She was consoled for the loss of her comfortable chair by the journey there and back, for she sat in the back seat of the Daimler between her soldier sons. The soldier sons, on the other hand, were only consoled by their lurking feeling that they were behaving damned decently, because they would greatly have preferred a different distribution of passengers. For in the Rolls-Royce James Hanson's large bulk was deposited between a young lady whom Nicholas had invited to the party, and a young lady whom Oliver had invited. One was called Miss Priscilla Mapledurham and the other was called Miss Marion Malindine. But which was which, nobody above the age of thirty-six could ever discover. To the elderly and undiscerning eye of anything between thirty-six and a hundred, accustomed to the demure but distinct types of Victorian and Edwardian beauty, modern young women all look pretty much the same. They are all exquisitely accoutred, and all are supremely capable of every twist and turn of the noble art of self-defence. They dance like the swift shadowy little leaves of autumn in a puff of westerly wind, and they drink like fishes. All the grace of Artemis is in them, with but little of the Huntress Lady's unattainability. They have been dowered with the gifts of Aphrodite and have got rid of some of the chiefest of them by slimming. But the goddess who stood aloof at their christening was the grey-eyed one, Pallas Athene, giver of wisdom.

Robert was perched in astrakhan splendour opposite these twin triumphs of mental and physical lacquer, and Eleanor went down in Major Jack Crawford's two-seater Rolls-Bentley.

Jack Crawford was second-in-command of Nicholas' regiment and, in consequence, loomed large in the affairs of the Hanson family. Very tall, very broad, very strong, very handsome with fair hair and a beautiful fair moustache, he had won the D.S.O. as a subaltern at the tank battle of Cambrai in 1917, in which he had taken part as a staff officer on the staff of the Forty-first Corps. He had also been mentioned in despatches and awarded the Belgian croix-de-guerre for his gallantry during the March retreat of 1918, when, as a staff officer on the staff of the Sixth Army, he had rescued single-handed the entire personal effects of his General, including his gramophone and two hundred and fifty records of contemporary musical comedy and revue, during the *sauve qui peut* from Army headquarters on receipt of the news that the Germans had captured the villages of Pozières and Courcelette, some ten miles distant to the eastwards.

With his superb good looks, his immense popularity, his magnificent war record, and the easy mastery which he exercised over every technical branch of his profession, Jack Crawford was marked out, at forty-one, for the highest honours of the military world. A future Chief of the Imperial General Staff, was the usual whisper about him as he rode gallantly with the Quorn, or strolled carelessly through the rooms of the Club, or threw a gracious word to a blushing dèbutante at a Mayfair ball.

The party reached with ease their allotted parking-place in the Rushmoor arena, thanks to the perfect efficiency and harmony with which the Army co-operates with the Automobile Association on these occasions, and proceeded to their seats. Here there was a considerable hitch, as Nicholas had left all the tickets on the table in the front hall of 44 Partington Crescent, and Mrs Hanson and Eleanor and the two girls, the friends of Nicholas and Oliver, and James Hanson, had to stand about while the three soldiers and the politician went in search of help in their predicament.

Mrs Hanson was completely resigned to the delay. She did not mind in the least whether she saw the Tattoo or not, and she was blissfully happy in the society of her family. La Mapledurham and La Malindine were not in the least resigned. They were not accustomed to being kept waiting, and they did not mind who knew it. So when Eleanor murmured, "Isn't it bad luck?" they both laughed shortly, simultaneously, as if they had been rehearsing it.

The next moment James Hanson suddenly produced an official out of nowhere, like a conjuring trick, and the party was allowed to go to its seats. The official promised to keep a good look-out for the missing quartette, and sure enough, within twenty minutes they had turned up, hot and apologetic, Robert worried, and Jack Crawford, Nicholas and Oliver quietly angry. They had tried to pull several strings and none had succeeded. "How the devil did you get in?" demanded Nicholas and Oliver simultaneously.

"I reasoned with them, children," replied James Hanson, focusing a field-glass upon a spirited representation of the battle of Agincourt, "I just reasoned with them."

The soldiers grunted and took their places. They were ruffled, but not for long. The splendour of the spectacle before them, the romance of the setting, the memories of the glorious British military past, the exquisite lighting effects, and the wonderful timing, orderliness, and efficiency of the whole Show, filled them with natural and legitimate pride. All sense of grievance died away.

The battle of Agincourt came to an end: the myriad French dead were shrouded in darkness: the searchlights switched on to that ever-popular item, the advance of the Highland pipers. A thrill of excitement was just beginning to percolate through the Hanson party, solidly English though they were, when suddenly a man in the row in front remarked, in a painfully clear voice, to the girl beside him, "These regular soldiers are first-class showmen. If they ran the London Pavilion, and Charles Cochran ran the Army, we might easily win a war one of these days."

The girl laughed a gay, deep laugh which seemed to encourage the blasphemer, for he pursued his obnoxious theme. "Look at the staff work," he said. "Look at the organization of the car-parks. Look at the slickness of it all. There's a brilliant staff officer at the back of all this. I wonder why they don't let him do military work as well."

"Perhaps they do, silly," said the girl.

"Silly yourself," retorted the man. "The Army can't move a couple of mules from Aldershot to Farnborough without either losing the mules, or losing the men in charge of them, or losing Aldershot——"

"Or losing Farnborough, I suppose," interrupted the girl with another gay contralto laugh.

"Precisely," replied the man. "Now here, everything goes like clockwork. At the Battle of Cambrai in 1917, the staff boys allotted one road through Havrincourt Wood to six brigades of artillery for one night, and the same road to seventy-two tanks for the same night. You never saw such a gorgeous muddle. Charles Cochran would never have done that."

Eleanor, listening to this conversation, suddenly became conscious of a number of curious emotions surging about inside her. She longed for an umbrella, or other blunt instrument, with which to bash this scurrilous brute on his black felt hat. At the same time she was entranced with the girl's deep laughter. She was furiously angry with the man for sneering at the Army, her Army, and yet she could not help blushing in the darkness at her brothers' audible indignation. And somewhere, she found something mildly comic in the idea of the showman-general as the rival of C. B. Cochran. And then she found herself furious for finding anything comic in such Bolshevik rubbish. But although it was Bolshevik rubbish, indeed just because it was Bolshevik rubbish, there was no excuse for the half-whispered, angry comments of Nicholas and Oliver. Fortunately there was a fine contrast at hand, and Eleanor was able to look up with pride at the tranquil dignity on the face of Jack Crawford.

The handsome young major looked down and caught Eleanor's half-despairing glance. He was puzzled for a moment, but when she threw a swift nod towards the man in the black felt hat, he understood and smiled a sympathetic, understanding smile.

"Just a box-wallah," he murmured with a sort of tolerance.

It was a perfect example of the *mot juste* gone wrong. Jack Crawford modestly thought it was a complete summing-up of the situation. Eleanor confidently knew it was. Both were supremely content for a moment.

But unfortunately in a lamentable interval in the skirling of the massed pipes the man in the black felt hat heard the words, and he sprang to arms at the challenge.

"I've got a notion," he said, raising his voice a little, "for bringing the fighting services into a proper perspective. Instead of having all these fancy titles — brigade-major, lieutenant-general, and so on, they ought simply to have the same names as the civil service. Thus a brigadier would become a first-class clerk, and a colonel a second-class clerk and so on. That would knock a bit of the glamour out of them."

"They'd still have their lovely coats and trousers," said the girl, obviously playing up to her companion. She too must have heard that unfortunate "boxwallah."

"Oh dear no!" replied her companion. "We'd announce to the League of Nations that in future the British uniform would be short black coats and striped trousers and steel helmets painted black and shaped exactly like bowler-hats."

"And you'd abolish medals and decorations, of course."

"All except the O.B.E., which would be compulsory for everyone above the rank of a second-class clerk." "It would make the medal-makers cross," said the girl.

"There's probably a secret Medal Ring somewhere," cried the man, delighted at the new idea, "which encourages wars——"

"And then sends beautiful girls round to all the camps to incite the troops to feats of gallantry——" put in the girl.

"And bribes generals to recommend chaps for D.S.O.'s——"

"And circulates photographs of proud mothers——"

Eleanor stole a quick glance at Jack Crawford. He was sitting bolt upright, gazing intently at the wheeling masses of Highlanders, and humming the pipers' march-tune with a gallant show of unconcern. Nicholas and Oliver were fuming and shuffling, and James Hanson, to Eleanor's distress, was leaning forward in his seat as if he did not want to miss a single word of the dialogue in front.

That was the worst of father, thought Eleanor gloomily. You never knew what he was likely to do next, and he had sometimes embarrassed her painfully in public by the most eccentric behaviour.

The Highlanders came swinging nearer and nearer, and the blare of the massed pipes made conversation happily impossible for a few minutes, but as the kilts receded, to the tune, of course, of "The Tangle of the Isles," which is the only pipe-tune the English recognize, Eleanor heard with dismay Nicholas saying to Oliver "these damned civilians."

The man in the black hat started off again at once. "Next time the oil-millionaires and steel-millionaires decide that we ought to go and die for King and Country, I think I shall join the Regular Army."

"They mightn't have you," said the girl.

"Oh, I wouldn't let on that I'd got any brains," he replied. "That would be fatal, of course. But if I just said that I played cricket for Eton, they'd let me in at once. And once inside, I could snap my fingers at the bloody millionaires and their bloody pipe-lines."

At that moment Eleanor's gloomiest forebodings were realized, for James Hanson lifted his hat politely addressed the young man.

"Speaking as a bloody millionaire," he said, "I would be delighted if you would come to supper with me after the Tattoo is over."

The couple in front turned round at once, and Eleanor could only see, in the dim light of the stars and a half-moon, that the man's face was thin, lined, and clean-shaven, and that the girl's face was pale, and that her chin was long and beautifully shaped.

"Thanks, Caliph," said the man easily. "And in what part of Baghdad does your Highness reside?"

"In South Kensington," replied James Hanson, smiling at the man's assurance.

"Capital," he turned to the girl. "My dear, allow me to present Mr Midas B. Croesus, a bloody millionaire. Croesus, my sister, Mrs Everard. Your turn, Helen, my dear."

The girl picked up her cue with a readiness that Eleanor could not help reluctantly admiring. "Mr Croesus, my brother," she said. "Mr Henry Winter." They solemnly shook hands.

"Croesus, my old," continued Mr Winter, "my sister and I accept your hospitality this evening, and in case you turn out to be completely bogus, neither a millionaire nor a South Kensingtonian, nor even an honest man, but the representative of a firm of Uruguayan white-slavers, of both varieties, allow me to tell you that I am heavily armed and that the Assistant Commissioner at Scotland Yard is my uncle by marriage."

"Splendid," said Mr Hanson. "You have a car here?"

"Oh yes, we too have our little hoard of ducats. Not on your level, of course, but enough to support a kind of mechanically propelled vehicle."

"Then 44 Partington Crescent about midnight."

"We shall be there."

All attention had now to be focused upon the Grand Finale in which some thousand picked soldiers were dressed in the uniforms of the late nineties and drawn up in squares to resist the blood-curdling assaults of five thousand of their comrades disguised as Mr Kipling's Fuzzy-wuzzies, and then came the singing of "Nearer my God to thee," by the entire audience standing.

The magnificence of the setting, the great roll of the hymn, the latent emotions which a display of armed might is always liable to evoke, and the consciousness, through it all, of the invincible strength of England, made Eleanor forget all the petty annoyances of the evening. She sang the first verse, but suddenly found that she could get no further without bursting into tears. Ashamed of her feminine weakness, she turned away from Jack Crawford to hide her face. Then she became aware that he too had stopped singing, and she nerved herself to look up at him. She was well rewarded, for two tears shone on his long silky eyelashes. Even so strong and so masculine a character could be touched by sentiment, and Eleanor felt a warm glow in her heart that such strength and such human pity should dwell in the same broad breast.

In front, Mr Henry Winter had obviously no such access of humanity, for he was singing with enormous gusto, his head thrown back and his voice echoing across his timider and more self-conscious neighbours.

Eleanor instinctively contrasted his voice and his assurance, both of which were remarkable in their own way, and his utter lack of feeling, with the tears on handsome Jack Crawford's eyelashes, and she was shocked and disgusted when, after the sonorous Amen had rolled across the Arena into the darkness, Mr Winter remarked in a clear voice, that seemed all the clearer in the solemn hush, "I thought they only sang that in the first-class smoking-room, just before the liner goes down."

Eleanor was more than ever angry with her father for inviting the strangers home to supper.

But on the journey home in Crawford's fast two-seater, the spell of the honest, simple soldier reasserted itself and the recollection of the creature in the black hat steadily receded from Eleanor's mind. It was not that Crawford talked much. He was unusually silent, even for a normally silent man. But he was so big and so sane and so reliable, so utterly and essentially a part of all that the British Empire meant to Eleanor, and he handled his car with such cool skill and confidence, that he projected his personality over the girl just as if he had been pouring out words of impassioned love in her ears. Eleanor felt like a yacht that was safely moored under the lee of a battleship, and she was content that neither of them spoke for a long time. When at last Crawford did speak it was with an apology for a platitude.

"It's a damned silly thing to say," he said, staring straight ahead at the headlights, "and that sweep in front of us would laugh like hell if he heard me say it, but all the same, a show like that does make one proud to be a Brit."

Eleanor laid her hand on his sleeve and looked up at him with shining eyes and nodded.

"After all," went on Crawford, swallowing a little, "it's the sort of thing we fought for in the Great War, and if necessary we'll fight for it again"; and he added with a show of lightness, "after all, we can't let the damned dagoes come and play old Harry with our girls."

He pulled out to pass another car and Eleanor for a moment saw his beautiful profile, soft and yet determined, resolute but not hard, against the lights. He looked the age-old type, far, far older than Achilles or Hector, of the complete fighting-man, ready at any hour to gird on his armour and go out to conquer or to die for his country, his women, and his God.

Nothing more was said and Eleanor went off into a sort of hypnotic dream, from which she was only awoken by the car's halt at Partington Crescent and the realization that she must try to be civil to the unwelcome supper guests.

CHAPTER IV

Mr Harry Winter is Invited to Supper

When Eleanor and Major Crawford arrived at Partington Crescent they found that the rest of the party must ave been more fortunate in their escapes from the car-parks than they had been, for they were already comfortably installed in the dining-room. It was easy to see that James Hanson was delighted with his new friends. He was standing on the bear-skin mat in front of the fire, his huge shoulders shaking with laughter as he looked down from under his shaggy eyebrows at Mr Winter. The latter, completely at his ease, was lying back in a comfortable chair, a chicken sandwich in one hand and a glass of champagne in the other, talking eloquently and cheerfully. The big dining-room table, covered with plates of sandwiches and bottles and glasses, had been pushed back to the end of the room, and Mrs Hanson sat behind it, as if she was presiding over breakfast, placidly knitting. Robert was on a sofa near Winter, listening to the talk with the eager air of a man who is mentally detecting fallacies and invisibly jotting down notes, with which, when his turn comes to catch the Speaker's eye, to pulverize the last speaker, and Mr Winter's sister sat on a big footstool near James Hanson's feet, with her back to the door. Her elbows rested on her knees, and the tips of her fingers were joined under her chin, palms downwards, and she turned her head alertly from speaker to speaker, just as a spectator at Wimbledon follows the flight of the lawn-tennis ball in swift rallies. The talkers' end of the room was illuminated by electricity, the sandwiches' end by four shaded candles, so that Mrs Hanson was almost invisible. From the drawing-room beyond came the sound of American music, of the shuffling of feet, and of gay laughter. The cavalry captains and their girls preferred dancing to dialectics.

Eleanor's spirits rose. No one had paid any attention to their entry, and Mrs Hanson had become so absorbed in the tricky negotiation of a heel that she had long since passed the stage of remembering her duties as a hostess. There was an admirable chance for escape in the dim shadows of the candles. Eleanor stood on tiptoe and whispered in Crawford's ear, "Let's slip through and dance." Her spirits fell again when he shook his head.

"Bad manners," he whispered back, and he sat down sideways on a chair beside the table and casually helped himself to a sandwich.

Disappointed, Eleanor sat down beside him and filled two glasses of champagne, and pushed one across to him. Crawford nodded and smiled, and lifted the glass to her, and some of Eleanor's disappointment evaporated under the smile.

"Must be polite to the old man," he whispered, and she was pleased by that too. Jack was not always so thoughtful of her father and mother.

Harry Winter was talking, and his sister, her back to Eleanor and Crawford, was gazing up at him. "The trouble with you, Croesus, mon vieux," he was saying, "is that you and all your brother Croesi can never see more than an inch and a half in any direction at any moment. Your sole idea is to make the world safe for plutocracy, and the way you go about it would make a cat laugh. And more than a cat, Croesus." He wagged a solemn finger at James Hanson. "Do you know that the antics of you and your confrères are depriving Comrade Stalin and all his merry boys in the Kremlin of their hard-earned night's rest, because they will keep on thinking about you, and the more they think about you the more they laugh, and the more they laugh the less they sleep. It isn't fair. It isn't right."

"I've made my own little world safe for my own little corner of plutocracy," replied James Hanson.

"The old story," answered Winter. "I'm up — pull the ladder up. And you call yourself a credit to Society." "Certainly not," said the millionaire, with a triumphant grin. "But I call my bank balance a credit to myself." "Fraudulently acquired, I doubt not," replied Winter airily.

"Partly fraud, partly violence," answered Hanson, his grin softening into an appreciative smile at the other's bland impertinence. "Fill your glass, St. Francis."

"You are a dreadful old scoundrel," cried Winter bouncing up from his chair and seizing a champagne bottle by the neck as if it was an Indian club with which he was about to attack his host. Crawford, once heavy-weight officers' champion of the Army, half rose to his feet but sat down again when Winter did nothing more violent than fill his sister's glass.

James Hanson was delighted. "I have been a dreadful scoundrel for forty years," he said, "and I suppose an old one for the last ten of them, and you're the first man who has ever said so."

"No," said Winter, slowly looking hard at the magnificent iron-grey head of the millionaire. "I withdraw the 'old.' You'll never be old, Croesus. Whom the devil loves live young."

"Of course Jim isn't old," exclaimed Mrs Hanson from the shadows. She had risen to the surface for a moment and had grasped the gist of the last two sentences. "I won't have Jim called old. Will someone give me a glass of lemon-squash?"

Crawford went efficiently and unobtrusively to her aid. Robert seized the diversion, cleared his throat quickly, and opened up his slow but accurate batteries.

"But Mr Winter, when you say that all power in the world rests with the controllers of certain commodities, and none whatever with the elected representatives of the great Democracies . . ."

Robert was soon in his stride, and Eleanor abstracted her mind from the sound and moved quietly to another chair from which she had a clear view of Mrs Everard. Mrs Everard's whole soul seemed now to be as completely absorbed by Robert's monologue as it had been by the shuttlecock exchanges between Hanson and her brother.

She was a woman of about thirty-five or perhaps a year or two more — almost certainly not less — and Eleanor instantly summed her up as a clever woman. She was not beautiful, but she had arranged her colouring in such a way that men would be easily deceived into forgetting about standards of beauty and into assessing Mrs Everard's face by standards of charm and striking unusualness. Instead of concentrating upon youthful bloom, Mrs Everard had increased her natural paleness. By contrast she contrived to make her deep-set eyes look black, and any man would swear that she had black eyes, although Eleanor saw at the first appraising that they were brown, and a rather ordinary brown at that. But her brown hair was swept carefully out of the way, and her brown eyebrows were plucked to the thinnest line, so that a white forehead accentuated the bogus blackness of her eyes, and so that brown hair was not allowed to accentuate the real brownness of them. The long black and silver Spanish earrings, too, helped the black and white illusion, and not only that; they most cleverly and subtly carried the eyes of the observer to the lines of the long and beautiful chin. And the lines of the chin, in turn, carried the eye on to her hands which were so cleverly placed beneath it, and thence to her slender wrists. A very clever woman, thought Eleanor, as she watched the apparently rapt interest with which Mrs Everard gazed up at Robert from her humble position at his feet and listened to his harangue. She seemed to be spell-bound by his wisdom and his eloquence, and then after a bit it seemed as if Robert was becoming a little spell-bound by her attention, for more and more he directed himself to her. He had set out to pulverize Winter, but he ended by preening his peacock eloquence before Mrs Everard.

Eleanor turned a little to see if Jack Crawford had noticed the little comedy. It was too good to miss. But Jack Crawford missed it, for his cold blue eves were staring, unwaveringly, unwinkingly, at Mrs Everard's profile which — owing to her half-turn towards Robert — he could now see for the first time.

Eleanor began to whisper something, and then stopped, startled. Twice she followed the line of his look to make sure, and each time she made painfully sure. Jack Crawford was, as he always was, completely impassive and completely master of himself, but there could be no doubt whatever that he was staring intently at Mrs Everard.

Eleanor suddenly felt cold. She jumped up and went to join the dancers, then realized that four may be company where five are not, and came slowly back to her chair by the table. Not even the sharp movement and unexpected return distracted Crawford from his absorbed, passionless, unemotional scrutiny.

Robert's speech came to an end and James Hanson said "Words, words." Mrs Everard swivelled herself on the footstool to face the new speaker.

"Deeds are your line, Croesus, aren't they?" said Winter.

"They used to be, they used to be. But you haven't told us what your line is, young man."

"Oh, I'm just a gas-bag," replied Winter.

"We all know that," retorted Hanson in a flash, "but in pursuit of what Noble Ideal do you expend your gas? And in return for what remuneration — if any?"

"Do you suggest that I would make money out of my Ideals?" cried Winter.

"Yes," answered Hanson.

Winter began to splutter in mock indignation. "After all," said Hanson with his demoniac smile, "I made money out of mine. Why not you out of yours?"

"Helen," said Winter, rising with dignity, "when Croesus starts talking about his Ideals it is time that honest folk like you and me were in bed."

"Have another drink," said Hanson, "and tell me what your profession is."

Harry Winter glanced with a half-waggish, half-rueful smile at his sister. She caught his eye — she seemed to catch everyone's eye with these swift, darting turns of her head — and laughed openly at him.

"I'm out of work just now," he said, "but for the last twelve years I've been business-man to my brother. He's an exporter."

James Hanson raised his bushy eyebrows sceptically at this vague statement.

"And what does he export, if one may ask?"

"Oh, he doesn't export anything now," explained Winter. "He's gone out of business."

"Broke, eh? No wonder you're down on millionaires. All failures are."

"Failures?" cried Winter indignantly. "We weren't failures. We made a packet."

"Why did you retire then?" demanded Hanson. "James, dear," purred Mrs Hanson, waking up again, "I don't think you ought to ask the young man so many questions. It isn't very hospitable. Won't you have another sandwich?" She addressed Mrs Everard. At the word sandwich, Crawford automatically picked up a plate and half rose to his feet. Then he sat down again and began to study the label on a champagne bottle as if he had not heard what Mrs Hanson said. But no harm was done, for no one paid any attention to what Mrs Hanson said. It was rare when anyone did, and nobody seemed to worry about it, least of all Mrs Hanson.

Harry Winter went on smoothly. "We went out of business because President Hoover was so ill-advised as to behave like a perfect ass and let President Roosevelt in."

"President Roosevelt," began Robert, gazing at Mrs Everard's dark eyes, "is a menace to all stability of——" His father interrupted, "You were rum-runners, eh?" Winter laughed. "There are no flies on you, Croesus. Yes, we were rum-runners. I attended to the purchasing end, in Glasgow, and delivered the stuff to my brother in the Bahamas. My brother attended to what you might call the delivery end. He used to be a professional sailor. Commander of a Q-boat at the age of twenty-two," he added.

"Well, I'm damned," said James Hanson slowly and with obvious admiration.

"Not yet, Croesus, not yet," cried Winter gaily and then he held out a hand to his sister and helped her up. "Come on, Helen, we must be going."

"Come again," said James Hanson, a great rumbling laugh exploding somewhere deep down in his barrel of a chest. "St. Francis the rum-runner, eh? The Idealistic boot-legger! Sir Galahad the hijacker! Thank God for a good laugh in this world. Master Winter, I may be an old scoundrel, but it seems to me that you're a pretty good specimen of a young one."

"What a partnership we should make," replied the irrepressible Mr Winter over his shoulder as he went across to the dining-room table to say good-bye to Mrs Hanson.

He was shaking hands with her and in the middle of a graceful sentence of thanks before he became aware of the presence of Eleanor and Crawford in the shadows. "Hello," he said, breaking off his thanks, "how rude of me. Why did no one introduce us?"

Mrs Hanson gave a squeal of fluttered distress and was on the point of launching into a flood of mingled introductions and remorse, when Helen Everard's deep voice cut in, "Why, it's Jack. Have you been sitting there all this time? How are you, Jack?" She held out her hand, and there were cries of "Good gracious, do you know each other?"

Crawford was completely impassive. He took her hand and held it for such a tiny fragment of a second that it almost looked as if he had not touched it at all, and said:

"How are you, Helen?"

"Dear me, what an echo of the past," she said. "I hope you left Bombay well, Jack. Come on, Harry"; and with a bright, comprehensive smile to everyone she led the way into the hall.

Jack Crawford did not even glance at her. He turned to the table and helped himself to a salted almond and crunched it with his gleaming, faultless teeth, and hummed a music-hall tune.

CHAPTER V

Eleanor's Thursdays

The day after her mother's birthday was Eleanor's Thursday. That day of the week was always called Eleanor's Thursday, or Miss Eleanor's Thursday, or my Thursday — according to the rank and identity of the speaker — in the Hanson establishment. The reason for this allocation of the day was that on every Thursday — except during certain unavoidable functions such as Wimbledon, Ascot Week, or Henley, and, of course, summer holidays in Scotland and winter holidays in Switzerland — Eleanor did her Social Work. It was a recognized institution among her friends, and one that had to be recognized by all new acquaintances if they wished to rise out of mere acquaintanceship, that Eleanor was always busy throughout the whole of the day on Thursdays, and was always thoroughly tired out in the evenings after the long day's work. No one, in consequence, ever bothered her with invitations for Thursday mornings, noons, or nights.

This Social Work meant a good deal to Eleanor. For one thing one had qualms about the size of one's own personal income when one compared it with the incomes of the people whom one met in East Stepditch. James Hanson was strongly opposed to the dependence of children upon their parents. He had been independent — through force of circumstances, it is true, but none the less independent — since the age of fourteen, and he loved freedom more than any other gift that his money brought him. And he intensely disliked the notion that his wife or his children should have to come creeping to him, hat in hand, whenever they wanted to buy something or spend something, or, worse still, the notion that they might be especially polite and kind and thoughtful to him when they thought they might thereby wheedle a few extra pounds out of him. Such mendicant flattery would be degrading to them and degrading to him. So each of the children had been made completely independent by the gift of a block of Preference Shares or Government Bonds as each came of age, a block sufficient to produce a considerable income. And the gifts had been outright and unconditional. Thus, at the date when this story opens, the two cavalry captains were each the possessor of a private income of five thousand pounds per annum. Robert too had five thousand a year, but, in view of his more important position and greater responsibilities and wider opportunities, James Hanson also paid the two thousand a year which the Westbourne Conservative Association demanded as the price of permitting themselves to be toiled for and slaved for by one of the most promising young men in the Party. Eleanor and Veronica each had an income of two thousand five hundred a year, and it was characteristic of Eleanor that, while it never occurred to her to think it unfair that her income was only half her brothers' — after all, why shouldn't it be? They were men, out in the fierce rush and competition of the world, while she was only a girl, living a quiet, sheltered life — nevertheless the Hanson blood ran fiercely in her veins whenever she thought of Robert's extra two thousand. For it was an extra two thousand. There was no way of getting round that. Their father did not pay club subscriptions for Nicholas and Oliver, although their clubs were just as important to them in their profession as Robert's seat was to him in his. He had not even paid for their polo ponies when they were stationed at Umballa, or their yachts when they went up to Naini Tal.

As for the argument that Robert's position was, or was ever likely to be, more important than theirs, that was sheer nonsense. Eleanor, only five years younger than Robert and therefore almost a contemporary in the nursery, knew exactly what Robert was like. He was nothing in comparison with the two heroes. She had pulled Robert's hair once and he had cried. Another time she had punched him in the eye and he had cried again. A lot of use he would be in a cavalry charge. He couldn't even ride. He could talk all right. He was a great hand at talking, but in the next war — and to judge from the mess Europe was in, the next war would be coming along quite soon — talking would not be half so useful as cavalry-charging. So Eleanor secretly resented that extra two thousand. And even more she resented the implication that it was deserved.

No one, except only the solicitors and James and Florence Hanson herself, had ever known how much James had settled on Florence. Now only the solicitors and James knew, for Mrs Hanson, who had accepted the money, but in her innermost heart hated the idea of not being utterly dependent on her man, had long ago forgotten.

This dreadful discrepancy between two thousand five hundred a year, plus a large and sheltered house, and the incomes of the poor, was one of the reasons for Eleanor's self-denying Thursday. She was often quite worried by it, and her way of absolution, of putting herself right with Heaven, was to go to the Welfare Centre in East Stepditch once a week and, furthermore, to contribute two hundred and fifty pounds a year to the finances of the Centre. She had fixed the sum partly owing to a childhood recollection of Biblical tithes, and partly because, from her earliest days up to the present, almost the only remark which she had ever heard her father make about business and business methods had been, "The world is built upon the secret ten per cent commission." She had never understood what it meant, nor had she ever known why her father's ironical smile had always accompanied the remark, but somehow the words had stuck in her memory. So she gave ten per cent of her income to the Centre and it comforted a great deal.

There was also another side to Eleanor's desire to help the world by working among the poor. Among all her friends — and she had a great many — there was one deep-rooted fear, one all-pervading terror. It was grimmer than the Kaiser of their War-nursery days, grimmer than the Bony of their great-great-grandfathers, grimmer than the Black Douglas ever was to the Border children. For it was intangible yet ever-present, vague yet hideously destructive, and it lurked round every corner of every year.

Eleanor and her friends rolled round London in their fathers' Daimlers, or in the sports cars of their young men; they played afternoon bridge in front of cosy fires; they were served by butlers, and by elderly dames who had once been their nurses; they had breakfast in bed; they danced decorously in each other's houses, and went to Commem. and May Week and the annual cricket match between the boys of Eton and the boys of Harrow, and the Grand National; and when they went to Carlsbad with their parents, there was always an announcement of their departure in the Morning Post and, later, of their return. But in spite of the apparently solid rock upon which their lives were built, they all shared this secret dread. They were prepared to face another war with equanimity — indeed it was one of their ordinary topics of conversation, and they joked gaily over the between-rubber toast-and-tea about gas-masks and germ-bombs and dug-outs and those dirty pacifist skunks — and sometimes they faced broken bones in the hunting-field, and they invariably travelled by aeroplane whenever they could. But they were, one and all, utterly, absolutely, unhingedly terrified of what they called Bolshevism. Eleanor was no less terrified than any of them. Her elder brothers spoke of it as a monster whose fifty thousand heads could only be dealt with by a good sharp cavalry sabre. Robert spoke of it as a fiend who could only be exorcised by a good sound Conservative majority. But though they differed between execution and exorcism as a cure, at least they agreed upon the essential monstrosity, or fiendishness — the distinction was too fine to quarrel about — of Bolshevism.

Eleanor and her friends would have been hard put to it to define what they understood by Bolshevism. It did not mean, as it did to most of their charming mothers, physical tortures usually applied by Chinese and Lett, or Lettish, torturers (Lett, or Lettish, sounds so incomparably more brutal, more refinedly sadistic, than the more ordinary word Latvian); nor did it mean, as it did to almost all their fathers, the forcible confiscation of oil-fields, with the consequent loss of paternal cash; nor did it even mean rape organized on national lines. Eleanor and her friends could not imagine themselves in the position of being tortured by Chinese or Letts. It was beyond all the bounds of reason. And their fathers seemed mostly to have so much money left, that it was rather surprising to make such a fuss over a few oil-fields. As for rape, whether organized or not, they did not belong to that queer class of young women which lives in flats, lounges upon orange cushions in pyjamas, and not only admits the existence of Bolshevik rape but openly discusses it.

No, to these sheltered, gently nurtured ladies, Bolshevism meant something infinitely more terrifying than any of these.

A generation accustomed, like a hundred generations before it, to take its fences or its medicine with a debonair gallantry, can look a Lett in the face. But what it cannot look in the face is the prospect that Parker, the lifelong butler, may suddenly say "You go to hell, Eleanor Hanson; you goddam little swine," and walk out of the house; the prospect that the head keeper at Achnaclorach Lodge might put his feet on the mantelpiece in the smoking-room and drink himself into a defiant coma; the prospect that policemen, bus-conductors, attendants in parking-places, girls in shops, servants in bridge clubs, hairdressers, manicurists, telephone operators, head waiters, hall porters, mannequins, all the tiny pebbles which made up the mosaic pavement upon which Eleanor and her friends walked every day of their lives, might turn and spit upon them, and, worse, refuse to work for them any longer; that was Bolshevism.

That was the Nightmare which haunted the Squares and Gardens, the Crescents and the Gates, which hung cloud-like over bridge-tables and brooded over fashion parades, which stalked invisible in Bond Street and dampened the air in theatre stalls.

This grim phantom had brought the only doubt into Eleanor's mind of her father's infallibility in the big things of the world. In the small things, he was, like Nicholas and Oliver and Robert, comically fallible, and Eleanor and her mother enjoyed many a gentle giggle, secretly shared, at the absurd prejudices and helpless incompetence of the four great, splendid men of the house. But in vast affairs, in the ruling of gigantic destinies, and, above all, in the cautious provision against unknown contingencies, men were supreme, and James Hanson was supremest among men. He had builded Number 44 Partington Crescent upon an unshakeable rock, and his vision had pierced the future and established against it a rampart of life insurances, trust funds, provisions for death-duties, tax-free inheritances, and lifetime bequests. No woman could do such a thing. No woman had the mental grasp of the practical affairs of life to look so far ahead and plan so fundamentally. It was all the greater shock, therefore, to Eleanor when she took her Bogey to her father, like a small child seeking comfort.

For James Hanson had laughed at her and her Bogey. Eleanor was scandalized.

"But, Father, it's nothing but barefaced robbery," she protested.

"It's just one system of barefaced robbery trying to get the better of another," he replied, with a glimpse of that smile that Eleanor could not find it in her heart to like, though she had tried with filial devotion to like it all her life.

"But this, all this," and Eleanor implied with a gesture all the Hanson prosperity, "isn't made out of barefaced robbery. It's — it's ours. They've no right to take it from us."

James Hanson laughed and said nothing.

"But you don't approve of Bolshevism," cried Eleanor, her foundations of faith quivering.

"If they can get my money from me, I'll admire them," said her father.

"Admire them?" her voice was almost shrill. "Certainly. I'd admire anyone who could do that."

Eleanor gave it up. "Well, thank God for Mussolini," she said, making for the door, in despair at the backsliding of a lifelong idol.

But worse was to come. Before she could make her exit on her big line, her father remarked, "Fascism — Bolshevism. It's all the same."

Unable to believe her ears, Eleanor turned and said in a tone of magnificent ice, "What did you say, Father?"

"You heard," replied James Hanson, who was never awed by his daughter's occasional soarings into the High Drama. "Think it out," and he returned to his study of the *Daily Herald*.

But Eleanor had lots of more important things to do than to waste time thinking about such paradoxical nonsense, and her filial devotion sagged a point or two after this conversation.

It was very puzzling, because Eleanor had never before imagined that her three brothers could take a saner and sounder view of a world problem than her father, and yet in this case they were unquestionably in the right and he unquestionably in the wrong. However, she reflected that everyone has a blind spot. Mr James Hanson was the only one among all the fathers of these timid and elegant ladies who seemed to treat Bolshevism lightly, and it was small wonder, then, that the ladies themselves were passionately devoted to any possible form of talisman against the terror, and to their lovely but bewildered eyes only three talismans appeared on the horizon — the British ballot-box, which permitted the deposit of a good, solid, true-blue Conservative vote; the character, personality, virility, black-shirt, and vital magnetism of Signor Mussolini; and Social Work among the Poor. The opportunity to use the first came but seldom. The second could only be assisted in his work by dinner-table praise. But the third offered scope to all.

And so Eleanor worked in East Stepditch on Thursdays, partly to ease her conscience and partly to save the world, except on those Thursdays, as previously catalogued, upon which social engagements had a prior claim over social welfare.

The Lady Anne Haselhurst almost always accompanied her to the East Stepditch Centre. Lady Anne was of the same age, the same elegance, and was possessed of the same terrors. She could not, it is true, contribute two hundred and fifty pounds a year to the Welfare Centre, for her father, the Lord Haselhurst, was not well off, but she brought an aristocratic poise, a sort of patrician tone, that was very nearly as valuable.

The arrangement had several advantages. Lady Anne, being of noble birth, cared nothing for money, but it was pleasanter to make the journey to Stepditch in a chauffeur-conducted Daimler as far as the Stepditch High Street, than to wrestle with buses, trams, and intersecting lines of subterraneous trains. Eleanor, for her part, was no snob, but she enjoyed the society of Lady Anne. And both girls found not merely pleasure in each other's company but mutual defence. For when they walked down dingy streets upon their various errands of mercy, and nasty little boys screamed appreciative but dubiously worded comments upon their smart costumes, they found it easy to appear unself-conscious by the simple device of chatting unconcernedly to each other. Whereas, alone, each would have been overwhelmed with shame.

It was not as if they looked in the least smart, for they always wore dowdy clothes that had not been remotely fashionable for at least two years and had never, even in their heyday, been ultra-smart. But somehow, however hard they tried, they never managed to look as if they had lived all their lives in Stepditch, and it was inevitable that small boys should sometimes express their admiration in unorthodox terms.

They tried to do as little walking as possible through the streets, but there was always the last half-mile to be covered, from the noisy, crowded thoroughfare where they got out of the car and sent it home, to the Welfare Centre. And there was the same walk back, of course, in the evenings.

At the beginning Eleanor had volunteered for the part of the work which involved visiting families in their houses, but she had been so appalled by the overcrowding, and the smells, and the dirt, and the torrents of small children, that after half a dozen genuine attempts to stand it she had asked to be allowed to work in the Centre itself. She felt a little ashamed of herself at first. If the paid worker, who was also a woman, could stand it, surely she ought to have been able to stand it too. But she was a little comforted by Lady Anne, who had also tried to visit the families in their houses and had also failed, when she pointed out that it was simply a matter of what you were accustomed to. "Miss Hondegger has been at it all her life, probably," said Lady Anne. "She doesn't see anything queer in six people sleeping in one room. We're different. We don't wear pince-nez and we don't have our hair tied up in a clump behind, and we don't like porridge. That's all it is. It isn't anybody's fault."

With this consolation ringing in her ears, Eleanor devoted her Thursdays, with the Lady Anne, to the weighing of babies and the noting down of the meagre weights upon charts, and to the distribution of nourishing foods to undernourished expectant mothers. They also had to listen a good deal to interminable stories about rent collectors and arrears and threats of eviction and instalments and rent restriction acts, which was all very complicated and very confusing, and not at all the sort of conversation they were accustomed to hear at home. Eleanor and Lady Anne could manage the babies fairly well, and the pathetic, humble, cow-eyed, expectant mothers with ease. But Rents they always handed over to Miss Hondegger. They felt that, as women, they could tackle babies and mothers instinctively. But Rents and Evictions and Arrears were essentially masculine and therefore belonged to Miss Hondegger who, if she was also a woman, was nevertheless accustomed to these things. Besides, Miss Hondegger could hardly be described as a woman in the sense that Eleanor and Lady Anne meant by the word.

And in the case of real, horrible emergency, of drunken husbands or enraged street book-makers or jilted lovers, there was always the Sergeant to fall back upon. The very existence of the Sergeant was a profound source of comfort. The Sergeant was the caretaker, cleaner, lighter-of-fires, washer-up, and janitor to the Welfare Centre.

He was not a Sergeant really, although once for a few weeks, long ago, he had worn the chevrons of that rank. Before the War a chauffeur, a gold prospector in Africa, a pot-boy in a Johannesburg drinking-den, a seaman, a chucker-out in a Durban music-hall, a hall-porter in a hotel in

Capetown, and again a chauffeur, Mick Barber enlisted in the Middlesex Regiment on August 5th, 1914. A little man, but as hard as flint, he was a great success as a boxing instructor and as a corporal, and, on being promoted to the rank of sergeant and transferred to the Machine-Gun Corps, he appeared to have reached high-water mark. Within a fortnight, however, a succession of amazingly brave and ridiculously impudent feats of arms in the March Retreat of 1918 brought him a commission on the field, and he was just as great a success as an officer as he had been as a boxing instructor. The dignity of the officers' mess could not abate one jot of his cockney accent, nor could the deadliest of dangers diminish his cheerfulness. Now, at the age of forty-eight, looking like a rather battered but undaunted cock-sparrow, he was officially caretaker, but actually general consultant in all delicate problems, to the East Stepditch Welfare Centre. And, from some innate sense of what is fitting, he concealed his one lapse into the higher walks of life and answered to the title of "Sergeant." There was no practical emergency for which the small sergeant could not find a remedy.

Thus on one occasion a rent collector, a ferret-like man with a pleading voice and tremulous hands and a perpetual, furtive look over his shoulder as if he was being shadowed for ever and ever by a fat, be-diamonded, claret-faced employer, came to the Centre and threatened fearful penalties against a poor woman who was behindhand with the rent of a room for herself and her five small children, and expecting a sixth, and her husband gone off with a drab from Wapping. Eleanor and Lady Anne could not be expected to wrestle with such unfortunate problems, but they used to keep their pretty ears open, and on this occasion they heard Miss Hondegger say to the ferret-face:

"You can't blackmail us into paying your rents, so put that in your pipe and smoke it."

"Blackmail?" cried ferret-face. "Did you say blackmail, Miss?"

"I did," replied Miss Hondegger steadily.

"Do you know what I would do to a man who called me a blackmailer?" asked ferret-face with sinister calm. "Blackmailer!" cried the Sergeant, flinging open the door, to which his ear had been glued, and leaping into the room like a diminutive jack-in-the-box; and there, after a brief but tense silence, the matter ended.

As Eleanor said to Lady Anne, "It's a great thing to have a man about the place," and Lady Anne agreed. On another terrible occasion it was a drunken husband who came to wring his wife's neck for deserting him and hiding in the Welfare Centre. It was not as if he had been unkind to her, he explained in his own particular jargon, every word and every nuance of which Miss Hondegger understood, for he had not beaten her with the buckle end of his belt more than twice in the last six beatings, and there weren't many wives in Paradise Alley who could say that of their husbands. Miss Hondegger, grey-haired, frail, but with eternal fires shining through her wobbly pince-nez, gazed up at him and replied that his wife was going to remain in the Welfare Centre until such time as the police arrived to scoop him in. Whereupon the man struck Miss Hondegger on the ear with the flat of an enormous grimy hand, and knocked her over like a muslin doll, and then the Sergeant came bouncing in to remonstrate. No one saw the actual form of his remonstrance, for Miss Hondegger had been alone with the husband in the room and the Sergeant had picked her up and put her outside the door and locked it, before registering his first objections to the man's conduct. But it appeared from conversation afterwards, that the Sergeant had counterbalanced the handicaps of six stone in weight, twenty inches in height, and eighteen inches in reach, by three quick foul blows which he had learnt in the ordinary everynight life of the Johannesburg pothouse. Anyway, after the ambulance had taken the husband away, the Sergeant had kept the door of the room locked until he had done a lot of scrubbing with a brush and a pail of water, singing quietly to himself all the while, a song of which the words were fortunately in the African taal.

After the first reactions of horror and terror were over, Eleanor and Lady Anne found that the whole thing had been really rather exciting, and for a moment or two they envied Miss Hondegger, elderly, plain, grey, salaried, though she was, that she had been fought for by men with naked fists.

And they summed the situation up in the words, spoken by Lady Anne on this occasion, that "it is a good thing to have a man about the place."

Miss Hondegger, pale but grimly unshaken, overheard and said sardonically, "It depends on the man."

"Oh, we mean a decent man," they cried simultaneously.

"I see," said Miss Hondegger, and went back to her work.

The Sergeant openly adored the two girls and always found time to help them with their baby-weighing. He was an expert in marshalling the mothers or elder sisters into queues, keeping the babies quiet on the scales with an endless variety of tricks, and maintaining a ceaseless flow of repartee with anyone who was rash enough to engage him in a verbal bout. He seemed to know three-quarters of East Stepditch by sight and name, and his sources of information about the ebb and flow of human life in those dreary hovels and grimy, sun-sequestered lanes, were widely ramified, for the most part reliable, and for the entire part highly irregular. But it was known throughout the bars of the pubs, and in book-making circles, and in burglarious circles, and in bashing circles, that the Sarge never tipped anyone off to the police for any misdemeanour in the world save two, wife-beating and cruelty to children. Everyone, including the Superintendent along at the station, knew that the Sarge had been present when Joel the Yid, the tick-tack man for Big Isaac, had had his throat cut in Antonelli's cafe on Christmas Eve, but everyone, including the Super, knew that it was useless to try to get any information from him. In the same way, the Sarge knew who killed the grocer at the corner of Lavender Walk and Rosemary Gardens, down by the River, and he could have identified the body of the man with ginger-coloured hair who was found in the Pool with his head bashed in. But it was a waste of time asking him about these things. Even when Soapy Joe, the safe-cracker, stabbed his partner Sam the Red for trying to betray him to the cops after Soapy Joe had double-crossed him over the Aldgate warehouse robbery, even then the Sarge kept his mouth shut, though it would have been a fine thing for Stepditch if Soapy Joe had been put away. "He's a good husband and he's a kind father," was all that the Sergeant would say, and Eleanor and Lady Anne marvelled at the loyalty of men to each other, and deplored the lack of that quality in women.

.....

It was a lucky chance that the day after Mrs Hanson's birthday was not only a Thursday, but a busy day in the Welfare Centre, for Eleanor was kept occupied all day and had not very much time in which to worry about Jack Crawford and the strange, clever woman. On the other hand, the rush of work cut both ways, for Eleanor had lain awake half the night before, wondering and wondering, and she was dog-tired before the day was out. She had known Jack long enough now — ever since that afternoon — she was seventeen at the time — when he had thrown her a careless, flashing, devastating glance at a polo match — to understand that his one unbreakable rule in life was never to show emotion. The more profoundly moved he was at heart, the more nonchalantly careless his outward demeanour became. His favourite poem, although he would never admit even that he knew of its existence, was Kipling's panegyric on the English character, to the gist of "Beware when the English grow polite." However deeply he might love a woman, Eleanor knew that he would never lose his head over her. "Funny old girl" — with a pat on the back of the head — would mean a lot from Jack Crawford. "Not a bad-looker" would have been his description of Venus Anadyomene, and Pallas Athene would have got "brain almost like a man's" from him. In just the same way Eleanor could picture him in a rain of German shells at Army headquarters, lighting a cigarette and rallying a panicky crew of temporary gentlemen with some cool metaphor from the hunting-field.

It was this knowledge of handsome Jack's character that kept Eleanor awake. For he had stared so long, and yet with such significant calm, at Mrs Everard, and at the end his manner had been so off-hand and composed, that his heart must surely have been thumping painfully and a less healthily florid complexion would surely have mantled with a blush. Jack would never have been so beautifully composed if Mrs Everard had meant nothing in his life. He would have come forward with his teeth shining in a smile, and all his easy charm of manner, and he would have asked how old So-and-so was, and whether she remembered that evening at the Ladies' Gymkhana, and had she heard what had happened to old What's-his-name. Jack was at his best on these occasions, especially when a pretty woman was concerned. And Mrs Everard was so clever that she would certainly attract a man's admiration, especially in the after-supper light of pink lamp-shades and scattered candles. But Jack's admiration had been carefully folded up and put away, and so Eleanor lay awake half the night, and so she found the busy day at the Welfare Centre at once a happy distraction and a weariness.

The reason for the pressure of work at the Welfare Centre was the new Slum Clearance Scheme. At last Lavender Walk and Princess Court were to be torn down with their rows of four-roomed, yellow-brick hovels, and were to be replaced by fine new five-storey blocks of flats, and a revolutionary proceeding such as this could not be carried out without creating a whole crop of problems. There were ground-landlords to be negotiated with, lease-holders to be compensated, mortgage-holders to be paid off, sub-leases and sub-sub-leases to be straightened out, and, of course, on the other side of the picture, there were the contracts for the new flats to be allotted, and the contractors vigilantly watched, and the sub-contractors vigilantly watched, and the money to be borrowed from the bank, and the interest to be paid on the loan, and a hundred and one intricate legal and financial hurdles to be surmounted or evaded.

All of which, as Miss Hondegger observed grimly to Eleanor and Lady Anne at their hasty lunch of soup and cake and cocoa, was of no concern to the Welfare Centre. The Welfare Centre was not designed for interfering in such high and important matters. Its only part in the great Slum Clearance Scheme was to look after the unimportant element, the side of the affair which Big Business was too busy to consider, the welfare of the men and women and children between the time of their humane eviction from Lavender Walk and Princess Court and their humane re-installation either in the new five-storied tenement flats, or in alternative accommodation somewhere in Greater London. For it was obvious from the start that all the occupants of the four-roomed hovels would never be able to crowd into the huge new blocks under the latest regulations of the Ministry of Health, which forbade a density of population of more than four to a room.

"It's a wonderful beginning," cried Eleanor enthusiastically. Lady Anne, swallowing her cocoa as if it was a Borgia draught, agreed with a little less warmth. Miss Hondegger agreed with no warmth at all.

"Yes. Seventy years overdue."

"But still, that's nobody's fault," said Eleanor. "The main thing is that it has started. I do think it's going to be a wonderful help against Bolshevism."

"They'll only keep coal in the bath," observed Lady Anne gloomily. "They always do."

"Yes, but even so," persisted Eleanor, "I think even to have a bath is a great thing against Bolshevism. I know my brother Robert thinks so."

"He was down here last Saturday," said Miss Hondegger, "speaking for Captain Clatworthy, our member."

"Captain Clatworthy?" said Eleanor, a wave of interest animating her pretty face. "What regiment is he in?"

"He isn't in the Army," replied Miss Hondegger. "He was a war-time captain. Got a D.S.O. and bar." Eleanor lost interest in the ex-gallant captain and returned to her brother.

"Robert talks a lot," she said. "I can't keep track of all his speeches. What was he talking about down here?"

"Oh, this Slum Clearance Scheme," replied Miss Hondegger. "They're very keen on Slum Clearance all of a sudden."

"But surely," protested Eleanor, "it isn't all of a sudden. I've heard Robert talk about it for years."

"Exactly," said Miss Hondegger, a spark of fire flashing through her pince-nez. "I've heard them talking about it for years and years and years. This is the first time that anything has been actually done."

"What do you suppose has made them switch over from words to deeds?" enquired Lady Anne in a rather bored way. Lunch-time was always the worst part of the day for Lady Anne, partly because of the really ghastly food and partly from the necessity of having to sustain an almost equally ghastly conversation with this very worthy, no doubt, very marvellous, no doubt, scarecrow.

"The Conservative Central Office," replied Miss Hondegger with a sort of polite savagery, "has at last discovered that if you put a man into decent living-quarters he is half-way to becoming a decent citizen. In a few years' time he'll be taking a pride in his job and his son will become a black-coated worker and the whole family will go Tory. Hence this sudden outburst of humanity."

"You talk as if you were a Bolshy yourself, Miss Hondegger," said Lady Anne with a rippling laugh. "I was a Socialist for twenty-five years, if that's what you mean," replied the grey-haired little lady. Eleanor and Lady Anne were aghast.

"But — but — you couldn't have been," they cried simultaneously.

"I never met anyone who'd ever worked down here for more than six months without becoming a Socialist," said Miss Hondegger.

"But not a— not a real Socialist?" implored Eleanor. She not only liked the little frail woman and admired her dauntless courage, but she always regarded her as a bulwark par excellence, the real and genuine type and model of all bulwarks, against the dread Russian menace. And now to find that all the time she had been a canker in the Rose of England, probably a paid agent of Stalin, certainly a distributor of seditious leaflets among the staunch troops in the Aldershot and Blackdown districts. Eleanor made one last groping attempt to restore her tottering world.

"You said you were a Socialist for twenty-five years. Does that mean——" She broke off with an almost pathetic look of entreaty.

Miss Hondegger understood perfectly. These were not the only tailor-made young ladies who had ever come to bring help and joy from S.W.7 to E.15, and she could handle them just as easily as she could an angry docker whose wife had just given birth to semi-Malayan twins.

"It's all right," she said soothingly, "I'm not a Socialist any longer." The two girls were too polite to sigh with relief, but they felt like doing so.

"Why did you change?" asked Lady Anne conventionally. A three years' experience of dancing in Mayfair and Belgravia with the flower of Britain's youth had made Lady Anne an expert in the automatic asking of conventional questions.

Miss Hondegger's sallow, lined face became grim again.

"I changed only three months ago," she said, "when I found that the Socialist candidate for the constituency, Councillor Holloway, had come to exactly the same conclusion as the Conservative Central office."

This seemed to the two inexperienced girls an inadequate reason for abandoning the convictions of twenty-five years, and their open mouths showed their perplexity. Miss Hondegger drank the remains of her cocoa, and began to pile the cups and saucers and plates.

"Do you mean that the Socialist turned Tory?" asked Eleanor at length.

"Oh dear no! Nothing so honest as that," was the sardonic reply. "But he also realized that better houses would mean more — what shall I say

— contentment, or apathy, or political inertia — and that would mean more Tory votes and fewer Socialist votes, so Councillor Holloway," and the little thin woman threw an almost terrifying sneer into the title "Councillor," "has been pulling every string he can on the Council to block the Slum Clearance that he's been advocating on the political platform for the last fifteen years."

Miss Hondegger slapped the crockery noisily onto a tray, and marched out to wash it up. Every day she started towards the tiny scullery with the intention of washing-up, and every day the little Sergeant bobbed up from nowhere and gently but firmly took the tray and did the washing-up himself, and every day Miss Hondegger went gaily back to her work with the feeling that there still was some goodness left in the world.

After the last baby had been weighed, and the last chart filled in, and the last notes made on the card-index, Eleanor and Lady Anne patted their hair and looked sadly at their hands and put on their hats, and set out on the half-mile tramp to the High Street where the Daimler would be waiting. It was past four o'clock and they were tired after their day's work. Miss Hondegger hardly noticed that they had gone. She gulped a cup of the Sergeant's strong-brewed tea, jammed a hat upon her grey wispy hair, and went out to investigate a rumour that a woman had been bashed by her husband down near the river, in a small dark street of villainous reputation called Lovers' Walk. The Sergeant, a knuckle-duster on each hand, followed at a discreet distance like a furtive and pugnacious gnome. It would have been fatal if Miss Hondegger had seen him, for she would certainly have sent him back to the Centre.

In the Daimler on the way home, Eleanor sat thoughtfully under the great tiger-skin rug for a long time, and then she said, "What a terrible story about that Socialist. What a swine."

"What can you expect from a Bolshy?" replied Lady Anne, and Eleanor agreed that it was all you could expect from a Bolshy, and then she dismissed from her mind all thoughts of Bolshevism and the destruction of the world, and, for the first time for many hours, she found herself free to dream of two tears glistening upon long, flaxen eyelashes, and to wonder, fearfully, about Mrs Everard.

CHAPTER VI

Helen Everard

Helen Everard was sitting in the corner of a deep sofa in her large and airy fourth-floor flat in Cleveland Place. It was half-past ten of a sunny morning, but she was still wearing pyjamas and a flowery dressing-gown. Only a pair of long gold earrings seemed to have been added to her toilet as a recognition that the bright dawn had come. Her brother Harry was standing in the open window, hands in pockets, gazing absently down at the gambolling children and dogs, the sedate nurserymaids, and, here and there, a civil servant, sauntering through the Green Park on his way to work.

"Any news of Bill?" asked Mrs Everard, drawing up a small bottle-covered table and beginning to varnish her nails.

"Not a line since he left Bucharest," replied Harry, without moving.

"He always was a rotten correspondent."

"He'd write quick enough if he had anything to write about."

"Things must be pretty slow down there," she observed. "My dear Helen, things are damned slow everywhere," her brother replied. "I don't know what's happened to the world."

"Don't get petulant, Harry darling. Something will turn up."

"Something's jolly well got to turn up," said Harry with a laugh. "We can't live on our bootlegging profits for ever. Damn and blast that Roosevelt."

"I'll start economising whenever you say the word, Harry. You know that, don't you?"

"That's all right, old girl. We'll let you know." "I can easily take a smaller flat, if you like."

"You may have to, if Bill doesn't land something within the next six months. But don't do anything drastic yet awhile. The world can't go on being sane for very much longer. There's only one thing I am a little afraid of." Harry Winter left his station at the window and came back into the room.

"What's that?"

"Well, you know what an impatient devil Bill is. If he can't find anything to smuggle in the Balkans, he may turn to drugs. There's no end of a market for them in Egypt, but it's so damned dangerous. I'd sooner shoot up that O'Bannion crowd off the Florida coast again than face a British Court for drug-running."

Helen Everard smiled up at him. "How would it be if you and Bill went in for a legitimate trade just for once in a while?"

Harry Winter grinned all over his thin brown face. "I wouldn't mind if I could find one. Bill never would."

"No. Bill never would. But you might — let's think — you might write a book about bootlegging."

"And leave poor old Bill in the lurch? No. I think we'd better stick together. Besides, I don't fancy my literary earnings would go far towards keeping a kid sister in the luxury to which she's been accustomed." He waved his arm round the flat. The conversation dropped, and Harry Winter resumed his contemplation of the urbi-rural scene below. The civil servants were slightly accelerating their speed as the hour drew on towards eleven.

At last Helen Everard broke the silence with the words, "I had a letter," she yawned slightly, "from Norman this morning."

Her brother spun round. "What does he want?"

"What do you suppose he wants? Money, of course. He's in Paris."

"I knew he was in Paris."

"Did you, Harry? How? I didn't."

"His being in Paris," replied Winter drily, "is one of the main reasons why he wants money and why he isn't getting money."

"Will you explain in words of one syllable these deep riddles to a poor female brain? In other words, what in hell are you talking about?"

"Bill and I made it perfectly clear to young Master Norman when you cleared out and left him to his breakfast brandies-and-soda, that we would give him five hundred a year because you asked us to and not because we loved his beautiful eyes. We also made it perfectly clear that the moment he started playing the fool in public, we'd cut it off. Dash it all, Helen, we're prepared to support your ex-boy-friend for your sake, but not his girl-friends for his. Be reasonable."

Mrs Everard sighed. "It's reasonable, I suppose, but it's hard-hearted."

"Bill and I don't feel soft-hearted about him. He did his best to ruin your life."

"Yes I know. But he was very lovely."

Harry Winter snorted. "Bill damned nearly shot him that time in Cairo. I wish he had."

"Bill's so impetuous. I was happy with Norman, you know, Harry."

"Yes, for the first three months of your married life. Three months isn't very long."

"Three months are better than nothing."

Harry Winter snorted again and brought the conversation back from these feminine side-tracks to solid, masculine reality.

"Anyway, he's living with a girl from the Opera Comique called Odette, and Bill and I can find just as good a use for five hundred quid as Miss Odette." Mrs Everard sighed again and slipped mischievously up the side-track again. She adored watching her brothers trying — in their own often-repeated words — to "stick to the point," and more laboriously still, trying to make her stick to it too.

"Poor Norman. He had such a beautiful moustache." This time her mischief had an unexpected and not entirely welcome result, for Harry, instead of ponderously trying to bring her back to the main topic of discussion, followed her up the side-track and exclaimed:

"Talking about beautiful moustaches, who was that chap last night that you knew?"

Mrs Everard found suddenly that she had finished varnishing her nails and she pushed the little table back and got up and walked across to the empty fireplace.

"I knew him in India," she said off-handedly. "Jack Crawford. He was in the Governor's Household. At least he was afterwards."

"Know him well?" The question was casual.

"Yes. Quite well." So was the answer.

"I thought so."

"Why? What do you mean?"

"A man doesn't cut a woman as dead as he cut you last night, if they've only been casual acquaintances." Helen Everard did not answer at once, and Harry gave a loud crow of triumph. "Oh, Nellie, I do believe I've embarrassed you. Yes — yes — I have. You're positively blushing."

"Don't be a fool, Harry," cried his sister, half-annoyed and half-laughing, and beginning to blush in earnest. "And don't be so clever. Men have no business to be clever."

"Come on," cried Harry, more delightedly than ever, tell me the whole sordid story of the lovely young married woman and the handsome A.D.C."

"He wasn't A.D.C. till afterwards," she murmured sombrely. "That was the point."

Harry Winter caught the sudden change in her tone and stopped chaffing. "Sorry; I was only ragging. Let's go back to what we were talking about — what the devil was it? — oh yes, Mademoiselle Odette and our five hundred hard-earned yellow-boys."

Helen Everard reached up her long graceful arm and pinched his ear and said, "You're a transparent old donkey, Harry, but quite a nice one when all's said and done. I'll tell you about Jack. There's no reason why I shouldn't now. It happened years ago and it doesn't hurt any more."

"Donkey be damned," cried Harry, massaging the lobe of his ear, "and cut out that Napoleon stuff. Come on, pitch your old yarn if you've got to," and he threw himself down on the sofa.

Helen put one elbow on the mantelpiece and crossed her small vermilion-slippered feet and looked down ironically at him. She had completely recovered her self-possession.

"You, my poor pet, being only a man, don't understand a great many things," she began, "and one of the things you don't understand is the attraction which a man has for women if he is big, and pink faced, and has lovely shiny teeth, and lots of fair hair, and a fair moustache, and is really stupid and really selfish. You, my sweet, being thin, and brown, and wiry, and sometimes not altogether half-witted, and never selfish, wouldn't stand a chance against a man like that, and you'd never understand why. I don't believe we really understand why either. But the first point is that we know it, whereas you'd never even believe it."

"At this point," murmured Harry Winter, beginning to fill a pipe, "the lecturer was interrupted by applause from all parts of the hall."

"Well, there it was," continued Helen. "We were up at Poona. I was having fun. Norman was drinking like a fish, and having an affair with a girl I'd known for years, and on the point of losing his job, and throwing plates at me from time to time, and intercepting my letters and so on — up to all his jolly tricks — when Jack Crawford came along. He was a captain then, and his regiment was sent to Poona.

"Well, he had all the qualifications I've just told you about, except that he was stupider than I had believed possible, and more selfish even than Norman. So, of course, I fell in love with him. In a sort of way. I mean I never loved him as I'd loved Norman, but he was a blessed relief from everlasting brandy-and-soda — Jack was practically a teetotaller — and I was at my wits' end, I was so unhappy. Anyway, there it was. He badgered me and badgered me to run away with him — and I suppose I didn't need much badgering — and finally I said I would. It was all arranged. We were to go for a week to Mahableshwar — Jack and I and his brother and his brother's wife — Norman had to go to Bombay on business — and at the end of the week Jack and I were simply to fade away together. We all went up on Friday night. Jack spent the whole of Saturday riding with his sister-in-law, and the whole of Sunday. On Sunday evening he told me he wasn't coming. It was all off. He was in love with another girl. I asked him who she was, and what she was like, and he got very confused. He was so stupid, you see, that he hadn't even bothered to get his details right. He wasn't accustomed to having to give details to women he was jilting. At last he lost his temper and said he was in love with his sister-in-law and had been living with her all the time he was making love to me."

"Oh! the swine!" said Harry under his breath. "That wasn't the worst, my dear child," went on Helen gaily. "You see, he wasn't in love with his sister-in-law at all and hadn't ever lived with her, but he just used her name to give corroborative detail to — to whatever the *Mikado* says — to an otherwise bald and unconvincing narrative?"

"Whew!"

Harry, seldom a tongue-tied conversationalist, could not find a word that was suitable at once for the situation and the company.

"His real reason, of course, was that on the Saturday morning he heard that he was going to be appointed to the Governor's Household and he decided that I wasn't worth his career. His sister-in-law spent the Saturday and Sunday in the hills trying to persuade him that I was. She was a decent child. I was terribly sorry for her."

"Why? For being Jack's sister-in-law?"

"No. But a native servant listened to all my talk with Jack and heard him boasting about her. He told Jack's brother and was sacked for his trouble. But it poisoned their lives just the suspicion of it. But Jack didn't care. As a matter of fact I don't suppose he gave it another thought. He was Comptroller of the Household by that time."

She laughed a gay, a genuinely gay laugh. "Dear me, what a storm in a tea-cup it all seems now. It was quite real at the time though."

Harry Winter got up and marched over to his sister.

"And why in the name of the foul fiend haven't we heard this story before?" he demanded truculently.

Helen smiled and pinched his ear again. "Because a girl has to be careful what she tells her kid brothers, when they're as violent as you and Bill, and as devoted to their sister."

Harry looked away awkwardly. "Oh! cut out the Napoleon stuff I tell you," he exclaimed, "and a little less of the kid brother, if you don't mind. We're five years older than you are, and don't you forget it."

"Little baby brothers," mocked Helen. "You're still only schoolboys and you'll never be anything else." At that moment the telephone rang and Harry answered it. After listening for a few seconds he reached out for a writing-pad and produced a pencil. "Telegram," he said, aside. He listened and wrote and, after hanging up, read out the result.

"It's from Bill, at last. From some damned place called Blut. Never heard of it. Anyway this is what he says: 'Am on track of good thing but may not have concrete results for another month but if it comes off we shall be sitting pretty write Poste Restante Blut love Bill'."

Helen had already pulled an atlas out of a shelf and was hunting through the index. It was a cheap atlas, of the kind which saves itself an infinity of explanation and extra colouring by pretending that Palestine and Mesopotamia and Tanganyika and Damaraland are all part of the British Empire, and that Syria belongs to France, but at least it could tell them that Blut was the modern name for Santa Olivia, the main seaport of the great modern country of Cimbro-Suevonia.

Helen Everard shivered elegantly. "What a nasty name — Blut," she remarked. "I hope it isn't a bad omen for us. Let's have a look. Where is it?"

"It's probably the Cimbrian for Bower of Lemon-Scented Verbena," said her brother, "and for all we know, Bernard Shaw goes bathing there every summer, and it's locally known as the Venice of the Balkans or the Blackpool of the Aegean or the Bognor Regis of the Levant."

The girl sat up. "I know where I've seen it. In travel agencies. They run cruises or something to it."

Harry Winter picked up the telegram and looked at it again. "It will be a sad come-down for poor old Bill after running guns for Carson and rum for himself all those years, if he ended up by running cruises for old ladies and gentlemen from Malvern."

Helen Everard laughed her deep, rich laugh. "Things would have to be pretty bad before that happened. But I don't think it's likely."

"It was that Carson business that ruined Bill," said Harry reminiscently. "Too much excitement for a lad of eighteen. Throw me over the atlas again. Let me have a look at Cimbro-Suevonia. A bit of European geography will do us all good for a change, after all these years of poring over the Atlantic seaboard. Dear me! I had no idea Romania was as big as that. It's grown a lot since I saw it last. And what the devil's this Kingdom of Serbs — Croats — Slovenes — oh yes! that's what we used to call Servia. 'Gallant Little Servia' was the technical term for a few years, so far as I remember. What a lot of quaint little countries! Well, if we're going to break the Customs and Revenue Laws of one of them, I suppose it doesn't matter much which it is. What did you think of that Hanson kid, Helen?"

"Oh! pretty," said Helen. "Very pretty indeed. Lived all her life in cotton-wool, I should think. But very attractive."

"I couldn't see much of her. She was in the shadow. But I thought she looked nice."

"She'd do very well for you—"

"Especially with a million or two—"

"No, but seriously, Harry—"

"Oh, rats! Where are the cigarettes?" He stretched and yawned. "Must say I hope Bill is going to land something at last. I'm getting a bit sick of doing nothing. Damn that Roosevelt."

"More likely to land you both in jail."

"And where will kid sister be then, poor thing?"

"She will sit in a bar and keep herself warm, and live on her immoral earnings instead of on her kid brothers' criminal ones."

"Damn it! Helen," cried her brother indignantly, "rum-running wasn't criminal."

"Oh I say, Harry, come come. What was it, if it wasn't criminal?"

"Tactless, perhaps, or thoughtless, or lacking in courtesy to the Federal Authorities, or even out of harmony with the spirit of international ethics. All those I am prepared to grant you—"

"Oh shut up, you great fool," and she threw a cushion at him which missed and knocked over a huge vase of Japanese lilies.

"You don't shoot any better than the O'Bannion crowd," Harry grumbled as he went down on his knees to retrieve the debris.

At that moment the telephone rang again, and Helen answered it. "Yes? Yes, speaking. Oh, really? What for? What about? Oh well, I suppose so, if you think you would like to. All right. Here in twenty minutes. Quarter-past eleven." She rang off and sat motionless for an instant with her hand still on the telephone, while Harry collected lilies.

Then she said briskly, "Run away, little man, I've had enough of you for one morning."

"Boy friend coming round, eh?"

"No. Face massage."

"That was a funny way to talk to a face-masseuse," said Harry drily, getting up and dusting the knees of his trousers. "It's not the way I talk to mine."

"Oh run away, you clown. Ring me up sometime."

"Dine to-night?"

"Maybe yes and maybe no. Ring me tea-time."

After her brother had gone, Helen slowly went round the room, tidying here and straightening there. At the window she stopped for a long time, until the chimes of Big Ben striking eleven aroused her. She shrugged her shoulders, gave a quick laugh, and ran across the room into her bedroom.

A quarter of an hour later she had changed into the gayest and brightest of flowered frocks, and was standing in front of the fireplace, when the porter of the block of flats announced Major Crawford.

He came forward with a graceful, lounging stride, the legacy of a youth of boxing and athletics, hand outstretched and, as usual, smiling. Helen, after a fraction of a second's hesitation, took his hand.

"Won't you sit down? Cigarette? Glass of sherry?"

"By Jove, Helen, you look marvellous," he replied, holding her hand for a moment longer and gazing down at her. "You haven't changed the tiniest bit."

"Did you expect me to in four years?"

"No, of course not. What I mean is you are looking lovelier than ever."

"Thank you," said Helen coolly. "Won't you sit down?" She went across to the sideboard and poured out two glasses of sherry and came back with them.

"It's a little too early for a drink," protested Crawford, shooting out his left arm so that a smart blue-and-yellow striped cuff receded from a tiny platinum wristwatch that was shaped like a hunting-saddle and kept in its place by a golden girth. "Only quarter-past eleven." He took the glass nevertheless and, with the words "Happy days, past, present, and future," drained it in a single gulp.

At the toast Helen's pale face went completely white and she put her sherry down without touching it. Crawford had stretched backwards to put his empty glass upon a table and saw nothing, and he turned again genially, with the words:

"Well, how's the world been treating you, my dear, since last we met?"

Even then he could not recognize the storm signals of a tightly shut mouth and a toe tapping on the fender, and added, "I often think of the old days."

At this Helen burst out, "Hadn't you better tell me what you've come about and get it over?"

Crawford raised his eyebrows a little and took a cigarette out of his be-diamonded cigarette-case and lit it.

"I really only came to renew an old — what shall I say?"

"Yes?" said Helen between her teeth.

"It was an unexpected pleasure seeing you last night at the Hansons'——"

"What is it you want?"

He blew out a long, slow cloud of smoke, and considered the point.

"Well," he said at last, "a lot of water has flowed under the bridges since you and I last met, and it seemed to me that it would be better for both of us if we let bygones be bygones."

"For both of us?"

"Well, don't you think so?"

"Can anything hurt me now more than you did then?"

"Oh come, Helen, I was only acting for the best. You know I was. Don't think for a moment that I didn't suffer too."

Helen made no answer to this and he went on, "Anyway, the point is, what's the use of raking up the past?"

"After your toast just now?"

"What toast?" He was genuinely puzzled but was content to let it go at that. Unlike the Winter brothers, he had long ago mastered the art of keeping women to the main issue in a serious conversation.

"Let the dead bury the dead and that sort of thing," he went on quickly, to prevent her answering his puzzled question. "Raking the ashes won't do either of us any good. Don't you agree?"

"Will it do us any harm?"

"Scandal's always unpleasant."

"What scandal?" cried Helen.

He instantly went into a soothing voice. "My dear Helen, you know what the world is. A story about a man is a bagatelle. About a woman, it becomes scandal. It's damned unfair that it should be so. But there it is, and you can't get away from it."

"You can get away from it," said Helen thoughtfully, "if you aren't afraid of scandal."

"All women are," he replied, tapping another cigarette on his case.

"And what if I said that I wasn't?"

He smiled tolerantly and struck a match.

Helen was so angry that she could not trust herself to speak. Then by a happy chance, her eyes travelled from the handsome cavalryman, whose diamond-monogrammed cigarette-lighter seemed to be giving a little trouble, to the telegram from her brother in Cimbro-Suevonia, and she had a quick vision of the tranquil, unshakeable Bill, the sailor and the smuggler whom no one could frighten or fluster or anger, and with a little smile of thanks to the absent hero, she turned again to Jack Crawford. "Then I take it," she said gently, "that if any rumour of our — our dead past — were to be spread, it would hurt me a great deal and you not at all?"

Crawford noted the little smile and reflected how extraordinarily like each other they all were, and how extraordinarily easy they were to manage if you knew how to go the right way about it, and said:

"That's exactly it, darling."

"And you simply want to protect me?"

"That's all. That's absolutely all. I mean, it's the least a man could do."

"It's terribly sweet of you, Jack——"

"Oh no," he interrupted, "it's the natural thing to do."

"But I don't really mind, you see," she went straight on. "I've dropped out of all the circles I used to be in, and nothing of that sort can hurt me now. In fact, in the circles I move in now, it might do me a lot of good if it were known that I'd been seduced by the great Jack Crawford, even if he did jilt me afterwards."

Crawford sprang to his feet, and strode to their window and back like a magnificent panther.

"That's it," he cried, "that's it. I don't mind the seduction, as you call it. That doesn't matter a damn. Nobody minds about a thing like that nowadays. It's the jilting that matters."

Helen threw herself into an armchair and laughed till the tears came, while Crawford fumed and swore at her and marched about the room and lit cigarettes and threw them away and stamped.

"Oh, Jack, I do think you're sweet," Helen gasped at last. She jumped up, gave one look at herself in a mirror, and fled from the room.

"God damn and blast all women," said the major moodily, and he drank three glasses of sherry in quick succession and felt better. The situation was not so bad after all, he reflected, as the generous wine of Jerez de la Frontera warmed his blood; that burst of laughter might easily have been a feminine device to cover up her emotion at seeing him again after all these years — he had known such things happen before — and she had definitely called him "sweet." He helped himself to another glass of sherry, straightened his tie in the mirror, stroked his moustache and awaited events.

Helen came back powdered, *soignée*, demure, sat down in an upright chair, folded her hands, Quaker-like, in her lap, looked sideways, mischievously, at Crawford, and said "Well?"

Crawford, always glad in affairs of this kind when the initiative passed to him, said, "Well, you see what I mean."

"Er — where had we got to?" she enquired guilelessly. "We'd got to the point," he explained patiently, "where we'd agreed that — that," he broke off and cleared his throat. Where exactly had they got to? Oh yes. "We'd agreed that it would be far better for your good name" — her eyes twinkled—"if we both of us said nothing about the old days."

Helen opened her eyes very wide. "But I thought we'd agreed that it would improve my social position enormously if everyone knew about the old days" — and she added, drily, "the good old days."

Crawford took two long, masterful strides across to where she was sitting, laid his hands, not very gently, on her shoulders and looked down at her.

"Helen," he said in a low, half-pleading, half-thrilling voice, "you were in love with me once."

"Yes. Once."

"And you are still."

"No, I'm not, Jack."

"Yes, you are. You may think you aren't, but you are. Listen. Listen. Don't speak for a moment. Helen, I'm in the devil of a mess. Money, of course. If something doesn't turn up soon I shall have to leave the regiment. I'm up to my ears in debt. And they're pressing me at last. God damn them. You aren't going to turn against me? You of all people?"

"Well? There's nothing new in that. You always were in debt. But you know how to get out."

"How?"

"Get a woman to pay them for you. I did it once, you remember."

"By George, so you did," exclaimed Crawford.

"Ah! So you didn't remember. Heigh-ho." Helen sighed a theatrical sigh.

"Of course I remember," he protested. "And what's more I can remember the exact details, eighty-four guineas to that damned breeches-maker in South Audley Street, a hundred and thirty pounds to the wine-man in Bombay, and sixty-one fifteen to that I.C.S. fellow who had such a damnable run at poker——"

"Oh stop! stop! stop!" cried Helen, despairingly, putting her hands up to her ears, and frantically trying to conjure up that vision of Bill who could be neither frightened, nor angered, nor flurried.

"How's that for a memory?" said Crawford admiringly, and then he came back to the point in his masterful way.

"But listen, darling, I've got a way out of all my troubles. I'm going to marry the most capital little creature, and after that everything will be plain sailing. But if she heard about — about us and the circumstances——"

"Not of the seducing but of the jilting?"

Crawford dropped on his knees beside Helen's chair and took her unresisting hands and kissed them in turn, fingers and palms.

"Don't be cruel to me, sweetheart. I'm in your hands, utterly in your hands. Don't tell anyone, my beautiful one. Be merciful, if you love me."

"I don't love you, Jack," said Helen. "I loved you once, but I don't love you any more."

"But you must, I know you must," he cried. "After all we were to each other, it's incredible, it's impossible, that you shouldn't love me any more."

"Do you love me, Jack?"

"I'm — I'm tremendously fond of you."

"Alas! Poor Jack." She stroked his shiny yellow hair in a moment of genuine pity. "You don't care a damn for me and I don't care a damn for you."

Crawford got up and pulled out his cigarette-case. "Very well," he said stiffly, "ruin my life if you like. I don't mind."

Helen stretched out a hand to him. "Oh Jack, did you never ruin mine?"

He turned on his heel savagely, ignoring her hand, and snapped, "Oh, don't go on harping about the past. I'm going." He had seized his hat and stick and reached the door before Helen stopped him.

"Jack."

"Well?"

"I've only told one person in the world and I promise you that I will only tell one more."

"Your brothers?"

"Yes. And I promise you that they will tell nobody. But — one thing Jack——"

"Yes?"

"Keep out of their way. They can be dangerous."

"To hell with that," said Crawford. "I can be dangerous too."

Helen nodded. "Don't say you weren't warned. They're rather fond of me."

Crawford went out, and Helen sat down, and slowly wiped his hair oil off her hand with a handkerchief, and burst into tears.

CHAPTER VII

Eleanor's Two Proposals of Marriage

When Eleanor reached home after her exertions as a pillar of the existing world-order and was proceeding, according to her established custom, to her room for a hot bath, and a couple of hours' sleep, and then dinner in bed she was annoyed to be halted on the stairs by the butler with the news that Mr Clifford Bray was waiting to see her upstairs in the drawing-room.

"Tell him I'm very sorry but I've gone to bed," she exclaimed a little crossly.

A slow, almost drawling voice spoke from the top of the stairs:

"You little story-teller!"

"Oh! Clifford! There you are, are you? I meant I was just off to bed."

"Why, you aren't ill, darling?" the young man enquired anxiously, coming down two steps to meet her.

"No, of course I'm not." Eleanor's petulance was increasing. "But it's my Thursday."

"Lord, yes, so it is," said the young man. "I'd forgotten all about it."

"Well, you oughtn't to have forgotten," cried Eleanor going past him into the drawing-room and throwing herself down upon a sofa with a great weariness. As he was there, she might as well make the best of a bad job and throw him a civil word or two before shooing him out of the house.

"Sorry, darling" — he followed her into the room — "but I've got such a lot of things to think about——"

"That you can't find time to think about me."

"Sweetheart, you know I think about you all day long——"

"But you manage to forget my Thursdays?"

"Eleanor, my adorable, I'm terribly sorry I forgot about your silly old baby-weighing——"

Eleanor sat up. Her blue eyes were wide open.

"My what?" she said icily.

"I didn't mean that, I swear I didn't." The young man wilted under her frosty gaze. "You know what I mean, your Welfare Work——"

"That's a little better." Eleanor lay back again.

"Darling, I'm terribly sorry. I said that——"

"For heaven's sake, Clifford, stop apologizing and tell me what you want. Can't you see that I'm absolutely exhausted."

He was all concern again for her. "My poor sweet," he cried, falling on his knee beside the sofa, and kissing her hand that hung down limply, "what on earth has happened to make you so exhausted? Late nights? Too many parties?"

Eleanor let her head fall back on the cushions and turned her eyes to the ceiling with an expression of misunderstood martyrdom, as though to say: "God, give me patience with this fool." The gesture was wasted, however, for Clifford exclaimed in alarm: "My dear, you do look terribly tired. You've been overdoing the social whirl. Too many cocktails, that's what it is. I shall have to speak to your mother about you."

Eleanor sighed, abandoned her martyr's crown which this idiot so miserably soiled by mistaking it for an aura of alcohol, and sat up again.

"Did you come for anything special, Clifford?" she asked patiently.

Clifford Bray rose from his knees and anxiously examined the fall and line of his beautiful trousers to see if his gesture of chivalry had caused any sartorial havoc, before replying: "I had to come and see your father about getting him to sign a letter to *The Times* — we're running a cruise this year to Cimbro-Suevonia and you know the old boy is president of the Anglo-Cimbrian Society — and as I was here, I thought I'd just hang about on the chance of seeing you. You're looking adorable, Eleanor."

"You said just now I was looking like an old hag," she said swiftly.

"I never said such a thing, I couldn't have, I mean it's monstrous to suggest, it's — it's — it's —" His protests died away when she relented a little and smiled.

"You're the loveliest thing in the whole world, Eleanor," he said wistfully. "Why won't you marry me?"

Eleanor laughed gaily. "Is that a proposal?"

"I suppose so."

"What's the score now, Clifford?"

"You always laugh at me," he said sulkily. "Why do you always laugh at me?"

"Come on, little man, what's the score?"

"About a hundred I should think."

Eleanor patted him on the cheek. "You're rather a pet, Cliff. I'm very fond of you really, you know. And now you must run away."

"It's always the same," he murmured, staring down at his brown suede shoes.

"Alas! and always will be, Cliff," she answered softly. Eleanor sincerely felt all the right feelings towards her unsuccessful suitors. They had paid her a great compliment, had done her a high honour, and she was grateful to them.

Bray looked up brightly. "Well, I'll still go on trying," he said in that slow voice which sounded so attractive when the world was going right, and so utterly maddening when the world was going wrong. "You'll marry me yet. And now I must return to my travel-shop and set about cajoling eight hundred and fifty ladies and gentlemen to go cruising together to Cimbro-Suevonia in our handsome steamship *Bactria*. Au revoir, darling."

"Au revoir," said Eleanor absently. As Clifford Bray went out, the butler came in, and Bray was only halfway down the stairs when he heard Eleanor's clear voice saying, "Major Crawford? Why, of course. Tell him to come round at once. No, of course I'm not tired." And then there was a swift pattering of feminine feet to the upper regions of the house, and the slow tramp of masculine feet downwards. Clifford Bray shook his head sadly and went on his way. It was not the first time in his four years of devotion that he had heard that change of tone in Eleanor's voice, from the bored to the eager, from the patiently resigned to the excitedly welcoming. "Ah! well," he reflected, as he walked back to the big travel agency in which he worked, "I've outlasted a good many already, and I'll outlast this damned Crawford too." After a few minutes more he thought, with a faint touch of bitterness, "She might have waited till I was out of earshot," and then, just as he reached his office, he thought, "But I don't suppose she even remembered that I was there." He went up in the lift to his room, and put the finishing touches to the letter which the President of the Anglo-Cimbrian Society had signed for *The Times*. On his desk was a large photograph of the President's daughter. Clifford Bray rang for a messenger and despatched the letter, and then sat for a moment with his head in his hands, looking at the photograph.

"Yes, I'll outlast them all," he said in his slow drawling voice, and then he settled down to a scrutiny of the passenger accommodation of the S.S. *Bactria*, bound, in the month of September, for the delectable Cimbrian shores, at almost the precise moment that Major Crawford was being shown into the drawing-room at Partington Crescent.

Eleanor, sprucely powdered and scented and *coiffée*, and in a very different sort of costume from her antique slum-wear, was sitting up alertly in a straight-backed chair, pretending to look at *Country Life*. Her blue eyes were bright and she was full of gaiety.

Crawford, on the other hand, seemed distrait. He sat down on the sofa and glared at the empty fireplace for a few minutes; then he went to the window and stared down at the traffic; then he engaged Eleanor in a desultory talk about the prospects on the Aberdeenshire moors during the approaching August; then he started a tirade against the High Command in India and broke it off abruptly; and then he frankly gave up all attempts at sociability and sat twisting an elegant silk handkerchief into knots.

Eleanor was pleased. He looked so handsome, so virile, so all-conquering, and yet so school-boyish. He had commanded great galloping squadrons and fought in vast wars, and there he was, as awkward in front of her as a puppy-dog. And he so desperately wanted to say something, and it was only her presence that prevented him from saying it. It seemed incredible that she, the small, humble Eleanor of a few years ago, should be terrifying almost to the point of incoherence one of the lordly ones, a strong and handsome soldier.

Crawford apparently could not speak. Eleanor would not break the lovely spell. So there was a long silence. At last the big soldier sprang up and exclaimed:

"Look here, Eleanor, I want to talk to you."

She lay back, in a haze of enchantment, and murmured, "Yes?"

"It's about that Everard woman," said Crawford.

The haze of enchantment vanished, and Eleanor felt frightened.

"Will you be seeing her again? Or that mountebank brother?" he went on brusquely.

She shrugged her shoulders. "Not if I can help it. But you know what father is. He's taken a fancy to them and that means he'll keep on asking them to the house."

Crawford received this statement in glum silence. Then he burst out, "Dammit all, I'd better tell you the whole story. Otherwise she'll start telling her damned lies all over the place. Look here, Eleanor, I knew her in India. She was married to a fellow in some trade or other, a box-wallah. Poor little devil. She did for him all right. She used to spin a yarn that he was unkind to her — drank, and so on — and I believed her. Lots of fellows did. It was her stock-in-trade. Well I thought I was in love with her — I wasn't, of course. I was just sorry for her. You know what I mean."

Eleanor nodded. He looked more school-boyish than ever, marching up and down the room, and shooting out staccato sentences with a woebegone look on his pink and white face.

"Anyway I promised to run away with her. It meant chucking my Army career, of course, but at the time it seemed worth it. At the very last moment, she wouldn't come. Found a richer man and ran off with him instead. I thought I was heart-broken. Luckily just afterwards," he coughed and repeated, a shade more loudly, "just afterwards, I was offered that job on the Governor's Staff, so I got a change of scene." He stopped and then added, "That's all."

"Poor old Jack," murmured Eleanor. "What devils women can be."

"Oh well," said Crawford, looking at himself in a glass and patting his moustache, "it takes all sorts to make a world." He felt better and bowled along more easily, "I heard afterwards that the poor little box-wallah had been a very decent fellow all along. He took to the bottle later on, of course, and I don't wonder. Don't let your father believe everything she tells him, especially when she turns on the hard-luck story."

"Is it only father who isn't to believe everything she says?" she asked.

Crawford turned away from the mirror with one of his brilliant smiles. "And you too, you little goose."

"I don't see that it matters very much what I believe or don't believe about you."

"That's a fine thing to say," he exclaimed, smiling more brilliantly than ever, "considering that you're going to marry me."

Eleanor gasped.

"But — Jack—" she began to stammer.

"Well, what's the matter now, little goose?"

"You haven't even asked me to marry you."

He laughed triumphantly. "I don't think it's necessary, is it?"

"No," said Eleanor in a small voice, and stood up to be kissed.

CHAPTER VIII

The Financial Secretary to the War Office

If it was perhaps a legacy of James Hanson's fire and swiftness and resolution, in those early days when he was the unofficial king of Cimbria, that made his two eldest sons gallop so straight at their fences, it was certainly his youthful determination to rise in the world that had been transmitted to Robert. Doggedness was Robert's essential characteristic. Some young men enter Parliament in the Conservative interest because their fathers and grandfathers have done so before them; some because they are well aware that they have insufficient brains for the mastery of a profession or a trade, and that therefore the making of the country's laws is the only career open to them; some for the subtle advancement of private industrial or financial interests; and yet a few others out of ambition to emulate those twin models of all that is worth while in public life, twin yet how dissimilar, Mr Disraeli and Mr Baldwin.

Robert was in this last rare category, and as if that was not sufficiently notable, he had a rarity all of his own. For he had come to believe, honestly, genuinely, and sincerely, after many hours of thought in the dark hours of the night, that Conservatism was in itself a Living Faith. He no longer regarded it, as he had in the first careless, thoughtless years of his membership for Westbourne, as a defence against Revolution, as a bulwark of South Kensington and all that South Kensington stands for, as the only decent creed which a public-school man could follow, as the essence of everything that is implied in the eternal words "British Empire." He had gone long past these petty notions. He detested, with a vehemence that would have surprised her, his sister Eleanor's idea of saving Society by weighing babies. His idea of saving Society was not to pamper East Stepditch in Welfare Centres, but to enlighten East Stepditch at street-corners. He even detested the name Conservatism, for it was so remote from everything which his creed meant to him. Conserve, by all means, but improve, improve, improve, all the time. That was Robert's creed and it irked him that he could find no name for it. Occasionally he even found himself envying the poor pathetic Liberals. They had no seats and no votes, and they still believed, God help them, that tariffs which diminish trade lead to a diminution of trade, but at least they had a magnificent name for their ex-Party.

It was this profound conviction that Conservatism was something alive which attracted the attention of the Party leaders to their singular adherent, the honourable member for Westbourne. A young man who really believed in all things which they had been saying for the last fifty years on platforms and in the House itself, at garden fêtes and whist drives, at tea-parties of Women's Conservative Associations and magic-lantern lectures of the junior Imperial League, was a perfect treasure. He was, indeed, exactly like what they would have been themselves if it had not been for the pressure of public affairs in connection with the Boer War. In those days work was work and there was no time for Idealism. But that was no reason why they should not recognize and applaud Idealism when they saw it. There was far too little of it about in these hard, materialistic times. Besides, an Idealist was a real asset to the Party, especially with that large amorphous mass of sentimentalists which was technically known as the Floating Vote. The elegant loungers of the Party and the sharp little careerists made no sort of appeal to the Floating Vote. But Robert Hanson was a different gun altogether. He could convey in a speech his passionate conviction in the essential rightness of Conservatism as a moral creed, and he was, in consequence, assessed by his leaders as the equivalent electoral value of four baronets, or six retired lieutenant-colonels, or one and a half athletic heirs to ancient peerages. The leaders were very skilful at the assessment of electoral values, and they knew a good thing when they saw it. And this was only natural, because they had been at the game for a long time. Too old to fight for their country in 1914, they did not feel themselves by any means too old to direct the affairs of their country twenty years later. They had no part, owing to the inexplicable madness of the populace in electing a Liberal Government three times running, in 1906 and in 1910, in the preparation for one war, but they were determined not to be backward in the preparation for the next war. And what could be better, from the point of view of the Floating Vote and the importance of catching it, than the appointment of an Idealist to a key position at the War Office? Lord Jukes of Glastonbury, the Lord Chancellor, had been the first to suggest it, which was only reasonable, as Lord Jukes was universally applauded in Conservative circles for his brilliant brain and his acknowledged astuteness. It is true that some of the Elder Statesmen of the Party, veterans who had been edged out of their native Idealism by the pressure of practical events at about the period of Majuba Hill and had never quite recaptured it, were a little dubious about his lordship's intellectual attainments. They admitted their existence — all the world did that — but they sometimes found it a little difficult to understand why so powerful a brain was to be found inside the true-blue ranks. It was without a precedent, and the Elder Statesmen nodded their antique heads in some dubiety, and consoled themselves with the reflection that occasions did arise when a little astuteness was a valuable thing. Lord Jukes's suggestion, therefore, was hailed with enthusiasm by such men as Lord Tubb of Ethandune, Lord Quigge of Walsingham, and especially by Lord Jones of Bannockburn, who doubled the parts of Secretary of State for Scotland and Treasurer of the Party Funds. Lord Jones, who had only been prevented by a truly terrifying outburst of Welsh indignation from taking the title of Lord Owen-Glendower on the occasion of his elevation to the peerage, had long been in hopes of tempting James Hanson to join him in the Upper House. Over and over again he had hinted that the Barony of Penistone could be conjured out of the vasty deep for a mere fifty thousand, or more picturesquely that the Viscounty of Loch Lomond might be arranged for seventy-five thousand, with Loch Katrine thrown in for guineas. But James Hanson had resolutely set his sardonic old face against ennoblement. Indeed on one or two occasions he had declined to change his name to that of a Yorkshire moor or a Scottish loch in such terms as to make Lord Jones of Bannockburn wonder if the man was a really staunch Tory after all.

"Think what we're doing for your steel trade with our tariffs," Lord Jones had once said plaintively.

"Think what I did for it myself without 'em, my boy," had been James Hanson's frivolous retort.

Another time Lord Jones had tried the high moral tone and had said, "Look at all these years of peace we've given to industry," only to be met with the deplorable reply, "Peace isn't any use to the steel trade. Give us a nice European war now—" Lord Jones, who had once been the member for a Welsh division and could not get out of the habit of thinking that he still had to conciliate the large Welsh peace vote, was shocked by this attitude. But he had never entirely given up hope of securing a substantial donation to the Party funds from the old steel millionaire, and the subject still cropped up at the periodical conferences between Lord Jones and Mr Sylvester Hildebrand. It was Mr Hildebrand's task in life to keep a suave lookout for gentlemen who might be disposed to do the State some service and thereby qualify themselves for the knighthoods, baronetcies, viscounties, earldoms, and the rest, which are the State's grateful rewards.

Whenever Mr Hildebrand discovered any such citizen, it was his duty to bring the pleasing news to the attention of the Treasurer of the Party, so that an accommodation might be arrived at which should be satisfactory to all concerned, especially, of course, the State. It was also a part of Mr Hildebrand's daily round to keep a watch for citizens who were so remote from the practical affairs of the world that they had never even vaguely considered the possibility that a seat in the House of Lords was within their reach. When Mr Hildebrand found such a one, usually a citizen of one of the three Ridings of Yorkshire or the neighbourhood of Manchester, he would gradually and gently try to break down the man's modesty and convince him that England had need of him as a hereditary legislator. An introduction to Lord Jones would follow in due season and the thing was as good as done. But James Hanson had been too tough a proposition even for so polished a persuader as Mr Sylvester Hildebrand, and the latter, like Lord Jones, welcomed Robert's promotion to ministerial rank. It might be possible to get at the father through the son.

The Radical press, naturally, was indignant at the appointment, and hinted darkly at a sinister connection between steel millionaires, political functionaries at the War Office, and contracts for rearmament. But then the Radical press was always so indignant about everything that nobody who counted for anything paid much attention to it. And its shrill, cocoa-fed yelpings were more than counterbalanced by the deep, drumming sonority of the *Morning Post*, which hailed the appointment as yet another example of the traditional courage of the Conservative Party in giving Youth its chance. The average age of the Ministry, pointed out the *Morning Post*, was reduced by the advent of this brilliant, erudite young man, typical of all that was best in the life of England and the Empire, from 69-85 years to 69-74.

.....

A few days after Robert's elevation to Ministerial rank as Financial Secretary to the War Office, the chairman of the Westbourne Conservative Association was invited to join the board of a newly formed, and quite obscure, company called the Perdurite Company Limited, and shortly afterwards he presented himself at the War Office and requested the favour of an interview with his brilliant young member.

Lieutenant-General Springton, C.M.G., C.B., D.S.O., was a man who had only come to believe in the essential Rightness of the Scheme of Things at a comparatively late period of life. Up till the age of forty-two he had never been able to detect the faintest shadow of Justice in the ordering of the Universe. But at that critical point in his career, his eyes had been suddenly opened and he had never again lost his faith.

On his forty-second birthday Major Springton, commander of the 250th Battery of the Royal Field Artillery, stationed at Aldershot, had taken bitter stock of his position in the world. His men disliked him because he was efficient; his officers distrusted him because he judged them by their gun-drill rather than by their polo; his superiors ignored him because he had no social influence. On the threshold of middle-age, he had no prospects of the military advancements that seemed to come so easily to others. If he had had the money to join the Cavalry, and the powerful friends in the drawing-rooms of Mayfair, he might have been a brigadier-general by now. Haig, the darling of the cavalry, and of the drawing-rooms, was only a few years senior to him, and look at Haig now — Inspector-General of Cavalry. So mused the tall, dark, ambitious, saturnine Major Springton savagely, on his forty-second birthday. Twenty-two years of the highest professional integrity had left him with nothing to look forward to except half-pay in the Channel Islands with his load of youthful debts.

Within three months of his forty-second birthday he had succeeded to the colonelcy of the brigade — the late colonel having been sniped through the forehead outside Landrecies — and within a year he was Brigadier-General Springton, D.S.O., commanding the Royal Artillery of a division of civilian soldiers. His pay was good, his allowances were lavish, and his opportunities of spending were small, and he calculated that if only the War would last another three years, he would be, for the first time in twenty-two years, entirely free from debt. It did, and he was.

General Springton made in every way an ideal commander of civilian troops, and gave the utmost satisfaction to his superior officers. The secret of his success lay in the one talisman — harness-cleaning. This secret had all the simplicity of genius, and it performed the double function of knocking the civilians into something like the shape of real soldiers, and it pleased the Higher Commands. Both were difficult and, in their varying degrees, important tasks.

The civilians, to take the lesser of the two problems first, had been disposed to treat the cleaning of harness, the whitewashing of the stones that marked the boundaries of the various horse-lines, and the polishing of buttons, as subsidiary matters in comparison with the accurate shooting of their eighteen-pounder guns. General Springton had soon corrected this amateurish delusion. His inspections of horse-lines were frequent and rigorous, and his command of invective became celebrated through three Army Corps. In a very short time few divisional artilleries had such highly polished curb-chains, or such glittering bits, or such pliable, flexible, malleable leather work. And of all the eight batteries in the divisional artillery, no curb-chains shone more brightly and no saddles were softer than those of the only battery that was commanded by a regular soldier and not by a civilian. And General Springton, in consequence, recommended the battery-commander for a D.S.O., which the battery-commander duly got. The civilian majors did the best they could, considering how long a time they were absent from their horse-lines and how long a time they spent in their gun-lines, but their best was not quite up to General Springton's ideal of military efficiency. So no D.S.O.'s came their way.

Nevertheless, civilian or regular, the divisional horse-lines instilled some notion into the amateurs' heads of how a war should be fought, and they were an ever-recurrent joy to the Higher Commands. For the Generals who commanded Divisions, Corps, and even Armies, felt from time to time, at longish intervals, a twinge of conscience at the inordinate number of kilometres which separated them from the troops which they so gallantly were in the habit of hurling against uncut barbed-wire entanglements. This twinge invariably reacted in a visit of inspection to the Front Line, or at any rate to somewhere fairly near the Front Line, according to the *savoir-faire* and tact of the local commanders. Some of these latter were so lacking in all the essentials of decent human feeling that they insisted enthusiastically upon piloting the Great Men, and their tail of be-medalled, be-tabbed, be-brassarded, perspiring, and reluctant young officers, right up into the Front Line and even — with so fearful a craziness had the High Gods touched them — into the deadly peril of a forward sap. And then they were naïvely puzzled — these poor, silly fellows — at their utter lack of subsequent professional advancement.

General Springton made no such mistake. He knew a trick worth two of that. On meeting one of his superior officers with his gorgeous tail, he always genially assumed that the argosy of military brilliance was on its way back from a triumphant visit to the forward saps rather than on its diffident way up, and, with an air of welcome to returning heroes that was exceedingly pleasant to the Great Man, and pleasanter still to his perspiring followers, conducted them to a display of burnished and soft-soaped harness, eight miles behind the Line.

Such a mixture of tact and soft soap had its natural consequences. General Springton, for the first time in his life, found himself popular with his superiors, men who knew a soldier when they saw one, and men, moreover, who were not slow to hand out the rewards of courage. Thus, when a young subaltern in one of the General's brigades, in private life a timber merchant in the north of Scotland, went forward with the first attacking wave of infantry in a battle and, after four hours, sat down under shell-fire and wrote out a masterly appreciation of the situation and despatched it by runner to Divisional Headquarters, General Springton promptly initialled the report and forwarded it to Corps Headquarters and was deservedly created a Commander of the Order of Michael and George. The subaltern's mother still cherishes the printed letter which the General sent her (and would, indeed, have personally signed, had it not been that he had an urgent harness-inspection on that day and told his clerk to sign all his letters for him), offering his sincerest sympathies upon the death of her gallant son who had fallen in the Cause of Freedom and Democracy.

Later on, when one of the civilian battery-commanders in the division, a country lawyer of some local distinction, simultaneously directed the fire of six six-gun batteries against German counter-attacks between Gavrelle and Roeux Chemical Works in the Valley of the Scarpe, and, by this feat of ballistical virtuosity, held a wobbly line single-handed against all-comers, General Springton was awarded the C.B. amid the acclamation of all those of his Woolwich contemporaries who had already got the C.B. It was particularly distressing for the General that he had not found it compatible with his duty to recommend the ballistical major for a Mention in Despatches. But only a week or two after the German counter-attacks along the Scarpe had been smothered by the flurry of shrapnel, it had been discovered that the week's pay for the major's battery had been stolen by a small driver and scattered, in one glorious, feverish, attempt to emulate the exploits of Casanova, among numerous discreet houses in the discreet quarter of Amiens. The little driver, reduced by his exertions to a shadow even of his former insignificant self, was removed to hospital prior to a spell in jail, and the major, who had been at the time of the theft, occupied on the fire-step of the Front Line with a periscope, was, of course, deprived of his command and sent home. Otherwise, General Springton would have unhesitatingly recommended him for a Mention, or even — who knows? — an O.B.E.

The high tide of the General's decorative fortunes arrived when the news gradually filtered through to Headquarters that he was in the habit of fearlessly maintaining a Forward Observation officer in No-man's-land day and night, whether or not there was anything to be observed or any chance of observing it. Come what might, the General was resolute. Whatever the risk, he would accept it; whatever the responsibility he would shoulder it. So long as he was commanding the divisional artillery a subaltern-officer would remain in No-man's-land. On the reception of this news at G.H.Q., enthusiasm was unbounded, and he was christened "Tiger" Springton on the spot, and his name was put on the list of those to whom foreign decorations should be awarded at regular intervals. As the War went on, these foreign decorations arrived in ever-increasing numbers, according as the various South American and Central American Republics made up their minds which way the cat was liable to jump, and it is hardly an exaggeration to say that as each Republic declared war upon the Central Powers in the name of Liberty, Democracy, and Humanity, and scooped in the German liners interned in its ports, so General Springton's manly chest acquired another piece of ribbon.

At the end of the War, the gallant Brigadier-General emerged with a magnificent reputation as a fighting-man, with three rows of ribbons, and without a single debt in the world.

Nor was he doomed to sink into the oblivion of half-pay, either in the Channel Islands or at Clifton. So useful a man could not be neglected, and the Tiger, for his nickname was famous by now wherever heroes meet together and talk about the deeds they did on Crispin's Day, successively served the Empire in command of the garrisons of the Seychelles, the Nicobars, South Georgia, and St. Helena, until his retirement in 1928 with the rank of lieutenant-general and the C.B.E. This then was the man, tall, dark, thin, benevolent, distinguished, who came to visit the new Financial Secretary to the War Office.

Robert was not the sort of jack-in-office to keep his local Chairman waiting. The General was shown up at once and, with the customary bluntness of a military man who was unaccustomed to the tangles of civilian circumlocution, he came to the point quickly.

"It's about this Perdurite," he said.

"Ah!" said Robert, who had no idea what he was talking about.

"Know what I mean?" said the general, cocking a dark eye.

"Well, yes," replied the young minister with a vestige of a knowing smile, as if to imply that what he did not know about Perdurite might just as well be written off as non-existent.

"Mind you," proceeded the military man of business, "not asking anyone to take anything on trust. Prepared to meet experts. More the better. Convince everyone."

Robert took up a pencil and jotted down "prepared to meet experts" on his memorandum pad.

"Passed all our tests," cried the Tiger. "Ready for yours." He whipped a bundle of documents out of his breast-pocket and passed them across the table. "Keep 'em. Duplicates," he waved his hand generously. Then he leant across and lowered his voice to an impressive whisper: "Must have a tariff though. Paramount."

Here Robert was on firmer ground. He was thoroughly grounded in the case for tariffs on any single article in the whole range of British manufacture, and he had himself used the very word "paramount" in this connection on a thousand hustings. Indeed, a more suspicious man than Robert, or one that knew less about General Springton's simple, straightforward character, might well have thought that his oratorical style was being slyly parodied by the soldier. As it was, however, he nodded vigorously several times and said, "Yes, I quite see that. Of course. I quite see that. A tariff is a sine qua non. About thirty-three and a third, I should imagine?"

"Fifty," replied the man of war.

Robert was dubious. "Fifty isn't so easy to wangle — I mean isn't so easy to negotiate. A plain one-third is the standard level."

"If we get the contracts," said the General, "we'd try to manage with forty," and Robert made another note.

"List of directors is there," went on the General, shooting out a long, thin forefinger at the bundle of documents. "Good fellows, all. Babs Cotterham was at Wellington with me. And Toby Stigge, of course. Commanded the Ninth when Bobo Gilkes had the Rawal Pindis. Don't know much about the others — business-men I fancy — but they're a decent-looking crowd. Met 'em last week. Not a Jew among 'em."

The Tiger bounded to his feet. "Well, mustn't keep you. Busy man now. Honour to the constituency." He held out his hand and barked, "Well, young feller, see you again. Let me know what you think some time," and he marched out.

Robert, after furtively rubbing his brow, rang for a secretary and gave instructions for the preparation of a précis of the general's documents, just to see what it was all about.

CHAPTER IX

Jack Crawford and Perdurite

It was partly because Eleanor lived for the next few weeks in such a remote, paradisal world of her own that she did not notice the comparative lack of enthusiasm of her family towards her engagement, and partly because the various members of it had lived their own separate lives and gone their own separate ways for so long that none of them expected much attention from any of the others.

Mrs Hanson simply said, "How nice, dear. We must get Veronica home for the wedding," and had gone on with her knitting.

Robert lifted his eyebrows and remarked, with fraternal outspokenness, "What, that ass?" but it is doubtful if Eleanor even heard him.

Her two eldest brothers were at first openly and blankly hostile. Their lower lips dropped simultaneously and they gaped at her for a moment or two like some of those odd fishes that are on view in the aquarium at the Zoo.

"But damn it," cried Nicholas, finding speech at last, "in three years Jack gets the regiment—"

"Yes, damn it," cried Oliver, "and you'll be Mrs Colonel," and simultaneously they cried, "Well, I'm damned."

"I know. Isn't it heaven?" murmured Eleanor absently as she drifted away upon a swan's-down cloud of romance.

It is only fair to say that Nicholas and Oliver quickly recovered their self-possession and, mutually consoling each other with the reflection that much may happen in three years, went in pursuit of their sister with the politest of congratulations and wishes of lifelong happiness.

Only James Hanson said nothing at all. He looked up from his book when Eleanor broke the news to him, and gazed at her thoughtfully, and then he nodded slowly, two or three times. Eleanor was not in the least hurt at her father's lack of comment. She knew that it was the usual thing for a father to be overwhelmed with sadness when a beloved daughter irrevocably left the paternal roof-tree, and she was rather pleased than otherwise at his attitude. She was a little surprised, however, a few days later, when James Hanson appeared to be reluctant to engage in the traditional talk with his prospective son-in-law.

"That's all vieux jeu," he said rather shortly, when the subject was broached. "I know what his income is — a cavalry major's pay and allowances — and I know what his prospects are — a cavalry colonel at forty-five and retired at fifty."

Eleanor flared up at this. "Jack won't be retired at fifty," she cried. "He's a marked man for big promotion. He'll be Chief of the Imperial General Staff before he's finished."

"All the less reason for me to worry about his prospects," was the unmoved reply.

Eleanor changed her tone. "Please, Daddy, talk to him. I know he wants to consult you about something. Please be a pet, Daddy."

"About what?"

"I don't know. He hasn't told me."

"Well, I'll tell you. About your money."

"It isn't about my money," Eleanor was up in arms again. "Jack doesn't care how much or how little money I've got. I think it's horrid of you to suggest such a thing."

"You can tell him from me that you've got £2,500 a year now, that you'll have another £1,000 a year from the day of your marriage, that the capital is so tied up that no husband of yours can ever touch it—"

"Father!" cried Eleanor, horrified and shocked at his lack of taste.

"And that I'll give you £1,000 for a wedding present and he can collar that if he can persuade you to let him. And knowing you as I do," he added drily, "and guessing he's what I think he is, I don't suppose he'll have much difficulty in that."

"I think you're hard and unkind," said Eleanor with cold dignity, moving to the door with her elegant head in the air.

"Oh, all right, all right," grumbled her father. "I'll see him. Send him along at six o'clock this evening, and tell Parkinson to see that there's plenty of sherry in the library before he comes. I don't want an awkward pause in the proceedings at the beginning."

.....

Major Jack Crawford, for all that his professional life lay exclusively among the male sex, without even the touch of femininity that a single lady typist gives to the dullest department of a City office, was always more at ease in a drawing-room than in a library, and a little of his habitual composure seemed to have deserted him as he sat down, sherry-glass in hand, to discuss affairs with his future father-in-law. He opened, however, on a confidently genial note.

"I'm afraid I want to take your daughter from you, sir," he began, with a glittering smile.

"Her money's all tied up, you know," was the rather disconcerting reply.

The long, silky eyelashes swept down as the Major blinked.

He tried again.

"Her money, of course, is her own. That has nothing to do with me."

"No. The trustees will see to that."

Crawford blinked again but refused to be put off. As one who would undoubtedly have been a resolute cavalry leader if his duties had ever taken him into the field of battle, he kept his eyes fixed upon his objective and galloped straight towards it, undeterred by hostile barrages or snipings.

"It's about myself I wanted to consult you, sir. I appreciate most tremendously your generosity towards Eleanor and £3,500 a year will, of course, be an enormous help. My only worry is that I won't be contributing anything like the same amount myself. I've only got my pay. No private means to speak of. I was wondering whether I ought to give up the Army and go into business."

There was a pause and then Mr Hanson said, "I understood you'd got a chance of becoming Chief of the Imperial General Staff."

Jack Crawford was delighted. The damned old fool must have heard something from somebody. Perhaps he wasn't such a damned old fool after all.

"People talk," he said modestly, "but it's only gossip. Anyway it would be many years before anything like that came along."

"What sort of business job do you want," asked Mr Hanson.

"Oh, directorships, of course. I don't mean learning how to be a stockbroker or chartered accountant or anything of that. I thought perhaps you might feel disposed to talk to some of your City friends about it. I've got a certain number of qualifications after all."

"What sort?"

"Well, I've got on pretty well in the Army for one thing, and you can't do that nowadays if you're a half-wit. And for another I know stacks of people, the right sort of people I mean. And I suppose, when all's said and done, that business is pretty much a matter of common sense. If you come down to brass tacks, I imagine that running a regiment is the same sort of thing as running a business concern. Am I right, sir, or am I just talking nonsense?"

"I have been out of harness for a good many years now," replied Mr Hanson, unexpectedly taking a cautious line and resisting the temptation to snap at such an opening.

"My idea," went on Crawford, "was that I could be pretty useful in the armament trade. I do know the ropes there. And this damned pacifist rot is collapsing right and left. I mean rearmament is obviously all the thing now, and there ought to be the chance for really big money. Do you know General Springton by any chance?"

"Only as Robert's chairman down at Westbourne."

"I was wondering if you could give me a recommendation to him. He's on to a pretty good thing from all accounts — a new secret metallurgical process that is going to be a real winner. Robert can't give me a line to him because, of course, he'll be concerned with it officially. But you could, sir, if you would be so kind. I'm sorry I can't tell you more about it, because it's being kept a dead secret. I only heard of it by chance."

James Hanson nodded and said, "Quite right. But it must be an odd secret if it can be picked up by chance."

Jack Crawford looked confused for a moment, a thing that could only have happened to him in the exclusive society of his own sex. But he quickly recovered and shrugged his shoulders.

"When I say 'by chance,' I mean, of course, 'confidentially' from someone in the know. The secret is quite safe with me."

James Hanson walked across to his desk, saying, "All right, I'll give you a note to Springton." He scribbled for a moment or two, scrawled his signature, and then sat for more than a minute in a brown study. Finally he jumped up, threw the note across, and said, "Look here. I'm going to give you a word of advice. Retired soldiers like Springton may be wonderful business men. On the other hand they may not. Don't put all your eggs into one basket."

Jack Crawford laughed gaily. "Thank you, sir. Even what they call a silly soldier-man can understand that. Well, sir, I'm enormously grateful to you for this talk, and for this note. If I can get in with General Springton, perhaps I might come back to discuss developments with you. There's no doubt, in my mind at any rate, that the whole future lies in armaments. That's where the big money is going to be made. Of course it's pretty good cheek my laying down the law like this to you, but in my position one is bound to be more or less in the swim, and you — I mean — as you said yourself, sir, well, I mean it's more or less inevitable that you should have dropped out a bit."

A little disconcerted by the older man's silence, Crawford made amends with a charming smile and the remark, "Why don't you stage a come-back, sir, and shake them all up a bit? That would give the world something to think about." This naïve suggestion at least penetrated Hanson's absent-mindedness, for he laughed and said, "You never know, I may yet."

"You'd have to take your son-in-law into partnership, sir," cried Crawford enthusiastically. "We could run a good show together," and on that flattering note he decided it would be prudent to terminate the interview. The Old Man was queer, devilish queer. It was sometimes difficult to know exactly what he was thinking about. It was even sometimes difficult to believe that he was thinking at all. Anyway it was best to clear out while the going was good. But the major's exit was spoilt after all, for, just as he reached the door, James Hanson said, "Got any debts?"

"Oh! None to speak of," replied Crawford a little crossly. It was a subject that he had purposely avoided. There was nothing he would like more than an offer from the old steel millionaire to extract him from his financial embarrassments, but, with a strong sense of the proprieties, he felt that such sordid arrangements ought to be postponed until the marriage ceremony had been duly — Crawford had almost used the word "safely" in his thoughts — concluded. He therefore answered the curt question with a curt "Oh! none to speak of."

"But do the creditors do any speaking?" replied the old man. "That's the point."

Crawford waved his neatly manicured hand, the hand that could control a mustang or launch a charge or stroke the back of a feminine neck, and said, off-handedly, "Oh! just damned tailors," and on that note, much less elegant than the other, he scrambled out.

The instant the door had closed behind his prospective son-in-law, James Hanson threw off his fit of abstraction and almost ran across the room to the bell.

"Has Miss Collins gone yet?" he demanded eagerly when Parkinson entered.

"No, sir," replied the butler. "I heard the typewriter still working as I passed the door of her work-room. But it is past her usual hour, sir, and she will be going at any minute."

"Catch her, catch her," cried Mr Hanson. "It's urgent," and he almost drove the stately Parkinson out of the room.

Miss Collins, the confidential private secretary, was only caught just in time, for she was wearing her smart little hat and her gloves and the beautifully cut dark-blue coat that went with her beautifully cut dark-blue skirt, and her neat despatch-case was in her hand. She was a girl of about twenty-five, fair-haired, with steady, confident, unsparkling blue eyes, tall, quiet, and unhurrying. She looked precisely what one part of her life was, an efficient, trustworthy private secretary. There are tens of thousands of them in Great Britain, and their employers, on the rare occasions on which they reflect upon the characters of their subordinates, are vaguely aware of that part of their secretaries' lives which comprise efficiency and trustworthiness. They know nothing of any other part.

In office hours the lady secretary is expected to be a gentle fund of understanding and of sympathy, and an inviolable repository of professional secrets. In the evenings, after office hours, she must be a machine, setting her face blankly against all enquiries and apparently knowing nothing of the supreme trust that has been confided in her during the day.

It is hidden, perhaps mercifully, from the employers that these ladies do not regard their twenty-four hours in precisely the same manner. To them, office hours are the time to be machines, registering secrets that appear to be wholly unimportant and sympathizing automatically with disasters which affect the welfare of mankind no more than the tears of a spoilt child.

It is during the rest of the day that they can be human beings, helping their unemployed fathers with the rent, dancing with their young men at suburban Palais des Danses, or putting their own babies to bed. That is the time for sympathy and understanding. And as for the betrayal of vast, professional secrets, the secretaries are loyal enough not to want to betray anyone, are not sufficiently interested to regard the secrets as of any value, do not know anyone who would pay them for betrayal, but would, of course, in an emergency betray the whole world if they thought it would benefit their unemployed fathers, their young men, or their babies. But the employer knows nothing of all this. He only knows that in the office there is a woman who can be persuaded to work long hours for a wretched wage, without whose infallible help and advice and efficiency he would be utterly lost.

Mr Hanson and Miss Collins were on slightly different terms. For one thing, he would not be utterly lost without her; for another he paid her a thousand pounds a year; for a third, when he did confide a secret to her, he knew, and she knew, that it was a secret of paramount importance. There was no concealment on his part nor indifference on hers. And for another thing, James Hanson's calls upon Ruth Collins' time and intelligence were not confined to strict office hours. For days on end, sometimes weeks, she would have nothing to do except to make out her own salary cheque. Then he might ask her to work late into the night four or five nights in succession.

Ruth Collins accepted it all with perfect equanimity. Her young men — and she had many — were resigned to the summary cancellation of a dinner-party or a dance, because they knew that Ruth, a charitable soul, would make up for it by a day on the river or a luncheon at the Ritz on her next unexpected holiday.

After Parkinson had intercepted her and brought her to the library, this self-possessed young lady stood and waited without a word. She never spoke first with her employer. On this occasion she had not long to wait, for James Hanson started off at once. "Miss Collins, listen. You must drop everything. I don't mean your party tonight — Ritz, Berkeley, wherever it is — I mean your work here, and concentrate on one thing. You know Jack Crawford?"

The girl nodded.

"And that damned old fool Springton who runs Robert's show down at Westbourne?"

She nodded again.

"Well, find out where the leakage of information is between Springton and Crawford about this new metal that Springton's on the board of. It's supposed to be a dead secret, and this Crawford turned up here a few minutes ago and knew all about it."

"What's it called?" asked Miss Collins.

"Perdurite. But don't write it down," he added sharply. She nodded a third time.

James Hanson ran his hand through his mop of coarse iron-grey hair and went on perplexedly: "It's very important, Miss Collins, and it's got to be done quickly, and I'm damned if I know how to give any tips about how to start. The only thing I can suggest is that it's unlikely that any man in his senses would give away any big secret to a quarter-witted young puppy like that—" He pulled up with his sardonic, twisted smile. "I'm talking, by the way, of my future well-beloved son-in-law. Anyway, my idea is that he must have wheedled it out of some woman or other. He's said to have rather a way with the girls."

"Yes, he has," said Miss Collins in a dry voice.

"Hey!" cried James Hanson, his eyes twinkling. "How do you know that?"

"We also have our secrets," replied Miss Collins gently. "Is that all?"

"Yes. Carte blanche about money, of course."

"Good night, Mr Hanson."

"Good night, Miss Collins."

CHAPTER X

Harry Winter makes a Proposal to Croesus

"Yes, but why bootlegging?" asked James Hanson. "Oh, for a variety of reasons," replied Winter, waving his cigar airily. They were sitting in the millionaire's study. A massive decanter of whisky, half a dozen bottles of Perrier, and a couple of tall glasses stood on a table between them. The younger man was, as usual, lying back at his ease in a big chair; the elder man was sitting forward alertly in his.

"Reasons such as?" enquired the latter.

"Well, for example, the shortage of legitimate jobs at the conclusion of Armageddon. After you gentlemen, the rulers of the world, had settled your little differences at the cost of ten million young men, the survivors naturally hoped to be allowed to return to peaceful vocations. You gentlemen had unfortunately forgotten to supply them."

"So you put all the blame on us?"

"You don't expect us to take it ourselves, do you, Croesus?"

"Wouldn't it be fairer to put some of the blame on to the existing system, or on to the sequence of history, or even on to sheer bad luck?"

"People like you were running the system, my dear sir," replied Winter, "and, if I may say so, profiting by the system. People like you were contributing to the sequence of history, and being nicely paid for your contribution. As for sheer bad luck—" He snapped his fingers.

"Very well," said Hanson imperturbably. "You couldn't find a peace-time job. Go on."

"I couldn't find a decent peace-time job," Winter corrected him. "When Liberty, and Humanity, and all the rest of the hi-tiddley-i-ti, were at stake, you made me a major and gave me a thousand a year and a few hundred men to command, and told me that you'd love me and kiss me when I came back again. When I did come back, and Liberty, etcetera, had been duly and handsomely saved, you offered me a job clearing out waste-paper baskets at a couple of quid a week. And if I complained, you patted me on the back in a damned decent, fatherly sort of way, and took me across to the office window and pointed down at all the other majors in the street who were playing barrel-organs, and selling matches, and wearing masks and so on, and told me how lucky I was to have a job at all, and how the pressure of world-economic-depression made it necessary for you to reduce my two quid to thirty-seven and six. Yah!"

"So having failed to find a decent legal job, you looked about for a decent illegal one, eh?"

"Cant, my good Croesus, sheer and utter cant. Legality and illegality don't come into it. There's only two things in this industrial world, Success and Failure, and there isn't anyone who knows that better than you do. You made millions of pounds, perfectly legally, by the deaths of millions of men. A world in which that can happen, perfectly legally, must be crazy. So let's leave the Law out of it."

"For a young man," said Hanson, with a sort of reflective admiration, "you have a larger fund of cynicism than anyone I have ever met."

"You give away your case," replied Winter with a grin, "by the phrase 'for a young man.' You naturally expect the old to be cynical, because they've had plenty of time to look at the world which they've created. Now there are a few survivors of a young generation who are cynical too. And you seem surprised."

"Well, never mind," said Hanson. "Go on."

"It is a perfectly simple story. One crazy performance of a crazy system had come to an end after feeding me fairly well, and clothing me in a costume that made me exceedingly glamorous to women, and giving me plenty of pocket-money, and trying to ensure that I should hardly ever risk my life except within five miles of a clergyman of the Anglican faith, also dressed in the same glamorous rig, by the way. Well, all that, as I say, had come to an end, so my brother Bill and I looked about for another crazy performance of the crazy system. We very soon found it, of course."

"Why didn't you go back to your old pre-War job? What was it by the way?"

"I was a handsome young mining engineer," replied Winter, "and doing remarkably well, allow me to tell you. I could tell zinc from sulphur, and dynamite from marzipan, at a single glance. As for sinking a shaft, or rigging a cage, there wasn't my equal from Dromore to Donaghadee. But after your heaven-born geniuses had rearranged the world——"

"There you go again," protested the millionaire almost plaintively.

"Had rearranged the world," went on Winter firmly, "what was wanted was unmining engineers."

"Whatever is an unmining engineer?"

"An expert in filling in mine-shafts so as to reduce the world's output of metals. That's what's called Rationalization. And if the rest of the arrangements of the world are rational, then I agree that that is rational too. But if the rest is all plumb crazy, then unmining seems to me to be plumb crazy too. Anyway, I couldn't get a mining job, and a gent called Geddes who had been a Major-General and a Vice-Admiral simultaneously, and for all I know an Air Rear-Marshal too, came along and drove Bill out of the Navy with the thanks of his Sovereign and the change out of six bob. So we pooled our resources and looked about for another public bug-house."

"Bug-house?" Hanson wrinkled his huge iron-grey brows in perplexity.

"Yes. Loony-bin, as a Mr Wodehouse calls it. Dottyville on the Dot. Mad-house."

"And did you find one?"

"Really, Croesus, I sometimes wonder how you ever got on in the world at all with that brain of yours. Your competitors must have sat about with straws in their hair watching the slugs go whizzing by. Yes, we soon found a public loony-bin."

"In Prohibition?"

"Yes. I've heard it called that. Quite one of the best jokes of our times. It is more correct to call it the Eighteenth Amendment to the United States Constitution. It was almost as mad in a different way as your Armageddon, Croesus."

"I wish you wouldn't keep on calling it 'my' Armageddon, " protested Hanson again. Winter laughed cheerfully.

"Oh, for the purposes of this conversation, Croesus, you don't exist in the flesh. You are a symbol, a synthesis of the Kaiser, and Berchtold, and the Drang nach Osten, and the Tsarist regime, and all the gutter-press of every nation—"

"Thank you," said Hanson drily.

"Not at all. And of the stupidity of the Serbs, and the legacy of Alsace-Lorraine, and Napoleon's invention of conscription, and Big Business, and Kipling, and the Navy League, and so on and so on and so on. Let us return to the point. What was the point? Oh yes. The Volstead business took a vast and jolly continent and handed it over on a dish to the dirtiest scum of filthy thugs that ever came out of Sicily and Naples and Ireland. Your business took ten million young men and handed them over to the worms. And both the thugs and the worms had the happiest and fattest time of their lives. And you did it in the name of Liberty, and the Volsteadites did it in the name of Decent Living. It's a lucky thing, Croesus, for people like my brother Bill and myself that in this world two Blacks don't make a White. That would be the devil and all."

"You live on the fact that two Blacks make a bigger Black. Is that it?"

"So do you, Croesus. So do you. At least you used to, from all accounts."

"Have you been looking up my past, you young scoundrel?" asked Hanson with a laugh.

"Oh, just glancing at it. Just glancing at it. A prosperous concern Messrs. Hanson, Wendelmann & Co. seems to have been in the old days."

Hanson laughed again. "Pour yourself out another drink, and take another cigar and tell me what particular brand of rascality you and your brother are going to go in for now?"

Harry Winter took a long pull at his second cigar, gazing at the wall opposite, and then he turned his head towards his host and said blandly, "We thought that might depend on you, Croesus, my old."

This piece of impudence staggered even the old millionaire out of his imperturbability. He sat straight up and stared incredulously at his visitor.

"You mean to say," he exclaimed, "that you have come here to ask me to finance some new iniquity."

"How you do harp on about Right and Wrong," said Winter in a plaintive voice. "Why can't you keep off the high moral tone for a bit. There must be some devilish Puritanical streak in you. I've come here to put an important financial proposition before you. That's the right jargon, by the way, isn't it?"

"You certainly are the most impudent young man that I have ever met in the course of a long and not unadventurous life," said Mr Hanson. "Come on. Out with it. What are you suggesting that I should do?"

It was Winter's turn to sit up in his chair and assume what he imagined to be a business-like attitude.

"Our idea is that we should form a small company, or syndicate — whatever you like to call it — of the four of us. My sister, Bill, and myself, and you. A snug little party. We would do all the work, and you would provide all the capital, and we would split the profits four ways."

"A very nice idea, I'm sure," said Hanson, nodding his great head. "And in what particular line of business would this — er — snug little party operate?"

"Any ideas yourself, Croesus?" Winter cocked an eye at him.

"No, no, no," cried Hanson, holding up his hands, palms forwards, in front of his face. "Supplying ideas comes under the heading of work, and that would be your business."

"I was afraid of that," replied the other, sinking back into his comfortable attitude again. "As a matter of fact, I confess I have been doing a bit of thinking on the subject. It is simply a question of finding a part of the world, or a section of society, or an institution, or a habit of thought, which is more particularly crazy than most of the others. You might think at first sight that it was easy. But the truth is, my dear Croesus, that almost everything is so dotty nowadays that it is jolly difficult to say which is the dottiest."

"But I gather you have come to some sort of tentative conclusions in this difficult problem?" enquired Hanson as solemnly as he could.

"Well, it's like this. Bill is an incurable smuggler and I know he's got a hankering after drug-smuggling. You see, ever since that blasted, cursed, muddle-headed busybody, Franklin D. Roosevelt, repealed the Volstead Amendment and took the bread out of honest men's mouths—" Winter stopped, took a deep breath, and went on apologetically: "I say, Mr Hanson. You would be doing me a great kindness if you stopped me every time I get on to the subject of Roosevelt. Whenever I think of that man and the way which he butted in and spoilt the finest racket that the world has seen since the days when you and the Kaiser were doing your stuff—"

"In that case," interrupted Mr Hanson, "if you're going to couple me with the Kaiser again, I'll ask you to stop talking about Mr Roosevelt."

"Capital," cried Winter. "Splendid. That's the style. Whenever I get on to Franklin D., you just get me off. It's a cardinal principle in the Winter family. Life without it would be impossible. Where was I?"

"You had just stated that your twin brother — er — Bill, has a hankering after drug-smuggling. I may as well say at once, Mr Winter, that I do not propose at my age to start financing drug-smugglers."

"I was afraid you wouldn't," said Winter, shaking his head gloomily. "At least, that isn't quite fair. I thought you might. But my sister, that kid Helen — you've met her — she was sure you wouldn't. But anyway there was no harm in suggesting it."

"Oh, none in the world," replied Hanson blandly. "Pray continue."

"Bill's old love," continued Winter, "is guns. He went as a kid with Carson and Smith and helped them to do the same identical thing that the same identical pair of fellows got Casement shot for, a couple of years later, and—"

"In all my life," interrupted Hanson smoothly, "I never heard a grosser distortion of historical facts."

"We were talking about Bill," replied Winter severely. "Please don't confuse the issue. Bill is a natural-born gun-runner. It took him months to get accustomed to gin and whisky. But in these days of wholesale public armament there doesn't seem to be much demand for illicit artillery. Or is there?"

"I don't know. Don't ask me." Hanson smiled. "My ex-partner Wendelmann might know. He's still in the trade."

"Will you recommend us to him," asked Winter, sitting up eagerly again, "as an old-established and reliable firm of revenue-dodgers?"

"Certainly not. I'm much too respectable to make such a suggestion and old Amschel Wendelmann is much too respectable to accept it."

"You wouldn't care to finance a high-class gambling-den in Mayfair?" enquired the young man wistfully. "Bill's a wonderful croupier and Helen would make a marvellous decoy."

"And what would your share in the undertaking be?"

"Oh! I'd look after the books and arrange them so that you'd get diddled out of your fair share of the profits."

Hanson's great frame shook with laughter as he jumped to his feet with a nimbleness that was astonishing in a man of nearly seventy.

"Run along, you young rascal," he exclaimed, holding out his big, thin hand. "I can't waste any more time on you. If there was a shadow of justice in this world, you'd have been hanged years ago. As it is, I'm afraid you're the sort of person who never will be. Have one more drink and write down your address and telephone number, and a list of your names, if you can remember them."

Winter paused with his hand on the siphon. "Why do you want my address?"

"Because although you're an infernal villain, you make me laugh. And any man who has a son in a Tory Ministry and two sons in the British Cavalry needs someone to make him laugh now and again. And also—" He broke off.

"And also?" prompted Winter.

"And also," finished Mr Hanson, thoughtfully stroking his chin, "I might, I say that I might, conceivably have a job for you and your brother in the fairly near future."

"Croesus," replied Winter, "if we aren't otherwise bespoke, and if we are out of jail, we shall esteem it an honour to march under the beneficent auspices of your shady oriflamme. Or do I mean shadowy?"

"Oh, get out!" cried James Hanson, his blue eyes twinkling. "And come again."

Harry Winter got out.

CHAPTER XI

Eleanor Resigns from the Welfare Centre

The world was a very lovely place for Eleanor. Everything in it was completely and absolutely perfect. And even if her family did not seem to be wildly excited about her engagement, her friends — and she had hundreds — rallied round her with enthusiastic congratulations. Clifford Bray was the one exception, but then his case was rather different. After all, he had loved her for four years with a constancy and devotion that would have touched the flintiest heart, and Eleanor's heart was far from flinty. But she did feel a little irritated by his attitude towards her engagement. She was prepared to make allowances for him — any woman in the same position would — but Eleanor could not help being vexed at his silliness. Clifford Bray treated, or affected to treat, her engagement as if it was an ephemeral fancy, the dilettante whim of an idle hour. He went from cocktail party to cocktail party, exquisitely dressed, carnation in buttonhole, and knowing the christian name and nickname of everyone, and at each and every party he said the same thing, "Poor darling Eleanor. It won't last." And then he would shake his head sorrowfully and ramble away, leaving his shaft to do its work. Eleanor at first laughed it away happily. Poor sweet Clifford! Heart-broken! Devotion of a lifetime! And so on. She, with her Jack, could afford to be charitable. But after a bit the thing became tiresome, and she sent for Clifford Bray and gently remonstrated with him. But he only gazed mournfully at her and said, "It's true you know."

"It isn't true," cried Eleanor, stung out of her gentleness. "What do you mean?"

"You'll marry me," replied Bray lugubriously, "when this midsummer madness is over."

"Oh, run away," said Eleanor, almost losing her temper, and Clifford Bray went off to a cocktail party. It was part of his professional duties to attend cocktail parties and he obtained many valuable clients for his travel agency's cruises at these strange functions.

But apart from the tiresomeness of Clifford, Eleanor found that life was good.

She gave up her work in East Stepditch, of course, immediately after her engagement. Somehow, now that she had Jack's broad chest to lean her head upon, and Jack's strong arm between her and the raging tempests, the menace of Bolshevism did not seem quite so insistent as before. Somehow the Kremlin and the Nationalization of Women seemed a little further away. She had intended at first to continue her subscription of two hundred and fifty pounds a year to the Welfare Centre even though she was giving up the actual work, but she changed her mind after a discussion with Jack about it, and sent them a banker's order for two guineas a year instead, and thanked the stars in their courses that she now had a man to advise her in affairs of business.

Indeed, after this discussion she had even felt a little ashamed of her activities in East Stepditch, for Jack had wisely pointed out to her the evils of pauperization and the dangers of indiscriminate charity. He had also explained, what Eleanor had not really understood before, that the true British defence against Bolshevism was not free bowls of soup, or free medical treatment for women who had been kicked in the stomach by their husbands, but a loyal, well-disciplined force of machine-gunners with the menace of cavalry in the background. "No rabble has ever been known to stand up against cavalry in the streets of a town," he explained. "That is why the Cossacks were always supreme in Russia. And that is the sort of thing we want over here. So long as the Army is loyal, we're all right."

"But the Army is loyal, isn't it?" she asked, gazing up at his eyes, and not caring in the least what the answer to the question was so long as it was spoken by his voice.

Down at the Welfare Centre, the poor little Sergeant was desolate. He liked the Lady Anne very much, and admired her shiny, metallic, good looks, but Eleanor had always been his favourite. She was so exactly the opposite of shiny and metallic. She had a word for everyone, and if it was not always the right word, it was a kind word. There was something about Eleanor that the Sergeant recognized and understood, something fundamentally like many of the poor women who came to the Centre for help and advice. The Sergeant could not put it into words, but he knew the fundamental likeness was there. He used to puzzle over it a lot, but the nearest he ever got to it was the vague soliloquy, "If the world got up and gave her a clip across the ear, she wouldn't know what had happened. Lady Anne, she's different. She'd up and give it a clip back." And another time he remarked to himself, "If she didn't belong to the officer class, she might get a husband who would kick her."

All the little man's pugnacious, protective instincts were aroused on Eleanor's Thursdays, and the prospect of no longer having to defend her, even in theory (for he had never had the occasion to unleash one of his famous Johannesburg fouls on her behalf), saddened him profoundly. Eleanor made him promise to come to her wedding. At first he protested, on the grounds that he would look a fine sight in a hired topper, but Eleanor insisted that he could wear anything he liked.

"An ordinary suit and put your medals on," she said. The little Sergeant brightened prodigiously.

"It will be in a posh church, won't it," he cried. "I could wear all my medals." Eleanor was puzzled. "Of course you could wear them all." She ran her finger along the faded row of ribbons on his jacket, "One, two, three, four, five; you'll look splendid, Sergeant."

The Sergeant was embarrassed and he looked round furtively to see if anyone was near enough to eavesdrop his shameful secret. Then he whispered, "I've got another one, but I don't like to wear it down here. I was an officer once, but I don't let on."

Mystified, Eleanor said, "Well, wear them all at my wedding, Sergeant," and passed on to other farewells. Miss Hondegger, who had seen many Eleanors come and go, said good-bye without emotion. She was more concerned about the two hundred and fifty pounds than with Eleanor's personal services. She had not yet heard the results of Major Crawford's sociological wisdom, but she had misgivings.

Eleanor, for her part, so long as she was actually in East Stepditch, felt uncomfortable about the money. It was not that she questioned for an instant Jack's essential rightness. But somehow, when he was many miles away, and his voice was no longer murmuring its incantations in her ear, the grime and poverty of East Stepditch seemed terribly real and terribly insistent. And somehow, she could not remember the exact words of his argument about machine-guns and cavalry. They had completely convinced her, naturally, because they were right. But would they convince the Sergeant, she wondered? And which side would the Sergeant be on, the tough, resourceful, trained machine-gunner, when the cavalry came smashing down the East Stepditch High Street? It was all very puzzling and very confusing, and, in any case, it was all essentially a masculine affair. Men understood these things so clearly, and were so admirably competent at settling them. So Eleanor settled her difficulty by not telling Miss Hondegger face to face that she was going to reduce her annual subscription by two hundred and forty-seven pounds eighteen shillings, and by offering to organize a Mammoth Ball at the Plantagenet House Hotel for the funds of the Centre. This solved all problems. Her bankers would do the awkward part, and her friends would buy enough tickets for the Ball to make up the financial deficit for at least a couple of years, and, by that time, anything might have happened.

Miss Hondegger accepted the suggestion of a Ball at Plantagenet House with what Eleanor thought was surprising equanimity. Miss Hondegger herself had never received an offer of this kind before, but a friend of hers who presided over the Welfare Centre in West Stockwell knew all about these charitable functions and had described them to her with a full account of their social repercussions and financial results. Miss Hondegger's equanimity was, therefore, all the more surprising.

Eleanor drove back from East Stepditch in the big Daimler for the last time with mixed feelings in her heart. She was sorry to give up the work which she had undertaken from the purest patriotic motives, and she was sorry to leave an atmosphere in which she had been regarded with a sort of veneration by everyone, except by Miss Hondegger, who seemed to venerate nobody except the Sidney Webbs, whoever they were. It was not that Eleanor wanted veneration. Far from it. But it was impossible to deny that an atmosphere of that sort was rather pleasing, especially when it emanated from a class that might at any moment break out into the worst excesses of the Russian Revolution. It was a warm, comforting feeling that her own personality, or rather her own love of human kindliness — for Eleanor had no false pride and was under no delusion that she had a powerful personality — had been able to overcome these instincts of savagery and convert them into an atmosphere of veneration.

On the other hand, she was thankful that she had been diverted from the unsound work of pauperization and indiscriminate charity before she had done any lasting harm to the labouring classes of East Stepditch. The Plantagenet House Ball, being only an isolated, ephemeral act of charity, could not really be put against her by the Recording Angel, and it would certainly please Miss Hondegger and the Sergeant and, Eleanor was honest enough to admit to herself at about the time that the Daimler was bowling down the Strand, it would salve her conscience over that small matter of the money.

When Eleanor reached Partington Crescent and, having thanked Bisgood, the chauffeur, with one of those quick, shy smiles that made worth while Bisgood's long and dreary adventures into the East End with his lovely, polished car, ran gaily up the stairs to her room for her last exhausted rest, she found the house in a sad turmoil and she knew exactly what had happened.

Her sister Veronica was back from Germany.

CHAPTER XII

Veronica Returns from Germany

The house was in a wild confusion. Suit-cases, opened hat-boxes, half-unpacked cardboard boxes, tissue-paper, fur coats, torn cellophane wrappers, string, straps, shoebags, lawn-tennis rackets, golf clubs, and quantities of other debris lay on the stairs, on the table in the hall, on the floor in the hall, and on every stray chair.

Parkinson was standing with his back to the front door, scratching his head humorously and examining the scene, while a twittering group of maids were huddled together over one of the suit-cases with many subdued oohs and aahs and smothered squeals of delight. Eleanor's neat and orderly mind found the confusion a little distasteful, and she said to the butler, "Couldn't you send some of it upstairs, Parkinson?"

The maids scuttled away to the subterranean regions like rabbits, the large white bows on their aprons looking just like white scuts, and Parkinson turned with a respectfully amused smile. "Miss Veronica's orders, Miss Eleanor. Nothing is to be touched till she comes down. Miss Veronica is in high spirits, very high spirits indeed. It's a pleasure to see it, Miss Eleanor."

Eleanor, with the faintest shrug, went upstairs to greet her sister. Veronica was a nice child, and some day or other she would settle down, but there were times when she was a little trying, especially when she insisted upon being the centre of every group in which she found herself. It was not that Eleanor wanted limelight. Far from it. But she did faintly resent being elbowed out of the way by a little shrimp of a younger sister. The modern generation had no sort of decent feeling about that sort of thing. "She can do what she likes after I'm married," thought Eleanor as she went slowly up the stairs — she was not going to hurry to greet Veronica, and, besides, it was her Thursday and she was entitled to be tired — "but until I'm married the stage belongs to me and I'm going to have it." The obvious delight of the domestic staff whenever Veronica came home was also a little irritating, especially as she gave ten times as much trouble as anyone else in the family with her erratic comings-and-goings and her thoughtlessness of others.

It was easy to tell by the sound of excited chatter, punctuated by bursts of laughter, that Veronica was in the drawing-room, and Eleanor went in. Her father and mother were sitting side by side on the sofa. Veronica was standing in front of them, talking.

"Hullo, Nicky," said Eleanor with deliberate sedateness.

Veronica clicked her heels and gave the Nazi salute and cried, "Heil!" and then she flung her arms round her sister's neck and hugged her vehemently. Then she held her at arm's length and rattled on: "Well, and how's the little bride? Radiant, of course. How are you, darling? You're looking lovely."

Eleanor gently extricated herself and smiled. "You look all right yourself, Nicky. How's Nuremberg?"

"Superb. Marvellous. Most heavenly place in the world. Divine concerts every night and divine processions of storm-troopers every day, hundreds of thousands of them, all singing the Horst Wessel song and stamping on the roads with enormous boots."

"I thought they only used their enormous boots for stamping on women," said James Hanson innocently. Veronica fell into the trap headlong.

"My poor, sweet, guileless, adorable Papa," she cried, flitting round the back of the sofa and patting the top of his iron-grey head. "Do you believe everything you see in print? All that stuff about atrocities is just lies. Communist propaganda, my pet. You know what Communists are, darling, don't you? I mean, you've been out of the world for such a long time that it's a bit hard to find out what you do know and what you don't."

"Veronica, dear," said Mrs Hanson admiringly, "aren't you being a little impertinent?"

"No, seriously, Daddy, that atrocity stuff is all rot. Hitler wouldn't allow it for a moment. He isn't that sort of man. A few Jews have been beaten up perhaps, but that's nothing. What are Jews for, anyway?"

"Every bit of food you've ever eaten," said James Hanson with unexpected seriousness, "and every stitch of clothing you've ever worn, young woman, have been paid for with money that I made in partnership with a Jew."

"Oh, old Wendelmann! He doesn't count. He'd be a pet if he wasn't a Jew. I mean the Jews who have ruined Germany, or rather who have tried to ruin Germany."

"And have been frustrated by the noble Adolf? Eh?"

Veronica stamped an incredibly small and incredibly high-heeled shoe.

"I won't have you sneering at the Führer," she cried. "He's the greatest man in the world."

Eleanor abstracted herself from the political discussion with the reflection "not so great as my Jack," and thought of other things. She did not even notice that she had been elbowed off the stage by the little shrimp of a younger sister within about thirty seconds of her entrance.

Veronica went on eagerly: "You ought to see them for yourself, Daddy, swinging down the streets in their uniforms and their steel hats — it's — it's — marvellous."

"I always have a sneaking fondness," said James Hanson comfortably, "for anyone who wears a steel hat. Probably I get a few pfennigs royalty on it. I don't remember who is making the German hats nowadays — I'm an old man and my memory is not what it was — but I expect I'm getting something out of them."

Veronica became petulant and pleading simultaneously: "Daddy, do be serious. I'm being serious. Don't you understand that modern Germany is just about the most important thing in the world just now? Can't you see that a nation is being re-created? Being given a new soul? It's most terribly exciting. Thank God I'm alive now and not in those mouldy old days of twenty years ago. Things are happening now. Everything is thrilling and wonderful. Daddy, I wish you'd come back to Germany with me and see it all for yourself You'd adore it."

"No, my dear, I fancy my travelling days to anywhere except Scotland and the Riviera are over. I prefer to listen to your descriptions of the world."

Mrs Hanson looked up from an intricate piece of woolwork and observed placidly: "I suppose you saw that Robert is in the Cabinet, darling. What is he, James? I never remember."

"Oh yes, I saw all about that," said Veronica, "the German papers are full of English news, especially about the War Office, and Robert isn't in the Cabinet, by the way, Mother—"

"Oh, well," was Mrs Hanson's vague defence.

"And doesn't it just show you, Dad." Veronica turned square to her father and almost put her hands on her hips — but not being that sort of girl she put them behind her back and screwed her fingers together instead.

"What does it just show me?" James Hanson's eyes were twinkling with delight that was caused partly by the truculence of his small, neat, elegant, bantam daughter, and partly by the confidence with which she explained the mechanism of the world to him.

"Why, it shows you what rubbish Democracy is. All this vote business and Parliamentary government and elections. Will of the People — my eye. Nobody in their senses is going to believe that the great British electorate rallied to the ballot boxes in order to put our Robert into the Government. Everyone knows that Robert is a pompous ass."

"Veronica, my dear," exclaimed Mrs Hanson, dropping a stitch.

"Well, if you don't know that Robert's a pompous ass, Mummy," proceeded the irrepressible bantam, "I bet Dad does."

"Robert," said Mr Hanson, "is a very worthy citizen."

Veronica clapped her hands delightedly. "Daddy, you are a pet," she cried, kissing the top of his head this time, "that's exactly what I mean. Worthy citizens are the curse of Democracy. You don't get worthy citizens under a Dictator. You don't want worthy citizens. All you want is men, lots of strong men in big boots."

Eleanor awoke from her day-dream and nodded approvingly. Veronica, silly kid though she was, occasionally had the right ideas. Jack looked magnificent in his resplendently polished field-boots. Eleanor returned to her day-dream.

"Dictators are the thing, Daddy," Veronica went on sagely, "take my word for it, and Germany's the country. Daddy, why on earth didn't we fight on their side instead of against them in the last war?"

"They hardly gave us the choice, my dear."

"They will in the next war anyway. They're tremendously pro-English. All my friends in Nuremberg are officers or in the reserve, and they all say the same. England and Germany together; that's the ticket, Daddy. The French aren't any use to the world. Never have been. Never will be."

"They were tolerably skilful at the defence of Verdun," remarked James Hanson. Veronica wrinkled her forehead for a second. "Verdun? Never heard of it. What happened at Verdun? Anyway, my point is that in the last war the whole world combined couldn't beat the German armies in the field——"

"Is that what they say nowadays in Deutschland?" interrupted her father.

Veronica opened her dark; green eyes very wide. "That's what they say everywhere. I mean, everyone knows that. It's simply a matter of record."

"That the German armies were never beaten in the field?"

"Of course they weren't. They were invincible. All the armies in the world couldn't beat them. Everybody admits that. The civilian population collapsed under the blockade. That is what lost the war. But the German armies were never beaten."

"How old are you, my child?" enquired Hanson. "Twenty-one, of course," replied Veronica, "and don't start telling me I'm too young to know better. I can read history as well as my neighbour."

"You were a nice little baby of three," murmured Hanson, "when the fellows bolted for their lives."

"What fellows?" asked the bantam in a voice like a frozen rasp.

"The German armies on the Western Front, my child, with all the Allies rushing after them as hard as they could. And even so they found it hard to keep up with the Germans. They bolted so fast, you see," he added by way of explanation.

Veronica impertinently yawned back at him. "Propaganda," she said with a sigh, "pure and simple propaganda. I expect it deceives a lot of people — people who are out of the swim," she added.

"You are a little monkey," said the old millionaire admiringly. "I don't think all these handsome young atrocity-merchants are really very good for you. I've a good mind to forbid you to go back to Nuremberg after the wedding."

"Only you know that that would be a fat lot of use."

"Well, maybe you're right. That's the worst of having generous instincts and making my daughters independent."

"I'm going straight back to Germany the day after the wedding," declared Veronica. "Why don't you come with me, Daddy, and learn how to say 'Heil Hitler' and see the whole thing for yourself? That'll convert you. I'll lay you six to one in Reichsmarks that in ten days you'll know the Horst Wessel song by heart."

"I am an old man," said Hanson with a humility which might not have deceived Eleanor, who knew her father only fairly well, which never deceived Mrs Hanson, who knew her husband from beginning to end, but which always deceived Veronica, who seldom could be bothered to try to know anyone except herself.

"Oh, there's life in the old dog yet," she cried encouragingly.

"No," said Hanson, shaking his massive head in a melancholy way. "I am an old man, or old dog if you prefer it. But old dogs are no good at learning new tricks. And so, if you don't mind, Veronica, I don't think I'll spend any of my declining years in learning the words and music of a song which commemorates the death of a loathsome little pimp in a brothel brawl."

Mrs Hanson kept her face bowed over her knitting.

She was a little distressed at the words which her husband had used in front of their youngest daughter, but she could not help smiling a little, unobtrusively, at the success of the old dodge. She knew so well that the humble tone of voice and the shrinking diffidence of manner was the invariable prelude to some devastating thrust, and it served Veronica right for being so cheeky that the trick had been worked on her.

Veronica herself went white with anger and she began to stutter. At last she managed to say, "Horst Wessel was a great patriot. He gave his life for his country."

"Horst Wessel," replied her father carelessly, "was a well-known pimp. And he gave other people's lives to the white slavers. Wendelmann showed me his dossier last year."

"Wendelmann!" exclaimed Veronica with relief, as one about to drown grabs an unexpected life-belt. She knew nothing of the truth about Wessel's horrible professional activities, and she felt on insecure ground in arguing about them. But the introduction of Wendelmann's name gave her an easy cue, and she took it with assurance.

"A Jew," she sneered. "Do you believe everything a Jew tells you?"

"I believe everything that Wendelmann tells me," was the placid reply.

"Trusting the Jews has been the ruin of the world." Veronica quoted one of Herr Streicher's few repeatable remarks.

"If you think it's been the ruin of me," said James Hanson with a cheerful laugh, "I would recommend you to visit a brain specialist before you return to Hunland.

"Father," replied Veronica quietly, drawing herself up to her full height of five foot and one inch in her heels, "I am not going to stay in a house where the Germans are called Huns."

James Hanson pulled a five-pound note out of his breast-pocket and held it out.

"This will pay your hotel bill for several nights," he said amiably, "and the Germans are Huns."

Veronica stamped her tiny foot again and her dark-green eyes filled with tears: "Dad, you're a devil," she cried angrily.

"Veronica, darling," protested Mrs Hanson, and James Hanson laughed again.

CHAPTER XIII

Sir Montagu Anderton-Mawle

The Chairman of the Board of Perdurite Limited listened with satisfaction to General Springton's soldierly report of his visit to the new Financial Secretary to the War Office, and read the letter, written subsequently to the visit, in which Robert Hanson stated that the War Office experts would be glad to meet a deputation from the Board of the Company, without prejudice on either side. The general position could then be discussed and arrangements made, if the general position was satisfactory, for more detailed examination and technical tests.

The Chairman was pleased with the new recruit to the Board, and even more pleased with himself for his acumen in selecting him for office. Sir Montagu Anderton-Mawle — for that was the Chairman's name — was a distinguished man. Although he was a comparatively poor man when he landed in England for the first time in the spring of 1914, he could not be in any way described as "self-made," for the Mawles were an old Tasmanian family, the first Mawle having been one of the pioneer settlers of the island. It was to the first Mawle that Sir Montagu in later life used to ascribe not only his financial acumen, but also the great physical strength with which he was endowed. For the enterprising settler had been a man of versatility and, on being unfortunately compelled to forsake the Old World of commerce and finance, had devoted his talents in the New almost entirely to manual labour in the woods and on the plantations. So strong is the force of heredity and so hard does the pioneering spirit die that it is not surprising to find that Sir Montagu — he was plain Mr Mawle in those days, of course — had been one of the first citizens to grasp the full implications of the scientific principles of commercial amalgamation, and posterity will probably record that he laid the foundations of Tasmanian prosperity by his famous merger of the island's eucalyptus and sassafras interests, an intricate transaction that was only completed in its final details the day before Mr Mawle left Tasmania for the Mother Country.

Arriving at Tilbury with nothing but a few hundreds of thousands of pounds in his pocket, his fee, of course, for effecting the timber merger, he was soon caught up in the whirl of war-contracting and he worked for eighteen or twenty hours a day in his passionate desire to destroy the menace of Prussian militarism for ever. It was not until 1917, when the War was becoming really serious, that Mr Mawle discovered that such ruinous overwork was unnecessary, and he closed his offices and discharged his staff with a kindly injunction to the female members that they should repair to the new munition works in the north of England, and a stern hint to the males that there was a war on in the north of France. He then hired a room in the Piccadilly Hotel, and for the rest of the War bought rifles which he never saw, from people whom he did not know, at prices which did not matter, and sold them to the Government for ten shillings per rifle more than the purchase price.

Unfortunately for the affairs of Sir Montagu Mawle — for he bought and sold so many rifles that he was speedily knighted for his trouble — an irritating Providence took a hand in the game towards the middle of 1918 and played him a very dirty trick. Working in her usual roundabout and unfair way, Providence used a singular weapon for this dirty trick. For she actually called into being the long-dormant conscience of a venerable French politician and dropped a single drop of decent feeling into it. That was all. But it was enough. M. Clemenceau obscurely and incomprehensibly decided that an army of a quarter of a million young men ought not to be commanded for more than two years by a sadistic maniac, who was suffering from several incurable diseases simultaneously, and so he recalled General Sarrail from the command of the Salonika Army of Allies, and replaced him with General Franchet d'Esperey. The new Commander had the strangest notions, for a professional soldier, of how to wage a modern war. He thought nothing about his decorations, his promotions, or his private debts. He did not use his position to advance the fortunes of the younger brothers of his mistresses, or to surround himself with a staff of the glittering lovers of elderly duchesses. He cared not a straw for political intrigue, and he even went so far as to reverse the cardinal point in his predecessor's strategy, which was to maintain a haughty reserve towards the enemy while engaging in a furious paper offensive against his principal Allies. Thus, to the astonishment of the enormous British contingent of the Salonika army, and of the British naval officers upon whom the whole existence of the Salonika army depended, General Franchet d'Esperey from the very outset treated them as if they were important parts of his command. Nor was that all. Having most unprofessionally welded his command into a homogeneous unit by a few kind words, he added the final touch to his unorthodoxy by suddenly attacking the Bulgarians with the utmost violence and crumpling them up in a trice. The Central Empires fell like a pack of cards, and Sir Montagu Mawle found himself stuck with two million rifles that no one in the world had any use for, least of all himself. For by an odd chance, Sir Montagu had never seen a rifle in his life, except upon the shoulders of the brave lads marching through the streets on their way to Victoria Station. It was a major tragedy. For after all, what can a law-abiding private citizen do with two million rifles. To make matters worse, a few weeks after the Armistice, an intimate friend and business associate of Sir Montagu's took umbrage at the discovery of a secret commission which Sir Montagu had been paying himself for some time out of the intimate friend's money, and he went off and sold the pass to the Excess Profits Tax people. In the end Sir Montagu reckoned himself' lucky to have got out of the whole thing with a quarter of a million saved. Such was the disastrous result of the dropping of a drop of decent feeling into the conscience of a French politician.

It was a sad finish to all his hard work for the Empire, and even the satisfaction of seeing the Prussians bite the dust could hardly console the poor Tasmanian for the loss of his millions.

But these pioneers of Empire are made of hardy stock. Where other men might have staggered under two such crashing blows, the loss of his beautiful rifle market and the treachery of a friend whom he had trusted, whom he had regarded as the essential Jonathan to his David, and might have reconciled themselves to a life of comparative penury, Sir Montagu was indomitable. Within three years he had amalgamated a large group of Lancashire cotton mills with such extraordinary skill that, to all intents and purposes, he put the industry on a new footing, and only the most scurrilous of slanderers ever suggested that there was the slightest connection between Sir Montagu's beneficent reorganization and the subsequent bankruptcy of the mills, the ruin of the work-people, the loss of the savings of lifetimes, the slow semi-starvation of men and women and children, the years and years of hopeless unemployment, and, in short, the utter destruction of a once prosperous and happy district. Such a notion was absurd. Everyone knows that such disasters cannot in the very nature of things follow from beneficent reorganization, but can only come in the train of a world-wide economic typhoon against which no amount of organization, however skilful, and no depth of beneficence, however warm-hearted, can possibly do more than ameliorate the suffering.

Sir Montagu, retiring from his three Lancashire years a multi-millionaire, bought a magnificent moated grange in the County of Essex, and, after a series of highly satisfactory interviews with the courtly Mr Sylvester

Hildebrand and a subsequent, and equally satisfactory, interview with Lord Jones of Bannockburn, added Anderton and a hyphen to his name and became a baronet. Although he never again visited Lancashire — just as he had never again visited Tasmania — nevertheless he invariably sent a cheque for twenty-five guineas to the Mayor of Boltington South End, in which town most of the unfortunate mills had been operating, for His Worship's Christmas Fund for the Unemployed. (And there is no doubt whatsoever that he would have done the same for the sufferers in the Tasmanian eucalyptus and sassafras merger, if he had realized the extent to which the world economic typhoon had struck that concern. But what with the War and all, he had somewhat dropped out of Tasmanian affairs.) It says a good deal for Sir Montagu's good nature that he was never in the least ruffled when the ungrateful Socialist Mayors of Boltington South End returned his cheque, as they had done now for the last six years, ever since they got a majority on the Town Council, with an unprintable word scrawled across it in large red letters.

"Twenty-five quid in me pocket and me duty done," was Sir Montagu's invariable remark on these occasions as he tore the cheque in half and rang for a secretary to cancel the counterfoil. "What more could a man ask of his Maker?"

Sir Montagu's inherited pioneering spirit had come out again over Perdurite. The young scientist who had invented this metal alloy, which was much lighter than the lightest aluminium and much harder than the hardest steel, had brought his invention to Sir Montagu as a likely man to take up the process and finance it. Like almost all important inventions in these days, the financing of it was the critical point. The new alloy was composed of a mixture of iron and zinc and a substance called Gloxite which was rather like pitch-blende in appearance and contained a good many of the mysterious mineral qualities of pitch-blende. Iron and zinc were comparatively easy to obtain. But the only deposits of Gloxite, except a few lodes of inferior quality in the mountains of Montana, USA, were situated in a remote mountain district of Cimbria, and a very considerable quantity of finance would be necessary before these deposits could be tapped, and their treasures transported to the British factories for compounding, in the correct proportion and by the correct process, with iron and zinc.

The young inventor could easily cope with the compounding, but he needed the help of a Sir Montagu to cope with the finance. The Tasmanian had been greatly impressed by the possibilities of the new alloy and, with his unerring acumen, had seen at once its potential value in an armament-ridden world. "We might knock the stuffing out of the steel boys," mused Sir Montagu, "if we ran it properly."

It need hardly be added that he did not thus muse aloud in the presence of the young inventor. He was not so foolish as to put ideas into the poor young fellow's head. Instead, he offered him a thousand pounds outright for the invention. After this had been refused, the pair settled down to a discussion of terms and the young man proved unexpectedly stubborn. Sir Montagu was chagrined to find that the youth was not penniless, was not supporting a pauper mother, was not trying to earn a few pounds with which to buy champagne and jellies for a beloved young wife on a cancerous or tubercular death-bed, was not, even, in the hands of money-lenders, and, in fact, was not really playing the game by its ordinarily accepted rules. The final bargain was ten thousand pounds in cash, a hundred thousand One Pound Ordinary Shares in the projected Company, and a two and a half per cent royalty upon the profit per ton.

There was no way out of the ten thousand pounds, and Sir Montagu paid it over with as good a grace as he could. The other two obligations were easily got round. The Durite Company was floated, and soon after flotation it was discovered that a mysterious Syndicate had acquired a three years' option on the total output of the Cimbrian Gloxite deposits, and without Gloxite it was impossible to make Durite. So the Company went bankrupt and all the shareholders' money was lost except that Sir Montagu got most of it, and money can never really be said to be lost that a friend gets. The Company was then bought for an old song by a second mysterious Syndicate which floated a new Company called the Perdurite Company. The unfortunate young inventor had no contract, of course, with the new company and his block of shares in the old company was worth just about the same as the undertaking to pay him a two and a half per cent royalty per ton. There was, in fact, nothing left for him to do but to take his ten thousand pounds and retire to the country and invent something else. This second mysterious Syndicate was apparently on the best of terms with the first mysterious Syndicate, for ample supplies of Gloxite were immediately available, and at the time of General Springton's visit to the War Office, the new Company was in a position to begin manufacture upon a large scale.

Sir Montagu was a man with a small body and a big head. The massiveness of the latter could not console him for the exiguity of the former, for no one knew better than Sir Montagu that beautiful ladies are far more liable to be swept off their high-heeled feet by big men with small heads than vice versa, and the sweeping of beautiful ladies off their feet was a passion second only in Sir Montagu's life to the making of money. Now at the age of fifty-three, he could look back on a long line of conquests, but candour compelled him to admit that he had been rather more successful with the exquisite but somewhat mercenary ladies from Kansas City, St. Louis, Oklahoma City, and elsewhere in the Middle West of the United States of America, who perform from time to time in cabarets in London's large hotels, than he ever had been with the daughters of the aristocracy. Unless, of course, he happened to meet a daughter of the aristocracy who was even harder up than most of the daughters of the aristocracy.

In consequence of this spiritual longing to be loved for himself alone, and the physical disabilities that made such an event unlikely — for Sir Montagu's enormous head was split from side to side by an enormous mouth and garlanded on each flank by a fine, outstanding ear — the little Tasmanian had come, after years of disappointment, to be obsessed with a detestation of tall men. He regarded every man of over six foot in height as a dragon who might at any moment snatch a fair maiden away without paying for her, or, worse still, snatch away a fair maiden who wanted to be snatched away, and this modern, chivalrous St. George hated all dragons. Whenever possible he employed small men in his numerous enterprises, and, if occasion arose when the indispensable man for a post happened to be tall, Sir Montagu treated him with the insolence and contempt that all dragons deserve at the hands of all saints.

But although General Springton was six feet two inches tall, and was universally known among fighting-men as the Tiger, Sir Montagu was courtesy itself to him. For the General might be a useful man to the Perdurite Company, and it would be downright folly to treat him with insolence and contempt while any of his potential utility remained. There would be plenty of time for that sort of thing later, when the contracts had been signed and the protective tariffs secured and the Government Subsidy voted. So Sir Montagu purred approvingly over the General's report and praised his dexterous handling of the preliminary negotiations.

They were sitting in Sir Montagu's enormous study — these two men who had, in their dissimilar but equally whole-hearted fashions, fought and suffered and sacrificed in the cause of Democracy between the years 1914 and 1918 — and the affairs of the Company lay between them on the table in piles of documents.

"You and I will go on this deputation, General," said the Chairman, laying down the report. "We'll need a third."

"What about Stigge?" suggested the General. "A good fellow. Used to command the Ninth when Gilkes had the Rawal Pindis."

"Yes. A fine fellow," agreed Sir Montagu, secretly wondering how General Stigge had ever escaped the attentions of the alienists.

"Or Cotterham?" went on Springton. "Good chap, Cotterham. Had Hodson's Horse when I was at Meerut with the Chestnut Troop."

Although Sir Montagu had long since got rid of the last trace — or almost the last trace — of his Tasmanian accent, he was racked by a spasm of hatred for this tall man who so confidently embarked upon a phrase like "had Hodson's Horse." He concealed it, however, and agreed that General Sir Henry Cotterham was a fine fellow, though he had never actually been able to make up his mind whether General Sir Henry Cotterham or General Stigge had been endowed with the more lavish equipment of brains.

"They're both fine fellows," he went on, lighting a fresh cigar and pushing the box across to the general who waved it away and pulled out a tobacco-pouch, "and it's a great weight off my shoulders to have them as colleagues on the Board. But I'm not at all sure that we wouldn't be better to have someone — what shall I say — someone who has concentrated a bit less on the practical side and a bit more on the legal side."

"Babs Cotterham was acting Judge-Advocate-General at Peshawur when I was at the Staff College at Quetta," replied the Tiger. "There wasn't much he didn't know about court-martials, I can tell you."

Sir Montagu must have looked a little doubtful at this, for the Tiger added, "Of course that isn't quite the same thing, I know, but what we always used to say in the old days was, 'a man who can understand King's Regulations can understand anything.' Rule of thumb. Lot of sense in it."

Sir Montagu laughed a rich, appreciative laugh at the other's playful humour. "Yes, you're quite right, General. There is a lot of sense in it. That's how we Britishers got our Empire, by rule of thumb and no nonsense about brain work or rubbish of that sort. But all the same—" He broke off and examined his cigar critically.

"Well? What is it?" enquired the Tiger gruffly.

"I was just wondering — it's a point on which I would value your opinion, General — I was just wondering whether we ought to embark on such a very intricate undertaking as getting the War Office to consider Perdurite as the new metal for this Rearmament campaign and yet rely simply on rule of thumb for our legal advice. All the business of drawing up contracts and so on — assuming that we get the contracts — will be pretty tricky, and I'm doubtful if General Cotterham's legal knowledge — extraordinarily able man though General Cotterham undoubtedly is," he added hastily as a dark look appeared upon the Tiger's face, "isn't just a little too highly specialized."

"I think I get you," said the General. "You mean we ought to take a lawyer with us?"

"Well, what do you think?"

"Excellent notion, my dear Anderton-Mawle. Capital idea. Haven't much use for lawyers myself. Lot of thieves. But in a case like this one can't be too careful."

"I think your advice is very sound, General," said the Chairman warmly, "and we can't do better than to act upon it. Now, who do you think we ought to take?"

The Tiger knitted his black eyebrows and cudgelled his brains. Suddenly he had an idea. "Isn't there a lawyer fellow on the Board?" he exclaimed.

Sir Montagu thumped the table with a podgy fist and hopped up like an enthusiastic goblin.

"General, you've got it," he exclaimed. "We'll take Andrew Hay with us. He's the very boy. And by a lucky chance he's coming to see me in a few minutes." The Tiger stretched his long legs out and began to fill himself another pipe. "One can solve most problems if one puts one's mind to them," he observed introspectively.

"How right you are," answered the enthusiastic goblin, sitting down again, and at that moment a dapper and extremely small young gentleman announced that Mr Andrew Hay had arrived.

"Show him in," commanded Sir Montagu brusquely, and then his tones changed to a winning cordiality as he went on. "Talk of the devil, my dear Hay. We were speaking about you this very minute. Delighted to see you. Sit down. Cigar? You know the General, of course."

"We met at the last Board Meeting, sir." Mr Hay addressed himself with a pleasing deference to the General.

"It was my first, sir," replied the latter, not to be outdone in courtesy, "and you must forgive me if I do not recall every face in that distinguished gathering. But I am proud to be a colleague of yours."

"I heard you had just joined us," said the lawyer, "and I was very glad to hear it, if I may say so." The General bowed, and the lawyer bowed in return. Mr Andrew Hay was a gentleman of about thirty-four or thirty-five years of age. Handsome in rather a dashing way, with an aquiline nose and sleek black hair and polished manners, he was not so short in stature that he could ever have been compared to an enthusiastic goblin, and not so tall as to arouse the Lotharian jealousy of Sir Montagu. He had all the cosmopolitan charm and elegance of a man who has been determined, over a period of many years, to conceal from the world the dreadful facts that his father was a large Dunfermline grocer, and was still a large Dunfermline grocer, and that his grandfather had been a very, very small Dunfermline grocer.

Sent first to a smart English preparatory school, where he lost his Dunfermline accent even more readily than Sir Montagu had lost his

Tasmanian one, young Andrew Hay proceeded to Eton and worked his way up the school to social, intellectual, and athletic pre-eminence. In his last year he was President of the Eton Society; he recited Gunga Din on the Fourth of June; and, though failing to get a place in the cricket eleven, was a popular captain of the ping-pong team, or, in Eton parlance, Keeper of the Table.

Trinity, Cambridge, followed Eton, and the Middle Temple followed Trinity, Cambridge. As a barrister, Hay had been a success almost from the beginning. He had many friends, both at Eton and at Cambridge. But he had never been the sort of man either to make use of his friends or to cultivate people simply in order to make use of them. That, to Andrew Hay's strict code of honour which had been born in Dunfermline and nourished at Eton, was not playing the game, and, besides, school friends and undergraduate friends were seldom in a position to be of real use. Their parents, however, were a very different story, and the ambitious young lawyer took enormous pains to be civil to those fathers and uncles of his young playmates who might be able to give him a helping hand. He was always at his best with old people, too — that is to say, with influential old people. An extraordinarily patient listener on important occasions, he would sit for hours over the after-dinner cigars, all ears to the tale of the early struggles of a now wealthy shipping magnate, or to the description of the hardships once endured by a now intimate friend of the present Lord Chancellor. Nor had this charming courtesy towards the Old gone entirely unrewarded. For briefs had never been lacking to Andrew Hay.

It was all the more curious, therefore, that his first real chance to show his calibre had come by chance, in the following circumstances, and not as a result of his assiduous good manners towards shipping magnates and friends of Lord Chancellors.

A certain well-to-do professional gentleman, conducting a large practice as an estate agent, surveyor, and, in general, a buyer and seller of Real Property, was arrested one day on the charge of having deliberately caused certain of his properties to be burned down in order to collect the insurance money. That the professional man had been careless was quite certain. That he had been criminal was quite another matter. Thirty-seven rogues were charged at the same time with complicity in the series of fires and all pleaded guilty of arson, because the case against them was so lamentably clear that they could not very well plead anything else without making the jury laugh; but the thirty-seven, while professing, one and all, the utmost readiness to turn King's Evidence against the other thirty-six, were unanimous in declaring that the thirty-eighth prisoner in the dock, the well-to-do buyer and seller of Real Property, was innocent.

The careless professional gentleman was defended by the famous Vernon Quick, K.C. (at seven hundred and fifty guineas and a hundred a day refresher), and Mr Andrew Hay. The case lasted for sixteen days, and for thirteen of those days Mr Hay sat in court and made notes and listened, while Mr Quick, K.C., flitted hither and thither from Court to Court upon other cases, now conducting vehement arguments about libel before the Lord Chief Justice, now expounding intricacies of the Law of Barratry to their Lordships of Appeal, now setting forth to the Law Lords themselves the sad wrongs which had been suffered by a worthy company of merchants, and now dodging into the Old Bailey to defend a murderer or two. On the fourteenth day of the trial, Mr Quick abruptly abandoned a client in the Court of the Master of the Rolls, and devoted four hours to a brilliant cross-examination of the Crown witnesses against his client, the careless professional gentleman. The fifteenth day of the trial was the crisis in Mr Andrew Hay's professional career. For on that day fell due to be played the fourth round of the Bar Golf Handicap, and Mr Quick, K.C., playing off a handicap of 24, had reached the fourth round for the first time in his whole career. To have expected Mr Quick to scratch and allow his opponent a walk-over, would have been to demand too great a sacrifice from any human being, and so on the fifteenth day of the trial Mr Vernon Quick, K.C., neatly attired in a suit of knickerbockers and a tweed cap and yellowish brogues, repaired in his large automobile to the golf links of the Royal Cinque Ports at Deal, and Mr Andrew Hay delivered the final speech on behalf of their innocent but careless client. It was generally admitted upon all hands that, for so young a man, the speech was a triumph of the forensic art, and Mr Hay was the recipient of innumerable congratulations. And everyone agreed that whereas Mr Quick might have got the careless but innocent business man off with three years, a less brilliant junior than Mr Hay would certainly have landed him with seven, and that, in consequence, justice was impartially and satisfactorily administered in the sentence of five. Nor did Mr Quick, K.C., ever openly rail against the ill-luck which condemned his client to two extra years in prison. Indeed Mr Quick, K.C., was inclined to feel that the sacrifice was worth it, for he not only defeated his opponent in the fourth round of the Bar Tournament but actually fought his way through into the final, where he was only narrowly defeated by a single hole by a King's Bench Master, playing off an unfairly low handicap of 3, and, what was even more unfair, playing down to it.

These three gentlemen then, representatives of three of the immemorial corporations of England, the Nobility, the Services, and the Law, formed the deputation which waited upon the Secretary of State for War to impress upon him the advantages that would accrue to the country and the Empire and, therefore, to Humanity at large, by the adoption of Perdurite, lightest and hardest of known metallic alloys, for armour-plating, steel helmets, bombs, bullets, asphyxiating gas projectors, bacteria-throwers, and all those other defensive weapons without which a modern Power would be quite incapable of waging a defensive war, against a brutal, barbarous, and unscrupulous aggressor.

CHAPTER XIV

Miss Collins makes her Report

The time between Eleanor's engagement to Jack Crawford and the day of the wedding sometimes seemed to pass quickly and sometimes to crawl most tediously. It was not that the time was very long, for Crawford, to Eleanor's delight and naïve surprise, was anxious to hurry the date forward. Eleanor would never have dared to suggest such a thing herself. She was prepared to wait for Jack till all eternity, and she was sincerely astonished that her demi-god should not only want to marry her but should be in a hurry to do so. The date was fixed, therefore, for a month after the engagement, as it was generally agreed by the family that this was the minimum length of time in which Mrs Hanson could be keyed up to adjust herself to the situation. There was also the organization of the wedding to be attended to, and at least a fortnight elapsed during which hardly any preparations were made. Mrs Hanson fussed vaguely about the house and did nothing. The three sons flatly refused to help in such ridiculous feminine nonsense, Robert on the legitimate ground that he was busy all day at the War Office and half the night at the House, and the cavalry captains out of sheer manly loftiness. Veronica excused herself on the score of political activity. Her friends in Nuremberg had asked her to examine, during her visit to London for her sister's wedding, the possibilities of forming an English branch of a new World Society that was being founded in Munich called the "Society for the Glorification of Holy Liberators." The idea of the Society was to celebrate the blessed memory of such men as Gavrile Princip who fired the glorious shots at Sarajevo, of ex-naval officer Kern, who exterminated the Jew Rathenau, of Hitler who so efficiently supervised the killing of Röhm in the Great Purge of June 30th, 1934, of the splendid Italians who killed the traitor Matteotti, of the French patriot whose well-aimed bullet cut short the infamous Jaurès' efforts to prevent the World War, of all those in fact who have sacrificed themselves, their lives, their fortunes, their families, to stamp out the twin evils of Socialism and Pacifism.

Veronica threw herself into the work with all her demoniac energy — for she was a true child of James Hanson — and had no time to spare for writing out invitation cards for weddings or choosing decorations for wedding-breakfast tables.

It so happened that at the end of the first fortnight, when Mrs Hanson and Eleanor and one or two of Eleanor's especial friends had between them reduced to chaos any semblance of organization which the ecclesiastical officials and the catering firms had opened the campaign with, Miss Ruth Collins, private secretary to Mr James Hanson, presented herself to her employer. Cool as ever, unsmiling, quiet, Miss Collins as usual waited for the first word to be spoken.

"Well?" said James Hanson.

"It took longer than I expected," said Miss Collins, and stopped.

The old millionaire looked at her sharply. "Something unpleasant, eh?" he asked.

Miss Collins very nearly forgot her professional manners so far as to smile. It was such a relief to come back from her crowds of charming, sweet, silly young men to this venerable demon with his swift mind. Tedious explanations were unnecessary with him, and a good deal of Miss Collins' leisure hours were taken up with tedious explanations of the obvious to attractive young gentlemen in immaculate clothes whose elegant figures were as thin as their intellectual attainments.

She suppressed her unprofessional smile, however, and nodded primly.

James Hanson's heavy eyebrows came down a little.

"A woman, eh?"

Miss Collins nodded again. "Springton's daughter."

"The worst occurred, eh?"

"Worse even than that."

Hanson started. "What do you mean?"

"She went into Sir Albion Featherby's Nursing Home two days ago."

"Not with——"

The girl nodded for the third time.

A flush covered the old man's face suddenly. "It's been going on right up — right up to——" He found it difficult to speak the words. Miss Collins said nothing, but Hanson knew her well enough to recognize the look of pity in her serenely beautiful face.

He sat down heavily and stared at her. "After the engagement as well? No, no, it's not possible. It's not true."

But he knew instinctively that with his prospective son-in-law all things were possible and he knew from the look in her face that it was true.

"Oh, what a swine," he said aloud to himself. "What a damnable swine. Poor little Eleanor. But what can I do? What can anyone do?"

As the questions were obviously not directed to her, Miss Collins said nothing. But James Hanson suddenly looked up at her and repeated, "What can I do?"

"Nothing," she answered evenly.

"Why not?" he almost barked.

"Because she is desperately in love with him."

"It won't last."

"I think so," the secretary replied, almost casually. James Hanson snorted. "I always thought you were a judge of human nature, Miss Collins. And you can stand there and tell me that a marriage on those lines is going to last?"

"I didn't say the marriage would last," she said placidly. "I said her love for him will last."

That silenced the old man and he looked at her for a long time. It was characteristic of the girl that she was not in the least put out of countenance by the long scrutiny. It was even more characteristic of her that her coolness was not due to any vast latent store of sang-froid, but because she knew very well that though her employer was gazing at her, he was not seeing her. His mind and his thoughts were far away.

"She won't be happy," he said abruptly.

"She will at first."

He thumped the table with his heavy fist. "That's not good enough for a daughter of mine."

"It's more than many get," was the almost inhumanly calm reply.

"But it means misery afterwards," he exclaimed. "Can't you see that?"

"You can't ever be really miserable if you've once been really happy," answered Miss Collins.

James Hanson laughed harshly. "Where do you young women learn all your philosophy?" he enquired. A ghost of a smile flickered on Ruth Collins' lips at last. "Such poor philosophy as we young women have," she said, "must be born in us," and then they both laughed.

"I feel better," said James Hanson. "Tell me all about it. I think I could stand it now."

"There's very little to tell that you haven't guessed," replied the secretary. "Crawford got on to Perdurite by chance. I mean he was living with Fiona Springton before he'd heard about it, and she told him about it. She'd got it from her father, and was rather proud of being able to give some important news to her lover. Poor kid!"

"And what's Crawford going to do about it?"

"Retire from the Army and bully his way on to the Board."

"No, no, I don't mean that," exclaimed Hanson.

"I know you don't," she replied tranquilly. "But I hoped you wouldn't ask me about the other."

"You mean he'll leave her in the lurch?"

"Can you describe the Nursing Home of Sir Albion Featherby as the lurch?"

James Hanson exploded. "Listen to me, woman. Do you think I pay you a thousand a year to talk like a West End comedy?"

"I think you pay me a thousand a year," replied Miss Collins, "to tell you things without having to talk."

There was another long pause after this. At last James Hanson said, "He'll get on to the Board, will he?" Even Miss Collins, in spite of her unshakeable poise and complete fearlessness, hesitated a moment before she answered, "Sir Montagu Anderton-Mawle is fond of giving lucrative seats on Boards to men who have just married pretty wives."

There was no explosion at this. And Miss Collins had known that there would not be one. She knew that James Hanson burst into flames over trivial affairs. Over serious affairs he became almost as cool as she was, and when he was as cool as that he could almost — almost but not quite — alarm Miss Collins.

"You're sketching a pretty future for my daughter," he said silkily.

Miss Collins said nothing.

"You're suggesting," he went on, with a deadly quietness, "that my daughter is going to share her husband's bed with a pack of other women, for a week or two, and will then be sold to Montagu Mawle for a seat on the Board of Perdurite. Is that what you're suggesting?"

Miss Collins continued to say nothing, but examined her beautiful finger-nails. Her hands were long and graceful and very white, and she was tired of hearing them described by her young men as butterflies or white water-lilies, or fragile lotus-flowers. There was nothing fragile about them. They were strong as well as beautiful.

James Hanson thumped the table again. "You heard what I said. Is that what you're suggesting?"

Miss Collins raised her tranquil blue eyes from her lovely fingers to James Hanson's flushed face and said, "Yes."

"And there's nothing I can do about it?"

"No."

"Why the. devil do you women fall in love with such damnable wrong 'uns?" he growled.

"That wouldn't matter so much," she began to reply, when he interrupted:

"If you weren't so damned faithful to them, eh?"

"Yes."

He threw up his hands in despair. "What fools," he cried.

"And what knaves," she answered.

"Yes. That's the tragedy of it. Folly can be divine, but knavery is just beastly. Listen, Miss Collins. I want you to take hold of the organizing of this wedding. The whole household are either silly or proud. And all of them are incompetent. Will you take it on?"

"Certainly."

"You're sure it can't be stopped?"

"Sure."

"Then for God's sake get it over decently and quickly."

"Is that all, Mr Hanson?"

"That's all. No. Stop. How did you find out about — about Crawford and Springton's daughter? Don't tell me if you don't want to."

"I met Major Crawford at a cocktail party and then at a dance," she replied coolly. "Major Crawford did me the honour to suggest that as Miss Springton was likely to be in the hands of Sir Albion for some little time, I might care to become her successor."

Hanson said nothing. He looked like an antique Greek statue, rigid, immovable, but full of living fire.

"And once a man has put himself in that position," she concluded, "it is easy to get his life story from him. In fact, it is almost impossible not to get his life story from him."

"Aren't there times when you rather despise men?" asked Hanson slowly.

Miss Collins gave a faint shrug. "It's the way of the world," she said indifferently.

"But do you think it's a good way of the world?"

"It might be worse."

"And you don't think that Jack Crawford is a blackguard?" he persisted.

"He's out to enjoy himself. If he succeeds, good luck to him. The world," she added casually, "can be quite a good place for the Jack Crawfords of it."

"I suppose because it is mainly run by people of that sort," said Hanson.

"I suppose so," Miss Collins agreed as she flicked a speck of dust off her dark-blue sleeve.

"And the Eleanors of this world go to the wall, eh?"

"I'm afraid so. If they're not careful."

"I see," said James Hanson heavily. "Well, good night."

"Good night, Mr Hanson," said Ruth Collins.

And the arrangements for the wedding were carried out with meticulous skill and accuracy down to the tiniest detail.

.....

The reasons why the month seemed to Eleanor to gallop at one moment and to drag at the next were that she was kept very busy arranging for the Mammoth Ball at the Plantagenet House Hotel for the East Stepditch Welfare Centre, and that she saw very little of Jack. While she was at work the time raced past; when she was sitting at home and wondering where he was and what he was doing, the time stood still. Even when he did drop in for a few minutes, he seemed absent-minded and worried. Eleanor never dreamt of asking him what the matter was. If he wanted to tell her, well and good. If he did not want to tell her, well and good. But it was not for her to add to his preoccupations by pestering him with unnecessary questions. So he came and went and hardly addressed five hundred words to his fiancée during the whole month of their engagement.

Organizing the Ball, on the other hand, was the greatest possible fun. All Eleanor's friends had rallied round her and formed themselves into a Grand Committee which met three or four times a week at each other's houses to drink a cocktail and discuss arrangements. At the beginning Eleanor had been a little doubtful of the competence of her friends to carry through such an undertaking. After the first three Committee meetings had taken place and nothing very definite seemed to have emerged from the deliberations, except the appointment of an Honorary Secretary who had unfortunately been compelled to leave for St. Juan les Pins after the second meeting, Eleanor had proposed that some young men should be co-opted on to the Committee. "Men always do these things so much better than we do," she said.

This had brought down a tornado of indignant denials from at least half of the Grand Committee, so that the other half, which held no strong views on the relative efficiency of men and women in the organization of charity balls, but which held strong views on the desirability of the presence of young men at cocktail parties, was completely shouted down, and the Feminist element triumphed. Eleanor, of course, was not in the least convinced, and she thought she had never heard anything so foolish as the remark of one exquisite lady who observed languidly, "Look, what a hash men make of everything."

Eleanor, contemplating a perfect world which had been designed and built entirely by men, could only pity a creature so witless or so warped.

The poor creature's views, however, carried the day and it was resolved to carry on without male assistance. A third Honorary Secretary was appointed to succeed the second one who had had to resign owing to an unexpected invitation to visit Antibes, and the work went briskly on. The core of the evening's entertainment was to be a Pageant of Historical

Ladies, and the main task of the members of the Grand Committee was to allot the various rôles to one another in such a way as not to disrupt the whole charitable undertaking. There was one lucky feature about the East Stepditch Ball, and that was the indisputable fact that it was to be Eleanor's night. Everyone was agreed on that. It had been Eleanor's suggestion; the Ball was to take place two nights before Eleanor's marriage; East Stepditch belonged to Eleanor; and all her friends suddenly realized what a lot she had done for them in the past, generously and unobtrusively, and how fond, in a half-humorous, half-genuine way, they were of her.

This spontaneous outburst of kindliness among these beautifully dressed young women, most of whom looked exactly like Miss Priscilla Mapledurham and Miss Marion Malindine, automatically smoothed over the one really intricate problem which arises on these occasions, and Eleanor was unanimously cast for the role of Helen of Troy. At first she protested against the honour, partly out of her natural modesty and diffidence, and partly because she knew that, although she herself was pretty — her modesty did not go so far as to prevent her understanding that — there were at least four girls on the Grand Committee who were so outstandingly beautiful that their photographs appeared every week in one or other of the illustrated weeklies, and young men sighed over them under almost every deodar, palm, giant gum-tree, eucalyptus, and mango in the Empire. But Eleanor's protests were firmly overruled by the Committee, none of whose members were firmer in their overruling than the four beautiful ladies, each of whom was desperately afraid that the coveted part might be captured, in some dirty, underhand way, by one of the other three.

After that awkward rock had been thus skilfully circumnavigated, the rest was plain sailing. The four beauties were allowed to grab, in order to avoid any unpleasantness, Cleopatra, Mary Queen of Scots, Ninon de l'Enclos, and Nell Gwynn, these being generally recognized in such affairs as being the next four after Helen, and the remainder of the Grand Committee scrambled for the Queen of Sheba, Marie Antoinette, Mrs Siddons, Anne of Austria, Madame de Montespan, Madame du Barry, Diane de Poitiers, Emma Lady Hamilton, Fanny Burney, Madame Récamier, the Mona Lisa, Beatrice d'Este, Clementina Sobieska, la Camargo, Flora Macdonald, Swift's Stella, Lucrezia Borgia, and the other stock beauties of history, and there was the usual scrimmage round the Empress Josephine. But everything sorted itself out amicably in the end, and even the small friction was smoothed over which had been caused when Anne Boleyn congratulated the Queen of Sheba on the ground that a black face and frizzy hair would go so well with her lovely, full lips. And Emma Lady Hamilton was a little distressed on being told by a member of the Committee, who wrote a gossip column for a daily newspaper and therefore sometimes had to read a book in the way of business, that her capture of Nelson took place when she was stoutish and over forty. But these were the merest trifles, and it was unanimously agreed that never had the work of organizing a charity ball gone so pleasantly and easily.

The price of the tickets was fixed at five guineas each, and it was announced that the Plantagenet House Hotel had agreed to make all the arrangements at the very moderate charge of five guineas per head. The Grand Committee then pledged itself to work unceasingly at the collection of donations with which to swell the Fund for the Welfare Centre, passed votes of thanks to Eleanor, to the Plantagenet House Hotel, to the three Honorary Secretaries, and to anyone else they could think of, drank one more cocktail, and declared itself dissolved.

.....

Veronica was full of contempt for her sister's charity ball, and she held her neat little upturned nose more loftily in the air than ever when she contrasted her own important mission with what she called Eleanor's amiable futilities. She herself was tearingly busy, dashing to the German Embassy in Carlton House Terrace, racing to interview possible adherents to the new Society, darting in and out of City offices, drawing up lists, despatching long reports to Munich, and allowing herself to be taken out to lunch and dinner either by anyone who might be useful to the Cause or by handsome young members of the German colony in London. She allowed the former to pay for her, and insisted on paying for the latter, an arrangement in which everyone gladly acquiesced.

The work itself called for the utmost tact, and Veronica found that it was rather more difficult than she at first imagined. She had supposed that her detestation for all Bolsheviks and Pacifists, or Reds and Runaways, as they were usually called in her circles, was shared by every right-thinking man and woman, and it had never occurred to her that there might be varying shades of opinion within the ranks of the right-thinking people themselves. Thus she was astonished to find, for example, that General Springton agreed cordially with her that Gavrile Princip, who fired the Sarajevo shots, was a man worthy of commemoration (without those crucial shots how would the Tiger have acquired his nickname and got rid of his debts?); that anyone who shot the Jew Rathenau, or any other Jew, was obviously a great man; that the only way to save the world from another war was by building up great armies, navies, and air forces; and that anyway another war would do the world a lot of good. But the

General drew the line at having anything to do with the Germans. "I spent the best years of my life fighting against them," he repeated over and over again, "and you can't come to what was practically hand-to-hand fighting with a fellow without knowing what sort of chap he is. I've been at pretty close quarters with the Boche, and I do happen to know what I'm talking about. I don't like Germans, and I never will." And then he added, over and over again, with a courtly expression on his dark face, "Of course a charming young lady like you wouldn't understand us old fighting men."

Veronica was in a furious rage when she left General Springton. But he was not the only Conservative to express that sort of view. Veronica found several of them. Their attitude, roughly speaking, was that Nazi Germany had done superbly in preventing "Communism on the Rhine" and that Germany ought to have been ruthlessly destroyed in 1919; that Prussianism was, as usual, the menace to Europe, and that Prussianism was Europe's bulwark against Moscow.

Veronica soon gave up this section of the Decent People as hopeless. And she was annoyed to find, almost at once, another section which was equally hopeless, but for a very different reason. Her friends in Munich and Nuremberg had earnestly advised and begged her to concentrate upon two sorts of person, the rich and the young. "The rich are important for their riches," they had explained with that lucidity which is the hall-mark of the German, "and the youth are important—"

"For their youth, I suppose," Veronica had interrupted flippantly.

"Precisely," had been the grave reply.

But though Veronica had been flippant, she knew exactly what they meant, and how perfectly right they were. Germany had to have money. And Germany's native Idealism would call to the Youth of the World like deep calling to deep. But wherever she went among the young people of Mayfair, she was disgusted to find that a miserable and sordid consideration prevented them from enlisting in her movement. It was not that they objected to the basic idea of the Glorification of Holy Liberators Society. Far from it. The young men and women of the drawing-rooms, the flats, and the little houses in fashionable mews were strongly in favour of anything that resembled even remotely the principles of Mussolini's Fascism. And they were eager to play a part in the establishment of a similar movement in Britain. But, however vehemently they expressed these views to Veronica in the privacy of boudoir or of sitting-room furnished to resemble a bar-parlour with high stools, dart-boards, and sawdusty floors, they one and all flatly refused to repeat them in public, and threatened Veronica with writs for slander if she quoted them as having indicated sympathy with the Glorification movement. The reason for this pusillanimity, this wretched refusal to stand up for their convictions, was that every single one of them was longing passionately for a job as actor or actress, as dialogue-writer or scenarist, as dress-designer or scene-painter, as sifter of manuscripts, or shifter of scenes in the Gaumont-British Film Company.

"A Jewish firm," cried Veronica scornfully, when at last she penetrated the reason for the blank wall of stubborn inertia with which she was faced. "Do you know what we do to Jewish firms in Germany?"

"That won't help us to get jobs at Shepherd's Bush," chorused the young elegants in reply.

"Aren't you ashamed of yourselves?" exclaimed the passionate little bantam, dark-green fire crackling from her eyes and the tip of her *retroussé* nose quivering.

"No," piped the young men, and "Not in the least," growled the young women.

Veronica impatiently left them to their lives of hypocritical slavery, or worse, of unwanted slavery, which was even more ignominious, for the Gaumont-British authorities did not seem to be rushing hither and thither in the streets of Mayfair to enlist the services of these talented folk, either as actors or as actresses, as dialogue-writers or scenarists, or sifters, shifters, or anything else.

Youth having thus lamentably failed to answer to the call of Youth, Veronica turned her attention to Wealth, and here found a much readier response. For she soon found two classes of rich men who were interested in any scheme for the closer co-operation of Britain and Germany, and who gladly subscribed to her Society on the sole condition that their names, and the amounts of their donations translated into marks, should be published in the German newspapers. Firstly, there were the financiers and bankers who had lent money to Germany for post-War reconstruction and could see no other way of getting it back than by lending some more. And secondly, there were the industrialists who had guns to sell to anyone who had money, or could borrow money, to buy them with. Both these classes of wealthy magnates consisted solely of patriots who were inspired by no other motive than the sincerest love of Great Britain. For those who had risked their money, or rather the money which they had been able to borrow from the general public, for the reconstruction of Germany, had done so in order to re-create a market for British goods and so help to reduce unemployment and add to the National Wealth of Britain. And it was obvious to all but the most obstinately muddle-headed of partisans that the more money which could be lent to Germany, the greater would be the increase of Britain's Wealth. These almost idealistic and certainly romantic patriots, therefore, were eagerly trying to persuade the general public to continue the policy of loans to themselves, and so to Germany, and they regarded Veronica's Society as a small but none the less useful advertisement for Anglo-German solidarity.

Nor were the gun-makers a whit behind the financiers in patriotism. Their sole objective was the maintenance in peace-time of a plant sufficiently large to fulfil Great Britain's needs in war-time, and the only way in which this was possible was to keep the plant going by means of foreign orders. In order to enable Britain and her far-flung Empire to defend themselves against potential aggression from Germany, it was absolutely essential for the gun-makers to maintain their factories at the fullest possible efficiency and modernity by selling guns to any and every foreign customer who might come along with the necessary cash. And it was quite irrelevant, though perhaps a little unfortunate, that the only large-scale customer, with any large-scale credit, at the moment happened to be Germany itself. But the principle was exactly the same as if the customer had happened to be San Salvador or Honduras. The Welfare of Britain was the only paramount consideration and the identity of the customer mattered nothing. So the far-sighted financiers handed the money of the public to the far-sighted gun-makers, who handed the guns to the Germans, and so everyone was satisfied. Thousands of British workmen were taken off the dole and given lucrative employment; the armament plants were kept working on a large enough scale to save Britain in the next war; Veronica got dozens of names and dozens of donations for her Society; her friends in Munich and Nuremberg wrote glowing letters of congratulation to her and hinted at the possibility of an official visit to the Führer himself when she returned to Germany; and even the German Government was satisfied with the arrangement, not having the far-sightedness of the London experts and therefore not realizing that by accepting money and guns they were simply playing into the hands of Britain and laying the permanent foundations of British financial and military supremacy.

James Hanson flatly refused to subscribe to Veronica's Society. Nicholas and Oliver each gave her a guinea because they thought she was a jolly kid, and Robert pleaded his official position as an impassable bar to subscription. Veronica did not ask Eleanor for a donation. Ever since early childhood she had refrained from asking for things from Eleanor. It was too like robbery.

.....

The charity ball was a great success. The Pageant of Historical Ladies down the Ages was universally agreed to be the most spectacular pageant of British girlhood since the Pageant of Historical Loveliness at the Montmorency House Hotel six weeks earlier. Cleopatra came in for a generous share of applause, though perhaps no more than Ninon de l'Enclos, while everyone admired the exquisiteness of Mary Queen of Scots and the lavish charms of Nell Gwynn. But enthusiasm reached a very high pitch when Sir Montagu Anderton-Mawle's special prize of a diamond-encrusted cigarette-case was awarded to Helen of Troy. Sir Montagu, who had not only offered the prize but had also contributed a hundred guineas to the Fund, claimed the right to do the judging for himself, and he sat in state upon a specially prepared dais while the procession of Beauty filed slowly past. His enormous head was sunk forward on his chest as he gazed absently at them. For he was not really looking at them. He was reflecting at one moment that he, a self-made man, great-grandson of a Tasmanian pioneer, was sitting in judgment upon the aristocratic beauties of the Capital of the Empire, and the thought filled him with pride, and at the next moment he was reflecting that he had paid a hundred and eighty guineas for the privilege, whereas at the Montmorency House Hotel six weeks before, the judge had been that young rascal the Marquess of Hascombe who hadn't a penny in the world but was a good-looking young man, besides being the eleventh Marquess of Hascombe, the sixteenth Viscount Ewhurst, the twelfth Baron Coneyhurst, and the twenty-second Baron Kiltartan in the Irish peerage.

When the procession was over, Sir Montagu, beaming like a beneficent and diminutive gargoyle, awarded the prize to Eleanor, to the enormous relief of Cleopatra, Ninon, Mary, and Nell, who had each been terrified that one of the other three might ogle the little bart. into giving her the cigarette-case.

Sir Montagu admired Eleanor's simple English prettiness and her charmingly shy smile. Besides, he was being pressed to take Jack Crawford on to the Board of Perdurite, and he could not remember an occasion on which he had so vehemently detested a man at first sight as he had detested the big, blond, silky-moustached, handsome young major whom Springton had brought to see him. So Sir Montagu awarded the first prize to Eleanor and presented her with his cheque for the Welfare Centre. If the big blond lady-killer was going to join Perdurite, he was jolly well going to bring his wife with him. That would square the account. So Sir Montagu awarded Eleanor the prize.

Eleanor was charmed with the great financier's generosity. She even thought his smile was delightful. Five hundred and sixty people bought tickets, and the Grand Committee collected three hundred and twenty pounds in donations from their fathers and uncles. The total profit for the East Stepditch Welfare Centre was three hundred and twenty pounds.

CHAPTER XV

Wendelmann Persuades Hanson to Come Out of Retirement

On the day after the Grand Ball at the Plantagenet House Hotel, Veronica returned from a successful afternoon's subscription-collecting in the City, and marched casually into her father's study at Partington Crescent. She was somewhat taken aback, and extremely cross, at finding old Amschel Wendelmann sitting in a deep armchair smoking a long fat cigar. Her father was leaning in his favourite position with his broad shoulders against the mantelpiece, and was looking down with an affectionate smile at his former partner. Veronica would have retreated as abruptly as she had entered, but her father mischievously hailed her with delight, and Mr Wendelmann politely hoisted his large body out of his chair. Veronica, much too proud of her cosmopolitan poise and polish, which she had acquired during her few months in Germany, to show the slightest distaste, bowed to him with her most charming smile — and Veronica's most charming smile was very charming indeed — and apologized for interrupting them.

"No interruption could possibly be more welcome," said Mr Wendelmann, also bowing, "nor could any interruption have been more exquisitely timed. Your Father and I had just reached a deadlock. A very stubborn man, your Father, very stubborn indeed."

James Hanson laughed gently and snapped his fingers at the old Jew. "And a very persuasive man is Mr Wendelmann," he said, "very persuasive indeed, but not very successful."

"Not yet, not yet perhaps" — Wendelmann drew a circle in the air with his cigar—— "but the toils are closing in upon you, old friend."

"This daughter of mine," said James Hanson, "has just returned from Germany. She is a great admirer of the Nazi regime."

Mr Wendelmann bowed again to Veronica, but it was to Hanson that he spoke with an unruffled smoothness. "I am sure that that is very nice for her, and I am sure that it is also very nice for the Nazi regime, but you surely do not expect to distract me from the point at issue by that sort of red herring."

Hanson laughed. "It was worth trying."

Wendelmann wagged a forefinger at him. "Hanson, you are always the same, just a schoolboy. How old are you? Eighteen?"

Veronica was interested, in spite of herself and of her international convictions and antipathies.

"What are you trying to persuade him to do, Mr Wendelmann?" she asked, cocking her head on one side in an engagingly impertinent way as she looked up at the two big men.

"To come back into the world, my dear young lady. That is all."

"All!" exclaimed Hanson indignantly. "A mere bagatelle, eh?"

"You speak as if auto-resurrection was an unpleasant process," said the Jew. "I should have thought that for a man of your temperament it would have been deliciously exciting. I never really understood why you committed suicide."

"For a quiet life, of course," retorted Hanson, and they all three laughed. Wendelmann turned to Veronica. "I was just explaining to your charming but somewhat slow-witted sire" — Veronica snorted, or got as near to a snort as her small nose would allow— "that as things are going now there will be no quiet lives for anyone in a year or two, and that the only chance for Europe is for people like himself to come back on to the bridge, so to speak, and help to steer the ship off the rocks."

The phraseology, so exactly what she had heard from a hundred political platforms, instantly struck a responsive chord in Veronica's mind, and she was ready with the next platitudinous move in the rhetorical game.

"But who is driving the ship on to the rocks?" she cried.

"That's rather a big question," replied Mr Wendelmann.

"With a short answer," snapped Veronica. "International Finance. People like you and father."

The old Jew sighed and rolled his dark eyes up to the ceiling. "Oh dear, oh dear, what a scoundrel I am," he murmured. "I was always afraid of it, and now I know."

Veronica stamped her foot angrily. "You're laughing at me," she cried; "I won't interrupt you any more." And she turned and made for the door.

"Listen, my child," said Mr Wendelmann mildly. "Three-quarters of the time of what you call International Finance is taken up in trying to persuade the industrialists of this sorry world not to provoke wars. It took me eight years to persuade your delightful but extremely dull-witted papa that there is much money to be made before a war and none whatever to be made after it."

"It took you exactly three minutes, you old scamp," said Hanson, with a deep laugh.

Wendelmann spread out his hands and smiled. "Three minutes or eight years — it doesn't matter. The principle is the same. You ought to have understood it for yourself. But you Aryans understand so very little. And just think of all the James Hansons of this world who haven't got their poor humble little Wendelmanns to look after them and explain elementary principles to them. They are the menace." He turned to Veronica again, and suddenly he looked very old and very worn, and there was a deep melancholy in his voice as he said, "It will not be long before the most highly organized country in the world consists entirely of James Hansons without any Wendelmanns at all."

Veronica was impressed in spite of herself, and instead of replying, as she certainly would have if she had not been impressed, "And a good job too," she asked, "What will happen then?"

"War," said Wendelmann.

"Is war such a dreadful thing?"

"I think so," replied the old Jew sadly.

"If I was a man I'd be a soldier." Veronica's voice was getting a little defiant, and she knew it and she did not like it. She wanted to be lofty, not defiant.

"To fight against your German friends?"

"Of course not," she cried. "We must have an Anglo-German Alliance."

"Don't you think when you hear that sort of thing that it is time you came back into the world, friend Hanson?" asked Wendelmann.

"Do you know, friend Wendelmann," answered Hanson, "I almost think it is." They all three laughed again, and Veronica took herself off.

After the door had shut behind Veronica, Wendelmann sighed and murmured, "The Blond Beast has a fatal attraction for young women." Then he went on, "It is not only the danger of war that worries me, though God knows that is bad enough."

"You mean Perdurite?" shot out Hanson. The Jew nodded.

"Mawle is a bold man. He works fast."

"What sort of fight are you putting up?" asked Hanson.

Wendelmann spread out his hands in front of him and shrugged his shoulders.

"You know what the steel trade was like in your day," he said. "Every man for himself and the devil gets the losers. No organization, no method, no combination, no elimination of waste, no common defence, no political unity. Well, it's exactly the same today. Nothing has changed in that way. But Mawle has changed everything else. In your day we fought each other because we had no one else to fight. Now that we've got a common enemy, we aren't organized to fight."

"What start has Mawle got? How far ahead of you is he?"

"At least a year."

James Hanson whistled, and the Jew nodded. "You may well whistle," he remarked. "I whistled myself when I discovered just how far ahead he was. You see what happened. It all depended on the gloxite. Nobody knew that except the inventor, and Mawle. Mawle bought up the Cimbrian deposits on the quiet. Nobody paid any attention. Why should they? Gloxite wasn't worth a sou a kilo in those days. It was only used for making a few synthetic lead pencils. Even when Mawle's syndicate dug out a thousand tons, we never suspected that it was anything else but a blind."

"You thought he was after our old copper working, I suppose?"

"Yes. It looked like it. Who would have thought that it was the gloxite he really wanted all the time?"

"So he's got some of his Perdurite manufactured already?"

"Thousands of tons. He's ready to go ahead at any moment with the sale of it to the Government." There was a long pause, then Hanson said thoughtfully, "If Mawle knocks out the steel trade here, there'll be the devil to pay."

"Can Germany let us re-arm with this wonderful alloy while she has to stick to steel?" replied Wendelmann.

"If Mawle creates this monster, is he the man to control it?" Hanson answered Wendelmann's question with another. The Jew replied with a third.

"Is he the man to want to control it?"

"You mean he'd welcome a war?"

"Mawle is a man for big profits and a quick get-away. He'll take all he can as fast as he can and then clear out."

"War would be disastrous for him," said Hanson.

"Of course. War would be disastrous for all of us. But Mawle isn't the man to see that. He can only think of men like Zaharoff."

"It's a deadly danger," said Hanson in an undertone.

"It is a crisis for the world," said the Jew gently, "and crises want drastic action——"

"And Mr Wendelmann is not very good at drastic action——"

"Precisely. Whereas Mr Hanson is very good at drastic action. Or at any rate was in the days long past."

"But is now too old, eh?"

Wendelmann smiled. "The eternal schoolboy. Eighteen I put you at."

"It certainly has all the makings of a crisis," said Hanson thoughtfully, "in a year or two."

"I give it two years," said the old Jew.

"Then if we're going to do anything," exclaimed Hanson energetically, "we must begin at once. Two years isn't long to catch up in."

Wendelmann noticed the "we," and he noticed the old vigour in his ex-partner's voice, but he said nothing and waited.

"I've got a good mind to," muttered Hanson. He glanced at himself in a mirror and then laughed cheerfully. "Too old at seventy, eh? All right, Wendelmann, I'll resurrect myself, and if I let you down it'll be your fault." The dark Eastern eyes of the Jew shone for a moment, but he only said, "I'll send round the papers."

James Hanson rubbed his great hands together. "Ha, ha! The good old phrase! How many times have you 'sent me round the papers,' eh? mon vieux?"

"And I'll send them round a good many more times I hope, mein lieber freund."

Hanson rested his massive head upon his hand and considered. "We'll need a go-between. I must get a man I can trust. The world mustn't know that the corpse is out of the coffin."

"'The old war-horse out of his stable' would be a pleasanter picture."

Hanson clapped his old partner on the shoulder. "It was you who started the mortuary metaphors," he cried gaily, and on that they parted.

James Hanson sat down in front of his fireplace and remained almost motionless for more than an hour, gazing steadily at the empty grate and thinking. Then he jumped up and rang for Miss Collins.

"How are the wedding arrangements?" was his first question, but he did not listen to the secretary's quiet report of the progress she had made.

"Listen," he interrupted abruptly. "I want you to get hold of a man called Harry Winter. You'll find his address in the telephone-book — somewhere in Westminster. If he's not in, try his sister — Mrs Everard — somewhere in Cleveland Place. I want to see him as soon as possible — urgently — either here or wherever he likes. Let me know what luck you have."

Miss Collins went out to the telephone and came back in a moment or two. "Mr Winter's man says that he has just left a few minutes ago to visit Mrs Everard. He will be there at any moment now."

Hanson went to the window and looked out. "Good. There's the car at the door. I'll go straight round. Tell whoever ordered the car that I've stolen it and they must take a taxi. If anyone wants me I shall be at Mrs Everard's."

Miss Collins looked thoughtfully after her employer as he almost ran down the steps and hopped into the limousine. "Something's happened to the old boy," she reflected, "and, whatever it is, it's taken twenty years off his life." She locked up the desk, arranged her neat little hat over one eye, and went off to the Ritz for a cocktail with one of her adorers.

CHAPTER XVI

Croesus makes a Proposal to Winter

"I don't see why you want to trot me out again after all these years," said Helen Everard, settling her head back against a cushion. "What's the idea of puffing away at dead ashes? They won't come to light, you know."

"No, not if they're really dead," replied Jack Crawford. He was sitting on the edge of a chair in the Cleveland Place flat, leaning forward and clasping one knee tightly with his manicured but sinewy hands. An ash-tray beside him was full of quarter-smoked cigarettes. "These are dead, I can assure you, my dear Jack."

"Mine aren't," he exclaimed eagerly.

"Listen to me, my good fool," said Helen. "Do you really expect me to believe that after the way you treated me——"

"Oh, I know it must have seemed horrible. But I've explained all that——"

She went straight on as if he had not spoken. "And after dropping me like a stone for six years and not making the slightest effort to see me, you want me to believe that you are still in love with me. And you think that you can start again just where you left off at Mahableshwar."

"Oh, I know it sounds funny, if you put it like that."

"How else would you put it? Isn't that the exact truth?"

Crawford looked hurt. "I've already explained the Mahableshwar business. I couldn't afford to marry you.

And afterwards I didn't see you because I was on service."

"Yes. Two years at Camberley when I was in London, and two years in Aldershot when I was in Paris. It isn't so very far from London to Camberley or from Aldershot to Paris."

Crawford brightened a lot at this, and the nervous frown left his face altogether. "So you followed my career," he remarked with satisfaction.

Helen Everard bit her lip for a moment, and then said composedly, "A woman likes to know how men who have jilted her are getting on in the world."

"I wish to God you wouldn't go on harping about the jilting," he exclaimed in an aggrieved voice. "I only did what any man in my position would have done."

Mrs Everard smiled. "You really are rather sweet, Jack."

"After all," he went on with his defence, "a man has to think of himself sometimes. If he always went about thinking of other people, God knows what would happen to the world."

"That would, of course, be quite disastrous," she agreed. "But luckily it isn't likely to happen."

"No, thank the Lord," murmured Crawford absently. The conversation had got on to the wrong lines and had to be got back somehow. By a fortunate chance the girl provided the opening herself. "And so you're going to be married next week, Jack?"

"Yes. Thursday. That's the whole point, sweetheart." It was easy to slip gracefully from his position on the edge of the chair on to his knees beside her. That is the great advantage of a leaning-forward attitude in a chair. When the psychological moment arrives, it can be converted into a chivalrous, and at the same time intimate, position in a single movement. So Crawford slipped gracefully on to his knees in a beautiful pantherine movement.

Helen smiled down at him. "You always were good at that, Jack, weren't you? Never mind. It goes to my heart just as surely as it did in the old days."

"Yes," said Crawford simply, "I expect it does," and then went on, "Yes, I'm to be married on Thursday. And that, sweetheart, is the whole point of what I'm trying to drive at. You see, she's a very sweet girl, pretty and charming and all that. And she's rather especially fond of me, though I say it what shouldn't. But — well — she isn't terribly exciting. Whereas——" he stopped.

"Yes."

"Whereas you are."

"This is so sudden," said Helen drily. "After six years."

"You see what this is going to mean for me," Crawford went on with a rush. "I shall be free and independent at last."

"That's rather a curious view to take of matrimony," she observed.

Crawford frowned impatiently. "You know what I mean. Eleanor has got money. I shan't be harassed at every turn for ready money as I have been for years. And I'm chucking the service. I've got a damned good job in the City. All that's what I mean by being free and independent."

"I see," said Helen slowly. "And what's all this got to do with me?"

"Nothing. Except that I love you. No, no, no," he almost shouted. "I won't have you laughing," and he clapped a strong hand across her mouth.

She tried to push the strong hand away. But the hand was too strong and it was reinforcement to slip the other hand round the nape of her neck and pull her against the silencing hand, and then it was the simplest thing to drop the silencing hand and do its work instead with a kiss.

After a moment Helen stopped trying to push him away. After a long kiss he whispered, "I love you, I love you, I love you. You belong to me and to no one else." She sank more deeply into the cushions, and he, still on his knees, leant across her and kissed her again passionately, and the door opened and Hanson and Harry Winter came in.

Crawford jumped up and automatically began to dust his knees, and there was a moment's silence. Then he automatically picked up a cigarette and lit it. Then Helen, still lying back among the cushions, remarked in her slow, deep voice:

"I think it's your turn to say something, Jack."

But Jack Crawford thought it more prudent to wait for someone else to begin the talking. He flicked ash into the fireplace instead.

James Hanson laid his hat and stick down on a chair and went across the room to her, hand outstretched. "Good evening," he said. "I wanted rather urgently to see your brother and they told me that he was on his way round here, so I ventured to come here too. We met on the mat."

Helen Everard sat up and took his hand. "Delighted to see you," she murmured. Hanson turned to Crawford. "Isn't it diabolical," he said with a pleasant air of man-to-man intimacy, "how incredibly quickly on these occasions women recover their self-possession? The unfortunate man is left stammering and stuttering, while the woman is as cool as a cucumber in a trice. It's most humiliating. Don't you agree, Winter?"

Helen laughed her deep laugh, and said, "Perhaps the reason is that we've never lost our self-possession."

James Hanson threw his hands up in consternation. "Worse and worse and worse," he cried. "It is humiliating enough to see you recover yourselves, but it would be fifty times worse to think that you had never lost yourselves. We can't allow that, can we, Crawford?"

Crawford, with black fury in his heart, mustered a gallant smile and said something about the parting of old friends and that there was no question of anyone losing self-possession.

Hanson had the tactlessness to pursue the distasteful subject. A gentleman, reflected Crawford bitterly, would have pretended to have seen nothing. What a cursed world it was, reflected Crawford, in which gentlemen were so harassed by debts that they had to marry into the clutches of these damned *chevaliers d'industrie*.

"But surely you're not parting from Mrs Everard," the old fool was harping on. "Whatever is the reason for doing a thing like that?"

Crawford shrugged his shoulders at such vulgarity and, turning away to show his distaste, squeezed out his quarter-smoked cigarette and lit another.

Mrs Everard came to the rescue. "Major Crawford and I have been friends for many years. He was a friend of my husband's in India." She smiled an innocent smile at the three men, and added, "He has just been bidding me what is called a fond farewell, before he vanishes for ever into matrimony on Thursday next."

Crawford shot her a look of gratitude. There was absolutely no limit to the loyalty of a woman who was in love with one, he reflected; provided, that is to say, that she is properly handled.

He blew a cloud of cigarette smoke, and remarked, "I must rush away now, Helen. I've got a tremendous lot to do."

"Many more fond farewells, I suppose?" She held out her hand.

"Dozens," he replied lightly, bowing over it in an intentionally theatrical way. "Did you know I'm dining with you tonight, sir?"

"No," replied Hanson.

"Eleanor and I are dancing afterwards. See you later." He nodded coolly to Winter. "Good-bye — er — sir," he said, ostentatiously forgetting Winter's name, and lounged out. Winter said nothing.

Greatly to Helen's relief, the two men made no further reference to the incident. Her brother walked briskly across to the sideboard and began pouring out whiskies-and-soda. Over his shoulder he said, "Well, Croesus, and what can I do for you?"

"I thought I might be able to put a little work in your way," replied Hanson.

"Lucrative, of course?" Harry Winter cocked an eye at the millionaire and stopped the flow of a siphon to hear the reply.

"I don't think that your brother is the sort of man to accept underpayment for services rendered," said Hanson to Mrs Everard.

"By thunder, you're right," cried Harry Winter.

"Then perhaps we could talk a little business," said Hanson, looking vaguely round, trying to suggest politely that either the lady or the men should retire to another room. Winter saw what he meant. "Don't mind the old girl," he exclaimed. "Bill and I always tell her everything."

"Except what I have to tell you and Bill," replied Mrs Everard, diving a hand down the back of the sofa and pulling out some sewing.

"Very well," said Hanson, "I'll explain. I've got a job I want done, and I must have someone I can trust. So I thought of you because you're so very untrustworthy, if you see what I mean."

"Hang it," cried Winter, "I don't see what you mean, and it's damned rot anyway."

"You see what I mean, Mrs Everard, don't you?"

She nodded. "Of course."

"That I'm untrustworthy?" shouted Winter. "You treacherous little turncoat."

"It's just the point of view," said Hanson soothingly. "If I pay you enough, you'll do anything in reason, inside or outside the law. That's all."

"Oh well, if that's all," grumbled Winter, subsiding. "What will you pay me?"

"Harry, darling," remonstrated Mrs Everard, "wouldn't it be polite if you asked first what sort of a job it is? You shouldn't be so greedy."

Winter grinned all over his thin brown face. "I thought it would be politer if I talked in Croesus' own language."

"You are a rude young puppy," said Hanson. "I'll give you two thousand pounds, and reasonable expenses, for one year, starting today."

"Two thousand! That doesn't go far among three," protested Winter.

"Three?"

"Yes. We run together, Bill and I and the jade over there. You can't hire one without the lot. Bill and I do the work——"

"And I provide the brains," murmured the girl.

"And, as I was just going to observe, Helen spends the takings."

"Bill's your brother?" said Hanson in an unexpectedly sharp voice.

Winter nodded. "Twin."

"What sort of chap is he?"

"How would you describe him, Helen? He used to be a sailor, very efficient, brave as a lion — you ought to have seen him shooting up the O'Bannion crowd off the Florida coast just before the damned Roosevelt——"

Helen held up a warning hand.

"All right, all right," exclaimed Winter plaintively. "I know I become a howling bore when I get on to that subject, but when I think of that man deliberately taking away the livelihood of honest, decent folk like Bill and me who never did a hand's-turn of harm to anyone in our lives — it fairly makes my blood boil. Where was I? Oh yes. What sort of chap is Bill? He's very quiet — one of the strong, silent sort — doesn't open his mouth, but a damned good fellow to have beside one in a row. You'd like him, Croesus. I know you would. Don't you think he would, Nellie?"

"I'm sure he would. Everyone likes Bill. Typical sailor. Masses of charm and the brains of a rabbit."

"Oh I say," protested her brother. "Bill's devilish brainy. He's twice as clever as I am."

"I know he is, Harry darling," replied Mrs Everard.

"Anyway, the point is," Mr Hanson interrupted the exchange of family amenities, "where can I meet the paragon of all the virtues and intellectual accomplishments?"

"Helen," said Winter severely, "the old rascal is laughing at us, and it is entirely your fault."

"My dear Harry," Helen laid her sewing down on her lap, "if there is any possibility of your accepting Mr Hanson's offer and earning an honest penny for a change——"

"Honest?" Winter cocked an eye at Hanson and grinned impudently.

"—For a change," went on Mrs Everard, unmoved, "I suggest that you keep a civil tongue in your head to your future employer."

"It wasn't in the bond," cried Winter. "Untrustworthiness, yes. Civility, no."

"Let us return to the bond," said Hanson blandly. "I will hire the three of you for one year, with an option on you for another year; civility not essential."

"And the money?"

"Three thousand between the three of you."

"Done," cried Winter, and was striding across to Hanson with his hand outstretched when he suddenly stopped, shuffled for a moment, looked uncommonly foolish, and then, with a half-shy, half-awkward smile, like a fourteen-year-old schoolboy, said, "I do feel a donkey now. But the truth is, sir, that — er — that, well, as a matter of fact, we've rather got into the habit — Bill and I — of — er — leaving this sort of decision to that package of nonsense on the sofa. It's not that she's got any sense, mind you — she hasn't — but it's some sort of queer instinct — do you know what I mean?"

"Of course. I quite understand," said James Hanson gravely, flicking a wink at the girl from under his great eyebrows. Helen Everard gazed at him with an air of profound seriousness for a moment, and then she said, also very gravely, "We accept your offer, Mr Hanson."

"Hurrah!" shouted Winter. "In the immortal words of Sam Weller, 'Take the bill down, we are let to a single gentleman' — or rather to a married gentleman."

"You haven't yet told me," said Hanson, "the whereabouts of your redoubtable twin. Or is it indiscreet to ask? You can't expect me to pay him a salary if he is — er — detained in Sing Sing or Leavenworth."

"No, it's not as bad as that," said Helen. "Not yet. The last we heard of him, he was trying to — what shall I say? — work up an honest, decent business connection in a town called Blut."

James Hanson started. "Blut? The place that used to be called Santa Olivia in my day. In Cimbro-Suevonia?"

"Of course, that is very much your part of the world, Mr Hanson. What a curious coincidence."

"It might be a coincidence, or it might not," said Hanson slowly. "Why did he go there?"

"To look for trouble," was Winter's prompt reply. "After that damned Roosevelt——"

Helen Everard again intercepted an anti-Presidential harangue. "There was no special reason that I know of for Bill to go to Cimbro-Suevonia. He simply thought that there might be opportunities of smuggling in the Levant."

"No one paid him to go?" Hanson shot out.

"No," said the girl, and Winter added, "worse luck."

There was a pause for a moment or two, and then the old millionaire said, "Well, I expect that many people would call me a fool to trust you, but your charming sex, madam, has not a complete monopoly of queer instincts. I've brought off things in the past by following my intuition that made poor old Wendelmann's beard go grey with horror. So here goes again. Listen to me, my children, and don't interrupt." He pulled a cigar-case out of his pocket and glanced enquiringly at his hostess. She nodded back and he lit it slowly and carefully. It was in full blast before he spoke again.

"I'm not going to tell you much," said James Hanson. "At least not now. The world is in a mess. That isn't news to you. But in about two years from now it will be in a worse mess. I retired from business nearly fifteen years ago to live quietly upon my — if you like, my ill-gotten gains. Now it has now been put to me, by certain people whose judgment I respect, that it is my duty to come down again into the arena and help to avert the smash. I have accepted the suggestion, and am going to return to active business."

James Hanson stretched his legs out and took two or three pulls at his cigar before he went on, with his sardonic smile:

"I should be doing myself more credit than is due if I pretended that my only motive is the welfare of the human race. There are new forces at work which, if they are allowed to develop, will not only encourage the war-makers but will deprive me and my friends of a large part of our capital. I do not want another war. But still less do I want to lose a large part of my capital. You see. I am being frank. I am not an idealist." He waved his cigar towards Harry Winter. "You were right from the first. You never thought I was one, did you?"

"Never," replied Winter, gazing at the ceiling.

"The wisest man I have ever known," continued Hanson, "made the same remark to me only an hour ago that he made forty years ago: 'The time to make money is before a war, not after.' Your true gun-maker wants nations to be afraid. It is only fools who want them to be angry. The true gun-maker wants to keep the peace — but only just. There are forces abroad now that do not understand that, or do not want to understand it. You think my cynicism is atrocious?"

"Atrocious, but rather fascinating," said Winter, still looking at the ceiling.

"The forces of today," went on Hanson, "are of exactly the same ignorance and stupidity as those of 1914. Last time we were helpless to stop them. This time we have a better chance. They say that the gun-makers made the World War. Don't believe them. The War brought to an end the halcyon years of the armourer."

"Halcyon!" murmured Helen Everard involuntarily. It was a very quiet murmur, but James Hanson's ears were not so old as to miss even a quiet murmur. "Yes, you're right," he said with a quick laugh. "I oughtn't to have compared gun-makers and king-fishers. All I mean is that I wished the Anglo-German Naval race would go on for ever, and I wanted Russia to build such a network of strategic railways that no one would dare to attack her, and Germany to have so many machine-guns that no one would dare to attack her, and so on. Everyone would have been safe, and I would have been the richest man in the world."

"And what good would that have done you?" asked Helen softly.

Hanson held up a finger. "Rule One of the Hanson Secretariat. No employee may entice the boss into a discussion of abstract philosophy. Listen. My partner, old Wendelmann, has dozens of young folk, trained, intelligent, trustworthy, really trustworthy" — he glanced at Winter to see how the thrust was received, but the ex-bootlegger made no sign— "who would do the job much better than you two, than you three I should say. But they all have a fatal drawback. They are known to be connected with Wendelmann, and if I so much as said 'how-do-you-do' to one of them in the street the news would be in the City within an hour."

He lowered his voice and spoke earnestly. "It is of the first importance that no one should know that I am coming back into the arena. It'll get out in time, of course, but every month that I can work without being watched is worth six months to me. That's why I've come to you. There's no connection between us, or between you and Wendelmann, or between you and anything that I might be supposed to be interested in. At first your job will be to act as messengers between Wendelmann and me. You'll pass everything to me via my secretary, Ruth Collins. But you must only know her socially. You mustn't come to the house. I'll tell her to get in touch with you. And cable your brother to stay in Cimbro-Suevonia till further notice. And write to him in some sort of code — you've got a code?"

"Yes. We did all our stuff in a code of our own before that blasted Roosevelt——"

"Yes, yes, quite," said Hanson hurriedly. "Then write and explain what you're doing. Be careful what you say. Miss Collins will pay your salaries. Pound notes. No cheques." He thought for a moment, and then said, "That's all I can think of at the moment. Sorry it's so vague." Then he looked at Mrs Everard, started to say something, thought better of it, and took his departure.

"Well," said Harry Winter, coming back into the drawing-room after showing Hanson out, "what do you make of it?"

"I think he's an old pet. I adore him."

"I said what do you make of it, not him."

"I don't know," she said thoughtfully. "But no man is going to pay us three thousand a year and expenses to hand messages to Miss Ruth What's-her-name over a cocktail-talk at the Mayfair Hotel."

"I sincerely hope not," said her brother. "That wouldn't suit young Bill very well."

"Or young Harry either."

"No, it would not."

"I'm going to dress for dinner now, Harry. Stay if you like."

"Got a date?"

"Yes." She had just reached the door when Harry said:

"I say, Nellie—"

"Yes."

Like Hanson, Harry Winter started to say something, and like Hanson he thought better of it. "Oh, nothing."

"I wouldn't have told you anyway, Harry," she said in a maternal sort of way, "any more than I would have told Mr Hanson."

"You don't know what I was going to say," cried her brother indignantly.

Helen blew him a kiss and vanished.

CHAPTER XVII

The Wedding

The wedding, thanks to the quiet efficiency of Miss Ruth Collins, went off without a hitch, as all weddings do that are under the supervision of the Miss Collinses of this world. The wedding presents included thirty-eight cocktail-shakers and two hundred and eighty-two cocktail-glasses, neither Mayfair nor Belgravia being especially strong in imaginative qualities, and they were rigorously defended against marauders by two plain-clothes detectives from Scotland Yard whose broad chests, healthy faces, clear eyes, and beautifully cut morning coats aroused several flutters in the breasts of young ladies and young gentlemen who had grown sorrowfully accustomed to the suede shoes and svelte figures of the masculinity — or near-masculinity — of Shepherd's Market and Ham Yard.

But the refined excitement caused by these stalwart upholders of the Law faded into nothingness on the arrival of Veronica with a companion. For the small, neat, bantam-like, youngest daughter of the house selected this day of all days as the occasion on which to introduce her *fiancé* to her family. It was a perfect specimen of stage-craft. An audience was gathered together, to applaud Eleanor. The stage was set, for the triumph of Eleanor. The limelight was ready, to illuminate Eleanor. And at the precise instant that the curtain went up, little Veronica tripped on to the stage with her *fiancé*, the six-foot-six, handsome, bullet-headed, duel-scarred, barrel-chested, high-well-born Freiherr Manfred Von Czepan-Eichenhöh, son of the former Commander of the Imperial Horse Guards and godson of the Emperor Wilhelm the Second. Eleanor bore no resentment. She had all the time expected that Veronica would produce a last-minute card, and as the days had gone by she had grown a little surprised at her little sister's inactivity. It is true that she had never dreamt that the card, when it did appear, would be quite so sensational, nor had she really thought that little Veronica would be brutal enough to produce it on the actual morning of the wedding. But when the deed had been actually accomplished, and the gigantic Prussian aristocrat was clicking his heels and kissing every fair hand that came his way — and many did — even then Eleanor only smiled. The mighty Graf might overtop Jack by three or four inches, and his titles might ring like a cavalry trumpet, but so far as Eleanor was concerned anyone might get hold of him and get engaged to him. So it was with completely genuine sincerity that Eleanor congratulated Veronica and, once again, left the centre of the stage to the shrimp-sister.

"What shall we do if the Boche pinches a salver?" whispered one of the plain-clothes men — he was a graduate of the Police College at Hendon and had been at Repton and Brasenose — to the other. The other — who was Marlborough and Trinity Hall — made a comic face in the direction of gigantic Freiherr and whispered back, "Give him a coffee jug to go with it. Who is he?"

"Name of Eichenhöh," whispered the first. "He was up at Magdalen in my time. The most dangerous fast bowler you ever saw." And the sleuths drifted back to their respective vigils over the phalanxes of cocktail-shakers and glasses.

The Hanson family had little time to devote to their rather formidable recruit at the moment. Mrs Hanson was so bewildered by the wedding and the crowds and the noise that she had no astonishment left for her new prospective son-in-law. If Veronica had introduced a dwarf to her, or a Senegalese negro, or a giraffe, Mrs Hanson would have been neither less nor more perturbed. Robert, of course, behaved with the utmost correctness, but left the Freiherr at the earliest possible moment to talk urgent public affairs in a corner with his friend the Financial Secretary to the Treasury, while the two cavalry captains mentally and simultaneously dismissed the vast Prussian as useless on a polo pony. Mr Hanson accepted the situation with a sort of grim thoughtfulness.

The wedding ceremony itself had gone off without a hitch, and hardly anyone noticed that the happy bridegroom brought the radiant bride down the nave of St. Margaret's, Westminster, on his right arm, a mistake that is almost always made by heavily uniformed bridegrooms. In any case such a trifle did not matter, for Major Crawford's uniform, and his medals for valour, carried everything before them, and the large crowd outside doted almost as fondly upon the gallant and gold-laced officer as upon the bride herself.

For it is a well-recognized axiom among professional frequenters of fashionable weddings that a civilian groom, however large his buttonhole, however classical his features, however exquisite his morning-coat, can never hope to receive a share of lachrymose admiration from the spectators one-tenth as deep or one-tenth as watery as that which is habitually accorded to any military gentleman.

The Guard of Honour, with their drawn swords and handsome little spurs, came in for a lot of favourable comment, and the bridesmaids, among whom a Mayfair boulevardier would certainly have recognized Helen of Troy, Nell Gwynn, Cleopatra, and La Camargo had it not been that they all looked identical in their dress and enamel, were greeted with the customary *oo*'s and *ooh*'s and *coo*'s of plebeian adoration.

One of the most prominent guests at the reception was Sir Montagu Anderton-Mawle, not because he thrust himself forward in any way, nor because his physical size made him an outstanding figure in the crowd. Quite the reverse, in fact. But he was prominent because he was the centre of an incessant whirl of movement. Whenever he stood, there was a bustle and an excitement, an eddying to-and-fro, a sort of subdued maelstrom of human endeavour. Those in the outer ranks were trying, with a mixture of gentility and bulldog tenacity, to push their way through to the heart of the matter, while those in the front ranks were trying, with rather less gentility and even more bulldog tenacity, to keep the heart of the matter to themselves. It was, in fact, a microcosm of a social phenomenon that is as old as recorded history, the behaviour of blue blood in the presence of red gold.

There had been a rumour, nothing definite, nothing more than a murmur on the air or a whisper on the westerly breeze, nothing that could be tracked to its conclusion or pinned down to its source, but none the less a rumour, intangible yet irresistible, growing in stature and momentum day by day, that Sir Montagu Anderton-Mawle was thinking of financing a cinematograph company. It was enough. Sir Montagu was a prominent guest at the reception.

General Springton was there also, tall, dark, urbane. He congratulated Crawford — now his colleague in the manufacture of Perdurite — on his wedding and apologized for the unfortunate absence of his daughter. "Something wrong with her inside," he explained. "Don't know what it is. Something got to come out, I expect. But modern girls never tell anything to their old fathers. Anyway I packed her off to Sir Albion Featherley. They tell me he's the best man for that sort of thing."

"Yes, I've heard that too," said Crawford impassively, and passed on to receive the congratulations of Andrew Hay, the brilliant young lawyer, who had been discussing the merits of the American polo team with one of the bridesmaids. Hay had never played polo, but he knew a great deal about it, having found a knowledge of its finer points very useful in certain wealthy circles, and a consideration of chukkas and handicaps had several times led to the discovery of mutual friends and, subsequently, an invitation to an influential dinner.

The best-dressed civilian at the wedding was poor Clifford Bray, who wandered about in a pathetic daze. He was completely unconscious of everything, even of the exquisiteness of his clothes, except his great sorrow. He had been a mixture of slave and squire to Eleanor for so long that it seemed incredible that it was all over. He drifted miserably from group to group — for he knew everyone at the wedding — and murmured all the time, "I wouldn't have believed it possible. I simply wouldn't have believed it possible." About half-way through the reception he was immensely cheered by a young lady who remarked, "Cheer up, Cliffie. It may not last, you know," and thenceforward he changed his tune somewhat and went about mournfully prophesying, "It won't last. I'm afraid it won't last. I don't see how it can last."

But the Freiherr von Czepan-Eichenhöh was the real hero of the reception. His mighty shoulders, his Ruritanian standard of old-world courtesy, his perfect command of English, put everyone else in the shade. Sir Montagu, for all his eager salon of beauty and talent, would have paid anyone a hundred pounds to remove the huge monstrosity and dump him in the Dagenham Sewage Farm. But as such a course was out of the question, Sir Montagu fell back upon a more civilized method of asserting himself and, pushing his way firmly through the crowd of aspirants to cinematographic fame and, more especially, fortune, he soon effected an introduction to Veronica and carried her off to a quiet corner with such an air of Napoleonic mastery that not even the most debt-ridden and film-struck daughter of the ancient aristocracy dared to follow and interrupt the *tête-à-tête*.

Veronica, who heartily despised the physical appearance of any male under about six-foot-three, was not so narrow-minded as to despise male intelligence simply because it was encased in a relatively dwarfish body. After all, no one could call the Führer particularly handsome, and yet what a mammoth intellect he had got! Dr. Goebbels was positively ugly, but look how he scattered the non-Aryans with his inner fires of patriotism and genius!

Veronica, therefore, settled down to talk to Sir Montagu with a considerable amount of tolerance, especially as he might very well come down handsome for the funds of the Glorification of Holy Liberators Society. Sir Montagu, for his part, was enchanted to find that she had a hobby — though he was much too clever and experienced in the ways of young ladies to make the mistake of calling it a hobby — to which he could subscribe a hundred guineas. How very convenient these Hanson girls are, he reflected, with their Social Clubs. Unfortunately he had not brought his cheque-book with him to the wedding, but if Miss Hanson would come round to his house — 12 New Park Lane — any morning between, say, ten and eleven, he would be delighted to subscribe to her most laudable and praiseworthy society. Sir Montagu had found that a strictly business hour for a first rendezvous was a most disarming gambit with certain types of young women. (Sir Montagu had long ago divided all womankind into types. It simplified life enormously, and if a woman came along who was a freak and did not fit into any of the pigeon-holes, why, throw her away and think no more about her. She would only cause worry and trouble.)

So Veronica and Sir Montagu sat and discussed international politics with especial reference to Germany and international finance, and both simultaneously made sly grimaces when Mr Wendelmann, looking very benign and very urbane, strolled past, and they each surprised the other's grimace and they both laughed an intimate laugh. Veronica thought she had not met such a sympathetic or quick-witted Englishman for a long time, and she said so. Sir Montagu was charmed at the progress he was making, and congratulated himself upon the brilliant stroke of betraying so unmistakeably, and yet so subtly, his antipathy to Jews. He had seen out of the corner of his restless eyes that his charming little friend's face had hardened suddenly upon Mr Wendelmann's approach, and his own intuition had done the rest. So when he was saying aloud, "But I'm not an Englishman, Miss Hanson. I'm only a poor crude colonial," his inner voice was saying, "You haven't lost your cunning, old boy."

At last the hour of departure approached. The honeymoon was going to be spent in Germany, at Sir Montagu's urgent and secret request. Indeed, so urgent had the request been that it almost amounted to an order from the Chairman of the Board to the newly joined assistant managing-director. Sir Montagu had given Crawford three or four brief letters of introduction and a great deal of confidential verbal instruction, and, in consequence, Messrs. Thomas Cook & Son had prepared tickets and arranged hotel accommodation for a visit to Berlin and a trip south to Munich.

Just as the happy couple was about to leave, a messenger-boy arrived with a small package for Eleanor and a note. It was from the Sergeant of the East Stepditch Welfare Club, and it was written in a neat writing, in pencil: "Miss, I got as far as Parliament Square, but there were too many toppers and uniforms, so I didn't go any further. I hope you will not be offended with me for sending a present with my respectful good wishes to you and the Major — The Sergeant."

The present was in the small package, and it was the Sergeant's Military Cross which he had won for valour on the field of battle in those secret days when he was an officer in the Machine Gun Corps.

CHAPTER XVIII

Perdurite gets its Tariff

It was generally agreed by those who had had long experience of these things that Andrew Hay's memorandum setting forth the reasons why the Government should place a fifty per cent *ad valorem* tariff on foreign Perdurite — if and when such an article should be produced — was one of the most masterly memoranda of its kind that had ever been produced in the long and glorious campaign for Protection. It stated the case in simple language, so that a large number of Conservative back-benchers understood it quite soon, and at the same time with such deadly logic that no answer to it was possible except of the feeblest and most futile description. Indeed, *The Times*, *Telegraph*, and *Morning Post* frankly made no attempt to answer it at all, but simply printed the memorandum in full and published leading articles admitting its devastating accuracy. Mr Hay started from the three eternal truths: Firstly, that the foreigner always pays, and that therefore the higher the tariff on Perdurite the more money would pour into the lap of the Chancellor of the Exchequer. (Mr Hay, like all barristers a purist in English style, would have preferred not to use such a hackneyed metaphor as the "lap of the Chancellor," but it was pointed out to him that the Conservative back-benchers would recognize the phrase, and might thus be encouraged to read a little further. For this reason also he was strongly advised by the drafting experts to refer to Free Trade as an "outworn shibboleth.") The second of the eternal truths was that a tariff on Perdurite would enable manufacturers very materially to reduce their cost of production, and, as the chief customer of the company was likely to be the Government, a substantial tariff would enable the company to make what was the practical equivalent of a substantial present to the taxpayer. And thirdly, of course, there was the truth, so obvious as to be almost a platitude, that every diminution of foreign trade must lead to an increase of employment at home.

Mr Hay then went on to details, and presented figures in conclusive proof of his general thesis. The memorandum was accompanied by a second document, drawn up with equal translucency and replete with equally cogent arguments, which argued that the existing tariff of thirty-three and a third per cent on foreign Gloxite ought to be removed entirely. Mr Hay pointed out that Gloxite was essential for the manufacture of Perdurite, that the import tax on it was inevitably borne by the home consumer, that it enabled the home producer of Gloxite to raise his price to an absurd and exorbitant level, and that the exclusion of foreign Gloxite inevitably increased the level of unemployment at home. In this second document, as in the first, Mr Hay presented figures in conclusive proof of his general thesis, and he had the satisfaction of seeing them both unanimously accepted by the Tariff Committee of the Conservative Party. Indeed, the only voices that were raised against the enactment of the two measures were the Liberals, who, unpatriotic as ever, did not hesitate to use the unpleasant word "ramp," and the two Tories who sat for the only constituencies in the country which provided Gloxite. This latter pair of gentlemen were in a hopeless position, however, for there were hardly three thousand families, all told, which were dependent upon the home Gloxite industry, and naturally no statesman could allow such a handful of people to stand in the way of progress. Besides, Sir Montagu Anderton-Mawle, although he had never been a Member of Parliament, was not such a tyro in the arts of government as not to know the value of an organized Lobby. His Sassafras Lobby in the old pre-War days in Tasmania was one of the most highly organized of these institutions in the world, and had often been compared in this respect to Tammany Hall in New York City. And although the purity of British public life is such that no Conservative Member can ever be influenced by pressure of any sort or description, whether from inside the Party or outside it, to vote against the dictates of his conscience, it is equally true that the impartial presentation of the truth will always cause him carefully to review, and, if necessary, to modify, any attitude that he may have taken up before he had had an opportunity to acquaint himself with the truth. Sir Montagu's Perdurite Lobby, carefully organized, presented the impartial truth with such authority that it easily swept away the shufflings of the hastily improvised and rather pathetic little Gloxite Lobby.

As for the Liberal wailings about the fifty per cent duty on Perdurite, no one paid any attention to Liberals any longer about anything, and the whole matter was quickly and satisfactorily arranged. For the Socialist Opposition gave very little trouble. It did not care in the least what size of tariff was put on to Perdurite or taken off Gloxite. The Socialist Opposition had always found a certain difficulty in tackling questions in which figures were involved, and had very wisely evolved a special technique for meeting this difficulty. Thus, in the twin cases of the alloy and its essential raw material, the Socialists argued that all the figures produced by the Government were, *ipso facto*, fraudulent, and would not stand an expert scrutiny for a single moment. Passing rapidly over their disinclination to produce expert scrutinizers, the Socialists hastened on to the second line of action of their well-tried technique, and argued that the tariff on Perdurite would, like all tariffs, transfer vast sums of money into the fur-lined pockets of the rich from the tiny savings of the poor and, in addition, would create a new wave of unemployment which would be another hideous disgrace to the callous capitalist system.

Thence it was an easy step to the third line of action, which vehemently denounced the removal of the tariff on Gloxite on the grounds that all removals of tariffs simply transferred vast sums of money into the fur-lined pockets etcetera, etcetera, etcetera.

It could hardly be expected that anyone would listen to such crazy stuff, and the Conservatives trooped victoriously through the divisions. Sir Montagu gave a wonderful dinner-party to the eighty-four members of the Lobby; Andrew Hay was congratulated by the Board of Perdurite Limited on his magnificent work, and at the same time was requested to draw up a memorandum to prove that a tariff of fifty per cent was insufficient and ought to be replaced by a tariff of eighty per cent, and another memorandum advocating a Government subsidy for Gloxite importers, both memoranda to be used later; and the English Gloxite pits were closed down and the three thousand families went upon the dole. This last minor result of Mr Hay's eloquent memoranda was considerably offset, however, by the wise action of the Government in despatching Robert Hanson to the affected areas to deliver a series of speeches advising the able-bodied unemployed to emigrate to Central Australia. Robert's obvious sincerity, his good looks, and his really touching description of the domestic life of the wallaby, saved him from being pelted with old tomatoes at any of his eight meetings except six.

CHAPTER XIX

Veronica and Freiherr Manfred Von Czepan-Eichenhöh

Veronica did not return to Germany immediately after Eleanor's wedding. This would have surprised anyone who had thought about it for one moment, but nobody did. The Hanson family went back instantly to its normal occupations of knitting, directing the affairs of the War Office, playing snooker's pool in the Cavalry Club, and meditating on the affairs of the world over a quiet cigar, with hardly a thought for Veronica and her Prussian colossus. Not that Veronica cared. Quite the reverse. She herself, a true Hanson, was so immersed in her own affairs that she never even noticed that her family was not immersed, or was even trying pathetically, as happens in so many families where the younger members are busy and the elder members are not, to be immersed in them too.

The reason why she did not rush back to Germany was the private business of the high-well-born Freiherr, who suddenly announced that he must remain in London for at least three weeks. He had urgent business, he said, and he went off and telegraphed to Berlin for a dozen suits, some more tail-coats and white waistcoats, and his golf clubs. But he flatly refused to tell Veronica what his urgent business was, and when she protested that there ought to be no secrets between them, he playfully pulled her uptilted nose and enquired blandly, "And what would the Führer say if he heard that I had told business secrets to a woman?"

"Women have got just as good brains as men," cried Veronica.

"Women have no brains at all," replied the Freiherr seriously. "When you are married to me you will realize that."

"When I am married to you, I shall tell you exactly what you ought to do and how to do it," retorted Veronica. The Prussian let out a huge laugh at the exquisitely absurd notion, and Veronica laughed out of pure pleasure at seeing her lover so happy.

"You must stay with us at Partington Crescent, Manfred," she went on, when she saw that he was obviously not going to tell her anything about his urgent business. "I will fix up a room for you, and you can just treat the house as if it was a hotel. Come and go as you like."

"That would suit me very well," said the German, "if you are sure that your gracious lady mother——"

"Oh, Mummy will be delighted," cried Veronica, and she tripped off eagerly to make the arrangements. The best spare-room was allotted to the distinguished guest; the chauffeur was despatched to the Ritz to pay the Freiherr's bill and collect the Freiherr's suitcases; maids were sent racing hither and thither for the various accoutrements of a spare-room; and Parkinson was commanded to produce a latchkey, and to stand by to put studs in the high-well-born shirt; and, in effect, the usual atmosphere of a typhoon, which invariably surrounded Veronica, swept up and down the house from attic to basement and back.

Mrs Hanson heard about the impending arrival from one of the housemaids, and nodded her mixture of resignation and pleasure. But there was an unexpected hitch when the news reached James Hanson. He knitted his eyebrows, thought for a moment, and then rang for Miss Collins.

"That German fellow," he said abruptly. "They've invited him to stay in the house. I don't want him. Make up some excuse or other and chuck him out."

Miss Collins, admirably self-trained to discipline in business hours, nodded and departed, and it was not until the door was safely closed behind her that she allowed herself a smile at the picture of herself chucking out the eighteen-stone German. But her methods of eviction, if not so spectacular as those of, say, the Sergeant in his Johannesburg pot-house, must have been equally effective, for within a quarter of an hour a small tornado shot into James Hanson's study, breathing fire and scattering lightning-bolts.

"What rot is this I hear, Father?" she demanded in a furious and imperious rage.

"It depends who you've been talking to," James Hanson put in neatly. Veronica was the only one of the family who would have burst into the study in this cyclonic way, deliberately challenging the head of the house to a battle-royal. On the other hand, when Veronica flew into one of her battle-royal rages, she was apt to forget that her father was the only one of the family who was not in the least afraid of her. Years of rough-shod riding over the rest of them had made the little bantam serenely confident in her fighting technique.

She therefore ignored the mild sally and drove straight on at the point.

"That Collins woman has been drivelling about Manfred not staying in the house. She says you told her to."

Hanson opened his eyes very wide. "She says that I told her to? She must have taken leave of her senses. I've never in my life told her to drivel."

Veronica punched the desk with her small but tough-looking fist.

"She says you told her to kick Manfred out."

"Oh, that?" said her father with maddening unconcern, and he picked up *The Times*. "Yes, I did that."

"Well, I've asked him to stay, and he's going to stay, and that's flat."

James Hanson laid down *The Times* and said seriously, "I've got a very particular reason for not wanting him to stay in the house just now, or anyone else for that matter. I'm very sorry, but there it is, my dear."

"What's the reason?"

"I'm afraid I can't tell you."

"Pooh! there isn't any reason, except that you dislike Manfred because he's a German."

"My dear child," replied Mr Hanson, "you greatly overestimate my antipathy to that muddle-headed and pugnacious race. I do not like Germans. I confess it. But I do not detest them so passionately that I would commit a breach of hospitality for my opinions. My only reason for refusing to welcome my prospective son-in-law at this moment is that I do not want to be disturbed."

"But no one's going to disturb you," cried Veronica.

"I know," answered her father with a twinkle in his eye. But his angry daughter was in no mood to respond to twinkles.

"Look here, Father," she exclaimed aggressively, "I've invited Manfred to stay here, and Manfred is going to stay here, and I don't care a tinker's damn what you or anyone else says about it. Manfred's going to be your son-in-law, and you've damned well got to be civil to him."

"I have only spoken to him once so far, and I was civility itself."

"Very well then. He comes to stay. I'll tell that Collins busybody." Veronica spun round and made for the door, her small, neat head carried at a triumphant angle.

"Veronica," said James Hanson gently. The girl stopped and looked back at him over her shoulder in a consciously theatrical pose.

"Well?"

"Abandon your delightful imitation of Sarah Bernhardt, my child," he continued, "and listen to me." Veronica dropped the pose with a furious scowl and turned round.

"I do not often give any orders in this house," he went on. "In fact I doubt if I have told any of you children to do anything for years and years. But if you think I would ever give an order and not make certain that it was carried out, you greatly misunderstand my character. If you bring your young man, or anyone else, as a guest into this house within the next six months, I shall close the house and send the whole establishment to Cannes, and I shall go to live at the Club."

Veronica threw herself into a chair and burst into floods of tears.

James Hanson rang a bell and Parkinson appeared. "Parkinson," said the master of the house, "the Freiherr von Czepan-Eichenhöh will not be staying here after all."

"Very good, sir."

"And bring Miss Veronica a few large handkerchiefs and some smelling-salts."

Veronica jumped up and scuttled out of the room.

"Parkinson," said Mr Hanson thoughtfully, "you needn't bring the handkerchiefs and the smelling-salts."

"Very good, sir," said the butler, looking his master straight in the eye. "Will that be all, sir?"

"That will be all," replied Mr Hanson. And such is the decorum that is invariably preserved between master and man on such occasions, that neither of these two elderly men winked at the other.

CHAPTER XX

Norman Everard, Gossip Columnist

Harry Winter found his new job very much to his taste. Every two or three days a packet of papers arrived, by circuitous routes from Mr Wendelmann's office, at Helen Everard's flat. Harry Winter picked them up there, arranged a rendezvous with Miss Collins at one or other of the large West End hotels, and surreptitiously handed the packet over to her. From time to time the process was reversed, and Hanson's answers went to Wendelmann's office.

The work had a twofold attraction. In the first place it was not work at all, and that exactly suited the ex-bootlegger's disposition. The other twin, the absent Bill, had inherited the double share of energy. And the second attraction was the regular rendezvous with Ruth Collins. Harry Winter admired her intensely from the very first meeting. She had so many qualities that he lacked and that he had always admired when he met them in others. She was cool and efficient and matter-of-fact. She never began a piece of work without carrying it straight through to the end, and she never could be lured away from work by the prospect of entertainment, however amusing.

"You simply aren't human," sighed Harry Winter plaintively at the fourth meeting, in a modernistic cocktail-bar in Clifford Street. Ruth Collins had just refused to leave a tedious evening's work, which consisted of filing press-cuttings, in order to accompany him to a theatre and a dance.

"You would give up everything for amusement, I suppose?" she replied.

"Of course I would. And so would anyone in their senses."

"Implying that I am ... ?" She raised her delicately narrowed eyebrows.

"Inhuman," he repeated.

"It might be that I am rather keen on my job." "But damn it," he protested, "not to the extent of preferring it to my society."

"It seems odd," she agreed.

"It seems damned odd."

"But nevertheless I fear, Mr Winter, that it is damned true."

"You might at least call me Harry," he grumbled.

"By all means," she assented with an exaggerated show of cordiality. "And if it would do anything to console you for the imminent loss of my society — in about seven minutes — you may call me Ruth."

Winter gave a cry of dismay. "Not seven minutes. Have a heart."

"Six and a half now. And I have."

"Made of ice. Junoesque. That's what you are. I hate Junos."

Ruth Collins smiled. "The remedy is in your own hands, my dear Harry. You don't have to spend your time with an ice-hearted Juno you detest. Your sister can come instead. It would be a pleasant change for me. I expect she has inherited the brains of the family."

"That is the sort of thing which I always ignore, woman," said Winter loftily. "Have another drink, and I hope it will muddle your brain so that you get all your filing and indexing wrong."

"Thank you," she replied. "I will have another drink, and I assure you that it won't in the least muddle my brain."

"No, I never really had any great confidence that it would," said Winter with another sigh, and he ordered two more cocktails.

Five minutes later, precisely, Miss Collins returned to her press-cuttings and Harry Winter strolled home to his sister's flat alone.

Helen Everard was waiting for him and for the sealed package of documents which had changed hands in the Clifford Street bar under an evening paper.

"You look melancholy," were her first words when her brother came in. "Are you falling in love again?"

"Again!" cried Winter. "You talk as if I made a habit of falling in love. I haven't fallen in love for years and years."

"What about that charming little lady at Deauville in June?"

Harry Winter clapped the palm of his hand to his forehead.

"True," he exclaimed. "Too true. Too damnably true. I had forgotten her. Yes. I am an incurable romantic. But this evening I have given up Romance for ever. From now onwards you see before you a stern realist. Heart-broken, perhaps; but never mind. A young man's dreams may be shattered-but what does it matter? Henceforward I am Winter, the Hard-headed Business Man. And by the time that I have put Mr Midas B. Hanson on the map of the world once again, I shall be known as the toughest kid on 'Change or the Kerb or wherever it is."

"What's up?" asked his sister casually. "Had a thick ear from La Collins?"

"A thick ear? I wish to heavens it had been. A thick ear from a girl friend is notoriously a token of affection all the world over. No. It was twenty times worse than that. Would you like to know what happened?"

"No. But I'm afraid I've got to."

Winter threw his black felt hat disgustedly on to the ground and jumped on it.

"Of all the unsympathetic beasts in this world, commend me to kid sisters. Very well. I'm going to pay you out for your callousness. I'm going to tell you what happened."

"I know you are," said Helen, picking up sewing. "And I won't spare your feelings."

"I'm ready. Shoot." And she yawned delicately.

"Then listen. La Collins jilted me tonight for a card-index. She walked out on me for a filing-cupboard. She swapped my society for a press-cutting. She gave me the go-by for a packet of paper-clips. She——"

"In fact, she went back to work?"

"What a wonderful thing is woman's intuition," said Winter bitterly. "Yes, in fact she went back to work. I can't think how you guessed it."

"She's very pretty, isn't she," murmured the girl absently.

Winter snorted. "Junoesque. I detest 'em Junoesque."

"You've never detested a woman in your life, my sweet child. You haven't got it in you. That's your trouble. Or at any rate one of them."

"If you're going to be impudent," said Winter with dignity, "I suggest that we change the subject."

"All right. I've got some news for you."

"Someone left me some money?"

"No, but someone wants to borrow off you."

"Pooh! There's no news in that. Who is it?"

"My late husband."

"To hell with him," said Harry Winter venomously, standing very still all of a sudden. "Where is he?"

"In London. He's coming round here at seven this evening."

"You don't have to see him, Nellie," said Winter earnestly. "I'll deal with him."

"I know you would, old boy. And that's why I think I'd better stay with you. Your ideas of dealing with poor Norman were always rather — what shall I say — violent."

"Violence is the only thing that poor Norman, poor sweet darling Norman, understands."

"Yes, I think I'd better stay," said Helen. "I don't want you to do anything silly."

"You don't want me to do anything sensible," grumbled Winter. "That's the devil about all you women. You will insist on turning the other cheek all the time."

"The devil?" murmured his sister. "What an odd person to associate with cheek-turning!"

"Oh! don't be so infernally clever all the time," Winter shouted. "You know perfectly well what I mean. Norman behaved abominably to you, and whenever Bill and I try to kick him downstairs, you turn on us as if we were absolute cads and make us give money to the poor little sweet lovey-dovey lambkin."

"You're perfectly right, Harry darling. What a brute I am."

"I wish you were a bit of a brute sometimes. Then people like Norman and that swine Crawford would get a little of what they deserve. Blast them."

The house-telephone rang and Winter answered it. He listened for a moment and then said sulkily, "Oh yes, I suppose you'd better show him up." He hung up the receiver and muttered, "I'd like to show him up."

Helen Everard shook a forefinger at him. "Harry! No nonsense now," she said in a warning voice. Winter made no reply, but planted himself on a chair in a corner of the room and thrust his hands into his trouser pockets. A moment later Norman Everard came in. He was a man of medium height, neatly built, with square shoulders and a good chest, and his sallowish complexion contrasted sharply with his glossy black hair, his black eyebrows, and his small black moustache. He was dressed in a smart new suit, carried yellow gloves and a black stick, and wore fawn-coloured shoes. His manner was self-assured almost to the point of jauntiness.

Helen Everard accepted his outstretched hand with a promptitude that conveyed, as it was intended to convey, a flat refusal to accept a more intimate greeting. Her late husband noticed the hint, smiled, and was in no way abashed.

He nodded affably to her, and then noticed Harry sitting in the corner. For a fraction of a second he appeared to be a little disconcerted by the grim appearance of his former brother-in-law. Then he quickly recovered and nodded to him with an equal affability.

"Hullo, Harry," he remarked, "or is it Bill? I never could tell you apart, even in the old days, you remember."

"I'm Harry," was the growled answer.

"You had slightly the better manners of the two, if I recall correctly," said Mr Everard airily, "or slightly the worse. I know it was one or the other."

"What is it that you want?" enquired Helen coldly. "Always the practical little woman," said Everard approvingly. "What is it that I want? Well, let me see. Firstly, of course——"

"A drink," snapped Winter.

"Give the clever gentleman a bag of pistachio nuts, my dear," proceeded the unruffled Everard, without taking his eyes off Helen. "He has rung the bell with his first cocoanut. I would greatly appreciate a drink, and after that I should like——"

"Money," snapped Winter.

Everard shook his head sadly. "I'm afraid the poor little gentleman does not qualify for the splendid cigar, my dear. What a pity!"

Helen's mouth opened a little, and then she said, "Do you mean to say you haven't come here for money?"

"Your incredulity, my dear Helen," replied Everard, "does small credit to the opinion which you must hold of your once-adoring and, if I may so far flatter myself, once-adored husband. Nevertheless, I must hasten to add that I have not come to ask you for money."

"I shall wake up in a moment," murmured Harry Winter.

"You will find the world a strange place," said Everard, turning towards him with a courteous bow, "after forty years of sleep."

Winter started furiously and was on the point of saying something, but Helen quickly intervened.

"Then what do you want if you don't want money?"

"I want help."

"Ah!" said Winter ironically.

"A curious snore your brother has acquired in his — er — forty years' winks," observed Everard. Helen again had to intervene before Harry could retort. A long experience of her brothers, before her marriage and after her divorce, had brought her skill in this kind of intervention to a high level. She sometimes felt a little guilty about it, because they always looked rather pathetically bewildered whenever they were headed off from a word or a deed which they had been on the point of uttering or performing. Even after all these years they never seemed quite to understand what had happened.

"What sort of help do you want, Norman?" she asked.

"I'll explain. Do you mind if I sit down?" replied Everard, sitting down. "It's like this. I've got a job." He held up a warning hand. "Please don't jump to the ordinary and slightly vulgar conclusion," he said severely. "I have descended to none of the last four refuges of the Public School man. I do not sell indifferent claret to indifferent stockbrokers on half-commission. I do not stand in front of expensive motor-cars in shop-windows. I do not exploit my skill at golf in order to dispose of bundles of peculiar shares in remarkable companies. Not that I have any skill at golf. At least I have been spared that misfortune. Nor do I exploit my — er — skill in the boudoir for the benefit of elderly dames on the Portuguese Riviera." He sipped his cocktail elegantly and proceeded: "So you see, I am fifth from bottom in the class. And that's what my new profession is."

"But you haven't told us what your new profession is," said Helen.

Norman Everard looked surprised. "But I've just explained. I'm fifth from the bottom. I'm a gossip-writer, of course."

Harry Winter gave a sudden loud crow of laughter.

"Still got the same enchanting ripple, I perceive," remarked Everard over his shoulder. "Just like April rain in a Devon orchard. Yes. I am a gossip-writer, or, rather, society columnist. I have a salary, an expense-sheet, a desk in a corner of a room about the size of the Green Park — the room, I mean, not the desk — and a titled employer. I have left Paris, and am now in residence in London."

"You don't sound as if you wanted help," said Helen. "You sound very prosperous."

"What I mean by help is a few introductions. I've been out of England for so many years now — what with our period of connubial bliss in India" — Harry Winter shifted ominously in his seat — "and my enforced residence out of London so long as I occupied the honourable position of pensioner to your delicious brothers, that I've dropped out of things a good deal in the metropolis of the Holy British Empire. And I shall not take my rightful place at the top of the columnist's tree if I don't know anybody to gossip about."

"Then how the hell did you get the job?" exclaimed Winter from his corner.

"Exquisite command of language, as ever," commented Everard. "What an intellectual treat it must be to have your brothers popping in and out all the time."

"If you want anything from us," said Helen wearily, "you aren't likely to get it by insulting Harry."

"I got the job," replied Everard, turning round and ostentatiously ignoring the last remark, "in a singular way. I had a delicious lady friend in Paris——"

"Yes. Called Odette. We know all about her," said Winter.

"Of course you do. I had forgotten." The columnist was not in the least disconcerted.

"Well, you know how these things are, Winter — or do I still call you Harry? What's the rule in these matters? — an exquisite beginning, glamour, romance, passion, and so on; then shading down into familiarity; gradually sliding into boredom, and thence to irritation, and so with a sickening thud to horror and detestation."

"What an utter and absolute cad you are, Norman," said Helen with a quiet absence of emphasis that made the words sound terrible.

But Norman Everard did not flinch. "I wasn't speaking of our married life, my dear," he said, "though, by Jove, now that I come to think of it, I well might have been. I was speaking of Odette. I had to get rid of her. A Greek offered me two thousand francs for her — he has a charming little establishment in Montevideo and I had almost accepted, though it was a damnable knock-down price, when dash my buttons if an English magnate didn't come along, take a fancy to her, and give me a two-year contract as a gossip-boy in exchange for her. I gave the Greek a kick in the pants, sold his name and address to a League of Nations busybody for a couple of hundred francs and got him chucked out of France, and here I am. Hired slave for two years to Sir Montagu Anderton-Mawle, proprietor of the *Daily Lightning*. Now, can you give me some introductions?"

"No," said Helen coldly. She got up and spoke across Everard's chair to Winter.

"It's time we were getting ready, Harry, or we'll be late for the theatre."

The visitor paid no attention to this intimation.

"Do you ever see anything of your old flame these days, Helen?" he asked. "The boy friend who — er — failed to come up to the scratch."

Winter jumped up impatiently and exclaimed: "For heaven's sake let me chuck the little swine out."

But Helen only shook her head. She was resolutely determined not to lose her temper.

"I see him occasionally," she said evenly.

"He's fallen on his feet, I see," went on the society columnist, "marrying old Hanson's daughter. Packets of money there. Do you know the girl?"

"Slightly."

"Do you know the old boy himself?"

"Slightly."

"You don't happen to know to what extent the old boy is financing handsome Jack, do you?"

"I think it's time you went away, Norman," said Helen in a voice of ice. "I'm tired of this conversation."

"Jack was always devilish fond of money, wasn't he?" mused Everard. Then he added plaintively, "I do wish you'd be a bit more helpful, Helen. This is the first assignment I've had in my new job, and I naturally want to make a success of it."

"What assignment?" said Winter sharply.

"To find out about Crawford. When I told the boss — little Monty — all about Helen and Jack and me — for heaven's sake, keep calm, Winter;

don't lose your head or you'll burst a blood-vessel — he got all hotted up with excitement. It appears that Jack has left the Army and got into one of little Monty's crook companies, and little Monty is worried about it for some reason or other. Perhaps he isn't worried. I don't know. Anyway, he's terrifically interested in Crawford's private life. I don't blame him. I was myself once. If you remember, Helen. But there — let bygones be bygones. Anyway, I've got to find out if Hanson has paid Jack's debts, and whether they get on well together, and so on."

"What on earth has that got to do with Anderton-Mawle's worries?" demanded Winter. Norman Everard sighed deeply. "And you call yourself a man of the world. Sweet Montagu didn't tell me any more than I've told you, but it's all as clear as crystal to me. What use is Jack to Anderton-Mawle if he is financially independent? If Hanson has paid Jack's debts, Jack can snap his fingers. But if he hasn't, Monty can buy them up and do what he likes with Jack for ever and ever. And also with Jack's wife. Eh? You follow me? Why, it's elementary."

"I'm afraid we can't help you," said Helen. "Goodbye."

Everard got up at last and looked keenly at the brother and sister for a moment. Then he said, "So long as I can hold this job of being a successful pimp to Anderton-Mawle, I shall be much pleasanter as a friend than as an enemy. Mawle is a rich man, and he appears to have almost as few scruples as I have. It's a point worth considering."

"Please go," said Helen.

Everard smiled, picked up his hat, stick, and yellow gloves, and went.

"Phew!" exclaimed Harry, wiping his forehead with his handkerchief. "Don't ever say again that I'm lacking in self-control. Lucky Bill wasn't here. Bill would have killed him stone dead."

"Bill would have done exactly what I told him to," said Helen absently.

"The room ought to be disinfected," growled her brother.

Helen looked up and smiled. "Anyway it's done you a good turn, Harry, so you oughtn't to grumble."

"Why? What do you mean?"

"Can't you see for yourself?"

"No, I'm dashed if I can."

"What are you going to do this evening?"

"Take you out to dinner and a cinema."

"Don't you think it's your duty to get hold of La Collins and force her away from her card-index and take her out to dinner and tell her that Anderton-Mawle is suddenly taking an acute interest in the affairs of the Hanson family?"

"Nellie," cried Harry Winter, "I always said you were a genius, and now I know it. Of course I must do that."

"Yes. It's your duty," said Helen demurely.

Winter grabbed the telephone and began to dial. Then he stopped and exclaimed, "But what about you? That'll leave you in the lurch for the evening."

She shook her head gravely. "You must sacrifice your pleasure to your duty."

Winter laughed cheerfully. "Devil," he observed.

"And think of Miss Collins' example. She also will be sacrificing pleasure to duty if she has to leave her card-index for the dinner-table with you."

"Fiend," said Winter, and went on dialling.

CHAPTER XXI

Sir Montagu Weaves a Web

The giant Freiherr von Czepan-Eichenhöh returned with his quantities of suitcases to the Ritz Hotel, and set about his discreet business in the City of London, while Veronica, making the best of a bad job, remained at Partington Crescent and went on with her energetic campaign for Anglo-German goodwill and mutual understanding through the memory of the Holy Liberators. Subscriptions were coming in so fast that Veronica was able to put in hand the first material representation of the great spiritual idea on which the whole movement was based. She was able to commission the first series of commemorative plaques for free distribution to all branches of Nazism or Fascism, in any country whatsoever, which might apply to the head office of the Society for one. The first plaque represented, in a tasteful bas-relief, the immortal scene at Sarajevo which liberated the purifying fires of war, and swept away the miserable cant and hypocrisy of Europe's Liberal tradition for ever. Round the edge of the central picture ran a frieze of naked Druids goose-stepping majestically past swastika-shaped bundles of mistletoe, their faces, though necessarily somewhat small, nevertheless rather cleverly suggesting the face of General Ludendorff. Above, on a scroll, was simply the name of the hero, Gavrile Princip, and below, also on a scroll, were the punning but immensely significant words: Facile Princeps. Veronica was delighted with it and was vehement in her congratulations of the Chelsea sculptor who had executed the design so skilfully. The sculptor himself, who had fought in the War and been severely gassed, and had accepted the commission solely because he and his wife were only seventeen pounds and a few shillings away from starvation, made the singular request that the plaque should not bear his signature, and that no one should know that it was his work.

At first Veronica had flared up at this request, and had accused him of being afraid of offending Jewry like the young film-aspirants of Mayfair. But the artist, after a lot of shuffling and evasion, finally admitted that the reason was personal, not financial. He had lost three brothers and a good many friends in the War, he explained, and he did not think very much of Gavrile Princip as a world benefactor. Possessing some hope, as artists with paint, stone, bronze, or ink, are so apt to do, of immortality through his work, the sculptor pointed out that he was not overwhelmed with a desire to be associated for ever and ever with a man whom he could only regard as a stinking wop. Veronica, her eyes flaming and her cheeks scarlet, faced up to him superbly and said that unless he instantly withdrew that remark and apologized she would refuse to take delivery of the plaque. The sculptor replied that she could take delivery or not of the plaque as she liked, and that he personally did not care two straws whether she did or didn't, but that if the money for it was not forthcoming within twenty-four hours she would hear from his solicitor. Veronica coldly wrote out a cheque for the full amount on the spot and, in her haughtiest manner, ordered the man to deliver the plaque to 44 Partington Crescent, SW7, immediately. "At the tradesmen's entrance," she added with a brilliant afterthought. But the sculptor had the best of it after all, for he took the plaque back into his studio and, before delivering it, engraved in minute letters upon the naked tail of each Druid, the words "Stinking Wop," and the inscriptions were not noticed until more than two hundred casts of the plaque had been erected in various towns and villages of Central Europe.

In the meanwhile Veronica turned her energetic attention to the choice of subject and design for the second of the series of plaques. Her original intention had been to immortalize the killers of Rasputin, but she had been warned off by her legal advisers, who cautiously pointed out that the alleged killers of the Russian monk had already been immortalized to some tune by a well-known film company which had been compelled to pay up a pretty considerable sum of cash for the indiscretion. The matter rested there, while Veronica turned over possible alternatives in her pretty little head.

Sir Montagu Anderton-Mawle rubbed his podgy hands together in some satisfaction. And he was genuinely entitled to feel a little pleased with himself. He had once again taken the long view, and once again the long view was proving the right one. Furthermore, it was not merely proving to be the right one, but it looked like being the right one on a colossal scale. Just as his little reorganization of the uneconomical timber trade of Tasmania had been dwarfed by his operations in rifles during the War, and just as his operations in rifles had been made to seem a small affair in comparison with his cotton exploits in Lancashire, so did it appear that Perdurite was going to put the cotton exploits in the shade. It really looked as if Providence knew a good man when she saw one.

Otherwise how could one rationally explain the sequence of coincidences by which the young inventor had brought his invention to Sir Montagu out of all the myriad financiers of London, at just the precise moment when a Patriotic Government had been returned to office with a thumping majority, when a wholesome and decent system of Protection had at last been almost universally accepted and strongly consolidated, and when the magic word Rearmament was in the air. As if that was not enough, Providence had thrown this plan into Sir Montagu's mouth when all the steel-fellows were in such a muddle that they wouldn't be ready for the great boom. It was such an exquisite sequence that some queer emotional feeling of thanksgiving welled up in the obscure depths of Sir Montagu's soul. The great financier had never set up to be a religious man in the orthodox sense of the word. He had simply concentrated throughout life upon doing what he thought was right. But the first Tasmanian Mawle, the pioneer who had doggedly worked his way up through the various stages of the official ladder until he was released on ticket of leave, and was allowed to exchange the convict settlement for the comparative amenities of a fifteen-hour day in the fields as a "Government-assigned man," had been the son of an ardent Plymouth Brother, and a personal friend of John Nelson Darby himself, the founder of the sect, and in great crises, such as now confronted Sir Montagu, it was only natural that the deep-seated, hereditary belief in Divine Guidance should find some queer, inarticulate outlet in the heart of the descendant of the Plymouth Brother.

So the financier rubbed his hands and beamed across the table at his colleagues — General Springton, Mr Andrew Hay, and the latest recruit to the Board, Major Jack Crawford.

Major Crawford had just returned from Germany and had presented an interesting report on the various interviews he had had with German industrial magnates. It is true that he had achieved no concrete results in the way of actual contracts, or even projects of co-operation with the Germans. But that was not surprising, for Sir Montagu had given him no such important tasks to perform. Sir Montagu had other ideas about the part which Major Crawford could play in the successful launching of Perdurite, and Sir Montagu, being a far-sighted man who took long views, was already preparing Major Crawford for his part, much as a Hollywood director "grooms" the embryonic star.

"In three months," mused the little financier to himself as he smiled paternally at the handsome ex-cavalryman, and congratulated him warmly upon the success of his mission to Germany, "In three months you'll have got the reputation on the Continent of being the silliest business man who ever came out of this silly country, and by God! you'll deserve it, and then you'll be of some use to intelligent folk like me." But there was no shadow of indication on his face that he had been thus musing when he turned from Crawford to General Springton and exclaimed genially, "Our new recruit is winning his spurs, eh, General?"

The Tiger, although he intensely disliked the use of a fine old military metaphor in a civilian's mouth, and a non-combatant civilian's at that, thought it would be more tactful to fall in with the Chairman's humour, and he agreed that Crawford had done admirably. Being a wise man, well versed in the art of being civil to Superior Officers, he refrained from asking what it was that Crawford had done so admirably in Germany.

"Czecho-Slovakia must be your next port of call," resumed Sir Montagu, moving with perfect ease from the military to the nautical metaphor. "I want you to go and make some contacts with the Skoda people, Crawford. Do you speak French, by the way?"

Crawford was surprised at the question. "French?" he said. "Good Lord! no."

"Oh well, it doesn't really matter," replied Sir Montagu, secretly delighted. His international contact-maker was going to turn out to be even sillier than he had dared to hope. "English will do well enough."

"I should think so indeed," replied Crawford with a scornful indifference.

"And then you might come back via Le Creusot," went on Sir Montagu, "and see the good folks there. Can you start tomorrow?"

"Dash it, I'm only just back," exclaimed Crawford. "Yes, I know, I know," said the Chairman soothingly, exerting his famous charm. "But we can't afford to let the grass grow under our feet, you know. We've got to get a move on. The new contracts will be out soon, and we've got to be ready for them."

"Precisely," said Springton, casting about vainly in his mind for a connection between the new contracts and Jack Crawford's peregrinations in Europe, but agreeing loyally, as ever, with his commander.

"Very well," said Crawford sulkily, "I'll start tomorrow if you like." The polo season was about to open in a week or so, and he had intended to suggest that it would be admirable publicity for the new company if he turned out for the Hurlinghampton Dragons — or some such team — in as many matches as possible.

"That's capital," replied the financier. "It's delicate work, you know, and you're exactly the right man for it." He sighed markedly. "It must be your Army training that gives you the knack of handling people. I wish I had it. You've got it too, General."

"It rubs the corners off us," said Springton tolerantly. "Sort of makes us understand the other fellow's point of view, if you see what I mean. No civilian can ever hope to get the same angle. I mean it isn't their fault but they obviously can't."

"That's hard on you and me, Hay," Sir Montagu smiled at the lawyer, who had sat impassive throughout the discussion. Andrew Hay nodded. "It's just too bad for us," he remarked drily.

Anderton-Mawle hastily changed the subject. "By the way, General, I'd like a word with you before you go."

Hay got up. "I'm off," he remarked, looking at his watch. "Coming my direction, Crawford? The Strand."

"The Strand?" said Crawford, puzzled. "No. What a queer place to go to."

"I work near there," replied the lawyer amiably, and he went out.

Sir Montagu detained Crawford for one more moment. "Come round to my house at six tonight. I'll give you some letters of introduction and we'll have a chat."

"Can't come at six," answered the new recruit. "I'm cocktailing. Make it seven."

The little financier gazed up at the big, good-looking ex-soldier and almost choked with fury. But he only said, "Very well. Make it seven. Try not to be late."

"Call it seven for half-past. Cheerio." And Crawford went out.

Anderton-Mawle swallowed hard, and then turned genially to the Tiger.

"Nice boy that," he observed. "He'll go far." And he made a mental note that once Perdurite had got some of the new Government contracts, and the whole thing had got under way, the nice boy would go as far as the metaphorical toe of Sir Montagu's metaphorical boot could kick him.

"Best type of young Englishman," answered the Tiger. "Those were the fellows who won the War for us. You can't get away from that. We older fellows simply had to keep an eye on them and give them a bit of advice now and then. They did all the rest."

Sir Montagu, however, was in no mood to listen to an eulogy of a damned young whipper-snapper who had had the goddam impertinence to fix his own hour for coming round for instructions, and he plunged into business at once.

"Sit down, General," he said. "Advice is exactly the right word to use. As usual, I find myself in the position of wanting yours."

The Tiger sat down and purred.

"And before I go any further," said Sir Montagu, "I want you to understand that this talk of ours is absolutely confidential. I don't want any of 'em, Hay or Crawford or Collingham or any of 'em, to know about it. It's your advice I want, not theirs."

The General's purring became almost audible.

"The point is this, Springton," and the baronet became very confidential and pulled a chair up close and tapped the other on the knee. "The point is this. If you chuck a stone into a pond, the ripples go all over the place. Properly handled, Perdurite is going to be one of the biggest goddam stones of modern times, and the ripples are going to be like waves, and some folks are going to get wet. And who's going to get wet? Why, the steel crowd, of course. And they aren't going to like it. No, sir. They're going to kick like hell. And I don't blame them. At the moment they aren't paying any attention to us, because we're new and they think we're small, while they're old and big. But when we start snapping up contracts from under their tomfool noses, they'll begin to sit up and take notice. And that's what we've got to be ready for. Do you get me?"

"I get you," said the General, assuming an air of preternatural wisdom.

"Very well. I want to be ready for them. So do you. So do we all. But what are we going to do? That's the point."

The General considered the point. "It'll need a lot of thinking out," he remarked.

"Yes, that's true," replied the Chairman, with a startled expression, as if the idea had not occurred to him. "And we'll all have to put our shoulders to the wheel," added the General.

"And that's precisely why I want your advice, General. There's one part of the — er — wheel where yours will be the only effective shoulder. I've been trying to foresee as many of the twists and turns that this thing is likely to take," continued Sir Montagu, "and I've come to the conclusion that one of the key places it may take us to is Cimbro-Suevonia."

"I never can remember the difference between Cimbro-whatever-it-is and Czecho-Slovakia and Jugo-Slavia," observed the General.

"Quite so," said Anderton-Mawle patiently.

"And why should Cimbro-what-do-you-call-it come into it?"

"Lots of iron there. Lots of steel interests."

"But surely our trouble is going to be with the home-grown article," said the General. "I don't see how the foreign ones will be dragged in."

"There's a lot of interlocking," explained Mawle laboriously. "Anyway, that is one of the conclusions I've come to, that Cimbro-Suevonia will be dragged into it sooner or later."

There was a pause.

"James Hanson used to be the uncrowned king of those parts, they tell me," mused Sir Montagu. The name touched off a spring inside the Tiger.

"Oh yes, rather. Young Robert Hanson's our member — I'm his chairman — great friend of mine — he's often told me about the old man. But he's retired many years ago."

"In 1924," murmured the other.

"Wendelmann was his partner. He's still in the business."

"In London."

"Oh yes. In London."

"He always was in the London end of it," said Sir Montagu thoughtfully. "Hanson ran the Cimbrian end. I was never afraid of Wendelmann," he added.

The General stared. "But you aren't implying that you ever were afraid of Hanson?" he exclaimed.

Sir Montagu shook his enormous head slowly. "I never met Hanson in business. He was out of it before I — well — before I was up in his class. But if I ever did come up against him, I should be very, very careful. I know where I am with the Wendelmann type. They're slow, and they're cautious, and they're safe. But Hanson, from all accounts, was another kettle of fish. Hanson was a buccaneer. A regular pirate. I wouldn't care to tackle him on his home ground."

"His home — oh, you mean in Cimbro-Suevonia?" Anderton-Mawle nodded.

"Well, you won't have to," said the General heartily, "if he's been out of business for twelve or fourteen years."

"He might come back," Sir Montagu almost whispered.

"He must be nearly seventy."

"That's nothing in these days."

"No. That's true."

"If Cimbro-Suevonia ever became the scene of action, that old man might be Steel's ace of trumps."

"Can't we get him into Perduralimin then?" asked Springton, and Sir Montagu just succeeded in not telling the redoubtable Tiger that he was a goddam fool.

"No," he said, shaking his huge head so vigorously that his sounding-board ears almost flapped.

"No. All we can do at present is to wait. But we must," he smacked a small fist into a palm and repeated, "we must get the earliest possible information about him if he does intend to come back. That's what I want you to do, Springton. Sound young Hanson — very carefully mind! — about what his father's doing. Ask him if the old war-horse isn't pawing the ground at all this programme of Rearmament, and that sort of thing. Find out if there's any special activity going on in the Partington Crescent house. Make an excuse to invite both of them to lunch in the City and see if the old boy has been down that way lately. See what I mean?"

"Perfectly," replied the Tiger. "But I should have thought young Crawford was more the man for the job."

Sir Montagu looked almost saintly as he gazed up into the General's dark, thin face. "I don't think I could ask a son-in-law to pump his father-in-law," he said in such a tone of gentle reproof that Springton was quite abashed, and the conversation came to an end on this high note of morality.

.....

Crawford interpreted the mystic phrase "seven for seven-thirty" as meaning roughly seven-fifty, and it was at this hour that he arrived at the huge house in Carlton House Terrace in which Sir Montagu resided.

Sir Montagu was an easily adaptable man, and managed to reconcile himself to most things, but nothing in the world ever completely reconciled him to subordinates who postponed appointments for an hour and then arrived fifty minutes late on top of that, and it required all his Tasmanian self-control not to fly out at Jack Crawford when he turned up at last. And not only was the ex-embryonic field-marshal fifty minutes late from a cocktail-party, but he was not even drunk. Anderton-Mawle, a scrupulously sober man himself, had at least expected to obtain from a man who had overstayed himself for fifty minutes at a cocktail-party, some vitally important news — or if not actual news, at any rate pointers towards news which an able man might be able to appreciate and assess. Instead of which, Crawford behaved exactly as if he was on parade. He was sober, cool, precise, and silent. He offered no apologies and listened to his Chairman's instructions in precisely the same bored and lofty way in which, as a captain and as a major, he had listened to the instructions of some foolish colonel or general, and he only brightened at the end when Sir Montagu, heroically suppressing a passionate desire to summon the help of half a dozen footmen and strangle the idiot with his own hands, whispered to him, "These are important matters, Crawford, that I'm giving you to handle, but they're nothing in comparison to what I'm going to give you later on. That is to say, if you turn out as I think you will, as you're shaping now."

But whenever Sir Montagu turned the conversation round to the two points on which this maddening man could have enlightened him, he met with a blank wall on the more important of the two, and only a flicker on the other. Crawford had no idea of his father-in-law's plans, and he did not appear to care what they might be, and he was not even faintly interested in Sir Montagu's studiously casual questions about them. And Sir Montagu could not be more than casual. If this monumental jackass with the long silky moustache got the faintest idea into his fat head, thought the little financier venomously, that I was interested in old Hanson, he'd probably spill the beans to the old devil tomorrow night at dinner without knowing what it all meant. And the old devil, thought Sir Montagu sadly and admiringly, would know all right what it all meant without the slightest hesitation.

Waiting courteously, therefore, until Crawford had finished describing the final of the Regimental Polo Cup at Lahore in 1928, with a modest reference to the winning goal which he himself had had the good fortune to score a moment before the end of the game, Sir Montagu deftly turned the conversation to the second of the two points on which he badly wanted information.

"Polo is a very expensive game, they tell me," he remarked.

"Very," replied the ex-idol of the cavalry.

"You were a lucky young devil to be able to afford it."

"Very."

"I've met lots of young chaps in my time who got into debt over it," pursued the financier, whose path through life had seldom, if ever, crossed the paths of polo-playing subalterns.

"Oh yes," said Crawford.

"And when I say debt, I mean debt."

"Rather," said Crawford.

Sir Montagu took a chance and was rewarded. "What a generous old chap your new father-in-law is!" he said suddenly, and a black cloud flitted across the blond face of the new son-in-law. It vanished in a moment, but it was enough for Sir Montagu. The generous old chap had not paid the debts, whatever they were, of the young cavalryman who had played polo on his pay. Sir Montagu had got what he wanted and he left it at that.

Half an hour later the Society Columnist of the *Daily Lightning* was ordered to leave his desk in the room that was about the size of the Green Park, and to present himself at the private residence of the proprietor of that important journal.

The proprietor did not invite Norman Everard to sit down, nor did he treat him with the smallest amount of courtesy. But Mr Everard had never in his life objected to the manners of any man or woman who seemed reasonably likely to butter his bread for him, on either side, and he was accustomed to this sort of thing.

So he stood, with a graceful air of nonchalance, in front of his temporary master.

"Find out," snapped Anderton-Mawle, "what your old boy-friend Crawford owes, and who he owes it to, and what it can be bought at."

"I've been so long out of London——" began Everard easily.

"That you're being employed on this job," interrupted his owner.

"That I am out of touch with the people who might supply me with information."

"Sammy Morris of Morris, Marks, Mance, & Styles. 630 Shaftesbury Avenue. Tell him I sent you. If anyone knows anything, he does."

"Crawford having married into the Hansons," remarked Everard, flicking dust off his sleeve, "you'd have to pay cent per cent, I should think."

"You're not paid to think. Get on with it."

With an almost imperceptible shrug, Norman Everard turned and strolled to the door. Sir Montagu barked after him, "And if you shrug your shoulders at me again, you're fired." Everard left the room without even looking back or pausing. His two-year contract with the *Daily Lightning* was snug in a solicitor's safe.

CHAPTER XXII

Sir Montagu Visits Eleanor at Lowbury Barn

Eleanor's natural reluctance to be out of the society of her husband for a single minute had one compensation. Her sadness at his frequent absences on the Continent was a little made up for by her pride in his extraordinary achievement. She, of course, had always known that Jack Crawford was one of those rare individuals who can turn their hand to anything at a moment's notice and defeat professionals at their own game, but even she had not contemplated the possibility that he would go straight to the top of the commercial tree quite so quickly. Within a month of leaving the Army, he had found an important post in the City. Within a month of assuming his duties in that important post, he had become the indispensable liaison officer between his Chief and the great Continental firms. To him were entrusted the most delicate missions and the trickiest negotiations. To him Sir Montagu turned in emergencies. He travelled, the ambassador of Perdurite, from Krupps to Skoda, and from Skoda to Schneider and from Schneider to Liège. It was amazing, and yet it was exactly the sort of thing that Jack would do.

There was another thing about the whole thing that delighted Eleanor's gentle soul. Her father's money, the money she had always lived on, the money she had married on, had been admittedly and frankly amassed by the sale of guns and shells. It was the profits of deathmongering. Everyone knew that. But Perdurite was different. Eleanor was far too sensible to discuss business affairs with her husband when he returned from his Continental excursions, and in any case she knew that the female brain was not so constructed as to understand the mysteries which were child's-play to the masculine brain; but she had grasped one essential point. Perdurite was a purely defensive substance. At first she had been a little distressed when Crawford had entered a trade which appeared to be exactly the same horrible, destructive affair as that from which her father had acquired his millions, and she had asked, very diffidently, whether it was absolutely necessary for her husband to be a gun-maker too. To her immense relief, Crawford had explained that Perdurite was the ideal substance for making armour against the products of the gun-makers. The more Perdurite there was in the world, the safer place the world would be. The steel shells and steel bullets of the old order would practically bounce off the Perdurite ships and Perdurite helmets of the new. The new company was practically a company of doctors setting out to fight against a deadly disease that had for centuries ravaged mankind, and generations of British soldiers would not only bless their names but would die in their beds instead of on the battlefield.

Eleanor was greatly comforted when this had been explained to her, and she exclaimed joyfully, "Oh Jack, won't it be marvellous when you're making so much money out of Perdurite that we can afford to give away all the money we've got from Daddy's guns."

"Why on earth should we do that?" exclaimed Crawford, startled out of his usual impassivity.

"Oh I know you'll think I'm only a goose," cried Eleanor, looking up at him, "but I do feel somehow that it's all tainted money. I'd be so enormously much happier if we could get rid of it and give it to the hospitals or something."

Crawford, fully in command of the situation again, smiled paternally and patted her cheek. "Little donkey," he murmured, "if tainted money is bad for you, it's just as bad for the hospitals."

"Of course; how right you are," cried Eleanor. "I hadn't thought of that."

"You never think of anything," replied Crawford. "Not now, when I've got you to think for me," she whispered happily, standing on tiptoe to be kissed. Crawford patted her cheek once more, and turned away with a careless laugh, and Eleanor sank down upon her heels again.

During her husband's trips abroad, Eleanor had plenty to do. They had taken a temporary flat near Berkeley Square, furnished, but Crawford had insisted upon buying a house in the country as well. It was summer, and he could not bear the idea of Eleanor sweltering among the asphalt fumes and carbon monoxide and airlessness of London, while she might be sitting on a deck-chair, on her own lawn, under her own apple-trees. Eleanor, who would have been happy anywhere, was enchanted with this thoughtfulness of Jack's, and she threw herself eagerly into the furnishing and equipping and modernizing of Lowbury Barn, a delightful old farmhouse on the heathery borders of Surrey and Hampshire. It had been Jack's idea to save her from discomfort, and Jack's idea that she should be happy in the country, and the house was Jack's present to her (at least it would be when he had earned money to pay her back the money he had spent on the purchase and fitting of it), and that was enough for her. She and Mrs Hanson fluttered excitedly round the electricians and plumbers and carpenters and painters inside the house, and round the gardener and his boy outside. It was an old stone house with a few oak beams in one or two rooms, and one or two big open fireplaces, and a large unwieldy kitchen. The garden had a lawn, sure enough, and apple-trees, and a herbaceous border full of delphiniums and lupins and evening primroses and columbines and the rest of the familiar cottage flowers of the English countryside. The wind brought the scent of heather across the commons which had been open to the peasants for a thousand years for the rights of pasturage and the rights of turbary and the rights of free-warren, but were now rigorously barred with barbed-wire and stake-posts against all-comers save those who came in tanks, and white butterflies and yellow butterflies wandered over the hedges from the daisied fields.

Wood-pigeons cried their laments in the beech-woods, and owls greeted the rising of the mist at sun-down. As twilight crept in from the east and dawn from the north, Eleanor could hear nothing but the distant cries of youthful cricketers upon the village green, and the rustle of starlings' wings as they jockeyed for the best places in the nests in the laurel shrubberies, and the drone of the homing aeroplanes, shining golden in the sunlight which they were high enough to catch, and sometimes the rat-tat-tat of a far-away machine-gun as it practised night firing on the military ranges away to the south. It was a peaceful, idyllic spot. There were peaches and nectarines on the south wall, and a great bed of strawberries, and plum-trees, espalier against tarred wooden fences, and the old-fashioned Victoria plum which needs no support against the blasts of Boreas but only an occasional protective scattering of small-shot against the marauding bullfinches, and an occasional Doyen de Comice pear, and, of course, the apples. There were brown bees too, swarms of them, which came up from the hives of the villagers to taste the pinks and the carnations when the sun was shining, and there was a pair of blackbirds in the ancient honey-suckle-tree at the corner of the kitchen.

Everything would have been perfect if only Jack had been able to spare more than an occasional flying weekend between his important missions abroad, but, as it was, Eleanor's pride in her man sustained her and she occupied her time by taking an active part in the affairs of the village. The Women's Institute, the Mothers' Union, the Girl Guides, the Lawn-tennis Club, all claimed her help. But it was the Women's Conservative Association which especially turned to her, as the sister of the Financial Secretary to the War Office, for sorely-needed sympathy and advice. For the W.C.A. was in a grave crisis. The chairwoman, who, like so many pillars of rural Conservatism in the South of England, was a charming and wealthy American lady, had a passion for all British forms of sport, and it was her habit, when she had nothing else to do, to stroll abroad in the ancestral park of her husband with a gun and a couple of dogs. Some months before Eleanor's arrival in the district, this high-spirited and mettlesome lady from Maryland was leaning over the fence which separated her husband's ancestral park from the parvenu park of Sir Tobias Jagg, MP, when she observed a pheasant of prodigious proportions taking the air in the Jagg demesne. Glancing hurriedly round, she found herself alone with her dogs, the pheasant, and her Maker, and it was the work of a few moments to add the noble bird to the bag. But alas! the glance round had been too hurried, for a couple of Jagg retainers came leaping out from behind trees, and the fat was in the fire. For months Conservative spectators on the marches of Surrey and Hampshire were scandalized by the action for trespass brought by a Conservative Member of Parliament against a prominent Conservative official. Sir Tobias won his case and the impulsive lady from Maryland was duly fined £10, and relations in the district were distinctly strained. The arrival of Eleanor, whom even the most bigoted adherents of both sides in the unhappy quarrel fell in love with at first sight, was a godsend to the distraught Association, and she was immediately and with acclamation elected vice-chairman to the poacheress. Nor was it only the two wings of the Episcopalian Party which fell under her modest charm. At the first public meeting over which she presided, the Maryland sportswoman having found it convenient to absent herself from the district awhile, the local Radicals and Socialists forbore to ask their ribald questions about the difference between law-makers and law-breakers, and whether the speaker was in favour of a tightening-up of the Game Laws, and what about America anyway. Eleanor's gentle diffidence made that sort of ragging impossible, even for Radicals and Socialists who have no school training in decency and fair-play.

So life at Lowbury was not uneventful. There were calls to be received and returned, and shopping to be done in Farnham, and curtains to be hung, and there was even a wonderful morning when Eleanor wandered out into the sun-bathed, bee-humming garden after breakfast and found a steel-helmeted platoon of the Grenadier Guards entrenched behind the laurels. Summer manoeuvres were in full swing, and a Blue Force was advancing, as the Blue Force always has advanced since the old days of the musket and the Duke of Cambridge, from the direction of Andover with their right flank resting upon Petersfield, and Lowbury Barn was assumed to be a nest of hostile Brown machine-gunners. The handsome and perspiring young men of the Grenadier Guards were representing this nest.

Eleanor was enchanted at this masculine break in the quiet routine of life, and, after the vicious assaults of the Blue Andoverians, represented by three infantrymen carrying rattles and a man on a big black horse, had been successfully beaten off, she insisted on entertaining the platoon to beer and biscuits on the lawn. The subaltern in command had heard of the famous Major Crawford of the Cavalry, and expressed his regrets, with a perfect courtesy, on hearing that the Army had sustained so severe a loss by his departure into the City. Eleanor thought that she had seldom met so charming and so discerning a young man, and she longed to tell him that, in a very short time, his handsome soldiers would not have to perspire quite so freely under heavy steel helmets, but that Mr Crawford — late Major of Cavalry — would soon be providing them with lighter and tougher helmets made of Perdurite. But Eleanor had never given away a secret in her life, and she was not likely to start now with her husband's secrets. So she just smiled gently, and said that the poor soldiers must be very hot.

When they marched away, to circumvent fresh Blue assaults by representing a cloud of poison gas in the neighbourhood of Hankley Common, they gave their hostess a resounding "Eyes Right" and smiled happily at her waving handkerchief. It was altogether a delightful episode.

There was another delightful episode when Sir Montagu Anderton-Mawle dropped in for tea one lovely September afternoon. He had been down to the neighbourhood of Southampton, inspecting the site of one of the new Perdurite factories that were springing up like Parma violets under the refreshing rain of Sir Montagu's energy, and he was on his way back to London when it occurred to him that a cup of tea and an hour of Mrs Crawford's society would be a wonderful tonic after the toil of the day. Jack at the time was in Italy, making valuable contacts at Spezia, Trieste, Fiume, and Pola, and sending Eleanor picture-postcards almost every week of the Leaning Tower, the Grand Canal, the Forum, and the Fiat Motor Works at Turin.

Sir Montagu was gently enthusiastic about Jack's work, and his charm, and his tact, and his extraordinary gift for getting on with foreigners.

"It was a lucky day for Perdurite, Mrs Crawford," he said with a gay but vast smile, "when we stole the most promising soldier in the Army."

Eleanor sighed a small sigh. She still had a faint twinge of regret for those polished field-boots, and that bemedalled chest, and the eyes of adoring sentries.

"In all my experience of the City," went on Sir Montagu, "I never knew a man take so quickly to business as your husband. Just like a duck to water. You'd have thought he'd spent all his life in Throgmorton Street. It's quite uncanny."

"I think it's just that he's got a flair for getting on with people," said Eleanor modestly, knowing very well that it was a great deal more than that.

Sir Montagu gazed into the far distance like a man who is straining to pierce a veil and capture a hidden secret — it was an attitude of which he was extremely fond, as it invested him with a strange sort of spirituality — and then he spoke, aloud but to himself: "Her father would never have let it happen. Never."

"Let what happen?" enquired Eleanor.

Sir Montagu started, and came back to earth. "I didn't know I was speaking out loud," he said confusedly. "But there's no harm done. All I meant was that if your father had still been in the saddle, the firm of Hanson & Wendelmann would never have let your husband slip through their fingers. Not they. He'd have been snapped up long ago. Your father was a great man. Wonderful vision. Wonderful! Still, their loss is my gain, and you bet I'm not complaining." Eleanor looked at the eager, vital, little man who was sitting bolt upright on the other side of the tea-table. He had neither handsomeness nor size nor the advantages of birth and breeding, but he had some indefinable twist of personality which made Eleanor understand a little of how he had hoisted himself unaided into the forefront of affairs. Within a quarter of an hour of sitting down under her apple-trees he had praised, with enthusiasm no less than with discrimination, the only two men that she really loved.

"The world's a queer place," he went on, shaking his big head thoughtfully, "a mighty queer place. And a mighty crazy place. It wants men like your father badly. I suppose he never thinks of coming back into affairs?"

"Good gracious, no!" exclaimed Eleanor. "He's been retired too long now."

"Doesn't old Wendelmann ever try to persuade him?" asked Sir Montagu.

"Mr Wendelmann came round a lot lately," said Eleanor, "and then he suddenly stopped coming. Do you think — do you suppose——?"

"I like Wendelmann," murmured the baronet. "Isn't that a green woodpecker over there? Is it — or isn't it? — yes, by Jove it is. Decorative creatures, aren't they, Mrs Crawford?"

"I love that odd swooping flight," said Eleanor. "And we get lots of stonechats here too. They sit on the gorse-bushes and twitter. But do you really think that Mr Wendelmann——"

"We've got wonderful bird life in Tasmania. Mrs Crawford, if I ask you a personal question, will you try not to think me impertinent? I'm an old man, and much may be forgiven to age? Tell me. Has your husband got something on his mind?"

Eleanor was dreadfully distressed. She had assumed, and it had never occurred to her to assume anything else, that Jack was deliriously happy. He was not of the forthcoming type, of course, and did not sing in his first-class carriage on his way to the City or anything of that sort. He was, in fact, the honest, straightforward, undemonstrative type of British husband which, if it lacks a little of the lovely fervour of the Frenchman, more than makes up for it by the solidity of its devotion and the unflightiness of its fancies.

She had seen no trace of worry on Jack's face, because there never seemed to be any trace of any emotion upon it whether of worry or of anything else. And here was this startlingly discerning little gnome of a man apparently detecting in a few short business meetings what an adoring wife had failed to see.

"Something on his mind, Sir Montagu?" she said falteringly. "Of course not. At least I'm sure he hasn't. I'm positive. At least — yes, of course he hasn't."

The little gnome leant forward sympathetically. "You see, I'm rather fond of him," he said gently. "In these few weeks I've learnt to do more than just respect him. And I think he's worrying. Mrs Crawford, are you sure that there is nothing I can do to help?"

Eleanor suddenly found herself going through the traditional routine of a self-controlled woman in distress, and rolling her handkerchief up into a variety of tight little balls.

"It can't be money troubles," purred the sympathetic goblin. "Your father must have paid off all your husband's youthful debts."

This shot in the dark was an immediate winner, and Sir Montagu hugged his small self with joy when Eleanor replied, her blue eyes startled into a look of panic, "But Jack hasn't got any youthful debts. And even if he had, Daddy wouldn't pay them." She swallowed hard. "Daddy doesn't — Daddy somehow — he doesn't like Jack."

"Doesn't like him," echoed Sir Montagu incredulously. "But that's impossible."

"I wish to God it was impossible," answered Eleanor sadly. "But Father is so — so intolerant of people who aren't his sort, and Jack isn't his sort at all. I don't know anything about Jack's financial affairs — it isn't my business, and I wouldn't understand them anyway — but I do know what Father told him when we were engaged."

"And what was that?" almost whispered Sir Montagu. He was getting very warm.

"He settled a lot on me, but he absolutely refused to let Jack have a penny except through me. It was horribly unfair," she added, her eyes shining with generous, maternal anger.

Sir Montagu whistled softly. "That explains everything," he said in a meditative tone. "No wonder poor Crawford is worried. Eleven thousand is no joke."

"Eleven thousand?" Eleanor went pale.

"I'm afraid that was the amount of his indebtedness when he left the regiment."

"You've been spying on him." Her tea-cup rattled in its saucer as her hand trembled.

Sir Montagu shook his head with a sort of Christian forgiveness. "I've given him a very good job. I was entitled to find out what his financial position was."

"And still you gave him the job, after you found out that he was eleven thousand in debt?"

"I liked him and I admired him," was the simple, dignified reply.

Eleanor was completely disarmed. She stretched her arm across the table and let her hand rest for a moment on his sleeve.

"I'm sorry," she said.

There was a small silence. Sir Montagu knew the immense value of these small silences, if allowed to fall at exactly the right moment over a *tête-à-tête*. The air was full of the song of blackbirds and a general atmosphere of noble sentiments and sympathetic generosity.

"You are going to let me pay them off," stated Sir Montagu at last in a tone of quiet, uncontradictable assurance.

Eleanor's eyes filled with tears, and she was about to protest against such magnanimity when the benevolent goblin went on: "I insist upon paying them off, partly from the business point of view — I cannot have my most promising recruit harried by a miserable eleven thousand pounds — and partly as a friend. At least, I hope I am your friend. Will you do this for me? Will you let me?"

Eleanor was overwhelmed. "Will you wait till Jack comes back?" she stammered.

"Will you, you yourself, quite apart from your husband, allow me to pay them off?" countered the baronet, summoning up all his powers of hypnotic mastery.

Eleanor gazed at him for a second and then said, "I cannot answer for my husband, but for myself I accept your most generous——"

"Good," cried the little financier, smacking his hands together. "Then that's settled. And I will answer for your husband. And now let's talk of other things. How is your small and vivacious sister?"

Although she vaguely resented for a moment the double implication that this man could interfere unasked in their private affairs and could so confidently predict that her husband would meekly accept the interference, Eleanor had not got it in her to be angry for more than a few moments, and she was soon chattering away about Veronica's campaign, about the ejection of the colossal Freiherr from Partington Crescent, about her father's sudden and inexplicable access of cheerfulness, about Ruth Collins' sudden friendship with Harry Winter, and such like trivialities.

Fortunately, Sir Montagu was one of those rare men who can take as great an interest, or at least can appear to take as great an interest, in trivialities as in major events, and he listened intently to all the chatter and even asked a number of questions. He seemed to be particularly interested in Mr Hanson's insistence upon von Czepan-Eichenhöh's departure.

"We could none of us explain it," said Eleanor. "He just said he would have no visitors in the house for at least six months. It isn't as if he was cross about anything. He is as happy as a sandboy. Goes about rubbing his hands all the time and raising all the servants' wages."

"Does he ever go to the City nowadays?"

"Never. He used to have some Board meeting or other — something quite formal — on alternate Tuesdays, but Mother says he's dropped even that nowadays."

Sir Montagu became very thoughtful at this harmless piece of news, and the conversation flagged for a moment or two. Then he enquired, "And so the good Wendelmann has suddenly stopped coming to the house."

Eleanor laughed gaily. "Yes. Veronica was furious with him. And you don't know what Veronica's like when she's furious. A little fiend."

"But why was she angry with poor old Wendelmann?"

"It's typical of Veronica. She jumps to the most outrageous conclusions. You see, the last time Mr Wendelmann came, Daddy talked to him for about an hour and then he kicked Veronica's German out of the house without a single reason and has been as pleased as Punch ever since. So of course Veronica goes about swearing that Mr Wendelmann told Daddy something about her precious Manfred, and she's livid with rage."

"How unreasonable of her," murmured Sir Montagu absently.

"Yes, isn't it absurd?"

"Just because Wendelmann happened to be there the same day."

"Yes, and apparently all that Mr Wendelmann was trying to do was to persuade Daddy to go out and about a bit more. Veronica heard him herself."

"Go out and about a bit more?" said Sir Montagu thoughtfully.

"Yes. Something like that." Eleanor laughed gaily. "Can you see Daddy in a white topper going to Ascot?" Sir Montagu joined in the laughter but he made no reply. His mind was moving, as it always did, at a great rate.

At last he said, "And Wendelmann hasn't been back since?"

"According to Veronica, he hasn't. And she's been looking out for him. She's a little hell-cat sometimes. We used to have the most terrible fights when we were kids."

"And I'm sure she always won."

Eleanor gave an indignant cry. "Sir Montagu! How can you be ungallant! I'm every bit as strong as she is."

"You mistake me," he answered softly. "I meant that you have far too fine a nature to want to fight with anyone. You are all for peace and friendship."

"I hate rows, certainly."

"This place is a perfect setting for you, Mrs Crawford. Peace and loveliness for a peaceful and lovely person."

Eleanor blushed a little and looked down. It was very wrong of Sir Montagu to say such things, and still worse of her to make no protest. But Jack had never said such a thing in his life to her, and it did sound rather nice. However, she concentrated upon the political rather than upon the physical epithet. "I think Peace is the only thing, don't you? I hate War. You don't think there is going to be another war for years and years do you, Sir Montagu?"

"Please God, no," he replied, with a faint upward glance that seemed to recognize the existence of a Deity that was ready to be pleased at the recognition. "And when we get Perdurite going, it will make war less likely than ever."

"All I want," said Eleanor, "is to be allowed to live here for the rest of my life with Jack."

"And bring up a nice large family, eh?" And he smiled his enormous smile.

"Well, Mrs Crawford, you've certainly got the ideal place for a peaceful family life," he went on, getting up to go. "Perhaps you'll do me the honour of dining with me one day in London?" Eleanor was unwilling to leave the country house that jack had so thoughtfully provided her with, was not anxious to dine out alone with a comparative stranger within a few weeks of her marriage, and, charitable soul though she was, could not entirely dismiss from her mind the rumours which she had heard about Sir Montagu's moral character. Nevertheless, she felt that she could not entirely rebuff a man who had just made her husband a present of eleven thousand pounds, and she agreed to meet the diminutive benefactor at the new restaurant off Charles Street, St. James's, on the following day. "We can start with a cocktail there," said Sir Montagu, "and go on to dinner somewhere."

.....

Throughout the drive back to London in his pale-green and silver Rolls-Royce, Sir Montagu's leonine head reposed upon his chest. A telegram, despatched from Guildford, brought Mr Andrew Hay round to his house to meet him, and the two men discussed the position for nearly an hour. In the end they resolved to assume that the certainty of James Hanson's active return to business had not yet been proved, and to take no immediate and hasty action in the meantime but to keep their eyes skinned. The two men also decided that it would be just as well not to make any mention of the whole affair to General Springton or to any of the naval or military gentlemen on the Board of Perdurite.

"It will only confuse their minds," said the Chairman with the faintest suspicion of a wink.

"Exactly," replied his legal adviser with that portentous gravity which is always recognized as the equivalent, in a Lowland Scotsman, of a burst of rocketing laughter.

CHAPTER XXIII

Herr Stanislas Negresco-Waldemar

At the time that the foundation-stone of the first Perdurite factory was being laid, near Southampton, Britain was enjoying the vast wave of prosperity which had been guaranteed by the election for the third time running of the Patriotic Government. This Government, with a parliamentary strength of four hundred and eighty members, of whom four hundred and seventyeight were gentlemen and two were ladies, was supported by all the right-thinking elements of the three Parties. This made for its extraordinary national strength and popularity, for it is an obvious truism that if the supporters of a Government are all the right-thinking people, the opponents must be all the wrong-thinking people. As indeed in this case they were.

The Patriotic Government faced its third term of office with the confidence that is born of a long spell of successful achievement. Unemployment had been reduced in ten years from the outrageous figure of two millions and a half — the legacy of the unhappy past — to the altogether reasonable and stable figure of two millions and a quarter, and the drift of industry from the derelict North to the warm South had been checked by an impassioned appeal from the Prime Minister which went direct to the hearts of the big industrialists. Sir Montagu Anderton-Mawle, MP, had almost broken down with emotion as he listened to it — for, after all, had not the foundations of his third, and so far greatest, fortune been laid in the cotton areas of Lancashire?— and there is not the slightest doubt whatever that, in response to that appeal, he would have planted his chain of Perdurite factories in the North of England if he had not been sorrowfully compelled to admit that the Perdurite case was somewhat different from the others, a conclusion to which all the rest of the big industrialists sadly arrived about their own industries.

But it is impossible to describe all the many achievements of the Patriotic Party. Several slums had been swept away in one or two cities. Education, so dear to the hearts of all Patriots, had been given a tremendous fillip, indeed almost a revolutionary fillip, by an Act of Parliament which made it compulsory for the children of the poor to remain at school until the age of fifteen, and which added a statesmanlike proviso that no child of the poor need remain at school after the age of fourteen unless it wanted to; and the health of the poor had been assured for ever by the simple device of raising the price of milk.

As a consequence of these far-seeing measures, with their rippling repercussions into every nook and cranny of British social life, there had never been so many Rolls-Royce cars in Piccadilly, never such a boom in the theatrical world, never such prosperity among the restaurants. From the top of Sloane Street, in Knightsbridge, to Piccadilly there was hardly a single beggar to be seen, except a few choirs of unemployed Welsh miners, and foreigners revisiting London after a period of years were astounded at the internal prosperity which had been induced by the Patriotic Government. In external affairs things were equally happy. At peace with the entire world, Britain was universally loved and respected by all the less fortunate nations, and, in order to preserve this universal respect, and to guarantee our shores against all those less fortunate nations which viewed us and our prosperity with ill-concealed jealousy and chagrin, the Government was very rightly undertaking a vast scheme of Rearmament.

Everyone was talking Rearmament and thinking Rearmament. The dust of the big scrimmage was beginning to arise, and the stockholders were darting in and out, like skirmishers on the fringe of a battle, and the armament shares were soaring, and fortunes were being made in a day, and occasionally a pacifist agitator would be put into prison for protesting against it all, and the newspapers descanted almost daily upon the colossal strength of old John Bull and how every foreigner loved and admired him, and the clang of hammer upon metal was heard from Glasgow to Sheerness and from Tyneside to Milford Haven, and everyone was happy.

It was into this golden world of opportunity that Sir Montagu Anderton-Mawle launched Perdurite. Never was there such a chance. Everyone wanted hard metal, and everyone had good, solid, Government money to pay for it, and the steel industry had not yet turned over in its long sleep. By the time the steel magnates had woken up, and had found that there was a vast demand for hard metal, and had found that their own processes were fifteen years out of date and that their entire industry was in a muddle—— "By that time" reflected the little Tasmanian as he rubbed his hands in the solitude of his huge dining-room, "we shall be there."

The only cloud upon the horizon was James Hanson. If he returned to battle, Sir Montagu would have to be very, very careful. For the key to the whole situation lay in the gloxite mines in the rugged hills and valleys of Cimbria, and James Hanson had once been a power in that primitive land.

And the position was additionally complicated by the fact that Cimbria was no longer such a primitive land as it had been in Hanson's early days. For it was now part, of course, of the great, progressive, and enlightened kingdom of Cimbro-Suevonia. And, just as the gloxite mines were the key to Perdurite, and just as Hanson might at any moment become the key to Cimbria, so was the kingdom of Cimbro-Suevonia the key to the whole European situation.

It is necessary to examine the causes, briefly, why this was so.

.....

The kingdom of Cimbro-Suevonia was basking happily under the rule of a benevolent Dictator. The King himself, descended by a variety of devious routes from Romulus (some even went further and said from Anchises through Aeneas), mostly via such noble courts as those of Coburg, Hesse-Cassel, Darmstadt, Pless, Teck, Weimar, Trier, Mainz, and Coblenz, had inherited the charm and the nose of the Caesars, but none of their energy. He was perfectly content to live quietly in the vast baroque palace in his capital Stz, called in earlier and less happy days La Nueva Ragusa, having been founded in 1306 by that romantic City of Argosies, and in the summer to retire to the mountain chalet at Brkòvdúktz, formerly L'Hospital de Nuestra Señora, and to leave the guidance of affairs to his energetic, brilliant, and benign Chief of State, Herr Stanislas Negresco-Waldemar.

Herr Waldemar was one of the most extraordinary figures in Europe. He had raised himself by sheer willpower, intellect, and personal charm from a humble position on a Chicago newspaper to the dictatorship of the most powerful of the newer States of Europe. Indeed, so amazing was the career of this modern Napoleon, and so astonishing his personal attainments, that the story of his life might be compared, and very often was compared in the cheaper journals, to a Romance of Fiction.

Born in a peasant district of Old Suevonia in 1886, young Stanislas soon showed such a spirited nature and such an untameable will that he was expelled at the age of seventeen from the country and was forced to seek refuge in Geneva. There he ran messages for the hall-porters of the big hotels with such speed and discretion that he was speedily offered, and accepted, a post in the Distribution Centre of the dope traffic which then, as now, had its headquarters in the city of Calvin. Stanislas rapidly acquired such a reputation as an efficient distributor of cocaine that the

Authorities repeatedly pressed him to apply for Swiss citizenship, and Lenin actually went so far as to cut him dead outside the Café Lyrique. Even in those days Lenin's austerity was being carried to such lengths that it was positively becoming a byword, and to be cut dead by him outside the Café Lyrique, or anywhere else for that matter, was almost a distinction. But however strongly and however flatteringly the good Swiss burghers pressed this brilliant young salesman to disregard the cranky Russian ascetic who actually disapproved of the cocaine business, and to become a Helvetian, there was always some mysterious inner prompting which made Stanislas Waldemar hold back. "Suevonia will have need of you, Suevonia will have need of you," the inner voice kept on saying, and the wisdom of the inner voice was amply confirmed when the mean-fisted Swiss burghers flatly turned down young Waldemar's suggestion that the patent of Swiss citizenship should be accompanied by an honorarium of ten thousand Swiss francs, as some small consolation for the sacrifice of Suevonian citizenship. But it is impossible to keep a brilliant man in perpetual submission, and Herr Waldemar rose resiliently superior to Lenin's ill manners, to the avarice of the Helvetian Confederation, and even to the terrible moment in the Brasserie Lindholt when he was mistaken for a local pimp by Trotsky.

Kind Fortune was watching over his destinies. A stupid Genevese watchmaker near the Hotel des Bergues allowed his shop to be burgled one night, and Stanislas Waldemar was on board an America-bound steamer in Genoa harbour before any of the dull, Calvinistic *gendarmerie* of Geneva had connected the burglary with the capable young cocaine-pedlar.

In America young Stanislas automatically became a crime reporter on the *Chicago Tribune*, and his series of articles on the drug traffic brought him an advance in salary, a considerable amount of notoriety, and a bonus of ten thousand dollars from the Drug Ring, of which the mayor of the city was the Patron and Visitor, on the understanding that he did not do it again. (Those were the days before the Sicilians and Neapolitans showed America that it was simpler, cheaper, and very much safer to shoot than to bribe.)

In Chicago he quickly became an influential member of the Suevonian Revolutionary Brotherhood, a society which existed to encourage political assassination in the Mother Country, and it was Brother Waldemar who first pointed out to the Inner Ring of the S.R.B., at their secret meeting-place in the Loop, that it would be far more economical to enthuse the patriots of Suevonia with pamphlets rather than with large gifts of dollars. And when the Chicago police finally were goaded into taking action against some of the more virulent of the European secret societies in their midst, it was Waldemar's almost uncanny sense of realism that made him understand, before any other member of the Brotherhood, that the game was up and that the only sensible course for a realist to adopt was to say "Kismet," to throw up the sponge, and to assist the police in the liquidation of the whole sorry business.

The fifteen thousand dollars which the Police Commissioner handed to him in recognition of his realistic common-sense enabled Waldemar to slip away to Philadelphia under a modestly assumed alias, without having to go through the painful formality of explaining to the survivors of the Brotherhood just how they had fallen short in that sphere of realism which is so essential for civic success in a great modern, bustling city like Chicago.

The European War — subsequently to become the World War — broke out while Waldemar was in Philadelphia, and he instantly responded to the eternal call of Patriotism. He threw up his job, an extremely pleasant and lucrative one in the very trade, by an odd coincidence, that Trotsky had mistakenly ascribed to him in the Genevese days, and flung himself wholeheartedly into the task of exhorting Suevonians to return to the Dear Old Country and enlist in the War that was to establish the reign of law and order for ever. For this purpose he collected funds from wealthy compatriots and founded a newspaper, which he edited himself, called *Advance, Suevonia!*

It might be said against Stanislas Waldemar, indeed in those early days it was said quite often by ignorant or malicious persons, that he did not show any great enthusiasm to return home and take up arms himself beside Noble Britain, Freedom-loving France, Gallant Little Belgium, Heroic Little Servia, and the rest of the Allies. But those who launched these petty insinuations did not take into account two essential factors. The first was that Waldemar, though longing to take his place, bayonet in hand and sword on hip, in the front-line trenches or even further forward than that, nevertheless restrained himself by the certain knowledge that whereas anyone can draw a sword, few can found and edit an *Advance, Suevonia!*

And secondly, those who allege that Stanislas Waldemar lowered himself to the level of the English squires and magistrates and landed proprietors who so eagerly persuaded others to go and die for them, make no allowance for the Suevonian Dictator's kindness of heart. The sight of blood, the sound of cannon, the feel of white-hot jagged bits of iron, were so repugnant to that humanitarian soul, that he could not bring himself to endure the agony of seeing, hearing, and feeling them.

Those are the true reasons why Stanislas Waldemar, Dictator of Cimbro-Suevonia, did not achieve the same war record as his brother dictators, Herr Hitler and Signor Mussolini. Men of tougher, or perhaps it would be more accurate to say coarser, fibre than he, the Führer and the Duce were able to sustain the long years of trench warfare, were able to lead innumerable forlorn hopes, were able to perform those dazzling series of exploits with which their biographers have acquainted the whole of the astounded world. Waldemar's contribution to the triumph of freedom was less spectacular, but perhaps even more effective, and, on the downfall of the Central Empires, there was no Suevonian whose name stood higher, if not throughout the whole world, at any rate in Philadelphia. Nor is it entirely fair to suggest that his prominence was only due to the fact that the Suevonian troops had consistently run away throughout the War, and that, in consequence, no Suevonian general or admiral had made a name for himself for anything except the conduct of quick retrograde movements.

At any rate the unassailable truth remains that, after the post-War discontent of 1919 and the spasmodic Bolshevik risings of 1920 had fizzled out and the country was returning to its normal mode of life, it was to Stanislas Negresco-Waldemar that the big industrialists turned when they saw that at last the country could be made safe for the People by the triumph of Industrialism.

The directors of the Suevonian Metallurgical Corporation, which had bought up the Suevonian properties of Messrs. Hanson, Wendelmann & Co. Ltd., took a prominent part in financing the *coup d'état*, and everything went smoothly according to plan. The industrialists hired a large number of unemployed, dressed them in smart new yellow jumpers, and sent them off to march on Stz, the capital. A few days later Waldemar arrived by Rolls-Royce from Switzerland, where he had been waiting for the signal, and took control of the Government. His first act was to summon the foreign correspondents and describe to them, modestly but nevertheless picturesquely, the severe wounds which he had received at the battle of the Marne as a poilu, incognito of course, in the French Foreign Legion, and the part he had subsequently taken in bringing America into the War on the side of the Allies. He then touched lightly upon the March of the Yellow jumpers on Stz, which he had led on foot all the way, and compared it to Mussolini's march on Rome and Napoleon's return from Elba, and finally dismissed the foreign correspondents with a brief eulogy of the noble profession of which he was proud to think that he too was a humble member.

On the following day Herr Waldemar went in solemn state to the Cathedral of St. Euschemon and swore the customary oath to maintain the Constitution, and in the afternoon he dissolved Parliament, imprisoned all the members of the Opposition, confiscated all the Press, shot all the leaders of the Trades Unions, exiled all professors, painters, musicians, and poets, and issued orders that all trains containing first-class carriages, which might therefore possibly contain tourists, must run punctually up to time. He then settled down to the exercise of a benevolent autocracy which hoisted Suevonia to a high pinnacle of prosperity, which made the regime of the Yellow jumper the envy of the incompetent democracies of western Europe and North America, and which raised the national self-respect of the Cimbro-Suevonians to such a prodigious height that it almost defeated its own end. Herr Waldemar certainly wished to persuade his compatriots to think well of themselves, but he had never contemplated the possibility of succeeding to the extent of making them esteem themselves to be invincible soldiers. Having attained this unexpected and sensational result, Herr Waldemar had spent twelve or fourteen years in scrutinizing the maps of Europe, Asia, and Africa to find an adversary on whom his Yellow jumpers might prove the truth of their opinion of themselves. So far he had not found one.

For the rest, Herr Waldemar was the idol of the middle-class homes of Britain and of the boarding-houses and hotels of the Suevonian Riviera. The secret visit of a famous Harley Street specialist had squared and extruded the Dictatorial jaw by a skilful operation, and a photograph of that virile countenance adorned the bedroom walls and dressing-tables of countless bourgeois maidens all over Europe, except in Spain, where the photographs of strange caballeros are not encouraged, even among the bourgeois. Even sceptical males, not so easily swept off their feet by square, extruded jaws, were forced to admit not only the strange new punctuality of the Suevonian trains but also the heroic feats on the Marne. And just as the outline of the jaw had altered somewhat with the passage of the years, and of the specialist, so also had the saga of the marshes of St. Gond. The exploits were more clearly drawn, the decorations for valour had grown more numerous, and the simple poilu had become, in accordance with the law which governs the previous military career of all Dictators since 1799, a Corporal.

It was, of course, inevitable that the epic of the Corporal of the Marne should, like the epic of Corporal Hitler of a thousand battles, and of Corporal Mussolini of a thousand battles, be compared in men's eyes, and even more in women's eyes, with the Little Corporal. It was not Stanislas Waldemar's fault that people called him napoleonic. He knew that he was napoleonic. But he did not arrogate to himself, any more than the other two Corporals had done, the magnificent adjective. It was forced upon him by the National Press. Waldemar knew perfectly well that the Corsican had done nothing which he himself could not do, except the dull routine business of winning some battles. But it was not for him to say so. If the world called him napoleonic, that was the world's affair. He himself would go on expending such small talents and energy as he possessed, in the beneficent government of Cimbro-Suevonia. He had found a poverty-stricken, miserable, groaning country. He had transformed it into a smiling, happy land. There was not a single groan to be heard from end to end of it, and the mere appearance of an official in a Yellow Jumper was the signal for gay laughter and the hanging out of flags.

If only Herr Waldemar could lay his hand upon an enemy who could be relied upon not to drive the Cimbro-Suevonian army into the sea within a fortnight of the outbreak of hostilities, his cup of happiness would be full. But he could find no such enemy, with the possible exception of the negro republic of Liberia on the west coast of Africa. And even there, maddeningly, there were difficulties. Liberia was a very long way from Cimbro-Suevonia; a war to civilize the Liberians would be a costly affair, and Herr Waldemar was a little hazy about the financial state of his country; the Firestone Rubber Company of the United States had extensive commitments in Liberia, and it might be awkward if they kicked up rough; and, most important of all, the Cimbro-Suevonians had got into the ineradicable habit of associating all negroes with the name of Jack Johnson, the former heavy-weight boxing champion of the world, and it was doubtful if their newly found self-confidence would carry them to the pitch of attacking a country populated entirely by negroes, even if they had been previously assured, by an intensive course of propaganda, that these particular black men were not really very handy with their fists and would certainly run at a great rate into the primaeval jungle at the first approach of an armed white man.

Reluctantly Herr Waldemar drew his pencil through the name Liberia, and resumed his forlorn study of the map of the world.

.....

And all the while Cimbro-Suevonia lay basking in the sun of fame and prosperity. She attracted vast numbers of tourists to her golden shores and her classical ruins; she had no unemployment (and naturally paid no attention to the whining sociologists of less fortunate countries when they maliciously alleged that a standing army of two million men was the equivalent of two million unemployed); and if she had not been granted the Permanent Seat on the Council of the League of Nations to which her prestige certainly entitled her, she had at least been elected to the next best thing, the tenure of a Temporary Seat in perpetuity.

This, then, was the potentially powerful force which lay athwart south-eastern Europe. Its standing army mustered a million men. It is true that the fighting quality of the men was doubtful, but their spirits were kept up by incessant parades of tanks, by incessant demonstrations of massed aeroplanes, and by incessant fiery speeches of Herr Negresco-Waldemar in which especial stress was invariably laid upon the heavenly and ecstatic beauty of being torn to pieces by red-hot metal on behalf of one's country. The Suevonian Navy, too, was heavily armed with the latest cruisers and destroyers and submarines. And although but few of these had ever been out of sight of the dear Fatherland for more than several minutes at a time, especially the submarines, and therefore their fleet-manoeuvring capacities had never been fully tested, nevertheless the known capabilities of the vessels were enough to make any German admiral's mouth water when he considered them, and any British admiral's knees shake.

Indeed German generals, as well as German admirals, cast envious eyes at Cimbro-Suevonian armaments, and in consequence, German diplomats strained every clumsy nerve to bring Herr Negresco-Waldemar within the orbit of Pan-Germanism. French diplomacy, never behindhand, and wielding its Ferrara blade with all its ancient Gallic swiftness and fire, strained every nerve to bring the Dictator into the web of the Quai d'Orsay. Italian diplomacy alternately fawned upon the third of the three famous modern Corporals and alternately published illustrated memoranda to prove that he, and all Cimbro-Suevonians, were barbarous savages who habitually poisoned their grandfathers with strychnine and shot their grandmothers with dum-dum bullets that were supplied to them — one packet with each ton of Welsh anthracite — free of charge by perfidious John Bull.

As a result of this triple diplomatic intrigue, Herr Waldemar was in clover. He could easily evade the bull-like rushes of the Wilhelmstrasse, and he found it child's play to juggle the Roman bombast against the Ferrara blade of the Quai d'Orsay, which, like all French diplomacy, invariably whizzed and flashed and darted in the wrong direction.

But although Herr Waldemar went on juggling with all the typical legerdemain an ex-crime-reporter of the *Chicago Tribune*, he could not prevent his country from gradually ascending in critical importance until it ousted Jugoslavia from the proud position of the keystone of the European arch. Not one of the three great competing Powers could afford to let either of the other two get a predominating foothold in Cimbro-Suevonia, and the tension had steadily grown and grown until it was no exaggeration to say that the killing on a frontier of a Cimbro-Suevonian chicken might easily plunge the whole world into a third Armageddon.

It was into this exquisite adjustment of diplomacy, finesse, delicate balancings, and beautiful crystal-clear thought, and subtle move and counter-move, plot, subplot, counter-plot, and marplot, that the young English inventor whose name flitted evanescently across the stage like a dim ghost, and is now for ever forgotten, dropped his terrible discovery, that an alloy of gloxite and iron and zinc would make the lightest and hardest metal known to the world.

CHAPTER XXIV

The Goblin's Plan at the Chichester House Hotel

The dinner-party for two which began with cocktails at the new restaurant off Charles Street, St. James's, was not a great success from Eleanor's point of view. From Sir Montagu's it could not have possibly gone off better. For urgent affairs of the Company made it necessary for the Chairman to recall his travelling emissary secretly from the Continent by aeroplane that very morning, and the Tasmanian's enormous Rolls-Royce met him at Croydon and drove him straight to the house in Cleveland Place where Anderton-Mawle was waiting for him. The financier-psychologist was in his subtlest and most patient form. He listened for three-quarters of an hour to Crawford's description of the insuperable obstacles which he had met — and surmounted — on his recent trip; of the prickly damned dagos whom he had so tactfully smoothed down; of the success he had been at the dinner-tables. And when the big, blond ex-soldier had at last exhausted the list of his triumphs, and had, in his turn, listened with an urbane tolerance to five minutes of unstinted praise from his Chairman, the latter at last was able to get to the point.

"Listen, my boy," he said. "I've got a very tricky job for you this evening so tricky in fact that you're just about the only man who could deal with it." Crawford twisted his silky moustache and gazed into the middle-distance. Anderton-Mawle saw the expression, and his small toes wriggled round inside his diminutive patent-leather, suede-topped, shiny-buttoned boots. However, he went on quickly.

"I've got a report that Hanson's secretary——"

"I know her," said Crawford, committing one of the unforgivable sins against his employer and interrupting him. "Damned nice girl. I knew her. I once thought of knowing her a bit better. In the biblical sense, if you see what I mean," he added.

Anderton-Mawle thought savagely, "Or the sense of my acquaintance with your wife in a week or two."

"Quite so," he proceeded. "As I was saying, Hanson's secretary has become very friendly all of a sudden with a certain Harry Winter whose sister was, I understand, once a friend of yours."

"And who did you understand that from, if I may ask?" enquired Crawford coolly.

"From the lady's husband, who is now employed on the staff of one of my newspapers."

Crawford smiled as one man of the world to another. "If you got it from young Norman Everard," he said negligently, "you'll probably understand that to say she was a friend of mine is — er — somewhat of an understatement."

"Quite so," replied Anderton with no answering smile. "Can you get hold of her tonight and take her out to dinner? I know it's short notice——"

"Eight hours, my dear Anderton-Mawle?" said Crawford, shooting his left cuff off his diamond, saddle-shaped watch, "I don't call that so very short. She'll come."

"And if you find any difficulty," muttered the ugly little man, with black fury in his soul at the twin torturing thoughts that the puppy was damnably self-confident, and that the puppy probably had every reason to be so, "you might suggest as an inducement that you might have some news which would interest her brother. It might be an ace of trumps."

"Good idea," said Crawford, stifling a yawn. "But there'll be no difficulty."

"And by the way," said Anderton-Mawle, "not a word to anyone else of your return to London. You haven't told anyone, have you?"

"Not a soul."

"Oh, come, Crawford," cried the little baronet, wagging a finger up at him — the interview was over and both men were standing up— "not even your lovely wife?"

The other stared down in surprise. "Good Lord, no!" he said, and went off to get in touch with Helen Everard on the telephone.

Helen was in some doubt at first whether to accept the invitation to appear in public with her former lover, and greatly to Jack Crawford's annoyance she asked him to hold the line while she consulted ostensibly her engagement-book, but actually her brother, who was at the flat at the time. But Harry Winter decided for her by unconsciously playing Sir Montagu's ace of trumps for him.

"I think you ought to go, Nellie," he said earnestly. "After all, Jack's in the Mawle camp and we're paid by Hanson. It's our duty to get all the information we can about the other side. I know the man's a bloody swine——"

"All right, I'll go," she said at once, and she accepted and hung up the receiver.

"What an extraordinary girl you are!" exclaimed Harry.

"Why, what's the matter now? Haven't I done what you wanted me to?"

"Yes, but when I was telling you what I thought you ought to do, you had a sort of reluctant look in your eyes. And the moment I called him a bloody swine, you perked up no end and accepted at once."

It was Helen's turn to look astonished.

"But, my sweet child, isn't that perfectly obvious?"

"No, I'm damned if it is."

"But surely — well, when you called him a bloody swine it reminded me of those days in Mahableshwar——"

"When he was a super-bloody swine!"

"Well, yes."

"Damnation!" cried Winter irritably. "I still don't see it."

"He wasn't always so bloody at Mahableshwar, you know," she said softly.

"And that's why you're going out with him tonight?"

She nodded demurely.

"And you expect me to see all that train of thought in a moment?" he cried.

"Oh, Harry darling, is that a train of thought? I am so glad. I didn't know that women ever had enough consecutive thoughts to make a train."

"Oh, God!" exclaimed her brother, clapping his hands to his forehead and sitting down in an easy-chair.

.....

Every move in the evening's programme went exactly according to the little goblin's plan. Crawford, having arrived at the Chichester House Hotel with his instructions to probe carefully and subtly into the possible connection of the Winter brother and sister with old Hanson and to collect and store in his memory every scrap of information, forgot his instructions as early in the evening as the middle of the *homard à l'armoricaine*, and began to make love to Helen with all his irresistible fire and dash. He brought all his batteries into action one after another. Beginning with a perfunctory sighting shot, which always consisted of the phrase, "How beautiful you are looking tonight, Helen! You really are the most beautiful woman in the world," he went straight on to a description of his work and travels on behalf of his new employers. He described his meetings with the uncrowned heads of Europe, the great armament-makers of France and Germany and Czecho-Slovakia, and told her the general gist of what they had said to him, and repeated word for word what he had said to them. He touched lightly on his sorrow at leaving the Army, and his sense of loss whenever he talked to a man who did not stand rigidly to attention "with the thumb in line with the seam of the trouser," and how he missed the gay chatter of the officers' mess over the pink gin after Morning Stables. But he also was at pains to point out the compensations of the new life.

"After all," he said, as he looked critically at the label on the champagne-bottle which the wine-waiter extended to him, and nodded in a way that suggested that the wine-waiter had only escaped a severe reprimand by the skin of his teeth, "in the Army days I was only running a regiment for the colonel, or perhaps a brigade when the brigadier had the sense to come and have a talk and ask my advice. But in this new job, after all, I am helping to run the world. And that's something, after all." Looking up from his partridge for a moment, he saw that Helen was on the point of saying something, so he hastily went on with the preparatory groundwork of his love-making by describing the part he had played in the choice of plans of the new Perdurite offices which were being built near Westminster Abbey, and by suggesting delicately that he and Mawle and Hay were the three people who counted. This lasted until his plate was removed and he could put his elbows on the table and gaze into Helen's brown eyes with his all-devastating blue ones.

"Do you remember what I said to you just before I got married?" he began in a soft voice that was designed to show that the skirmishing was over and that the serious attack was about to be launched.

Helen Everard, trying very hard not to laugh, lowered her eyes modestly and said, "No. What was it?"

"I can see that you do," said Crawford with a light laugh. "You always did find it difficult to hide things from me, didn't you, darling? But seriously, don't you think it would be a wonderful thing if we — if we came together again? Just as we were in the old days. I was a good lover, wasn't I, sweetheart?"

Helen suddenly lost her inclination to laugh. She nodded.

"And I would be a better lover than ever now, because I love you so much more now than I did then."

"Didn't you love me in the old days, Jack?"

"Of course I did. But not so much as I do now."

"I wonder why."

Jack Crawford pondered and finally decided to offer no solution. He changed the subject.

"You're very lovely, Helen. And terribly alluring. There never was a woman so alluring as you are."

But Helen was not to be put off. She gazed at him as if he was a problem-picture which she was trying to understand.

"But why do you love me more than you did six years ago?"

Crawford suppressed his annoyance and started to ponder again. At last he said, "It must be because I've missed you so badly all these years." It did not sound very convincing, but it was the best he could do. To his surprise and relief, Helen seemed to accept it, for she replied after a moment, "Yes. I suppose that must be it."

"Yes, of course, that's it," he clinched the matter eagerly. "I've missed you terribly. I've been horribly lonely without you, Helen. Life without you is damnably dull. It's all — it's all sort of lonely. And dull," he added.

"Why not go away for another six years?" she suggested. "You might come back really in love with me then."

He seized the opportunity. "But I am really in love with you now, darling. Don't you believe me? What can I do to make you believe me? I'm crazy about you. I've never been crazy about anyone in my life before."

This was too much even for Helen to pass. Her momentary sadness at the sudden conjuring-up of old memories and happy days vanished, and the temptation to giggle returned. Luckily she remembered that she was drawing a salary from James Hanson and that it was part of her job to get news for her employer. By dropping her hands into her lap, and digging a long, scarlet finger-nail of one hand into the palm of the other under cover of the table-cloth, she managed to keep a serious face. But she could not help exclaiming, at this last statement, "Oh, I say, Jack!"

Crawford's handsome face assumed a look of intense seriousness as he leaned forward and said, "It's true. I swear it. I've often said that before to women — after all, it's part of the game——"

"Part of the routine," she murmured.

"Yes, exactly," he replied simply. "And I expect I've often thought it was true. You know, deluded myself into thinking it was true. But I know that I was wrong. Because I feel quite differently towards you from anything I've ever felt before."

"And what do you feel, Jack?"

"I can't describe it. I feel — oh! it's just one of those things you can't put into words. But it's just that I'm crazy about you."

Again, to Crawford's surprise, this explanation was accepted, and his spirits rose. This weak absence of critical enquiry, and the refusal to score nasty dialectical points, could only mean one thing. It always meant one thing. The girl was falling under the magic spell and would believe anything she was told because she was so anxious to believe it. He called for an 1868 liqueur brandy for himself and a "sticky liqueur for Madame, you know the sort of thing" — he and the wine-waiter exchanged amused smiles which covered the whole range of the feminine palate for wines — and went on, moving easily from the key of intense seriousness to the key of schoolboyish appeal.

"You do like me, sweetheart, just a little? Say you like me. Say you don't think I'm a brute for making love to you like this" — he amended the slip hastily — "for being in love with you like this. After all, it's not my fault that I'm in love with you. It never is anyone's fault."

"Then why should I think you're a brute, Jack?" Helen asked innocently.

Crawford started to explain, stopped, and then went off elliptically.

"I wish to God I had married you instead. I would have. You know that, don't you? But I had to marry money. Listen, sweetheart. I've got money now. Not much, but enough. More than I've ever had before. And if only my god-damned old father-in-law would pay off my debts, everything would be perfect."

"Hasn't he paid them?" Helen was genuinely surprised.

"No, blast him. But he's got to. I'll find a way of making him. Dammit, what does he suppose I married Eleanor for? She's a nice girl, couldn't be nicer. But nobody can say she's a world-beater, either for looks or for anything else. I'm tremendously fond of her, mind you, and nobody's ever going to hear me say a word against her. One goes into these things with one's eyes open, and one plays the game. But this is what I was going to say. I've got money now — a salary of my own, and, of course, my half-share in Eleanor's income — and I'm taking one of those new flats in Arlington Street. Eleanor is parked in the country, and everything is perfect."

"Perfect?" murmured Helen.

"Yes, for you and me, lovely one. Will you come and see me in my new flat sometimes? I want you so terribly badly, Helen. Will you? Say you will. Say you will, sweet one. Say you will live with me again, sweetheart, when I've got my new flat."

It was good generalship by which Sir Montagu Anderton-Mawle contrived to take Eleanor to the same restaurant that Crawford had taken Helen — a private secretary had followed Crawford and reported his movements by telephone — but it was the sheer good luck that so often attends upon good generals which brought him and Eleanor to Crawford's table at the precise moment when the ardent lover was, as it were, throwing in his Imperial Guard at the most critical point and pressing the attack home.

Crawford was so earnestly concentrated upon the matter in hand that he repeated his "Say you will live with me again, sweetheart" twice before he noticed vaguely that someone was standing by the table. Imagining the interrupter to be a waiter, he waved him away without looking up. But the hearty greeting of "Hullo, Crawford!" in the slightly Tasmanian accent of his Chief, brought him swiftly to earth. He looked up into the incredulous eyes of Eleanor.

.....

Crawford had designed to spend the first part of the night at the restaurant of the Chichester House Hotel, the second part of the night in Helen Everard's arms, and the remainder, if any, at the club. Only the first part of the programme went according to schedule. The second was compulsorily frustrated, and Crawford, like a wise tactician, voluntarily gave up the third, and went back with Eleanor to the spare-room at Partington Crescent. There had been a look in Eleanor's eyes, a look of pathetic bewilderment, and at the same time a look which contained a faint suggestion of the pugnacious spirit of her redoubtable father, which Crawford mentally decided must be smoothed out as quickly as possible. He at once, therefore, insisted on driving to the club and collecting his bag *en route* for South Kensington. For a few moments there was silence in the taxi. Crawford had been in difficult situations before, and he knew that the cardinal rule is not to open the discussion with a volunteered explanation. To begin with a defence is to invite an attack. There was also a faint possibility that no explanation or defence might be necessary. Eleanor was not a suspicious person. Indeed her simplicity had been one of her chief attractions for Crawford, for he had long ago resolved that if he ever had to marry, it would be essential to marry a wife who would believe anything.

It all depended on how long she had been standing with the damned little crook beside the table, and how much she had heard. If she had heard the last three sentences, not even Eleanor's simplicity would stand the strain. Crawford lay back in his corner of the taxi and tried very hard to remember exactly the words he had been using. There was just a chance that they might have been sufficiently ambiguous to be carried off with some vague explanation about business.

But this hope was extinguished by Eleanor's first words. Poor Eleanor had never been in this kind of situation before, and she had no notion of the required tactics. She too had huddled herself up into her corner of the cab and waited, miserably, for the explanation which she imagined her husband would immediately start to give her. But nothing happened. Neither explanation nor grovelling apology was forthcoming from the other corner, and Eleanor grew more and more miserable. Then suddenly her misery was turned into a cold anger. It was the very first occasion in her whole life that she had ever experienced cold anger, and she trembled violently. For Crawford was humming gaily to himself. His silence had not been due to shame, or to the difficulty of finding words in which to apologize. And he was not going to bother to invent an excuse. Instead, he hummed.

Eleanor looked straight in front of her and said in a small hard voice, "I didn't know you were taking a flat in London."

Crawford, though glad that Eleanor had abandoned her strong tactical position of silence and had advanced to battle, was nevertheless furious to discover that the worst had happened and that Eleanor had overheard a remark which could not possibly be carried off with an airy reference to business. His fury was divided into two sections, a moderate amount being directed at his own folly in having landed himself in such a mess, and a very large amount being directed at Eleanor for her damned stupidity in arriving at the table at the fatal instant.

He kept his temper, however. In situations of this kind it is fatal to lose one's temper except at the right moment. This moment needs to be very carefully chosen and usually comes towards the end of the discussion.

Crawford shrugged his shoulders slightly and replied casually, "I thought I'd told you."

"It wasn't me you told," said Eleanor. "It was your friend Mrs Everard. How pretty she is," she added icily. Crawford relapsed into silence. If Eleanor would only maintain the intensity of her anger, everything would be simple for him. The trouble would be if she became tearful too soon. He went on humming.

"I was sorry to interrupt," continued Eleanor, "before you got the answer to your question to Mrs Everard. I hope it will be a satisfactory answer when it does come."

"Sarcasm doesn't suit you, my dear," said Crawford coolly, pulling out his cigarette-case.

Eleanor shrank back into her corner as if she had been struck, and silence fell again and was unbroken until they reached Partington Crescent.

The rest of the family had gone to bed. Crawford snapped on electric lights and went into the dining-room for a whisky-and-soda. He felt that he had earned a whisky-and-soda after his emotional experiences of the evening, and also that a little stimulant would be of some help against the emotional experiences that were still to come. Eleanor followed him into the room. She waited till he had poured himself out the drink, had taken the first mouthful, and had put the glass down again.

Then she gazed up at his handsome face and said mournfully, "It's just some ghastly nightmare. Tell me that it isn't true. Tell me that I've made some idiotic mistake. Tell me that you were joking."

"I'll tell you anything you like," said Crawford, folding his arms and leaning back against the sideboard.

"I love you so terribly, Jack," she said despairingly. "Why did you do it?"

"I was only making conversation." It was his first acknowledgment that any explanation was necessary.

"Helen Everard is that sort of woman. She expects to be made love to by everyone."

"It makes me so cheap," she murmured. "'Six months married, and her husband already making love to other women.' That's what they'll be saying."

"It doesn't matter what they say."

"It matters what I think," she cried, with a return of spirit.

"Oh yes. Of course that matters," he agreed soothingly.

"You knew her in India, didn't you? Were you ever her lover?"

"Never," said Crawford smoothly.

"Yet you want to be her lover now." Eleanor looked like a small bewildered child.

"I tell you I was only making conversation." Crawford spoke a little irritably for the first time. What on earth was the use of a woman solemnly swearing to love, honour, and obey a husband if she began to doubt his word within six months of their marriage. He had told her twice that he was only making conversation to Helen Everard, and she still seemed to be doubting his word.

"You looked terribly earnest."

"My good woman, there's no earthly sense in pretending to make love, even to make conversation, if you don't act the part."

"Do you swear that's true, Jack?"

"Of course I do. I've said it over and over again. How many more times do you want me to repeat it?"

"It all seems so strange," said Eleanor forlornly. "Didn't you ever think of me when you were making — making conversation to that woman?"

"Of course I think of you all the time."

"Didn't you feel you were being disloyal to me?"

This was a very easy one, and Crawford had the answer pat.

"If I had been seriously making love to Helen, of course I should have felt most damnably disloyal. But as I wasn't, I didn't. Why should I?"

"She must be laughing at me," murmured Eleanor.

"She might be envying you."

There was another flicker of spirit in the reply, "Perhaps she has no cause to envy me."

"Meaning?"

"That she can take you from me and that she knows it."

Crawford began to get cross. The conversation was becoming tedious, and to be so long on the defensive was galling to his pride and bad for his temper. He poured out another drink and said stiffly, "if I have caused you any worry by attempting to entertain Helen Everard with idle chatter, I apologize. There. Will that do? I can't say fairer than that."

Even that handsome *amende* did not close the absurd incident, for Eleanor still continued to gaze up at him sadly.

"Why did you come back to London without telling me? You might have sent me a wire."

"Oh! So that's another grievance, is it? Well, just permit me to explain. I went abroad on business. I went as part of my job, which is the only way I have in which to work for you and make money for you, so that you can live in comfort and idleness. I'm not complaining about having to work and make money for you. That's part of the marriage contract. Every husband does it — or ought to. But one thing I do object to, and that is when you deliberately try to interfere with my work. No. Don't interrupt. I'm doing the talking just now. I got a wire from Anderton-Mawle telling me to come back secretly — without a word to a soul — for a very important meeting this morning. I wasn't even to tell you. If I had told you, I might have lost my job. Now you turn on me for not risking my job. Dammit, it's a bit hard."

Eleanor began to waver. She had been unjust to him about one point. Perhaps she had been unjust about others. And he was looking so gloriously handsome. And she was so madly in love with him. Her heart began to turn away from anger. She made one more show of resistance, half-heartedly, before surrendering.

"Was it part of your secret business to dine with that woman?"

Crawford scowled. "Oh for God's sake shut up!" he exclaimed. "And if you really want to know, it was part of my secret business to dine with the lady that you graciously describe as 'that woman.'"

Eleanor capitulated. It was not very nice of Jack to shout at her and tell her to shut up, but she had goaded him to desperation with her silly questions and unreasoning suspicions at the end of a hard and important day's work and it was all her fault. She took a step towards him and put her arms up round his neck and whispered, "I'm sorry, darling. I didn't mean to be so silly. Forgive me, darling. It's all my fault. But I do love you so much, and I just got silly notions into my head when I saw you in the restaurant. I was all flustered and upset, because I never expected to see you suddenly like that when I never even knew you were in England."

The decisive moment had arrived. The crisis had been reached. Jack Crawford could have cried out with joy at his own superb talents, with sheer admiration at his own virtuosity. He had kept his head, and saved his powder, so that he was ready for the crisis when it came at long last. Now was the moment for the counter-attack, horse, foot, and artillery.

He took Eleanor's arms away from his neck, folded his arms again, and opened: "That, my dear girl, is a matter which still remains to be considered," he said. The words were harmless enough. The gesture of taking her hands from his neck was not. It was compact with hostility.

A look of terror came into Eleanor's soft brown eyes.

"What do you mean? What matter?" she whispered fearfully.

"The small matter that you did not know I was in England, and so you chose the occasion to dine out with Montagu Mawle."

"But — but — there's nothing wrong in that," she stammered. "He asked me to."

"I expect he did. It's a habit he's got," said Crawford drily. "I had no idea you were on such intimate terms with him. Why didn't you tell me?"

"He only asked me yesterday."

"What were you doing in London yesterday?"

"I wasn't in London. He came in to tea at Lowbury. He was passing."

"I see," said Crawford with a really skilful sneer. "He was passing, only somehow he didn't pass. He dropped in to tea. Was it the first time, may I ask?"

Eleanor stiffened. "What are you driving at, Jack?" she asked steadily.

"I'll tell you exactly what I'm driving at," cried Crawford, raising his voice. "When I'm away on business, trying to make a living for you, you go and take up with the most notorious woman-hunter in London. He goes secretly down to visit you in the country, and you come secretly up to visit him in London. By the Lord God, Eleanor, you've got a bit of nerve to throw my quiet little business dinner with Helen Everard in my teeth when all the time you're gallivanting about behind my back with that dirty little seducer."

"But, Jack darling," cried Eleanor, by this time almost in tears, "I don't like him. I don't like anybody in the world except you. You know I don't. You must know I don't. I didn't ask him down yesterday to the country. He just came. And when he invited me to dinner tonight I couldn't very well refuse."

"Why not?" he asked in a grim, quiet voice.

"Because, after all, he is your Chief and you depend on him for your position and your salary. And also——" Eleanor broke off, and a great light of joy shone on her face, and she stood on tiptoe with her hands clasped behind her back. "Darling," she cried, "what a goose I am and what an old silly you are! Here we've been bickering and quarrelling for hours all about nothing, and all the time I've had the most wonderful bit of news for you and never told you about it. It just shows how much I love you, darling, that you can put everything else in the world clean out of my head. Listen. Do you know what Sir Montagu is going to do?"

"What?" said Crawford coldly. The temptation to score a neat point by suggesting what he thought Sir Montagu wanted to do, and by wondering whether Sir Montagu was going to do what he wanted to, was difficult to resist. But he resisted it.

"He's going to pay off all your debts, darling. Isn't that marvellous?"

"He's going to do what?" ejaculated Crawford. He was completely dumbfounded.

"Pay off your debts, sweetheart."

"But — but how much is he going to pay, I mean how does he know I've got any debts — I mean — I mean..." Crawford found himself stammering and he intensely disliked the sensation. He liked to be in full control of all scenes. Worse was to follow, for he lost his temper with himself for stammering and naturally covered it up by pretending that he had lost it with Eleanor for her stupidity.

"What the devil are you talking about?" he shouted furiously.

"Darling, darling, hush! You'll wake the house," whispered Eleanor. "If Daddy comes down he'll be furious. He's forbidden any of us to bring guests home here for the next six months."

"Damn your father!" said Crawford savagely, but in a distinctly quieter voice. He was having enough trouble for one evening without having to face that damnable old man. "Will you kindly explain what you mean?" he went on between his teeth.

"Darling," cried Eleanor, the light of joy beginning to fade from her eyes a little, "why are you so cross with me? I only mean that Sir Montagu is worried that you should be worried, and he wants to help you. He's found out somehow or other — I don't understand these things — that you owe about eleven thousand pounds—"

Crawford started at the uncanny accuracy of his Chief's information.

"—and he's going to send you a cheque for the whole' amount. That's all. I think it's marvellously generous of him."

Two emotions tumbled over each other in Jack Crawford's breast, or rather two variations of one emotion. Many times in his life he had felt that a Divine Power was hovering protectively over him. It was not only that the Divine Power had endowed him with good looks, and good health, and an irresistible charm for women, and a graceful seat on a horse; it had also saved him many and many a time when things looked uncommonly black. Crawford had only to think of one of dozens of occasions, and recall the crisis in his life, years before, when he was on the point of being sued for breach of promise by that schoolmaster's daughter, whose name he never could remember, near Camberley. A suit for breach of promise, with a plaintiff who was obviously going to have a baby at any moment, would have ruined his professional career for ever, and it was the direct intervention of Providence that made her throw up her suit and herself, instead, into the Thames. It was odd that he could remember her father's face — she was an only child — but not her name. However, it was an unimportant point. The important point, the superb, the magnificent point, was that he could hear once again the sound of the beating wings of his guardian angel. And what an efficient guardian. With a single stroke it had extricated him from two very tight corners. Sir Montagu's gift had torn away the millstone of debt that had weighed so heavily upon him since his earliest days as a subaltern, and the way in which the news had arrived had secured for ever his position on his own domestic hearth-rug.

"If I understand you correctly," he said slowly, in a voice of steel, or perhaps of Perdurite, "Anderton-Mawle is going to pay off my debts to the tune of eleven thousand pounds."

All the joy had vanished from Eleanor's face by this time, and she looked up at him unhappily.

"Yes, but darling, what's the matter? Have I done something wrong? But I haven't done anything at all."

"May I ask why Mawle is indulging in this charming act of philanthropy?"

"Because he likes you, I suppose."

"Oh, for my beaux yeux. That's it, is it. Or is it for yours?" he added sharply.

"What do you mean, darling?" Eleanor was frightened. Her handsome, adorable lover was angry with her for the first time, and she was frightened.

"I'll tell you what I mean," he said coldly. "I go away to the Continent to work for you. I come back to find you entertaining the most notorious woman-hunter in London at our house in the country, dining with him alone in a London restaurant, without so much as a single word to me——"

"But he only asked me yesterday," she cried. "How could I let you know?"

He waved the interruption aside.

"And you accept eleven thousand pounds from him and think I'm going to believe he's getting nothing in return."

"Jack!"

"Sir Montagu Anderton-Mawle give something away and get nothing in return!" Crawford laughed. "Well, I may be a mug, but, damn it all, I'm not such a mug as all that."

Eleanor had no spirit left for the outburst of furious anger which still might have saved the day. Besides, it was the man she loved who was in such dreadful distress, and it was her part not to trample on him but to comfort him by convincing him that he had made a mistake. And she saw how foolish she had been in accepting Sir Montagu's invitation, and how everything had been her fault and hers only. So, instead of trampling she grovelled.

"Jack, I swear to you——"

Crawford knew instantly that the game was won. "Swear away," he said ruthlessly. "I'll believe anything you tell me, of course. I'm just the silly sort of mug who would. Anderton-Mawle dropped in yesterday to talk about the crocuses, and he's going to give me — a man he's only known for a month or two — eleven thousand quid because he likes the way I call my hand at bridge. Is that it? Or is it because he's suddenly given up girls and gone all pansy?"

Eleanor burst into tears.

"And I must say, Eleanor," he went on, "I do admire your nerve in going for me because I was dining out with Helen Everard. Pretty good show, I call that. Let me tell you, my dear, that henceforward I shall dine out with as many Helen Everards as I damned well choose. I don't see why the fun should all be on one side. And, by the way, I ought to have told you before — you're wasting your time crying. I've never believed in female tears and I'm not going to begin now. That's right. Mop them up and run along to bed. Tell them to send my early tea to the dressing-room. Considering all things, I think I'll be sleeping there."

It was a lucky circumstance that this final blow so appalled Eleanor that she forgot her tears and could only stand and stare pitifully at him, for the next moment the door opened and James Hanson walked in. He was wearing a scarlet-and-gold dressing-gown that had been originally made as a ceremonial robe for a Chinese mandarin, a pair of bright-green moroccan slippers, and blue silk pyjamas, and the flamboyance of the colouring exactly suited the flamboyance of the old man's Beethoven-like head.

"Hearing a powerful masculine voice," said Mr Hanson blandly, "I guessed it must be you, Crawford. I hope you are well." He was addressing his son-in-law but it was at his daughter that he was looking. Eleanor, desperately conscious that her last tear was only two seconds old and was still lingering upon her eyelashes, turned away from her father and said nothing. There was no chance that the terrible watchfulness of the old man might miss the tear. There was no chance whatever that it would miss the sob in her voice if she spoke before she had recovered herself. Crawford, however, who was completely in command of himself, was able to step smoothly into the awkward breach.

"I am sorry to have disturbed the household," he remarked. "We were just going upstairs to bed."

James Hanson lifted his great eyebrows. "Were you?" he enquired in a puzzled voice which clearly implied that the question was not simply a conventional one.

Eleanor wheeled round. The urgent necessity of defending her man against a very heavy piece of ordnance had driven away both tears and sobs.

"It's my fault, Daddy," she cried. "I know you don't want visitors staying in the house just now. But Jack's not a visitor. He's one of the family now. He's only this minute back from the Continent, and I insisted on his coming here."

Crawford at once became the courteous, anxious-to-please man-of-the-world.

"Good heavens!" he exclaimed. "This is dreadful. I had no idea you didn't want visitors, sir. I'll go off to the club at once. Eleanor darling," he turned to her with a loving reproachfulness, "you really ought to have told me."

Eleanor's hard-won composure cracked for a moment and she cried in a voice of anguish, "You can't go to the club now. It would be too cruel."

James Hanson heard the note of anguish and understood that he had come into a crisis of some kind. He did not know, could not know, what sort of crisis it was, but one thing he did know: that for his daughter it was a matter of desperate urgency to speak to her husband again that night, and that for his son-in-law it would be vastly pleasanter if he could escape to his club. Eleanor's voice had been too feverish, Crawford's offer had been too anxiously ready, for the old man to make any mistake.

"I insist upon your staying here," he said at once. "Of course you are one of the family. It is true that I ejected Veronica's young man somewhat offensively, but he has not yet been dragged to the altar by that vehement child. Take him upstairs, Eleanor, and look after him. Good-night to you both."

Hanson was confirmed in his estimate of the position by the especial warmth — it might almost, he reflected, be hysterical warmth — of Eleanor's hug, and the faint clouding of Crawford's blond, well-mannered brow. But he remembered Ruth Collins' wisdom. There was nothing to be done. A father could only help a daughter when she came to him for help. He could not go to her with it.

Hanson's heart was heavy as he watched them go up the staircase together. Then he turned and went slowly into his study and locked the door behind him. For the next ten minutes he searched through the roll-top desk for documents and, having made a neat bundle out of certain of them, he opened a brand-new small safe which had been recently installed in a corner and put the bundle inside and carefully locked it again.

"My esteemed son-in-law might be able to break into a wooden desk," he reflected grimly, "but I doubt if he could manage a safe." He switched out the light and was just going upstairs when another idea occurred to him. "Anderton-Mawle would stick at nothing," he said aloud, and he picked up the telephone and dialled a number. After a minute or two of buzzing, a sleepily indignant voice said, "Who the hell is that at this god-awful hour of the morning?"

"It's your employer," said Hanson.

Harry Winter's voice instantly sprang to life as he said quietly, "I'm with you."

The old millionaire did not miss the speed with which Winter had gone from the daze to the alert, and he nodded approvingly. That was the sort of man he had used in the old fierce buccaneering days in Cimbria, when the Hanson, Wendelmann Company was being formed in the teeth of all Europe.

"Come round," was all he said, and when Winter had said "Right," Hanson added, "and bring one of those things you used in argument with the O'Bannon crowd off Florida."

Winter said "Right" again, and they rang off.

It was a warm September night, and Hanson strolled quietly to the front door and stood on the top of the steps in his dressing-gown. There was to be no bell-ringing or door-knocking. Ten minutes later a taxi drew up at the far end of the crescent, and again Hanson nodded in appreciation of the caution of his subordinate. Winter paid off the taxi and came down the street swiftly but without a sound. He was wearing rubber-soled shoes.

A grin flashed across his thin brown face as he saw the gorgeous scarlet-and-gold figure on the top of the steps, but he said nothing and followed Hanson into his study.

With the door locked behind them and the household secluded in their bedrooms, Hanson began to talk at once.

"It's that son-in-law of mine," he said in an urgent whisper. "He's here — in the house. Arrived at about one o'clock. Eleanor brought him, or else he made her bring him. I don't know which. But, whatever it is, I don't trust Anderton-Mawle an inch. I wouldn't put it past him to have a couple of safe-crackers outside now, waiting for Crawford to let them in. I've got stuff in that safe that they'd like to see."

"Right," said Winter. There was nothing in his face now except hard, almost ruthless, resolution.

"I'm too old," went on Hanson, "for a single-handed rough-house, and if I put police on outside, Mawle will know that I've got something afoot here. But you and I together, eh?"

Winter shook his head. "Leave it to me. I'll deal with them." He pulled an automatic pistol out of his right-hand coat-pocket, and another out of his left, and laid them on the table. "You go off to bed, sir," he added.

After a moment Hanson nodded and went out, and Harry Winter settled down to his vigil.

Next morning an envelope was lying on the hall-table addressed to James Hanson. The pencilled message in it ran simply, "5 a.m. Sun shining. All O.K. Gone home."

CHAPTER XXV

The Nazi Shows his Hand

That same day, a few hours after Harry Winter had gone home in the five o'clock sunshine, one of the evening newspapers secured an immensely valuable scoop, by no merit or initiative of its own, but simply because Ruth Collins rang up the editor and asked him, in her cool, impersonal voice, if he would care for an exclusive interview with Mr James Hanson on the future of Perdurite and its relation to the steel trade of the world, together with an exclusive statement about Mr Hanson's own future. The editor replied that he would care for such an interview very much indeed, and he despatched his star reporter to Partington Crescent.

The result was a terrific shouting of newsboys, an immense display of posters with the words Steel King's Sensational Statement, and a furious rushing to and fro of the newspaper's motor-vans, driven at a speed that was almost as sensational as the statement.

The gist of the story was that, thanks to the unparalleled acumen of the staff of the newspaper, to its perseverance, to its flair for news, and, above all, to its resolute determination to let nothing stand in the way of its determined resolution to serve the British public with the best, and the best only, Mr James Hanson had been persuaded to give an exclusive interview.

The gist of the interview was that the retired Steel King prophesied that the new alloy, Perdurite, would totally ruin the British steel trade, that all the Great Powers of Europe would be forced into war in order to obtain a share of the Cimbro-Suevonian Gloxite, without which Perdurite could not be manufactured, and that he himself was going to step down into the arena once again to organize the defence of British steel and avert the calamity of another world war. "'Curiously enough,' added Mr Hanson to our representative, 'I used to be interested in the iron of Cimbro-Suevonia in the old days, but not, of course, in the Gloxite. Gloxite was of no commercial value in my day. By the way, I'm President of the British branch of the Anglo-Cimbrian Society. It is rather ironical that I should be congratulating that country, for whom I have the deepest affection, on this immensely valuable discovery, and at the same time deprecating its discovery on the ground that it will ruin our own steel trade.' "'Do you ever re-visit Cimbro-Suevonia?' asked our representative.

"'I have not been there for some years,' replied the veteran industrialist, who looks, by the way, many years younger than his age. 'But by an odd coincidence I had arranged to lead our Society's delegation to the celebrations in Stz this autumn of Herr Waldemar's fifteenth anniversary in office.'

"'Are you going?' the grizzled magnate was asked.

"'I may and I may not,' replied the Steel King. 'Besides,' he added with a twinkle in his blue eyes, 'when they know that I am to fight Perdurite, I may not exactly be persona grata with Herr Waldemar.'"

This interview although it was not published until after the Stock Exchange had closed, caused a profound sensation that evening in some circles, and no sensation at all in others. These latter were circles composed of young men to whom the name of James Hanson meant nothing. To them a pre-War figure was as shadowy as a pre-Flood figure, and a man of seventy might just as well have been a man of a hundred and seventy. So they yawned at the news, and smiled at the notion that a long-retired ancient could emerge from his Victorian dignity and affect by one iota the hustling, rushing, efficient, modern world. They also made a mental note that, if this ancient Hanson was the best card which Steel could play, it might be worth while to buy Perdurite Ordinaries, even though they already stood at sixty-two and sixpence.

But the older men, who had been contemporaries of the buccaneering and the vast expansion, before the War, of Hanson, Wendelmann & Co., shook their heads and wondered, in the clubs of the West End, in the big houses of Avenue Road and Fitzjohn Avenue, and in the variegated palaces of brick and plaster and fancy wood-carvings which look out over Wimbledon Common, what was likely to be the upshot of it all.

But to no one in London did it cause a more profound sensation, and to no one did it bring a greater occasion for head-shaking and wondering, than to Sir Montagu Anderton-Mawle. For that astute psychologist was under no illusions about the capacity of his opponent. Indeed he had very few illusions about anything, including himself. A man whose advances had been so consistently rebuffed, over such a long and continuous period of years, by such a variety of youthful, graceful, and beautiful ladies, unless those advances were accompanied by a substantial gift, either in cash or in diamonds, was not likely to entertain the rosiest notions about himself if he was anything at all in the nature of a realist. And whatever else Sir Montagu might be, he was most certainly a realist. And he had a genuine fear of James Hanson. He read the newspaper interview over and over again, as if making certain that he had extracted the last shade of meaning and the last implication, but he always came back to the same point. What did the old fox mean by dragging in that stuff about a possible visit to Cimbro-Suevonia? That was the crux of the whole thing. Sir Montagu instantly dismissed from his mind the ludicrous notion that it was a coincidence. Obviously that was only the old fox's little joke. It was a cross of some kind. But was it a double-cross, or a treble, or even a quadruple? Was Hanson really going to Stz? Or was he trying to focus the attention of the Perdurite Board on their precious Gloxite mines while he launched some deadly attack elsewhere? Or was it so absurdly obvious that Hanson could not draw the eyes of the world to his visit to Stz and then expect to go there unnoticed, that no one would believe for a moment that he would try to go there, and so he would go there after all?

It was all terribly difficult. But of one thing Sir Montagu was certain: James Hanson had had a very good reason for bringing in the subject of his possible visit. There was nothing for it now but to strain every nerve, and maintain every vigilance, to discover what that very good reason was.

In the meantime there was one counter-weight that could be set in motion. He could despatch his roving ambassador, Jack Crawford, with a message to the Home Secretary of Cimbro-Suevonia. No one would pay the slightest attention to Crawford's departure to Stz, owing to the masterly policy of exposing to the world — that is to say the world that mattered, and that is to say the magnates of the armament firms and their subsidiaries — the thinness of the gallant ex-major's intellectual equipment. The world had summed him up as a man who, rightly, was never entrusted by the Perdurite Company with work of any importance whatsoever. But this time things would be different.

Eleanor was greatly distressed when she read the interview that evening. It was a bad day for Eleanor. First of all, she had lain awake until nearly four o'clock, unhappy and wretched, her only consolation during the long weary hours being the knowledge that her beloved husband had not been prevented by her brainless idiocy, from snatching a little sleep — for she could hear his snores from the dressing-room. Then she had woken up at eight o'clock and found that she was all alone in the big spare bed, and the memory of the dismal evening and the hateful quarrel came rushing up at her like a wave in a nasty, grey, choppy sea. Then she had crept humbly into the dressing-room to beg her husband's forgiveness for her stupidity, and had found that he had already dressed and gone downstairs. In a dressing-gown and bedroom slippers, Eleanor had fled on the wings of terror down to the dining-room, where she found a maid who told her that the Major had said he did not want any breakfast as he was in a hurry and would breakfast at the club.

Twice during the morning she telephoned to him at the office, and each time a secretary told her that Major Crawford was "in conference." If it had been in Eleanor's nature to notice such things, she would have detected a note of derision in the girl's voice. Then, at five o'clock in the afternoon, Parkinson brought in the evening papers, neatly folded and warmed, according to the old-fashioned custom, and coughed in a discreet but nevertheless marked manner. Eleanor, knowing the exact meaning of that cough, dutifully looked up from her dreary novel — any novel would have been dreary that afternoon — and in two seconds had grasped from the blaring headlines that her father had taken the field against her husband, and the only two men in the world whom she really loved were to be mortal enemies.

She ran down to her father's study, newspaper in hand, and found him studying a large blue chart covered with white lines running all over it.

"Daddy," she cried, "what does all this mean?" She laid the paper down in front of him.

"What it says, I trust, my dear. I haven't seen it yet. Ah yes. There it is. Well, well, well," he gazed at the front page admiringly, "they've certainly done me proud."

"But, Daddy, you can't mean that you are going to attack Perdurite — why, it's Jack's livelihood — it's his business — it's his great chance. You can't be going to fight against your son-in-law. It's — it's inhuman."

James Hanson looked at her sadly. "You love him very much, don't you?" he asked.

She nodded two or three times.

"I'll see that he won't lose financially," he said. "And if Perdurite comes out on top he'll be a very rich man, and it's I who will be ruined."

"Oh, Father, you don't understand," she cried. It really was extraordinary how stupid men could be, for all their brains. "Don't you see, it isn't the money I am thinking of. What does money count for? It's that you and Jack will be fighting against each other. It means that nothing will ever be the same again. It's the end of all our lovely family life."

"That came to an end when you married, my dear. You have started your own family life. It's the way of the world."

"But I wanted the new family and the old to be all one. I wanted you and Mummy to love Jack, and him to love you. And now it's all spoilt."

"Things never do work out like that," said Hanson gently. "Each generation must do the best it can for itself."

Eleanor turned on him with one of her rare flashes of revolt.

"Then why can't you leave the new generation to run the world? Why must you come back into it?"

"Because I do not believe the new generation is running the world very well, my dear."

"The old always think that. Did you run it so well when you were young?"

"Touché," replied Hanson, "undeniably touché. So you think I am wrong to interfere again?"

"I think you are utterly and absolutely wrong to try to destroy Perdurite. It's simply a defensive metal. There is nothing aggressive about it. Oh! there's nothing to smile about, Father; I know what I'm talking about. Listen. Would you sooner a British soldier went into battle protected by a weak steel hat rather than a strong Perdurite one?"

"The answer is 'yes,'" said Hanson steadily. Eleanor stared at him incredulously. "You would send a young Englishman to die when Perdurite might save him?"

"If I succeed, young Englishmen won't have to go out to die in a steel hat or a Perdurite hat or any other."

"But, Father, surely you must see that this new metal is going to make the British Empire supreme for ever."

"So that the other Powers must inevitably fight before we're completely re-armed with it."

"No one would dare to attack us," cried Eleanor proudly.

"That is what I propose to try and arrange," said her father drily. "I wish I had the same confidence in the altruistic motives of Sir Montagu Anderton-Mawle as I have in my own."

"Altruistic motives!" said Eleanor, with the nearest approach to a sneer her gentle soul had ever been able to muster. "Your motives seem to be a desire to destroy the British Empire, the British soldier, and your son-in-law's future, at one blow."

Hanson sighed. "Put like that, it sounds dreadful," he admitted. "But I can only do what I think right." And that was the last word of the conversation. Eleanor's heart was too full of misery and bewilderment to argue against such a fantastic theory that such devilry was right.

She went slowly to her bedroom and went to bed. She had endured enough for one day. Cold hardness from one of the two men she worships, and diabolical evil from the other, is enough in twelve hours for any woman.

.....

After Eleanor's sorrowful departure. James Hanson sighed again deeply and returned to an intensive study of his huge blue chart map. The telephone in the butler's pantry rang incessantly, and Parkinson explained over and over again that Mr Hanson would speak to no one. A footman, stationed at the front door, performed the same office for callers.

But at half-past six one of the members of the family arrived and had to be admitted. It was Veronica, and she brought with her the Freiherr von Czepan-Eichenhöh. Veronica was wearing a most fetching costume of black and white that was designed to suggest the glorious anti-Semitic swastika. The dress itself was a shimmering white, but a black sash, with a long black tassel, and a black panel down the centre, and two skilfully arranged posies of black artificial roses-one nestling against a slender neck and the other against a small breast — most elegantly conveyed the idea of the sacred Hakenkreuz. Impetuous as usual, she ran eagerly on her tiny shoes with absurdly high heels into her father's study, hauling the colossal Prussian after her.

It might have suited her purpose better, and it certainly would have suited the Prussian's, if she had not been quite so impetuous. For James Hanson recognized in a flash the quick pitter-patter of those small and impulsive feet, and he had whisked his blue chart over so that it lay face downwards upon his desk, before even the door opened.

The Freiherr confessed afterwards that he would have given ten thousand marks for a sight of the other side of that sheet of paper.

"Dad," cried Veronica, as she shot into the room like a miniature typhoon, "this is the most exciting thing that has ever happened. You must shoot the whole story, off your chest. Manfred is thrilled to the marrow, and you've only got to give him one look to realize that a thing has got to be pretty hot to get through all that mountain to the marrow-bones, and so here we are. What's it all about? Have you got a half-nelson on those goddam Perdurite crooks, and if so, how? We're with you to the last button, aren't we, my sweet lambkin?"

Von Eichenhöh smiled a tolerant smile at her, and then bowed to Hanson.

"Your interview, sir, is very interesting to me."

"I had guessed that it might be," replied Hanson.

The German was taken aback. "But — but — but —" he stuttered. "Why should you guess that? I was — I mean I am on a secret mission."

"Yes. Representing the Krupp-Reichsbank Combine, and trying to negotiate armaments contracts in Newcastle and Birmingham without having to pay for the stuff," retorted the terrible old man. The German flushed scarlet, and small veins began to bulge on his forehead in a rather dangerous way.

"There are traitors somewhere," he said at last, his beautiful Oxford accent sinking into a Teutonic guttural.

"There are traitors everywhere, thank God," replied Hanson briskly. "That is how honest men like you and I get all our information, my dear Freiherr. But I understand you want to talk to me. Sit down. And you, little rascal, perch yourself on the arm of that easy-chair."

"Veronica," said the Prussian, "go."

"Very well, Manfred," the little bantam said meekly. "One moment," cut in James Hanson in his blandest tones, "I think I am right in supposing that you heard me invite my younger daughter to seat herself upon the arm of that chair."

"I've come to talk business," replied von Czepan-Eichenhöh shortly, "and women have no place in business. Veronica!" he added in a peremptory voice.

"I am an old man, Count," said Hanson urbanely, "much stricken in years, but you make a grievous error if you suppose I am not still master in my own study."

The Prussian frowned sullenly. Then he shot a glance at Veronica which so clearly implied that she would hear all about it when he got her alone, that Hanson rose to his feet and went on, always with the same old-fashioned courtesy:

"But as I perceive, my dear Count, that you are likely to visit the sins of the father upon the head of the daughter, I will not press the point. But let me explain that if you wish to conduct business with me, you must first see my partner, Mr Wendelmann."

Veronica instantly went round to the side of her man. "Father," she exclaimed, "you can't insult Manfred like that! It's absolutely monstrous. It's — it's a damned shame."

"Always these damned Jews," shouted the German, losing his head and thumping the table with a vast fist, just as Parkinson opened the door and announced, "Mr Wendelmann to see you, sir."

"Alas! yes," said Wendelmann sadly, "always these damned Jews. Damned to all eternity." He bowed to Veronica and to the German. The former bowed faintly. The latter clicked his heels and then turned away and ostentatiously examined a shelf of books that was at least seven feet from the ground.

"You have come at the right moment for a business conference, my dear Wendelmann," said Hanson. "The Freiherr von Czepan-Eichenhöh has come to ask something from the firm of Messrs. Hanson, Wendelmann & Co. He has begun by insulting both partners of the firm within five minutes."

The German spun round.

"I have not insulted either of you," he said haughtily. "I have come to talk business on behalf of my company——"

"The German Government, in fact," said Hanson. "If you like to say so," was the stiff response. The German was furiously angry and had no technique for concealing his emotions. "The position is simple. Our chemists — the finest chemists in the world — have analysed the new alloy. Their report is final. For war purposes — and we in Germany are not interested in any other purposes — Perdurite supersedes steel. Our choice is twofold. We must secure our share of the Gloxite of the world and manufacture the alloy ourselves, or we must prevent those who have the Gloxite monopoly from manufacturing it."

"War either on Cimbro-Suevonia or on the British Empire?" said Wendelmann softly.

"Not necessarily. Why not war of the combined steelmakers of the world against this new alloy? That would be simpler and cheaper."

"Steel-workers of the world, unite!" murmured Veronica.

Von Czepan-Eichenhöh glanced at her angrily. For a woman to be present at a business talk of men was bad enough; for her to open her mouth was an outrage; but for her to make a reference, even by way of parody, to a Communist slogan was not only quite monstrous but was the direct route to the concentration camp, the torture-chamber, and the rubber truncheon.

However, he managed to swallow hard and keep to the matter in hand.

"You have given us a lead, Herr Hanson," he said, picking up Eleanor's evening paper, and slapping it with his hand, making a noise like the back-fire of a high-powered motor-cycle, "why should we not follow?"

"What is your idea of a plan of campaign against Perdurite?" enquired Wendelmann.

It was typical of the Freiherr that he had recovered his self-assurance sufficiently to start insulting the old Jew again, and he deliberately directed his answer to Hanson.

"We and you and the Comité des Forges ought to be strong enough if we pool resources."

"Strong enough to do what?" asked Hanson. "To — to — to — smash this thing."

"You may have noticed," said Hanson with elaborate irony, elaborate enough to penetrate even a Prussian's consciousness, "that this country is about to spend five hundred million pounds sterling in rebuilding its navy and its air force. The Perdurite people have already secured the contracts for the armour for two super-dreadnoughts, six light cruisers, and a flotilla of destroyers. More will unquestionably follow. Can you draft out a scheme, my dear Freiherr, for smashing a concern which has the potential backing of five hundred million pounds. If you can, I shall be delighted to give it my most earnest consideration."

The German stared down at Hanson, his eyes bulging a little from his head so that he looked like a gigantic and helpless salmon.

"Then we also must make Perdurite," he said at last.

"Where will you get the Gloxite?" asked Hanson grimly.

There was a long pause, and then von Eichenhöh said slowly, "Then it means war."

Hanson nodded. "That is the logical sequence. It is going to be my business to see if I cannot prevent war."

"You cannot. It is inevitable. There is no third course. All must have Perdurite or none."

Old Wendelmann took no part in the conversation, but kept his dark, shining eyes fixed upon the face of his partner. Veronica's eyes darted backwards and forwards from speaker to speaker.

"Will your people," said Hanson, leaning forward across his desk to emphasize the gravity of his next words, "hold their hands from war until I have tried to solve the Perdurite problem? Will they give me two months?"

"Two months," said the German, "is a long time. Your country is six months ahead already. In two months a highly industrialised country like Britain can build many aeroplanes."

"Will they give me one month?"

"One month might be possible."

"Would you carry that message back to your Leader?"

"To hold our hands for one month? And if you fail——"

"You can open the lock-gates and destroy civilization."

"War never destroyed anything except what was effete and miserable," said the German proudly, and Veronica murmured "Hear, hear," and clapped her hands once, gently.

"I will not argue that," replied Hanson. "Will you take the message?"

"I will."

"At once? Time is vital. My car will take you to Croydon and my secretary will telephone for an aeroplane to be ready for you."

The German was visibly impressed by this precipitation. "Mein Gott," he said, "you do not waste time, Herr Hanson, or words."

"It never was his custom," murmured Wendelmann.

"Very well," said the German. "Nor will I. Come, Veronica."

When they had gone out, Wendelmann turned to Hanson and looked at him gravely.

"Ah! but you are a bold man, mein lieber freund," he said. "What is going on in that piratical old heart of yours, I wonder."

Hanson picked up the chart and set it down face-upwards.

"I must go to Cimbro-Suevonia," he said.

"To see Waldemar?"

"I may have to see Waldemar. But it is not essential." He paused and then added, "There are other more important things to see in Cimbro-Suevonia than that crook."

"You have a dark and sudden mind, James Hanson," said the Jew.

"Dark and sudden?" cried Hanson, leaping up energetically. "What the devil do you mean, you old rascal?"

"I mean dark and sudden," replied the other. "And now I must go."

"I shall leave this day week," went on Hanson, talking like an eager schoolboy. "We must call a conference of all the big steel-men for the day after tomorrow, and you and I had better meet at the office tomorrow. We must get ready for those new contracts."

"What new contracts?"

"The two super-dreadnoughts, and the rest of them, that will come back to steel when I've smashed Perdurite."

"Ah! You villain," said Wendelmann with a laugh, and he went away to summon the steel-makers of Britain to conference.

.....

"Miss Collins," said. Hanson a few minutes later, "get an aeroplane to be ready for that fool of a Boche in an hour to take him to the loathsome metropolis of the Hun. Get that feeble little lizard whose name I forget — what are you writing down, Miss Collins?"

"Get Clifford Bray," she replied impassively, and Hanson burst into a great thunder-clap of a laugh.

"Yes. That's him. Get him to keep sleepers for me and Harry Winter for next Tuesday on the Orient Express for Stz. Get Winter round here now. Tell the Anglo-Cimbrian Society that I'm going. Tell the Press. Tell everyone. Ring up Anderton-Mawle and tell him I'm going."

"I think that would hardly be wise," said Miss Collins in her smooth, decisive voice.

"Dash it, it would give him something to think about," protested Mr Hanson.

"I fancy the evening paper has already done that."

"By the way, Miss Collins, what do you think about it?"

"It makes me think that the world is an even madder place than I had imagined," was the disconcerting answer. Even James Hanson was, for once, taken aback.

"Do you think I'm mad?" he enquired at last in a voice that almost sounded humble.

"I didn't say that," she replied patiently. "I said I thought the world was mad. And so do you, or you wouldn't be coming out to try and save it."

Hanson caught on to her words with a pathetic eagerness. "You do know that I'm trying to save it, don't you? You do know that?"

"Yes."

"And do you think I'll succeed?"

"No."

Hanson stared at her beautiful, flawless, impassive beauty for what seemed a long time, and at last he said, "Tell me one thing more. Do you think it's worth trying to save?"

"I am a woman," was the calm, even reply, "and so of course I think it's worth trying to save it."

"I'm very nearly in love with you," said the old millionaire abruptly.

"I know."

"I think I've been nearly in love with you for a long time."

"I know."

He turned away suddenly. "Will you get that aeroplane now?"

"Yes."

She left the room, and the old man returned to his chart, and his mind went back to happy, far-off days, when the cherry orchards were in bloom in the pleasant vales of Cimbria, and he and all his world were young.

CHAPTER XXVI

Rearmament

Rearmament was in full cry. The shipyards and the forges were all a-clatter. The furnaces blazed, the hammers banged and clanged, the giant lathes whirred like mammoth pussy-cats, and everywhere the shareholders in the heavy industries sat pretty. There were so many orders that there were, for once, enough to go round, and Tyneside temporarily gave up its intensive campaign of propaganda to prove that the Clyde was not navigable for big ships, and Clydeside temporarily gave up its intensive campaign to prove that the workers on the Tyne could not drive a straight rivet. Birkenhead called a truce in its war with Belfast, Birmingham exchanged compliments with Sheffield, and the Lord Provost of Aberdeen, on hearing of the contract for mine-sweepers which a firm in his city had secured, was publicly seen to nod to the Lord Provost of Dundee. And the latter, who had just heard of the vast order for sandbags which had been placed with a firm in Dundee, mustered up a sufficient geniality to nod back.

Directors of Aircraft Manufacturing Companies bought bigger and bigger cigars, and uglier and uglier mansions, some in Watford, some in Wealdstone, some in Stanmore, and the remainder, of course, overlooking Wimbledon Common. Air Marshals were even more plentiful than Marshals had been in the high Imperial days, when a Marshal was a man who led his stormtroops from in front and not a kind of super-clerk who sat in a polished office a thousand miles from danger, with about sixteen medals and about fourteen telephones. Air Vice-Marshals were as common as parsons, and, when in uniform, much more picturesque, and as for Air Commodores, the sky was literally, as you might say, blue with them.

For there was no question of half-measures about the Patriotic Government. Very often it could be accused, indeed often was accused, of doing nothing. But when it did nothing, it did it in the grand manner. It could ignore a social injustice with the same superb indifference that Lord Chesterfield would have shown to an agricultural labourer or Lord Byron to a modern pansy gentleman. It could turn its back on a good cause with a grace that made the world admire its back rather than deprecate its behaviour. It could fail to hear noble words and generous appeals in a way that Odysseus would have dearly liked to manage when he was sailing past the island of the Sirens.

But there are two sides to every penny, even a bad one.

The Patriotic Government could be slow to move, or even impervious to suggestion that it should move. But when it did make up its mind to do something it sprang to action galvanically. It became like a swarm of bees. It became like an American baseball crowd. It became like the proverbial flea upon a hot saucepan.

And so it was with rearmament. Everything else was swept aside to make way for the new crusade. Peter the Hermit himself was not more single-minded than the Cabinet of the Patriotic Government. Each Cabinet Minister donned the casque of Bayard. "*Sans peur et sans reproche*" might well have been the motto of each, if each had not been so frightened of the future and if each had not been reproachable for so many mistakes in the past.

They began by disembarrassing themselves of all superfluous and hampering activities. Thus they cancelled, for a start, all their slum-clearance schemes. There is no point in building houses for men if you are trying to make them air-conscious at the same time. It is true that the Government was not trying to make the women and children air-conscious too (except in so far that gas-mask drill was made compulsory throughout the country), but the women and children, after all, had to sacrifice something for the sake of their beloved country. It could not be left to the men to make all the sacrifices. The women and children themselves would not have liked that.

Then again, a double economy was effected by reducing the new school-leaving age to thirteen, thus saving the country a sum of money in education which would build two submarines and a flotilla-leader every year and would still leave enough to mechanize a squadron of Life Guards, and thus ensuring also a regular supply of juvenile labour in the munition factories.

But it is impossible to do more than hint at the wide range of economies which the Government managed to make in order the more vigorously to prosecute their defensive rearmament. The subsidies in aid of the National Gallery and the British Museum were reduced; the scheduling of Ancient Monuments was abandoned; the pensions on the Civil List to elderly and indigent — and therefore useless — painters, writers, musicians, sculptors, or their elderly and indigent widows, were abolished, thereby saving the equivalent of the cost of one smallish torpedo per annum; the lands which had been presented in perpetuity to the National Trust were taken back and sold to the Tudor and Half-Timbered Bungalow Construction Company for a sum that would bring in a complete battle-cruiser, all except the forward turret of eighteen-inch guns; the new National Theatre in Long Acre was converted into a News Reel Cinema and leased to an American Corporation for the equivalent of the lime juice ration of the entire Navy (rum having been abolished after the National Temperance Council had proved so conclusively that even one noggin of it reduces a gun-layer's efficiency by as much as 2.45 per cent); and the Ministry of Infant Welfare was abolished altogether, and the Ministry of Maternal Welfare was absorbed by the Post Office.

Nor was the Government's activity confined to the purely negative sphere of economy. The length of the legal working-day was raised from eight hours to ten for men, from eight hours to ten for women, and from eight hours to ten for children. The BBC was instructed to broadcast poignant little stories three times a week of the human side of the great Crusade: how, for example, little Billy Spigot, of Allenby Road, Oldham, found a threepenny bit in the street and took it to the Lord Mayor of Oldham and offered it towards the cost of the new Mustard Gas Containers which were being made in the town; or how little Rosemary Spavin's dying words —she was badly mauled when an eighteen-inch naval shell, which she was filling with tri-nitrotoluene, exploded — had been, "To hell with George Lansbury"; or how little Gussie Jobbes, captain of the juvenile section of the New Cross and East Deptford Church Lads' Association, blew his leg off with a Mills bomb in the local factory where he was working, and only murmured as he was being taken to hospital on a stretcher, "'It is lawful for Christian men, at the commandment of the Magistrate, to wear weapons and serve in the Wars.' Article 37 of the Articles of Religion." These and many more poignant heart-throbs were duly committed to the ether by the most refined of accents.

Nor was the BBC's invaluable aid only enlisted for the world-wide diffusion of human heart-throbs in the most refined of accents. Stern realism was not forgotten. Thus the children's hour one Tuesday would be taken up by a description of the effect of the new poison-gas upon the skin of anyone who might attack the British Empire; on the next Saturday, again, the concert hour might be filled by gramophone records which gave the exact sounds of an aerial torpedo wiping out a crèche of alien children, even including the guttural whines and un-British yelps of fear of the little brutes.

Official photographs of the new defensive heavy guns appeared in all the newspapers; official descriptions of the new defensive tanks were published every fortnight or so; while the new defensive germ-sprayer was, as *The Listener*, the BBC's gay little journal, said, "literally on everybody's lips."

But of all advertisements for the Rearmament Campaign, none was so ubiquitous and none so effective as Perdurite. The new metal, the triumph of Empire brains, the defensive saviour of, if not mankind, at any rate the British part of the English-speaking Union, the revolutionizing factor in world politics, Perdurite was the toast of the hour.

The shares soared phenomenally. The factories rushed skywards like any helicopter. And Sir Montagu Anderton-Mawle toiled for the Empire sixteen hours a day. His other eight were divided in the proportion of one hour for Miss Clytemnestra de Valois (whom he had bought from Lazarus Finkelbummer, the bucket-shop man, for a thousand pounds down and fifty ordinary shares in Perdurite Ltd.), six hours for sleep, and one hour for deciding where to invest his perfectly magnificent profits.

For money was pouring in upon the great Tasmanian in a vast flood. Not only was he getting the dividends from the millions which he had been rightly given for reorganizing the Lancashire cotton trade; not only was he drawing £20,000 a year as chairman of the new company; not only was he making a tidy packet out of the manipulation and sale of ordinary shares in Perdurite; but he was also raking in money at an almost unbelievable speed from the sale of Cimbro-Suevonian Gloxite (the entire output of which he owned under the rather non-committal name of Barclay's Bank, Nominees) to himself acting as buyer, on behalf of Perdurite Ltd. The seller fixed the market-price of Gloxite. The buyer did not haggle. And the Nation paid.

There was no doubt about it. Prosperity was in the air. The clubs of the West End during the luncheon hour were thick with the smoke of huge cigars and aglow with the rosy beams of countless benevolent faces. The consumption of kümmel had not reached such a high index-mark since the year when King Edward the Seventh won the Derby with Minoru, and it was only the timely discovery of a synthetic Stilton cheese, manufactured in Newfoundland, that saved the ugly situation which had been caused by the serious shortage of the genuine article. And old club servants hailed with quietly decorous satisfaction the return of the good old days in a distinct recrudescence of gout among the members.

The activity in the War Office, Admiralty, and Air Ministry was prodigious, and Tiger Springton was inexpressibly delighted at the number of old cronies of his who were being rapidly promoted on account of the expansion of the armed forces of the Crown. Men who had dared all, and won, in the desperate days at Army Headquarters at Querrieu, Albert, St.

Pol, or Cassel, were coming into their own at last, and many an old-time captain at G.H.Q. at Montreuil was now a lieutenant-general, his chest glittering with the rewards of long-ago valour. There was dear old Toby Sniggleton, for instance, who had got the D.S.O. for his suggestion of a method of improving discipline in the Territorial Army. "There's no use sending the blighters home in disgrace when they've let the Army down," Toby had said. "They love being sent home. Stop their leave. That's the dodge." And the dodge it certainly was, and good old Toby got a D.S.O. for it, and a damned fine D.S.O. it was too, and now the dear old boy was G.O.C.-in-C. the South Central Command. The Tiger wired him a long message of congratulations, and sighed a little enviously. But his regret at being too old for an active part in all the military excitement did not last long. After all, he was doing his bit too.

Robert Hanson, the Financial Secretary to the War Office, was living in a sort of well-ordered and well-appointed paradise. He was right in the centre of things, he was making a name for himself as an administrator, and he was winning the respect of all parties by the quiet dignity with which he answered questions in the House. Even the hullabaloo which a handful of extreme Socialists raised about the Financial Secretary to the War Office being a son of a steel magnate and the brother-in-law of a Director of Perdurite did him no harm. For one thing it was obvious that the double connection was a clear guarantee of impartiality, and for another, any gentleman who is howled at by extreme Socialists is always certain of sympathy from his fellow-gentlemen, of whom there were four hundred and seventy-eight on the Ministerial Benches. The two ladies, who completed the Ministerial four hundred and eighty, were not so sure. But then, not being gentlemen, they did not count, except in divisions.

CHAPTER XXVII

Eleanor and Helen

While the steel-makers of Britain were being summoned by Mr Wendelmann's secretaries by telegraph and telephone to meet on the following morning in the boardroom of Messrs. Hanson, Wendelmann & Co. to hear what James Hanson might have to say to them, Eleanor was ringing the bell of Helen Everard's flat. It was not that Eleanor pocketed her pride in seeking an interview with Helen, for Eleanor had no vain pride of that sort to pocket. She was simply prepared to do everything that lay in her power to keep the affection of her husband, and it seemed to her that one of the things which she might do was to pay this visit. There was only one question which she wanted to ask Helen Everard. Some women might have thought it undignified, or cowardly, or defeatist, or ignominious, to ask it. To Eleanor it seemed a perfectly plain and obvious thing to do. No man, in reversed circumstances, could ever ask the question of another man without feeling that he had surrendered his birthright of domination. Eleanor's dignity was so serene that nothing could make her undignified, and her high simplicity of heart could surrender everything without surrendering anything.

And when she said at once to Helen Everard, "Do you want to take my husband away from me?" Helen felt as if someone had hit her violently on the heart. Her face became paler than ever, and she found it difficult to breathe for a moment. Then she cried in a gasping, half-stifled voice, "Oh! my dear," and she flung her arms round Eleanor.

"What a pretty flat you've got!" was the next thing that Eleanor found herself saying as she dried her eyes and gazed vaguely round. Everything was so misty that she could not see whether it was a pretty flat or not.

"Yes, isn't it," replied Helen as she dried hers. Everything was misty to her too. They were somehow, without much notion of how they had got there, sitting on a sofa. "You see, I love him," said Eleanor. Helen touched her hand with the faintest gossamer touch. "And he's so important and so popular and so awfully brilliant that — that it's difficult to see — difficult to see how he is going to settle down." Eleanor found it easier to keep her eyes fixed upon the open window rather than on this woman whose brown eyes were so full of understanding. She had broken down and cried once, and she did not want to cry again. So she resolutely looked at the fading autumnal leaves in the Park and went on: "I've lived in London all my life, but I'm really a country mouse. Jack is a cosmopolitan. He likes restaurants and houses and gaiety and musical comedies. Of course you may say that I knew all that when we got married, and that I ought not to have married him. But that never really has anything to do with it, has it?"

"Never."

"You see, I've been in love with Jack for so many years. He was my — oh well, you know what I mean. My eldest brothers were subalterns in the regiment when he was the senior captain — with a D.S.O. and an M.C. and the background of the War — and he used to come to the house and I used to go to dances at Aldershot, and — you can't blame me for being in love with him."

"I least of all women," said Helen very softly.

Eleanor was so engrossed in her almost confessional mood that she did not notice the implication in the words.

"I'd wanted to marry Jack ever since I was fifteen. I used to pray every night of my life that he would fall in love with me. And when he did——" She broke off and clenched her fists very tightly and stared at the fading autumnal leaves with a desperate intensity. Helen Everard could have burst into tears, real, uncontrollable, scalding tears this time. There was something magnificent about this unflinching facing of facts, about the quiet courage with which a gentle heart was telling, in few, simple words, the tragedy which would last so long as the heart continued to beat, about the pride which made no pretence at pride. She hoped passionately that Eleanor would leave unsaid the last part of the sentence, but she knew that in the presence of that unflinching courage and that pride her passionate hope was a vain hope.

"I am wrong," said Eleanor steadily. "I ought not to have said 'when he did fall in love with me.' I ought to have said, 'when he asked me to marry him,' I felt that my prayers had been answered, and that there was a God in heaven. I was wrong of course."

"Don't you believe in God?"

"I don't mean that I was wrong about that. I know that there is a God. But I was wrong in believing that my prayers had been answered. Jack is not in love with me. He never has been and he never will be."

A conventional denial would have been worse than stupid. It would have been cruel. So Helen said, "He never has been in love with anyone and he never will be in love with anyone."

Eleanor nodded because she could not find the voice with which to say that Helen was right.

Helen murmured, "That's his tragedy."

Eleanor faced her at last, with eyes wide open. "You know that too? You know that?"

"Any woman would," said Helen.

"Yes, of course. But somehow it doesn't make things easier."

"Because you know your tragedy, whereas he doesn't know his?"

Eleanor shivered. "Because Jack doesn't believe that it is a tragedy for him. That is the worst of all."

"Oh! men, men, men," cried Helen, jumping up and going across to the sherry decanter. "It's only eleven in the morning, and two honest, decent women ought not to drink sherry at eleven o'clock in the morning. But when you're trying to grapple with the male sex in the abstract, when you're trying to understand one-fiftieth part of the reasons which make them do the utterly insane, utterly childish, utterly wicked things they do do, you need a glass of something strong. And yet they can be so adorable, damn them!"

"Yes, that's just the trouble," said Eleanor in a small voice.

Helen laughed. "Let's drink to the damnation of men, and to their charm, damn them!" She drank her glass off. Eleanor took a sip our of hers and put the glass down.

"But what am I to do?" she said.

Helen shrugged her shoulders. "What can you do? What can any woman do who finds out that she has hitched herself to the wrong star? She can't unhitch herself. That's flat. Men can, nine times out of ten. Women only once in a hundred. That's why we get the worst of it, and the best of it too. Would you like to have been born a boy instead of a girl?"

Eleanor was jolted out of her single track of thought by the question.

"No, of course not," she said in surprise. "Would you?"

Helen smiled. "Good heavens no," she said. "But almost every man in the world is convinced that every woman in the world is secretly sorrowing that she is not a man. I am never quite sure whether it is a fundamental cause of their stupidity, or just a manifestation of it."

"Stupidity!" protested Eleanor, shocked by the heresy. "Men stupid! You can't possibly say that."

"Perhaps I shouldn't say stupid. What I mean, perhaps, is childish. Whatever it is, it's the quality that makes them do unbelievably cruel things to women and then forget all about it. That's a childish knack. If a man does a cruel thing to another man, he doesn't forget about it. He's on his guard against him for years and years, in case of a come-back. But if he hurts a woman, he isn't afraid of a come-back and he finds so many reasons in his own mind which completely justify him in hurting her, that in a week or two-presto! it's all forgotten."

"Except in the woman's mind," said Eleanor sadly. "Except, as you say, in the woman's mind," was the dry response.

"But why — why — why — should they be like that? Are they all like that?"

Helen Everard shrugged her shoulders. "There may be exceptions. But they haven't come my way. Perhaps I've been unlucky."

Eleanor abandoned the abstract and went back to her personal woes. "He — he — said dreadful things last night." Her eyes filled with tears.

"That's a good sign anyway," cried Helen. "He can't be wholly bad."

Eleanor was so astonished at the first part of this statement that she completely missed the black slander contained in the second.

"A good sign!" she exclaimed. "What on earth do you mean?"

"It shows that he knew he was in the wrong. When Norman — he was my — what shall I call it — my lord and master — got exceptionally drunk, he used to accuse me of the most awful things, and used to try and kick me sometimes, or hit me on the ear with his open hand, and I always knew that so long as he did that he was not completely dead to all decent feeling. But after we'd been married for about eighteen months he stopped cursing me when he'd done something particularly foul, and then I knew that everything was over. He either didn't notice what he'd done, or else he didn't care."

Eleanor's blue eyes were wide-open in horror.

"He used to kick and hit you!" she exclaimed.

Helen laughed her deep laugh. "Don't look as if you'd seen the devil, child. It's years ago now and all forgotten. Anyway, he only once landed a kick. It was just bad luck for him that it should have got me in the tummy."

"Bad luck for him!" The horror in the blue eyes was deeper than ever.

"Well, you see, I got over it in a couple of days. It took him at least a week of complete teetotalism before he recovered from the shock. And then it took him three weeks to recover from the week's teetotalism."

"I never heard of anything so ghastly," said Eleanor under her breath.

"Men aren't all quite as bad as that," replied Helen lightly. "I think I drew a particularly rotten card from the pack. But you haven't come here to talk about me."

Eleanor's horror disappeared and her nervousness returned.

"You don't think — you can't think — that Jack is stupid in a childish way," she said timidly.

"Abysmally," was the vehement reply, and Eleanor was just about to bristle up like a maternal hedgehog when Helen added, "but only a very little more abysmally stupid in a childish way than most men. When you're with a man, what does he talk about? Himself. Venture a small contribution to the conversation, and watch the mask of boredom snap into place. You've seen it a thousand times. Out comes the mechanical "Oh yes? Oh yes?" until you've finished, and then — pouf! away goes the mask and out comes the really interesting subject again. Go to a dance — any dance. Every man — even if he weighs eighteen stone and is perspiring like a torrent and has only danced once in his life — is absolutely confident that he is conferring an honour by dancing with any girl even if she is a combination of Aphrodite and Pavlova. And you know it."

"Ye-es," said Eleanor doubtfully, watching some long-cherished illusions vanishing.

"Meet a well-known man and his wife at dinner," went on Helen with a rush. "Who does the talking? The Lion roars all the evening, and the pretty little Lioness who has heard it all ten thousand times before, and who is probably fifty times more amusing and clever than the Lion is anyway, listens to every word, and laughs at every right moment, and gazes at him admiringly all the time. What do you suppose she is thinking?"

"I don't know — I suppose she is admiring him," stammered Eleanor, caught unawares by the sudden question amid the flow of words.

"Eleanor Crawford, you are nothing but a humbug," said Helen severely. "You know perfectly well that if she isn't wondering about her next new hat, she is thinking that her little fellow is speaking his piece very nicely and being a great credit to her among all these grown-ups. You've done it yourself a thousand times."

"I haven't been married long enough for that," protested Eleanor, laughing more cheerfully than at any moment in the conversation so far.

"But you've done it with your father and your brothers——"

"But how could I think of Daddy as a little fellow?"

"What's that got to do with it? They're all schoolboys. Hasn't your father seemed rather young to you?"

"Oh, yes of course, but——"

"Well, there you are then." Helen lay back among her cushions in triumph. But still Eleanor refused to give in entirely.

"Men have got fifty times the brains we've got. There isn't a single thing, apart from babies and that sort of thing, which we can do that they can't do better."

"They can make much nicer wars than we would ever be able to," conceded Helen, "and they can build much slummier slums, and they can lift much heavier weights, and they can spend far more of their wages on drink than women can——"

"Oh! you're ridiculous," cried Eleanor. "Think of the whole organization of Society——"

"That is precisely what I am thinking about," said Helen drily.

"Women could never run banks, or insurance companies, or the Stock Exchange."

"I agree with you. I doubt if it would ever occur to us to produce a lady Hatry, or a girl Whitaker Wright, or even a female Anderton-Mawle."

"Then what do you think men are good at," cried Eleanor, tired of having her illusions attacked, "besides fighting and building slums and weight-lifting?"

"Writing poetry, of course," Helen replied promptly, "and designing our dresses, and inventing new dishes, and writing plays, and painting pictures, and directing films, and tasting wines — all the trimmings of life, all the fripperies, all the lovely and unnecessary little luxuries."

Eleanor was so enchanted by this theory that she again forgot her woes for a moment or two and laughed gaily.

"I think you're lovely," she cried. "I honestly believe you're pretending to think that men are unpractical."

"Listen to me, you silly child," replied Helen, "and try to clear that pretty head of yours of some of the nonsense it's crammed with. Answer this question. Do you think it's practical to bring the world to the very edge of another war that might destroy everything? Do you regard that as a triumph of masculine statesmanship?"

"No — but ——"

"Answer another one. Don't you think it's nauseating hypocrisy for parsons to preach the Sermon on the Mount and wear a military uniform? Women aren't good enough to be parsons, but I doubt if we would ever be quite so awful as that."

"You sound as if you hated all men."

Helen smiled a little grimace of a smile. "No, I'm a woman too, and I love them. And that again is the worst of it — and the best of it."

Eleanor was angry with herself to find that she had no arguments left except the old defensive one, "But would women do any better?"

"I don't know," said Helen, "if they would do any better. But one thing I do know, that they could not do any worse. Men are a worthless crew really, but horribly attractive."

"Jack isn't worthless," Eleanor flared up, and then she remembered her woes again, and her face clouded.

"Were you — are you — were you ever in love with Jack?" she stammered. "I've no right to ask, and I'm a fool to ask it, but——"

"Yes, I was," said Helen steadily.

"And — and — now?"

There was a long pause. Then, "I was the hundredth woman, my dear, who could unhitch herself from the star."

After Eleanor had gone, Helen stood for a long time at the window watching the children playing in the Green Park. At last the autumnal air of the afternoon grew a little chilly and she shut the window. "I wish to God I was the hundredth woman," she said, and she went off to drink a cocktail with Harry.

CHAPTER XXVIII

Give the Englishman my Solemn Word of Honour

The day which had been such a momentous one in the lives of a handful of comparatively obscure personages, was not yet finished.

Sir Montagu Anderton-Mawle had an interview with Crawford, and gave him his operation-orders for his visit to Cimbro-Suevonia. And they sounded like operation-orders. The little baronet's voice rang like a rather tinny clarion. The pretence of good-fellowship and heartiness was abandoned, and the Chief dictated his orders to his subordinate.

"You will not talk to Waldemar," he rapped out, thrusting his right hand into the breast of his jacket. "Waldemar is, unfortunately, incorruptible. He has grabbed a whole country, so he doesn't want any cash. It's a pity, but it can't be helped. Do you understand that?"

"Yes," said Crawford sulkily. He did not like being spoken to like this.

"You will concentrate upon the Minister of the Interior and the Minister of Commerce and the Minister of Police. You will hand each of them a draft upon the Amsterdam-Batavia Bank for fifty thousand pounds. Got that?"

Crawford nodded.

"You will tell each of them that I will pay them a royalty of one pound for every ton of Gloxite that is shipped to me. You will tell them that I will pay on the nail. You will emphasize the fact that no one else will pay them as much or as promptly. You may have to square the Minister of Communications as well. Got that?"

"Yes."

"It hasn't taken you long," said the financier, "to drop the Army trick of saying 'sir' to your superiors."

Crawford started and flushed with anger. Sir Montagu turned away to conceal his grin of delight. To make any big man squirm with helpless rage gave him an exquisite pleasure, and the pleasure was raised to an intensified keenness when the big man happened to fancy himself as a lady-killer.

He went on sharply, "Now be kind enough to repeat your instructions."

Crawford, wriggling with rage, repeated them. At the end, Sir Montagu, glowing with pride at having made him look, and feel, like a schoolboy, reached up and pinched his ear in the best Imperial style.

"Run along now," he said. "Catch the night aeroplane to Paris. Square those fellows and I'll give you a thousand pounds."

"By the way — sir," Crawford gulped the hateful word, "talking of money, I believe I — er — I ought to thank you——"

Sir Montagu pushed him towards the door in a humorous sort of way, and wound up with a parting shot: "Nonsense, my boy. Delighted to do anything I can for that charming wife of yours."

.....

Another little scene took place at Partington Crescent when Harry Winter arrived.

"We leave for Cimbro-Suevonia on Tuesday," said Hanson. "Will you telegraph to your brother to be ready for us?"

"I will," said Winter.

"You really have been a mining engineer?" shot out the old man suddenly.

"Yes, but not for twenty years."

"You remember how to do it?"

"Yes, pretty well."

"I am going to do a little experimental work, prospecting is the word I believe, in Cimbro-Suevonia. I rely on you for technical assistance."

"If it's anything big," said Winter, "hadn't you better get someone who is more up-to-date?"

"Can you lay a blasting charge?"

"Oh yes."

"And fire it?"

"Yes."

"That's all I shall want."

"Have you got the dynamite?" asked Winter.

"Your brother must see to that."

"And a better man for seeing to dynamite you couldn't find in a month of Sundays," remarked Winter heartily.

"Good," said Hanson absently, and then he nodded. "That's all."

In the hall Winter met Ruth Collins.

"Are you going on this party of the Governor's?" he asked.

"Yes."

"I say——" he began earnestly, but she cut him short.

"If you are going to say anything about what you call 'this party of the Governor's,' don't say it here where anyone might be listening."

Winter seized her by the arm and almost dragged her into the empty dining-room.

"Will you marry me?" he said.

She regarded him gravely. "I don't think so," she said after a moment.

"I thought — I mean I should like to protect you when the row starts."

"What row?"

"Well, it looks as if we're in for a bit of a dust-up. What with dynamite and all."

"And you want to marry me, simply to protect me?"

"Well, of course I'm in love with you too."

She smiled a quick, mischievous smile.

"Oh, well. That's always something." And with that she ran past him and vanished into Mr Hanson's study.

.....

A meeting took place on that same evening between the Hochwohlgeborn Freiherr Manfred von Czepan-Eichenhöh and his Leader.

"Give the Englishman my solemn word of honour that I will do nothing for a month," said the Leader, and when the Freiherr had left for the aerodrome with this message, the Leader was free to study the plans which the General Staff had drawn up for sudden air attack upon Cimbro-Suevonia on the following Thursday. The plans involved a triple assault. A thousand aeroplanes were to bomb the Gloxite mines, a thousand the railway connecting the mines and the port of Blut, and a thousand the port of Blut itself. The General Staff calculated that if the worst came to the worst and only one of these three were successful, the supply of Gloxite would be held up for six months, and if two were successful, for eighteen months. They did not ask, or expect, all three to be successful. A delay of six months, the General Staff concluded, would enable the Reich to catch up with British Rearmament. A delay of eighteen months would enable the Reich to win a world war.

.....

Jack Crawford told the porter at his club to telephone to Mrs Crawford at 44 Partington Crescent, and tell her that he had left on urgent business for the Continent, and that he did not know when he would be back. There was a letter waiting for him at the club, in a writing that was very familiar to him. The notepaper was also familiar to him, for it was the blue, with mauve edgings, of the Nursing Home of Sir Albion Featherby. Crawford tore it up without opening it and went upstairs, whistling gaily, to the smoking-room for a couple of quick drinks before setting out.

CHAPTER XXIX

The Steel-Makers Meet

The steel-makers from east, west, north, and south had answered the summons of telegram and telephone and sat at the long shiny table in the board-room of Messrs. Hanson, Wendelmann & Co., and waited for James Hanson to begin. There was an atmosphere of mingled tension and eagerness — tension because every man present knew that a crisis of the first magnitude had arisen in their trade, and eagerness to hear what Hanson had to propose. At least seventy-five per cent of those present had been contemporaries of Hanson's in the old days — some indeed were his seniors — and knew him personally. To the younger men he was an almost legendary figure. The tales, by this time embroidered and exaggerated no doubt, of his spectacular feats, of his lightning strokes, of his direct and sensational cutting of Gordian knots, had made him into an epic figure, a sort of Viking of steel and iron.

The meeting had been called for eleven a.m., and at five minutes to eleven everything was ready. There was the usual hum of conversation which precedes the business on such occasions — exchanges of greetings, enquiries after lumbago, golf handicaps, wives, and youngsters — but as the board-room clock struck the hour the hum died down and faces turned towards the end of the table where Hanson was sitting. For at least a minute there was silence. Then Hanson pressed a bell and whispered to the secretary, who answered it. There was another pause. Another secretary came in and there was more whispering. At five-past eleven the first secretary came in with a note. Hanson read it, frowned for a moment, and then rose to address the meeting. "Gentlemen," he said, "I must first present to you the apologies of my partner, Mr Wendelmann. Mr Wendelmann has just sent me a note to say that he is detained on unexpected business of the most vitally urgent nature, and that he will join us as soon as he possibly can. He begs — indeed the word he uses is 'implores' — us not to separate this morning before he has had an opportunity of laying this matter before us. Those of you, gentlemen, who know my partner will readily appreciate that he does not use such emphatic language without good cause."

There were murmurs of assent, and the tension noticeably increased.

"There is no need for me to go into details of our position," continued James Hanson. "We all know it. The country is going to spend five hundred million pounds on armaments within the next few years. Perdurite is a better substance than steel. Perdurite will get the contracts. I might argue that if this happens British armaments will be at the mercy of the foreign supply of Gloxite, and thus pose as a patriot. I might argue that great hardship will be suffered by our shareholders, especially by the widows and orphans, and pose as a philanthropist. I will do neither. I will be frank and say that great financial losses will be suffered by you, gentlemen, and by me. I personally do not propose to suffer that financial loss without putting up the strongest and most vigorous fight that lies in my power."

Again there were murmurs of assent.

"I have worked out a scheme," went on the leonine old millionaire, "which, if successful, will hamstring Perdurite during the next two years, the crucial years of Rearmament. The nature of the scheme I do not intend to disclose to you, gentlemen, or to anyone else except my own — er — secretariat, which will have to help me to carry out the details of it. You must trust me to do the best I can. And if you do not trust me, I shall do the best I can anyway, and be damned to you."

The steel magnates shuffled their feet and nodded and exchanged glances. Seventy-five per cent of them thought, "Just the same old Hanson"; twenty-five per cent of them thought, "He is exactly the Viking of the legend."

"I will take my part in the spiking — almost literal spiking" — Hanson smiled to himself for a moment "of the Perdurite guns. You must take your part in what follows. That is why I have asked you to meet me here. I have not asked you to come here to give me advice. I want no man's advice except Wendelmann's. I have asked you to come so that I can tell you something. The British Empire must rearm." His voice rang out like a resonant gong. "And if it does not rearm with Perdurite, it must rearm with steel. And we, gentlemen, must be ready to play our part. If I spike Anderton-Mawle, you must make your contribution too. There must be co-operation between us all, pooling of secrets, pooling of patents, pooling of resources. Otherwise Germany will see her chance, and another world war will engulf us.

"War, gentlemen, is the Armourer's catastrophe. Preparation for war is the Armourer's paradise.

"If you will co-operate to seize this mighty opportunity, and to seize it quickly, I will provide you with the opportunity."

There was a long silence after he had sat down, and then a simultaneous outbreak of murmuring in all parts of the room.

Then an elderly man rose and said, "Mr Chairman, I see in today's *Morning Post* that you are leaving for Cimbro-Suevonia on Tuesday. That can only mean that you intend to attack Perdurite through Gloxite. And if I can draw that deduction, so can Anderton-Mawle. Every official in the land will already have been bribed against you. You are a strong man, James Hanson, and a bold one. But I do not believe that even you can hammer Gloxite on the Stz Stock Exchange, or can cause a general financial panic in Cimbro-Suevonia, against Mawle, against his bribed friends in Stz, and against the resources, which the Government contracts are already buttressing, that are ranged behind Perdurite."

The elderly man sat down amid a ripple of unwilling agreement.

James Hanson stood up again.

"The point of this discussion," he said coldly, "is not what I can do. It is what you are going to do. My part is settled. It is perfectly true that I am going to Stz to attack Mawle through Gloxite. Whether I can hammer Gloxite is my affair. What are you going to do when I've hammered it? That is the essential question."

A younger man jumped up briskly. "I move, gentlemen," he cried in eager, confident tones, "that we accept Mr Hanson at his own estimation, and that we appoint a committee here and now to draw up a scheme for the pooling of our secrets, our patents, and our resources."

A hubbub broke out at once. Hanson sat at his end of the table and surveyed the excited men from under his heavy eyebrows. He was incomparably the coolest man present.

There may have been something hypnotic about his coolness, or about his arrogant treatment of men who had not encountered arrogance in others for a great number of years, or it may have been a combination of the three. At any rate, after a few minutes' buzz, one of the oldest men present — he was ninety-one, and was on the board of forty-two companies — excused himself for not standing up, and seconded the motion.

There was a flickering show of hands, at first held up in uncertain ones and twos, and then gaining in confidence and numbers, just as sheep do on leaping through a gap in a hedge to get from one field which they dislike to another field which they do not know, until almost every man present had signified his agreement, and at that moment Mr Wendelmann came in.

He looked old and tired, and his black eyes were heavy. James Hanson shot one glance at him and saw that something terrible had happened.

He jumped to his feet and put an arm across his partner's shoulders and patted them.

"Thank you," said Wendelmann, half under his breath. "I do not need to ask you for help. You are always ready."

The next moment the old Jew had recovered his nerve and was addressing the meeting in his quiet, unemotional voice.

"I have just come from an interview with Sir Montagu Anderton-Mawle," he said, and the atmosphere, strained and difficult before, became electric.

"There have been developments, very recent developments, in the matter between his associates and us, which have completely altered the situation. Two days ago, Sir Montagu was approached by Imperial Chemical Industries with the information that a young scientist in their employ has made an epoch-making discovery. This young man, after eight or ten years of research, has discovered a way of reducing Gloxite to its essentials, just as Madame Curie reduced pitchblende. I am probably using the wrong terms — I am no scientist — but, in effect, just as Madame Curie discovered that so many tons of pitchblende could be made into a gramme of radium, so has this young man discovered that so many tons of Gloxite can be made into a certain cure for cancer in women."

In the rattle of chatter that broke out no one noticed that James Hanson was sitting immobile, silent, staring at his partner with a look of almost fear in his magnificent old face. Wendelmann raised a thin yellowish hand and went on:

"Imperial Chemicals have offered to buy as much of Anderton-Mawle's Gloxite interests as he will let them have, and have also offered a guarantee that they will not make a profit out of the cancer cure. Anderton-Mawle has entered into the same spirit of philanthropy," the Jew's voice hardened, "and has offered one-fifth of the entire output of the mines to Imperial Chemicals as a personal present from himself for the betterment of mankind — or rather of womankind — and the remaining four-fifths of the output at cost price."

After a momentary gasp, the entire meeting demanded simultaneously:

"Then what about Perdurite?"

"Sir Montagu Anderton-Mawle," said Mr Wendelmann, "told me half an hour ago that he is only interested in humanity. The vast profits which he would certainly make out of Rearmament mean nothing to him in comparison with the benefits which this cancer cure will confer upon the world. Money is no object to him. All he wants is to do good. He is prepared to scrap Perdurite, to close his factories, to discharge his employees, and to go into voluntary liquidation, if we, the steel group, will also contribute. He suggests that we find a sum of three million pounds which will enable him to pay off his shareholders approximately at the rate of seven shillings in the pound, which he appears to consider a more than adequate rate for any shareholder, and that we should add a secret bonus to him as a small token of our appreciation of all his philanthropy, a bonus about which his shareholders would know nothing, of twenty-five million pounds."

The uproar was instantaneous, but it died away very quickly as these shrewd, experienced men of affairs realized the full implication of the dilemma. All eyes turned towards Hanson.

"I need hardly say," added Wendelmann, "that the word of the men in ICI is beyond suspicion. The cancer cure is genuine. ICI's offer to forgo their profits is genuine."

James Hanson lay back in his big, upright, leathered chair and half closed his eyes. "I find something almost luxurious," he said quietly to Wendelmann, "in the contemplation of that Mawle fellow's cleverness. His cleverness is so clever that it bears the stamp of genius. Either we pay up, in which case Anderton-Mawle clears out with twenty-five millions and the golden aureole of the greatest benefactor the human race has ever known, or else we fight him and reap the execration of the world. It has all the beauty of a mathematical proposition. Well, I won't give in to the fellow."

He stood up suddenly and said, "Gentlemen, a resolution has been proposed, seconded, and carried, that a committee be set up to co-ordinate our resources, while I do my best to prevent Gloxite from reaching the world. Is there any other business?"

"But — but — but——" stuttered the old man who had seconded the resolution, and then his words ceased to flow. Another man, a big Sheffield man, tried to say something, and he also dried up. A third managed to get out the words, "But a cancer cure!"

The spell was broken, and the talk became general again for a moment or two.

"We must reconsider our position," cried a man from South Wales. "One human being in seven in this country dies of cancer, Mr Chairman. In terrible agony, Mr Chairman, I tell you." His Welsh accent, which was usually kept under control, had got unleashed in the excitement.

"Indeed, my God, yes," cried another Welshman. "We are all good Christians."

Hanson shot a wicked glance at Wendelmann, but his partner's melancholy face did not respond.

A man from the South of Scotland said heavily, "It is a terrible decision to have to make. Could we not bargain with the man Mawle?"

"Mawle holds the cards," said Hanson. "Why should he bargain? He'd be a fool if he did."

"Mawle's no fool," said a Lancastrian, who knew a good deal about the Tasmanian's famous reconstruction of the Lancashire cotton trade.

"Mr Chairman," said the Scotsman, "what is your own opinion?"

"Fight to the last," replied Hanson, raising his voice for the first time, and striking the table.

"You mean that you would carry out your scheme to ruin the Gloxite syndicate, just as if Mr Wendelmann's news had never arrived and the cancer cure never discovered."

"Precisely."

"But man alive," cried the second of the Welshmen, leaning across the table, "think, think! One life in seven!"

"General Sir Herbert Lawrence, the Chairman of Vickers," replied Hanson steadily, "in giving evidence not so long ago before the Enquiry into the Private Manufacture of Arms, said, 'We greatly exaggerate the sanctity of human life.' I agree with the Chairman of Vickers."

"I also agree with the Chairman of Vickers," cried an old man from the far end of the room. "What are we? Sentimentalists? Woolly-headed old women? Spinsters? Painted young night-club women? Of course we are not.

We are business men, we are realists. We must face facts. Here's a man wants to ruin our trade either by cutthroat competition or by blackmail. Smash him then, say I. Smash him into pulp. Smash him into dust. And if we smash this cancer cure at the same time, well — it's a pity. But it can't be helped. There are too many women in the world anyway. Everybody knows that." He sat down amid a definite murmur of approval.

The two Welshmen were still whimpering a little, and one of them moved an adjournment of the meeting for further consideration. Hanson refused to accept the motion.

"If we do not strike quickly, Germany will attack Cimbro-Suevonia. Will Germany use the Gloxite for a cancer cure for women?"

"Ah! that's the point," exclaimed a man, and there were murmured remarks of:

"That clinches it."

"Of course she won't."

"That's unanswerable."

The fiery old man from the far end of the room jumped up again.

"We've passed our resolution, gentlemen. I move that this meeting, having concluded its business, dissolves. The committee can be set up in the usual way."

The motion was seconded and carried *nem. con.* The two Welshmen, three men from Durham, and Wendelmann did not vote. The meeting dissolved in complete silence, leaving only Hanson and Wendelmann in the room.

"Well, my friend," said Hanson grimly, "and what do you think of the sanctity of human life?"

"I am an Oriental, but you frighten me, James Hanson," replied the old Jew. "My race ought to be accustomed to cruel and violent death by now, but somehow I find it difficult."

"Face the facts," cried Hanson almost brutally. "These Gloxite mines are a permanent temptation to the warmakers of the world. I am going to destroy the mines."

Wendelmann started. "The mines themselves? Or the finance of the Syndicate?"

"The mines themselves."

The Jew smiled an ironical smile. "Face the facts yourself, my friend. Will you be allowed to walk up to the pit-shafts and drop dynamite down them? Don't you suppose that Master Mawle has got every official in the country bribed, and the whole place bristling with troops and gendarmerie?"

"That had occurred to my poor intelligence also," admitted Hanson. "Half-wit though I am, I had just succeeded in envisaging that possibility."

"Well?"

Hanson looked round. "Walls, in the old days of the proverb, never really had ears," he said, "but in these up-to-date scientific days they might really have microphones. Come and stroll across the Park with me." Wendelmann's Rolls-Royce dropped them in Birdcage Walk, and the two old men went into the Green Park.

"They sank the main shafts of the Gloxite mines during these last two years, if I am not mistaken?" said Hanson, when they were clear of passers-by.

"Yes."

"On the south side of the great Cimbrian range of mountains?"

"Yes."

"And before that, no one knew if there was any Gloxite there, and no one cared?"

"A little had been found further to the east," said Wendelmann, "but it wasn't till the Durite alloy was invented that people remembered it. Nobody had ever worked the deposits before, and no one knew the extent of them,"

"Wrong on both points," replied Hanson. "The Romans had worked the deposits, and I knew the extent of them."

"Perhaps I was wrong in persuading him to return to active affairs," murmured Wendelmann. "The strain of the morning has proved too much for him. He is seeing hallucinations. Very sad." He tapped his forehead and added, "Everyone knows that, except for that one small disused pit, there were no workings, and never have been any workings, along the whole south face of the mountain range."

"Precisely," said Hanson with triumphant suavity, "but I broke into the old Roman galleries from the north face of the mountain range."

Wendelmann stopped and stared at him. "What are you saying?" he exclaimed, and then he added simply, "Tell me."

"I'll tell you. It was fifty years ago —fifty years! whew! it's a long time. I went up looking for iron ore. I was working for Penistone's in those days — it was before you came along — and I had a notion that we might find an ore body on that north face. So we did. It was a small one, but it encouraged me to go on. I went on. I drove a long gallery into the mountain and I found a little more iron, and then one day I cut into someone else's gallery. There were skeletons of men wearing chains and a couple of coins of Trajan and a lot of Roman bronze tools of the fourth century. The British Museum verified it for me. I went down the gallery and found lots of other workings. The place was honeycombed with them."

"What were they mining?"

"Copper, I think. I found some here and there. And there was a mass of this Gloxite everywhere. I had some analysed, but when I found it was commercially no use I paid no more attention to it. I spent three months altogether there, looking to see if the Romans had left any copper behind worth picking up — they hadn't of course. The Romans very seldom did leave anything behind worth picking up — and I made a map of their workings. There were scores of miles of them. The interesting thing was that as you went south into the mountain, the drier the galleries became. When we started, on the north face, the galleries were very wet. Full of water. We had to pump all the time. But to the south they got dry. I found out the reason in the end."

He stopped and lit a cigar. Wendelmann smiled a little to himself. He understood his old partner so very well. He knew that he was approaching the crucial point in the tale, and he knew that the lighting of the cigar was not because the story-teller wanted a cigar, but because the story-teller wanted to keep his audience in true dramatic suspense.

"Last week," continued James Hanson, puffing away, "I bought for two thousand pounds, through the good offices of one or two old friends of mine, a large-scale map of the new Gloxite Syndicate's workings, into the south face of the mountains. One of the Chief Engineers of the Syndicate had been gambling on the Stock Exchange in Stz, and was embarrassed for ready money. You know how it often is."

"Oh, quite, quite," murmured Wendelmann. "We all know how it often is."

"The new workings are not a long distance from the lake," said Hanson in a negligent voice, swiping at a dandelion with his umbrella.

Again the old Jew was startled. "What lake?" he exclaimed.

"Oh, didn't I tell you?" asked Hanson in elaborately innocent surprise. "I thought I had. The water from the Roman galleries as we went south all drained into a rather jolly lake in a huge underground cavern. Rather like Rider Haggard's stuff. Or those big grottoes in Austria. Anyway there it is. And that's all." Wendelmann, his face pale and fear in his eyes, clutched him by the arm and brought him to a standstill.

"In God's name, Hanson, what are you going to do?"

"With a strong charge of dynamite," said Hanson, "I am going to let the lake into the new workings."

"But the workers, the miners! Hanson — don't you know — women and children as well as men work in the mines in Cimbro-Suevonia. They will all drown like rats."

"We greatly exaggerate the sanctity of human life, Wendelmann," said Hanson firmly.

The old Jew turned away with a gesture of despair.

"I cannot escape my share of Nemesis," he said. "Any good things I have ever done in this sad world, I have done with money which you have helped me to make. I cannot refuse to accept my responsibility for the bad things. When we throw a stone into a pool we cannot say we have not caused the ripples."

"But I want to cause the ripples. I am proud of causing the ripples." Hanson's voice was full of his vital energy.

"That is the difference between us, Hanson," said Wendelmann. "You are big. You can see clearly the vast issues. It always was your strength. But I am weak. I can only see the widows and orphans of those miners, or if you like, those women who are dying a dreadful death of cancer. That has always been my weakness. But I tell you this, James Hanson, and I say it to the only man in this world that I have ever loved, I wish in the name of the God of Abraham, and of Isaac, and of Jacob, that I had never met you, all those forty years ago."

"And I say to you, Amschel Wendelmann," replied Hanson, "the only man in the world that I have ever loved, that I thank the Almighty God that I met you. And that, as you say, is the difference between us."

"We must go forward," said the Jew sadly. "We are as Jonathan and David. Nothing can take away the love we have for one another."

"You would not have me turn back from my resolution?"

"Not if you think you are right."

"I know I am right. The only ultimate horror is war. The peace of the world must be maintained."

"And you can maintain it?"

"I can destroy a fatal cause of war."

"Is there no other way? Must you kill those men and women and children in the mines, and must you doom all those other women to a lingering death?"

"Do you think I'm a monster of savagery?" burst out Hanson. "Do you think I want to kill women and children? Can't you see that I want to save the world from another war? Can't you see that I must sacrifice this handful for the welfare of the rest? If one woman dies of cancer, six will live to bear children. Bring on your world war, and six will be killed by gas bombs and the seventh will bear a rickety starveling. Don't you see, don't you see" — he seized Wendelmann's shoulder and shook it vehemently— — "that I am killing one woman to save six? Good God! Do you suppose I look forward to having that one woman's death on my soul? But I would sooner face that than face the responsibility of having failed to save the six. Wendelmann. Amschel. Don't you see?"

"Yes, James, I see."

"And are you going to desert me?"

Wendelmann took Hanson's great gnarled right fist between his two thin parchmenty hands, and said, "The Lord do so to me, and more also, if ought but death part thee and me."

"I am glad, old friend, that you said that," said Hanson, "because the parting is very near."

"Ah!" The Jew stroked his iron-grey beard and his dark Eastern eyes looked into the vivid blue eyes of the Englishman. "Is the parting so near?"

"Yes. You see, I do not exaggerate the sanctity of my own life."

"You have a dark and sudden mind. I said it once before, you remember."

"I remember." There was a pause.

"Well, auf wiedersehen," said Wendelmann. "And God be with you Jonathan."

"I will not say 'auf wiedersehen,'" replied Hanson, "because it would be false. But I will give you the English version of 'God be with you.' Good-bye — David."

The two old men shook hands in a momentary handclasp. Neither looked at the face of the other. Then they turned abruptly and walked away, Wendelmann back to his Rolls-Royce, which was waiting in Birdcage Walk, and Hanson towards Piccadilly, to pick up a taxi to take him back to Partington Crescent.

.....

Ruth Collins was in the study when Hanson got back. He laid down his umbrella on a chair with a gesture as if it was the sword of a vanquished knight surrendering to invincible forces. He took off his grey gloves and threw them down beside the umbrella, like a vanquished knight stripping himself of his own gauntlets. Then he sat down in his chair like an old man who had lost his last hold on life.

Ruth Collins knew very well that a tragedy was at hand. Her employer, the man who was almost in love with her, the greatest man she had ever met or was ever likely to meet, was nearly at the end of his tether. It was as if this splendid, famous old man was a small child and she was his elder experienced sister.

"What is it?" she whispered, dropping on her knees beside his chair. "What is it? Tell me."

He put his hand upon her brown hair and said in a queer, half-choked voice, "Ruth, do you think that we exaggerate the sanctity of human life?"

"No," she cried strongly.

"Are you too against me, my beautiful?" he said sadly.

She saw instantly where the tragedy was, where the end of the tether lay, and she dropped the vehement tone of her first "No."

"Listen, my lover-that-almost-was," she said softly. "Some time or other I think that — with the grace of God — I shall bring a human life into the world, out of my body. Do you think that it will be possible for me to exaggerate the sanctity of that human life?"

For several long minutes James Hanson stroked her soft hair.

CHAPTER XXX

James Hanson in Cimbro-Suevonia

Darkness was falling, the sudden, violet, rose-scented darkness of south-eastern Europe, before the three men left the Hotel de l'Univers et Penistone, in the main square of Stz. It had been a long and rather tiring day, for the return of the great James Hanson to Cimbro-Suevonia, even on a brief visit, had been a red-letter day for the newspapers of the capital. Reporters, photographers, and cinema-men had swarmed round the hotel for hours. There had also been a luncheon at the British Embassy, and a tea-party at the Foreign Office.

But the evening had been kept free. Hanson had pleaded the infirmities of a septuagenarian who had just come off the Orient express, and had refused an invitation to dine with the British Chamber of Commerce, four invitations to official receptions, and sixteen invitations to unofficial private supper-parties.

From six o'clock onwards the old millionaire sat in his private sitting-room and waited for the darkness, and with him sat Harry Winter and his twin brother, Bill. It was a silent party. Hanson had pulled his chair to the window and stared out over the great city to which he had come as a boy of eighteen more than fifty years before, when the streets were paved with rough pebblestones and the oxen pulled the rattling, springless carts between the rows of gaily painted, wooden, two-storeyed houses, and the lichen had shone, ochre-coloured, in the sun, and the girls had worn their lovely peasant dresses, and the tinkle of sheep-bells and the sound of wind in fir-trees had never been far distant.

Now everything was concrete, and chromium, and bowler hats, and American motor-cars, and be-frogged and be-spurred cavalry officers, and loud-speakers. Below, in the square, was all the hustle and bustle of a great modern cosmopolitan city. It was no longer sleepy, happy, picturesque Santa Leonora, but Stz, the Paris of the Balkans, the Chicago of the South-east, the Buenos Aires of Europe.

Harry Winter did not disturb his employer's long reverie, and Bill Winter was by nature a silent man. At last Hanson moved. He stretched out his arm and said, "Look! The evening star." The pale gold of Hesperus stood high in the heavens above the huge copper-green dome of the new Casino, and the western sky was fading its Mediterranean blue into a haze of amethyst and topaz. A faintly chill breath of wind shook the curtains, and Hanson got up suddenly and stretched his arms above his head.

"'And the sun went down and the stars came out far over the summer sea,'" he quoted. "It is very beautiful, my Cimbria, don't you think?"

"Were you happy here?" said Harry abruptly. Hanson looked at him queerly. "Why do you ask that?" he said in an odd half-choked voice.

"I don't know," replied Winter. "But you looked somehow as if you were thinking of happy times long ago."

"Happy times long ago," repeated the old man slowly. "Yes, I suppose I was. I was eighteen when I first came to Santa Leonora — eighteen, and all the world to play with. There was an apple-tree at that corner over there — where the Guaranty Trust Company's office is — and old Tom Macadam lived in the house behind and he used to hitch his horse to the tree when he came in from work. Poor old Tom. He died quickly. That is one good thing."

"How?" asked Harry conventionally. The old man was talking to himself, but it would be tactful to pretend to take an interest in what he was saying. To Harry's surprise, Hanson swung round and answered the question energetically.

"How did old Tom die? I fancy you would say that I killed him."

Bill Winter, thin, brown, hard, alert, compact, shot out, "And did you?"

"I sold the shell which killed him," said Hanson sombrely, "and I sold the gun which fired the shell, and I made the war in which the shell was fired. Do you call that killing him?"

"No," said Bill Winter.

"Yes," said Harry.

"When I was eighteen years of age," went on Hanson, folding his arms across his chest and gazing down almost fiercely at the twins from under his iron-grey eyebrows, "this country of Cimbria, and this town of Santa Leonora, were lovely, quiet, soft, timid places. If ever a land had a soul, that land was Cimbria. Look at it now" — he turned and threw out an arm towards the straggly, grimy, shoddy town that stretched away into the distance—— "that is my doing. There is no soul in Cimbria now. Did I kill that soul?"

This time Bill Winter said nothing. Harry firmly said "Yes."

"Well, Mr Gun-runner, what say you?" Hanson faced Bill Winter squarely.

"Places have no souls," was the blunt reply.

"Ah! You think that?" murmured the millionaire. "I wish I could believe you."

"If you had it all over again, would you do the same as you have done?" asked Harry Winter.

"I wonder. I wonder. I wonder." The old man swung round and faced the open window again. The setting sun was turning the silvery peaks of far-off mountains into gold. The pine-woods on the slopes below were already in shadow, and the arc-lamps were flaring in the streets of the city.

"I made great wealth for the people of the land," said Hanson thoughtfully, "but I also prepared the way for that — that monstrosity. The money I gave to hospitals eliminated the disease of typhus, and my mines introduced the disease of miners' consumption. I taught the peasants how to read and write. I also taught them how to fight. When I found them, they did not always have enough to eat. When I left them, they had enough to eat — out of Chicago tins. I found them free and I left them — well, Mr Winter — what did I leave them? Slaves?"

"Very nearly," said Harry sombrely.

"But damn it, man," cried Hanson, "the world must go on. If I had not done it, someone else would have. The iron was here and the coal was there. Someone had to bring them together. It happened that it fell to me."

"But does the world go on — I mean does it go onwards?"

"It must," exclaimed the old man vehemently. "It must go onwards. That is why we are here tonight. That is why we are going to do what we are going to do. Do you think I would destroy the cancer cure if I wasn't utterly convinced that I am saving something infinitely more important? Gloxite may be found elsewhere. Other cures for cancer will be discovered. But if another world war is loosed, then all, all will be destroyed. Socrates and Copernicus and Newton and Galileo and Velazquez will have lived in vain, and the four Gospels might just as well have not been written."

"And Christ?" Bill Winter shot out unexpectedly.

"Might just as well have never lived," replied Hanson in a firm voice. He was not in the least taken aback by the unexpectedness of the question.

"You a Christian?" the ex-sailor shot out again.

Hanson smiled a twisted, unhumorous smile. "Your brother would deny that gun-makers can be Christians." Harry Winter nodded.

"That's no answer," said the other twin shortly.

"No. You're right," admitted Hanson. "It isn't an answer. And it's a difficult question to answer honestly. But I'll try."

There was a long silence. Harry Winter smoked a cigarette in quick, feverish puffs, threw it away and lit another, and smoked that too in the same way, flicking ash on to his toes, his trousers, his waistcoat, and the carpet indiscriminately. Bill Winter, the inscrutable, brown, thin adventurer, sat absolutely motionless. His hard, wiry hands lay on the arms of his chair as immobile as the hands of a long-trained actor. His pale-blue eyes were unwavering upon Hanson's face.

James Hanson himself looked out over the toadstool city, where once old Tom Macadam had hitched his horse to the apple-tree and filled the glasses with peach-brandy beside his adored, deep-breasted Cimbrian wife.

At last the old man turned and smiled, a gay young smile, full of his ancient demoniac twinkle and his boyish joy of life.

Twin sons of Belial," he said, "I will bequeath to you my last will and testament. There is no money in it — such money as is coming your way will be paid to you by my lawyers — and there is no real interest in it. But you have asked me a question, and I will answer it. Not for your sake, but for my own. I must be my own confessor before I die."

"And give yourself absolution?" said Bill Winter.

"I want no absolution," cried Hanson with a magnificent pride. "If I'm due for hell, I'll find Achilles there."

"Croesus," murmured Harry Winter, "I find it in my heart to put you beside D'Artagnan."

Hanson threw his large bulk down into a chair. "I have been, in my time," he said, concentrating his gaze upon the carpet, "fawned upon, flattered, made much of, damnably buttered, complimented, and, in general, lied to, but no one has ever, in my seventy years of life, paid me such a supreme compliment as to compare me to D'Artagnan. Achilles will be impressed — when I meet him." He got up again and bowed, half seriously, half ironically, to Harry Winter. "Moriturus te saluto," he said.

"Moriturus be damned," replied Harry. "We're all going to die, but you'll outlive the lot of us."

"And the answer to the question?" said Bill.

"Ah! the question!" Hanson ran his fist across his mass of hair that looked like silver veins in a black quartz.

"Am I a Christian?" he said meditatively. "Well, it is a long story, this confession of faith of mine. But you, sons of Belial, will have to lump it. When I landed in Cimbria, two-and-fifty years ago, I wanted one thing, and one thing only, and that was Money. It was easy to get and I got it. Then I looked further on, and I saw Power. I went to get Power and I got it. Then I met Amschel Wendelmann. We became partners. We became more than partners, we became friends. And then I began to learn." Hanson got up and went across to the window again, as if the concrete, jerry-built fantasy, on which the dark shadows of circling night were quickly falling, had some mysterious attraction for him, and put his hands in his trousers pockets.

"It took me years to begin to understand," he went on meditatively, "and I don't think I really understand now. But Wendelmann taught me that Money is not everything, and that Power is not everything. I grasped all that, in time. It was difficult, but I grasped it. But what took me years to grasp, was the thing that really was everything. Everything, everything, everything," he repeated. "And it was simply the words of another Jew, 'Thou shalt love thy neighbour as thyself.'"

The old man turned and faced the twins. He spread out his hands and said very gently, "And that is why I am a Christian."

There was a silence. Then, "Do you judge me, you two strong young men?" he cried, as if their silence was a condemnation. "Have I done more harm than good? Will Achilles draw in the hem of his garment from me? Will D'Artagnan tell Cyrano that I am not fit company for a musketeer?"

"Who are we to judge you?" said Bill Winter. "You are a man. Ten thousand times more a man than we can ever hope to be. Don't look to us for judgement."

"I made this country," cried Hanson in a strong voice, as if he had got encouragement from the young adventurer's homage, "I made it, for what it is worth. I have done great harm, but I have tried to do great good. I have tried to master the high gods, and sometimes I have succeeded, and sometimes I have failed. But ever since I understood what Amschel Wendelmann was trying to teach me — I have tried, desperately, to love my neighbour. There is only one sin against the Holy Ghost, and that is cruelty. And there is only one way in which that sin against the Holy Ghost can get universal expression, universal triumph, and that is war."

James Hanson struck the table with his old blue-veined fist three times and repeated, at each blow, "War, war, war."

"The old boy's fey," Bill Winter shot out of the corner of his mouth at Harry.

"I made a war once," went on Hanson, dropping his voice so that he seemed to be talking to nobody in particular, "and many young men were killed in it. It meant nothing to me. I made money. I amalgamated the iron and the coal. I became the uncrowned King of Cimbro-Suevonia. And then that Jew came and dropped his poison — or honey, whichever way you look at it — into my ear, with his 'Thou shalt love thy neighbour,' and nothing has ever been the same since.

"And that," he went on with a great gust of laughter, "is why we three are going out into the mountains tonight to drown men and women and children. Christians all. Neighbours all. Come, lads. The mantle of night has descended upon the gentle vales of Cimbria, and also upon the Casino, so let us shog. Is the car ready?"

"Yes," said Bill Winter.

CHAPTER XXXI

Once more in the Cimbrian Mountains

Bill Winter drove the hired Mercedes — with a cool, undemonstrative efficiency — along the great high-road that ran from Stz to Blut and circled round the east shoulder of the Cimbrian mountains. Harry was beside him, Hanson behind. Two large packing-cases were strapped on the luggage-carrier. The moon had risen and the high snow was a cataract of silver. The only words spoken were an occasional curt word of direction from the old millionaire.

It was nearly eleven o'clock before the car left the main road and began to climb steadily upwards by a side-road through the pine-woods. The big head-lights illuminated the feverish terrors of rabbits and stoats and hares. Once or twice a sleepy bear, honey-drunk, stumbled away into the woods, and deer gazed with sad, limpid eyes at the roaring, flashing monster. As they climbed and climbed, in twisty hairpins and spirals, through long pine-arched tunnels and sometimes on the edge of a clear, sheer drop, with Stz a glimmer of incandescence far away and below, James Hanson began to lean forward more and more alertly, searching the moonlit slopes for old familiar landmarks. Twice he started to give a direction, and twice he checked himself. The third time he was certain. The car stopped. The Winters shouldered the packing-cases and followed Hanson into the wood.

For a quarter of a mile the old man led the way up a narrow path between the trees until he came to a clearing at the foot of a rocky cliff. "This is the place," he said, looking round him in the moonlight. "The entrance to my gallery must be underneath those creepers." He pointed to a myrtle-covered pyramid at one side of the clearing. "There is my old soil-dump," he went on. "Yes. This is the place."

The Winters deposited the packing-cases and went forward into the dense mass of creepers and undergrowth. After a few minutes of hacking and cutting, Harry called out, "Right again, Croesus. Here's the gallery.

What a wizard you are!" Bill Winter backed out of the undergrowth and said, "What a navigator you'd have made, sir."

Hanson smiled. "The time for compliments is over," he said. "But all the same, I thank you. I will lead, with the torch. You needn't be afraid of gases. The Romans knew how to ventilate."

The old man switched on the torch and plunged into the mass of creepers. The twins lifted their packing-cases and followed.

.....

"Is everything set?" asked Hanson quietly. He was standing at a gallery junction, fifty yards from the underground lake.

The brothers were coming towards him from the lake. "Everything," said Harry Winter. He had a stopwatch in his hand. "We gave it ten feet of fuse. That's about five minutes. Best to be on the safe side."

"Three and a half minutes more," said Bill. He also had a stop-watch.

"Three and a half minutes," murmured Hanson. "And then the mines will be flooded and the night-shift of men, women, and children will be drowned like rats. And the cancer cure for women will be set back for years. How much longer?"

"Two minutes, fifteen seconds," said Bill Winter.

"Moriturus te saluto," said Hanson very quietly. "Good-bye, my friends. At least I do not greatly exaggerate the sanctity of my own life," and he walked, erect and proud, down the old Roman gallery towards the underground lake.

Bill Winter made a motion to stop him, but Harry laid his hand on his brother's shoulder. "Let him be," he said, "I understand."

"I don't," said Bill, "but I'm off. Come on."

They ran back up the gallery towards the moonlight. The mountain trembled and rumbled.

.....

But all was in vain.

The news of the destruction of the Gloxite mines reached Germany just as the three air fleets had been mobilized for the triple bombing of Cimbro-Suevonia. As the whole reason for the triple bombing had now been removed, the Leader wished to cancel the war. But his military experts assured him that this was impossible for technical reasons, and that a bombing expedition, once planned, must be carried out. So the air fleets started off. And the air fleets of France, Czecho-Slovakia, Belgium,

Romania, and Poland were instantly mobilized for defence against this unheard-of aggression and, having been mobilized, could not for technical reasons be demobilized without doing some sort of defending, and so they bombed Berlin. And the Italian air force bombed Belgrade, and the Russians bombed Tokyo, and the Japanese, furious at their inability to bomb Moscow, took it out of Singapore and San Francisco and Melbourne, and the two halves of the English-speaking world sprang to arms and lent each other large sums of money without the slightest intention of repaying any of it, and Portugal, uncertain of the rights and wrongs of the whole affair, but knowing exactly which nation drank the most port-wine, joined in the fray on the British side, and sent an aeroplane to bomb Andorra — the only target within range which was unlikely to indulge in reprisals upon Lisbon.

And so Armageddon began once again.

Sir Montagu Anderton-Mawle, understanding more clearly than ever that Pippa was right and that God was in His Heaven, sacked the entire board of the now defunct Perdurite Company except Mr Andrew Hay, and took his old room in the Savoy Hotel and resumed his old trade — with Hay to draw up the contracts — of buying and selling. Only this time it was not rifles that he dealt in but germs.

Crawford returned to the Army as a temporary colonel and won a bar to his D.S.O. a fortnight before a new regulation laid it down that D.S.O.s could only be awarded for actual service in the field.

Nicholas and Oliver Hanson, cavalry captains, became infantry colonels in a twinkling and were killed by a bomb from an Albanian aeroplane while sitting in the American bar of the Berkeley Hotel, and Robert Hanson went from political strength to strength until he became Under-Secretary of the Board of Works with an M.V.O. (third class).

The Freiherr Manfred von Czepan-Eichenhöh was so blistered by a gas-bomb in the Alexanderplatz in Berlin, a bomb, incidentally, which had been dropped by mistake by a German aeroplane, that little Veronica found it very difficult to go on loving him, and the Sergeant, the pillar and prop of the East Stepditch Welfare Centre, re-enlisted at the age of forty-nine and, to his intense embarrassment, soon won a commission for the second time, and for the second time a Military Cross.

The Winters, in spite of their detestation of President Roosevelt, emigrated to the United States and Helen went with them. The Mexican border offered them scope for their peculiar talents, and Europe, after the death of the greatest man they had ever known, was a bitter place of crackling thorns under a pot. And Helen ruthlessly decided that the sight of Crawford in all the recaptured glory of his medals and polished boots and red tabs must be cut out of her life for ever and a day. "Yet will I love him till I die," she sang gently in the smoking-room of the liner in Southampton harbour, and she dried a single tear, her last, on the lashes of her dark-brown eyes.

And after the new Armageddon had been raging its gaseous and germiferous way for six months, the gentle Eleanor died of cancer.